PENNILESS CINDERELLA FOR THE GREEK

CHANTELLE SHAW

BACK TO CLAIM HIS ITALIAN HEIR

KATE HEWITT

MILLS & BOON

First published in Great Britain 2023
by Mills & Boon, an imprint of HarperCollins*Publishers* Ltd,
1 London Bridge Street, London, SE1 9GF

www.harpercollins.co.uk

HarperCollins*Publishers*, Macken House, 39/40 Mayor Street Upper, Dublin 1, D01 C9W8, Ireland

ISBN: 978-0-263-30682-8

06/23

MIX
Paper | Supporting
responsible forestry
FSC™ C007454

This book is produced from independently certified FSC™ paper to ensure responsible forest management.
For more information visit: www.harpercollins.co.uk/green.

Printed and Bound in the UK using 100% Renewable Electricity at CPI Group (UK) Ltd, Croydon, CR0 4YY

PENNILESS CINDERELLA FOR THE GREEK

CHANTELLE SHAW

MILLS & BOON

In memory of Julia, my wonderful mother-in-law.

CHAPTER ONE

'WHAT CAN I get you, sir?' The barman dropped the cloth he had been pushing in a lacklustre fashion across the counter and stood straighter when he saw Dimitris. 'I hope you don't mind me mentioning that you look a lot like the celebrity chef Dimitris Kyriakou.'

'I have been told there is a resemblance,' Dimitris murmured drily. He had learned to live with the public recognition that fame had brought him, but this evening he was preoccupied and not inclined to chat to the barman. 'Give me a bottle of champagne and a couple of glasses, will you.'

'Certainly, sir. If you are a hotel guest I can arrange for the champagne to be delivered to your room.'

'I'll take it with me.' Dimitris smiled, but his eyes were hard. 'I'm planning a little surprise.' He masked his impatience while the barman placed two flutes on a tray, scooped ice into a bucket and took a bottle of champagne from the fridge.

'Are you celebrating a special event?' the young man asked chattily.

'Something like that.'

If his sister Eleni's suspicions about her fiancé were

proved correct she had vowed to break off her engagement to Matt Collier. In Dimitris's opinion it would be a cause for celebration. He'd made some discreet enquiries and learned that Collier had a reputation for cheating on his previous girlfriends.

Eleni deserved to marry a man who would be a faithful and loving husband. Dimitris felt a pang when he thought of his parents' happy marriage before their lives were cut tragically short. He had agreed to help Eleni discover if Collier had a mistress because it was his duty to take care of his younger sister. After all, it was his fault that she had been orphaned when she was ten years old.

Dimitris was fourteen when their parents had been killed and Eleni had sustained life-changing injuries in a car accident. Amazingly he had escaped from the wreckage virtually unscathed. In the mirror behind the bar he could see the faint white line of the scar that ran down his cheek and was partially hidden by the dark stubble on his jaw.

Although his physical scar had faded he was still haunted by his guilt that he had been responsible for the accident. In the past eighteen years Eleni had undergone numerous operations and for a long time she'd had to use a wheelchair or walking stick. Pioneering surgery meant that she would be able to walk down the aisle unaided on her wedding day, in three weeks' time, unless Dimitris found evidence that Eleni's slick advertising executive fiancé was a cheat.

'Matt has been acting strangely lately. I know it was an awful thing to do, but while he was in another room

I looked at his phone and discovered that he has been in regular contact with a woman he calls S,' Eleni had sobbed. *'Matt told me he is going away at the weekend to play in a golf tournament, but his messages show that he has arranged to meet S at a hotel. I have to know the truth. You will help me, won't you, Dimitris?'*

Earlier, Dimitris had driven to the country house hotel a few miles out of London where Eleni's fiancé had arranged a secret assignation. Collier's car was in the car park and his phone messages to the mysterious *S* had included a room number. Dimitris had endured a mediocre dinner at the hotel, hoping to spot Collier and his companion. But they hadn't appeared in the dining room so he would have to implement Plan B.

He carried the tray with the champagne out of the bar and stepped into the lift.

'I'm going to take a quick shower, baby. Don't go anywhere!' Matt winked at Savannah and she forced a smile, but her face clouded over as she watched him saunter into the bathroom.

She couldn't go through with it. She could not sleep with Matt even though it was their third date, and everyone knew that the third date meant sex. It was one reason why she'd never got further than a second date in years. She'd disliked the pressure to rush into a sexual relationship. The truth was there had always been something missing when she'd dated other men and it hadn't been a difficult decision not to see them again. With Matt she'd felt a spark of attraction, and his open, friendly nature had allowed her to relax her usual wariness.

She reminded herself that they were both single, consenting adults. So what was the problem? The hotel suite's impersonal décor added to Savannah's sense that what they were about to do was sordid rather than romantic. Perhaps she would have felt better if Matt had suggested they could spend their first night together at his flat. He'd told her that he owned an apartment in Canary Wharf, but the decorators were in and the place was a mess.

Matt had arranged for them to have a private dinner in the suite. It was a thoughtful gesture, but Savannah had felt too uptight to eat much. Now she was relieved to be alone, although it was a temporary reprieve. She wandered around the room and raked her fingers through her hair—an unconscious habit when she felt tense.

You are being idiotic, she told her reflection in the mirror.

She tried to reassure herself that it was natural to feel apprehensive about having sex after a long gap. She could list her previous sexual experiences on the back of a postage stamp, but once she got started she would be fine.

Getting undressed would be a start. Her dress was a slinky wraparound style. She never usually wore red, but she'd chosen the seductive scarlet dress to boost her confidence. It hadn't worked and her fingers were unsteady as she untied the belt and the two sides of the dress fell open to reveal her black lace push-up bra, also new and bought in the hope that the sexy underwear would give her libido the wake-up call it needed.

Savannah cast her mind back to a couple of weeks ago when she'd met Matt Collier through her job as a food photographer. Her assignment had been to take pictures for an advertising campaign Matt had devised to promote a new tapas bar in Soho. She'd been drawn to his laid-back charm, and after the shoot it had seemed natural to stay on for a few drinks in the bar with him. In fact anything had been preferable to going home to face the dire financial situation her father had left behind.

Over dinner on their second date Matt had explained that his last relationship had ended a few months ago. Savannah had enjoyed his company and agreed to his suggestion to meet him at a hotel. Everything else in her life was going spectacularly wrong and she'd welcomed the distraction of a new relationship. Besides, she was twenty-eight and it was time she stopped hiding away from life.

'No one does old-fashioned courtship any more,' her agent and friend Bev had stated a few days ago when Savannah had confided that she was considering moving her relationship with Matt up a notch. If you like this guy, go for it. From the sound of it your ex-fiancé was a jerk, and you need to get over him.'

Years ago Savannah had ended her engagement to Hugo when she'd realised that she wasn't in love with him. Discovering that he had used her for his own nefarious reasons had been humiliating, but Hugo hadn't broken her heart. That honour went to the man who still invaded her dreams ten years after he had cruelly rejected her. Thinking about *him* had made her furious and she'd resolved to take Bev's advice and give Matt a chance.

But when Matt had ushered her into the suite and she'd seen the king-size bed she'd had an attack of doubts, or nerves, maybe both. It was too soon, and she wasn't ready to have a sexual relationship with someone she hardly knew. Maybe it was ridiculous to hope she would one day meet a man who made her heart pound and know she would willingly follow him to the ends of the earth. With a flash of clarity Savannah realised that she wasn't prepared to settle for less.

She heard the sound of the shower and briefly considered making her escape while Matt was in the bathroom. Her conscience pricked that it would be unfair to run out on him. He was a nice guy and deserved to know that the problem was her, not him.

A knock on the door of the suite gave her hope that the hotel was on fire, although presumably the fire alarm would be ringing. With any luck a sinkhole had opened up on the driveway and the guests were being advised to evacuate the hotel. Whatever the reason, the interruption was perfectly timed and would give her a chance to explain to Matt that she had changed her mind about them becoming lovers.

Savannah hurried to open the door and belatedly remembered that the front of her dress was undone.

The lift stopped at the fourth floor and Dimitris walked down the corridor and knocked on the door of Room 402. 'Room service.'

'Just a minute,' came a female voice from the other

side of the door. 'Matt, did you order…?' Silence and then Dimitris heard her mutter, 'I suppose he can't hear me in the bathroom.'

The door opened, but the woman did not look at him while she fumbled to tie the belt of her scarlet dress. Dimitris wondered if she'd pulled her clothes on in a hurry. The front edges of her dress did not meet properly, affording him an enticing glimpse of the pale mounds of her breasts spilling over the top of her bra.

He took in her blonde hair that fell in messy waves to just above her shoulders, before raking his gaze over her slender figure and finally down to her long legs and scarlet stiletto-heeled shoes. The lady in red was a sexy little number. Her perfume was evocative, floral notes mixed with something deeper and more sensual that stirred a distant memory in Dimitris's mind, but it remained elusive.

'I'll put the champagne on the table, shall I?' He strode into the room without giving the woman time to reply. Rage burned in his gut. He was glad he'd persuaded Eleni to stay at home. His sister would be devastated when he confirmed that the man she loved did indeed have a mistress, but at least she had been spared the humiliation of coming face to face with the fragrant woman who, from her dishevelled hair and clothes, Dimitris assumed had moments ago been in bed with Eleni's fiancé.

A door that must lead to the en suite bathroom opened and Matt Collier emerged, wearing a bathrobe. His jaw sagged when he saw Dimitris. 'What the bloody hell are you doing here?'

Dimitris did not answer. He had realised why the woman's fragrance was familiar. It had haunted him for years. *She* had haunted him for years. She lifted her head and looked at him, and recognition flared in her hazel-green eyes as they widened with surprise.

'*Dimitris?*'

'Savannah O'Neal.' Shock ricocheted through him. He narrowed his gaze to hide his reaction as his brain, and more pertinently his body, acknowledged that the pretty teenager he'd dumped ten years ago had grown up to become a stunningly beautiful and very sexy woman. 'It's been a long time.'

Dimitris's effect on Savannah was as shattering as when she had been eighteen. Her heart was pounding and her mouth was dry. She had seen him on TV many times, hosting his hugely popular cooking programmes. His rock star looks and charismatic personality meant that he was regularly invited to be a guest on chat shows. But nothing had prepared Savannah for seeing him for real. His sex appeal was off the scale.

She had often imagined meeting Dimitris again and she'd planned on being cool and sophisticated, unlike the teenager who'd had a massive crush on him. The years fell away and she was the gauche girl on the cusp of womanhood who had daydreamed that the handsome Greek god working in his family's restaurant would notice her. For eleven magical nights her fantasy had come true. But there had been no fairy tale happy ending, just a cold dose of reality that had forced her to grow up.

At twenty-two, Dimitris's swarthy good looks had made him seem exotic and gorgeous compared to the few boys of her age Savannah had known. She'd had a sheltered upbringing and been privately educated at an all-girls' school, and she had been ill-equipped to deal with Dimitris's potent masculinity. When he'd laughed, the wicked glint in his eyes had been irresistible. But there was no hint of laughter on his chiselled features, and he looked as though he'd been hewn from granite or cold, hard marble.

Now in his early thirties, he was even more devastatingly attractive than she remembered. The scar on his cheek had faded over time. It did not detract from his good looks, rather it gave him a piratical air that added to his intrigue. His square jaw was uncompromising and his cheekbones sharply angular. Eyes a fathomless dark blue were shaded by thick black lashes and his heavy brows met over a strong nose. But it was his mouth that held Savannah's attention. The full lips that promised heaven and had delivered, she remembered. His kiss was imprinted on her psyche.

She told herself that Dimitris, breaker of a thousand hearts besides her own, would have no memory of their first passionate encounter on a sultry summer's night a decade ago. But the gleam in his eyes made her wonder if his mind had revisited the pool house on the night of her eighteenth birthday party.

'It's not what it looks like.' Matt's voice jolted Savannah back to reality.

Matt!

She felt guilty at how easily she had forgotten him. It

had been sweet of Matt to order champagne. Perhaps he had planned to celebrate after they'd made love for the first time, she thought guiltily, knowing that she still had to have an awkward conversation with him and tell him she'd changed her mind about sleeping with him.

But why on earth had the famous chef and TV personality Dimitris Kyriakou delivered champagne to the suite? Utterly bemused, Savannah wondered if Matt had arranged to surprise her with a visit from a celebrity—a bit like a stripper-gram, although Dimitris showed no sign of removing his clothes. A memory of his muscular naked body pressed against hers brought a flush of warmth to her face.

She looked at Matt and then back at the impressive Greek who dominated the room with his sheer presence. One of the few things Dimitris had told her about himself years ago was that his mother had been English, and he had inherited his six feet plus height from her side of the family.

At eighteen Savannah had been painfully naïve, and unaware that men like Dimitris were a rarity. Now she knew better. Now she knew that every man faded into insignificance compared to Dimitris. Her confusion grew when she sensed angry vibes from him.

'What's going on?' Savannah asked Matt. But he did not look at her and spoke to Dimitris.

'I know it must seem suspicious that I'm at a hotel with a woman. But Savannah is a work colleague. She suggested meeting up to discuss a project and I had no idea that she'd booked a room with the intention of trying to persuade me to sleep with her.'

Savannah gasped. 'That's not true. You know full well that you asked me to spend the night with you.' When Matt avoided her gaze she appealed to Dimitris. 'Will you please tell me why you are here?'

Eyes the unfathomable blue of the deepest ocean swept over her and set every nerve-ending on her body alight. Dimitris's penetrating gaze gave Savannah the unsettling notion that he could see inside her head.

'Do you expect me to believe that you did not know your lover is engaged to be married?' he asked curtly.

'I expect you to believe it because it's the truth.' Her brief spurt of temper fizzled out as she tried to make sense of what Dimitris had said. 'There must be some kind of mistake. Matt isn't engaged to anyone. Are you... Matt?'

Matt's sheepish expression turned sullen and there was no need for him to say anything. Savannah released her breath slowly as her shock and disbelief morphed into anger and mortification. *Fool*, she castigated herself. Would she never learn that all men were liars? She included her father in that sweeping generalisation, and now she knew it was true of both men in the hotel suite.

She felt sick when she looked at Matt, with his hair damp from the shower he'd taken before he'd planned to have sex with her. She wondered how he would have reacted if they hadn't been interrupted and she'd admitted that she had changed her mind. Would he have tried to persuade her to sleep with him, knowing that he'd promised to marry someone else?

'Matt and I are not lovers,' she told Dimitris. He

looked disbelieving and, following his gaze down, she discovered that the tie on her wrap dress had come loose again and the front was gaping open, revealing her bra and an embarrassing amount of cleavage. Blushing furiously, she jerked the edges of her dress together.

'It's the truth,' Matt confirmed quickly. 'I haven't slept with Savannah, and she means nothing to me. Meeting her tonight was a stupid mistake.'

'That's not the impression you gave me,' she said sharply. Ironically, she'd had second thoughts about sleeping with Matt because she did not know him well enough. It was bad enough to be humiliated by Matt, but for it to happen in front of Dimitris made her wish she could wake up from what must surely be a nightmare.

Matt ignored her and spoke to Dimitris. 'Look, mate, I don't know how you found me, but there's no need to tell Eleni about tonight's little indiscretion, especially as nothing happened.'

'I am not your *mate*, Collier.' Dimitris's voice dripped with icy disdain. 'My sister read messages on your phone and discovered that you had lied about attending a golf tournament and planned to meet someone you referred to as S. I assume that person is Savannah.'

'Matt is engaged to *Eleni*?' At last Savannah understood the reason for Dimitris's barely suppressed fury. Years ago, he had been fiercely protective of his younger sister. 'I didn't know,' she whispered.

Odd little things made sense now. Matt had used her initial in texts, joking that typing her name took too long. She'd believed him when he'd said he was taking a break from social media because constantly being online sucked out your soul. Matt had gone to great lengths to deceive her, and she'd fallen for his lies.

Dimitris scowled at Matt. 'The wedding is off, Collier. My sister will want nothing more to do with you after this.'

'Is that really Eleni's decision or have you decided for her, Kyriakou? I'll talk to her and convince her to give me another chance.' Matt's bravado slipped and he took a hasty step backwards when Dimitris's jaw hardened aggressively.

'Keep away from Eleni. I will do whatever it takes to protect her from scum like you,' Dimitris growled.

He flicked his cold gaze over Savannah. 'Does your lover know you are married?' His lip curled when she looked startled. 'Not long after I left London years ago, I heard that you had become engaged to a member of the English aristocracy. The wedding was expected to be the society event of the year.' He shook his head. 'You and Collier deserve each other.'

Before Savannah had a chance to gather her wits and defend herself, Dimitris strode out of the hotel suite. In his wake it felt as though an earthquake had struck, leaving her dazed and disorientated.

'You didn't mention anything about being married.' Matt had the cheek to sound affronted.

'I'm not,' she muttered. 'I was engaged, but I called the wedding off.'

'It looks like my engagement is off.' Matt seemed annoyed rather than upset. 'Kyriakou has never approved of me marrying his sister and Eleni will do what he says because he pays for everything, including the luxury flat in Canary Wharf that was meant to have been a wedding present for us. It's damned inconvenient. I've already given notice to leave my rented flat and I'll have to look for somewhere else to live.'

He moved closer to Savannah and ran his finger down her cheek. 'Perhaps I could come and live with you at your big house near Hampstead Heath. What do you say we open the champagne and drink to new beginnings, baby?'

She jerked away from him in disgust. 'You've got a nerve. I hope I never see you again. Anyway, it's my mother's house.'

But in fact Pond House did not belong to her mother, Savannah thought bleakly. It had been yet another shock to discover that the title deed of the house only bore her father's name, meaning that the property was an asset of Richard O'Neal's. His creditors were demanding that the house must be sold to pay his debts.

Savannah remembered how Matt had been impressed with the house where she had grown up, and had returned to live after her mum had become ill, when he'd dropped her home after their second date. He had remarked that properties in the area were worth a fortune. Pond House, with its private swimming pool, tennis court and extensive grounds, had recently been valued at several million pounds. The sale of the house should raise enough money to clear her father's debts, but Savannah knew it would break her mother's heart to leave the home she loved.

'Get lost, Matt.' She did not know who she loathed

most—Matt for being a creep, or herself for having been so gullible. 'Why did you start dating me when you were planning to marry someone else?'

He shrugged. 'It was obvious when we had drinks after the photoshoot that you were available and a bit desperate. I thought I'd covered my tracks and Eleni wouldn't find out. Most blokes will seize an opportunity if it comes their way,' he said sulkily. 'Kyriakou can't take the moral high ground. He's a notorious womaniser and lurid details about his personal life regularly appear in the tabloids.'

Savannah had seen photos in the newspapers of Dimitris with a seemingly never-ending supply of beautiful women. Since his meteoric rise to fame as a celebrity chef who had amassed a multi-million-pound fortune from his bestselling cookery books, numerous TV appearances and a chain of hugely successful Greek restaurants, Dimitris was regarded as a highly eligible bachelor. Unfortunately for his legions of female fans, he was determined to maintain his single status and was on record saying that he had no desire to marry and settle down.

He'd said the same thing ten years ago when Savannah had laid her heart on the line and told him that she loved him. Remembering how naïve she had been made her cringe. She was dismayed that Dimitris still had a seismic effect on her. Her body was tingling all over, and he made her feel more alive and aware of her femininity than any other man ever had.

'What's the story between you and Kyriakou?' Matt sounded petulant. 'Why did he recognise you?'

'I…knew him a long time ago.' Her short affair with Dimitris had been passionate and intense, and she'd been obsessed with him, but she had not really known him. Savannah wondered if any woman had managed to break through the steel barrier around his emotions.

She was angry that he hadn't given her a chance to explain how she had been duped by Matt. She did not care about Dimitris's opinion of her, she assured herself. But she had been friends with Eleni, and she wanted to set the record straight about her involvement with Matt Collier.

'Don't try to contact me again,' she told Matt as she gathered up her bag and the shreds of her dignity and hurried out of the suite. Up ahead she saw Dimitris was about to step into the lift.

'Wait!' Savannah tore along the corridor. The doors were sliding closed, and she shoved her hand between them so that they automatically opened again. Time juddered to a standstill as she stared into the lift at Dimitris. Her nemesis.

His black hair was cut shorter than Savannah remembered, but it still had a tendency to curl. He was a work of art, beyond merely handsome. Anger emanated from his whipcord body. 'I don't have time for this,' he grated. 'I must go to my sister.'

Savannah's eyes were drawn to the glint of the gold watch on his wrist that contrasted with his olive-toned skin. His sleeves were rolled up to the elbows and his forearms were covered with black hairs. Wearing black trousers and a shirt, and with a scowl on his face, he was a dark avenging angel, determined to protect his sister from being hurt by *her*, Savannah thought bleakly. She had been an unwitting accomplice in Matt's cheating. It did not make her feel better knowing that they hadn't actually had sex.

'I didn't sleep with Matt,' she repeated. There was no softening of Dimitris's hard features. Savannah bit her lip. 'Please don't tell Eleni that you found me with her fiancé. She and I were friends before we lost touch, and I would never do anything to hurt her.'

Dimitris's silence was damning, but with a jolt Savannah recognised a gleam of awareness in his eyes. Ten years ago their chemistry had been white-hot. She moved her hand up to the front of her dress to check it was still fastened and the lift doors instantly closed. Cursing, she jabbed her finger on the button to open the doors again, but the indicator arrow showed that the lift had started to descend.

She sagged against the wall, breathing hard as if she'd run a marathon. It was crazy how hurt she felt by Dimitris's refusal to listen to her. He had accepted at face value finding her with his sister's fiancé and had judged her unfairly. Even worse, seeing Dimitris again had forced Savannah to face the truth that she had tried to deny to herself since she was eighteen. She had never got over him and she compared all other men to him.

CHAPTER TWO

'IS SHE PRETTY?'

Dimitris raised an eyebrow. 'Who?' He was aware that he was playing for time before he answered his sister, but he wanted to be sure his emotions were under control. He did not like surprises like the one he'd had earlier tonight.

'Matt's other woman, of course.' Eleni wiped away her tears. She'd been crying ever since Dimitris had returned to his house in Richmond upon Thames, where his sister had come to stay while she prepared for her wedding, and gently broken the news that he'd found Collier at the hotel with a woman who was evidently his mistress.

'I did not take much notice of her.' Dimitris hated deceit, but he made no apology for the lie. *Theós!* He wasn't going to admit to Eleni or himself that when he'd recognised Savannah his heart had crashed against his ribs with the force of a runaway juggernaut. He saw no point in revealing to his sister that her now ex-fiancé's mistress was none other than Eleni's old schoolfriend.

It was not the first time Dimitris had seen Savannah since he'd broken off their relationship, but photographs could not fully capture her intriguing mix of innocence and sensuality. Her image had graced billboards in major cities around the world when she had been 'the face' of a well-known cosmetics company and she'd also modelled for a designer brand of eyewear.

Savannah possessed exquisite facial features and her hazel-green eyes were mesmerising. Dimitris knew that their stunning colour had not been enhanced by the latest photographic technology. Her eyes were the first thing he had noticed about her when she'd been a teenager and had applied for a summer waitressing job in his grandfather's restaurant.

'Savannah is not like most of the other rich girls at school,' Eleni had assured him when he'd been doubtful that the daughter of a wealthy businessman would be willing to work long hours for low wages. Hestia's Authentic Greek restaurant, situated at the rough end of the high street in a north London borough, had been struggling to attract customers since several fast food places had opened up nearby.

'She has never made me feel embarrassed about being the only scholarship pupil at Brampton Girls Academy, or that I use a wheelchair,' Eleni had said. 'Savannah is my friend. Please give her a chance, Dimitris. I'm sure you won't be disappointed with her.'

Dimitris swore silently as he was bombarded by memories of Savannah's shy smile, her slender figure and pert curves, and the way she'd blushed when he had caught her watching him. At twenty-two he had been used to receiving attention from women, and he'd dated widely but never exclusively. He had told himself that Savannah was too young, and her air of vulnerability made her off-limits. He could not offer her a meaningful relationship that he sensed she hoped for.

It was a pity he hadn't listened to the warning voice inside his head, he brooded. Their affair had been short-lived, and Dimitris had moved away. But he'd never quite forgotten the heady passion that had burned out of control between them. Ten years was a long time and people changed. He certainly had, and he should not be surprised that the half-undressed siren he'd discovered in a hotel room with the man Eleni had hoped to marry was different to the sweet girl he'd known a decade ago, who had affected him more deeply than he cared to admit.

A couple of months after he'd broken up with Savannah, he'd been working as a chef at a hotel in Rhodes and had flicked through an English newspaper. He'd been shocked to read about her engagement to the son of an earl or a duke—Dimitris could not recall the exact details. He had felt gutted that she'd made plans to marry another man so soon after she had declared her love for him. But he'd reminded himself that he did not deserve to be loved after he had destroyed the two people who had loved him most.

He guessed that Savannah's father had approved of her marrying into the aristocracy. Thinking of Richard O'Neal reminded Dimitris of the deal he had been forced to make with Savannah's father, and the secret that he'd kept from her.

He forced his mind from the distant past and frowned as he replayed the scene in the hotel suite. Savannah had denied knowing that Matt Collier was engaged, and she had seemed shocked. But they lived in an age when most people's personal details were plastered over social media. She *must* have known that Collier had promised to marry Eleni, Dimitris thought grimly.

'I bet Matt's girlfriend doesn't walk with a limp.' Eleni's face crumpled. 'I know you had doubts about Matt. I wish I had listened to you. I'll have to call the caterers and the florist and all the guests to tell them the wedding is cancelled. I was due to have a final fitting of my dress, but I won't get to wear it now.'

'Hush, *paidí mou.*' Dimitris put his hand on his sister's shoulders that were shaking with the force of her sobs. He had spent his whole adult life taking care of Eleni, but at this moment he felt helpless. Her distress fuelled his anger with Matt Collier and Savannah for hurting her. 'I will deal with everything and cancel the wedding arrangements. Go to bed and try to sleep.'

Guilt, his ever-present demon, slid a knife-blade between his ribs as he watched Eleni walk stiffly across the room. It was a miracle she was able to walk at all. For the past decade Dimitris had regularly worked eighteen-hour days, he'd seized every opportunity that had come his way and he was the first to admit that he'd had some lucky breaks. He had poured his passion into cooking and earned a fortune, and he was driven by a desire to try to recompense his sister for ruining her life.

He would never forgive himself for causing the accident that had destroyed his happy family. If he hadn't distracted his mother, so that she had taken her eyes off the road, their car would not have swerved into the path of an oncoming lorry.

After all this time Dimitris still suffered flashbacks. He had been a troubled teenager, torn between his Greek and English cultures, and he'd felt he did not belong anywhere. He'd been drawn into a gang of older boys who had used and sold drugs on the streets. With hindsight Dimitris realised that his parents had been trying to protect him when they'd refused to let him stay out late, but at fourteen he'd resented their rules and curfews.

On that fateful day his parents had been taking Eleni to her dance class, and he should have ridden his bike to football training, but he'd overslept, and his mum had agreed to give him a lift. The argument had started in the car.

'Would you mind helping in the restaurant this evening, Dimitris? One of the waitresses is ill.'

'Oh, Mum. It's Saturday night, and everyone's meeting at Jack's house.'

'Well, you can go out with your friends, but I want you home by eleven. Dad will collect you so that you don't have to walk back on your own.'

'Stop treating me like a kid. No one else's parents make a fuss. Can I at least stay out until midnight?'

'It's too late. And you've got homework to finish tomorrow. Eleni said she saw you playing games on your computer instead of getting on with your history project.'

'Thanks for snitching, Eleni. Stay out of my room in future.'

Eleni had started to cry. Both parents had turned their heads to look at Dimitris in the back of the car.

'Don't be mean to your sister,' his mother had told him. Her voice had softened. *'Your family are concerned about you because we love you.'*

Dimitris had seen the lorry the split-second before the crash. *'Mum—look out!'*

His jaw clenched as he fought to block out his agonising memories. He focused on Eleni when she paused in the doorway. 'I want to go back to Greece,' she said in a choked voice. 'At least I hadn't relocated my business to London. What will happen to the flat in Canary Wharf?'

'I'll sell it or rent it out.' Dimitris sighed. 'I know it's hard to believe now, but one day you will meet the right person who will make you happy.'

Eleni sniffed. 'You haven't.'

'Ah, but I don't want to fall in love.'

'I'm not sure we can control these things. Love just happens and it creeps up when you are least expecting it.'

'Not to me it doesn't,' Dimitris said firmly. He had decided when he was fourteen and racked with grief and guilt that he must spend the rest of his life alone. He did not deserve the things that most people took for granted, such as falling in love and having a family of his own.

'Will you come to Rhodes with me?' Eleni pleaded. 'I can't face telling *Γιαγιά* that my wedding is cancelled.'

Their grandmother Hestia was a formidable matriarch even at nearly ninety. Dimitris shook his head regretfully. 'I must stay in London to take part in the photoshoot for Philpot's. As soon as I am free I'll join you at the villa.'

After Eleni had gone upstairs, Dimitris checked his messages on his phone. He had agreed to become the brand ambassador for Philpot's, the UK's biggest supermarket chain, in return for their support of his charity Food for All, which was involved in a number of projects to encourage young people to learn to cook instead of relying on fast food.

There was an email from Philpot's PR executive regarding the photography session the next day, when Dimitris would cook the dishes he had created for the supermarket's Healthy Meals campaign. The recipes and accompanying photographs of the food would be published in the autumn edition of Philpot's magazine. He had left all the arrangements to their PR team while he'd been concerned about his sister, and this was the first time he'd looked at the details of the shoot.

Philpot's had commissioned an up-and-coming food photographer. Dimitris cursed as the name jumped out at him. Savannah O'Neal. *Seriously?* What were the chances that there were two women with the same fairly unusual name? Fate had a warped sense of humour, he thought grimly.

Savannah woke to blinding sunshine streaming through the half-open curtains. She squinted at the clock on the bedside cabinet and groaned when she realised that she must have switched off the alarm and fallen back to sleep. It was eight a.m., and she had a full-on day at work in front of her. She'd packed her camera gear last night, but there was an element of secrecy around the shoot, and she hadn't been told yet where it would take place. Hopefully the location wasn't miles away.

As she scrambled out of bed her phone rang. Guessing it was her agent with details of the photoshoot, she flung her hand out to pick up her phone and knocked over a glass of water. *'Dammit.'*

'Bad news, I'm afraid,' Beverly Wright, owner of Wright's Photographic Agency and known to everyone as Bev, greeted Savannah.

'I've had my quota of bad news for this century.' What else could go wrong? Savannah ran her mind over the events of the past year, when her father had been arrested and convicted of corruption. Before he could begin his lengthy prison sentence he had died from a heart attack. Savannah was still trying to come to terms with his death, and the shocking revelations in court that her apparently respectable and successful businessman father had committed fraud on a breathtaking scale.

Dating Matt Collier had allowed her to temporarily forget the stress of dealing with her father's financial affairs and her worries about her mum. But Matt had shown himself to be as unreliable as every other man Savannah had known.

As for Dimitris, she had been stunned when he'd appeared in the hotel suite, and horrified by her body's instant response to him. Forget Sleeping Beauty who had been woken by the handsome prince's kiss. All it had taken was one searing look from Dimitris to re-kindle her libido. Memories of the shockingly erotic dream she'd had about him last night evoked a flood of warmth between her thighs.

'What news?' she croaked into her phone.

'Philpot's have cancelled.'

'But the shoot was meant to be today. Are they going to reschedule?' Savannah sank down onto the bed. 'Let me know the new date and I'll make sure I'm available.'

Her work diary was not brimming with assignments. When she'd started out as a freelance photographer she'd realised it would take time to build her reputation, and she'd been lucky enough to have the back-up of her savings from her brief modelling career. But since her father's arrest, and after Richard O'Neal's assets had been frozen, most of her money had gone on household bills; her mother did not have money to pay for the upkeep of Pond House.

'The photoshoot is to go ahead today, but Philpot's have asked for a different photographer,' Bev told her. 'I'm sorry, Savannah. Tara Brown, head of brand communication, called me late last night and said that the request for you to be replaced came from the very top. As you know, the shoot is for the campaign Philpot's are planning for the autumn, when they will reveal that their new brand ambassador is the hot Greek chef Dimitris Kyriakou.'

Savannah made a muffled sound somewhere between a sob and hysterical laughter, but Bev did not seem to hear her.

'Actually I shouldn't have let that slip. Philpot's want

to keep his identity under wraps until the launch, but I know I can trust you to keep it to yourself. Kyriakou prefers to work in his own kitchen studio and the photoshoot will be at River Retreat in Richmond, where his recent cooking series was filmed. I have no idea why he asked for a change of photographer. Perhaps he wasn't keen on your portfolio, although Philpot's loved your work. I tried calling you last night to let you know, but you didn't answer your phone.'

'I must have been in the bath.' After Savannah had left Matt at the hotel and driven home, she'd switched off her phone before taking a long soak, hoping it would help her relax after what was up there as one of the worst evenings of her life. Today wasn't proving to be much better.

'Luckily Philpot's are willing to use another photographer from my agency.' Bev was a businesswoman first and foremost. 'Jason Bloomfield will take your place. I've sent your portfolio to the editor of a lifestyle magazine who is planning an article about artisan bread.' Her tone softened. 'I know you must be disappointed about the Philpot's assignment, but these things happen.'

After the call from Bev, Savannah resisted the childish urge to hurl her phone across the room. The photoshoot for Philpot's would have raised her profile as a food photographer. Losing the assignment was a disaster both professionally and for her bank balance that was currently in the red.

She wasn't just disappointed; she was furious with Dimitris for being so petty and demanding that she was replaced by a different photographer. She had done nothing wrong. Matt Collier had deceived her as much as Eleni. Even so, she felt guilty that she had unwittingly been partly responsible for ruining her old schoolfriend's wedding plans. Her heart ached as she imagined how distraught Eleni must be feeling.

At eighteen Savannah had been devastated when Dimitris had bluntly told her that he was not in love with her. He had broken her heart, and now he had the power to potentially damage her career—unless she could convince him that she was not his sister's fiancé's mistress. Last night, when he had found her with Matt in the hotel room, Dimitris had been understandably angry and protective of his sister. But perhaps by now his temper had cooled and he would allow her to explain.

She did not have much time, Savannah realised. The photoshoot was scheduled to start at ten o'clock, but the team of assistants, food stylists and technicians would arrive earlier. If she left immediately and the London traffic wasn't too bad she could be in Richmond in just over half an hour. She prayed that her car would start. It was old and had been playing up recently, but the precarious state of her finances meant she couldn't afford to buy a newer model or take the car to a garage for it to be serviced.

Without wasting any more time, Savannah pulled on her usual work uniform of black trousers and tee shirt, scooped her hair into a ponytail and waved a mascara wand over her eyelashes before she ran downstairs. She met Cathy, her mother's live-in carer, outside the drawing room that had been turned into Evelyn's bedroom since her mobility had become affected by multiple sclerosis.

'Is Mum awake? How did she sleep?'

Cathy nodded. 'She had a fairly good night. I'm going to make Evelyn a cup of tea. Would you like one?' It had become a morning ritual for Savannah to spend time with her mum before she went to work.

'I can't hang about this morning. I've got to dash.' Savannah stepped into the room and felt a surge of love and concern when she noted how frail her mum looked, propped against the pillows.

The traumas of the past few years had taken a toll on Evelyn's health and mental wellbeing and her MS symptoms had worsened. It was hardly surprising after she'd had to cope with her husband's arrest and trial, his shocking death, and the dramatic change to her financial circumstances. Savannah tried to keep the truth of how broke they were from her mum. She had prioritised paying Cathy's wages because Evelyn needed the help of a carer as her health deteriorated, but finding the money was a struggle.

She walked over to the bed and leaned down to kiss her mother's cheek. 'I've got an early start this morning, Mum.'

'Oh, yes, today is the photoshoot for Philpot's, isn't it? Do you know which celebrity chef you'll be working with?'

Savannah tried to sound casual. 'I'm not supposed to tell a soul. He's Dimitris Kyriakou.'

Evelyn wasn't fooled. 'Be careful, darling. He upset you badly when you were younger.'

'I admit I fancied him like crazy for a while. I doubt he'll remember me, and all I'm going to do is take pictures of his food.' Except that she wasn't, Savannah thought after she'd left her mum. The assignment had been given to another photographer, but if she could persuade Dimitris to look at her portfolio and endorse her work, Philpot's might employ her for their future campaigns.

Richmond upon Thames was renowned for being an affluent area of south-west London, where millionaires were drawn to the leafy suburb close to the capital. Recently, an interview with Dimitris and photographs of him at his London home had been published in the magazine supplement of a Sunday newspaper. Savannah had bought the paper because it featured an article about photography that she'd wanted to read, or so she'd told herself. Admittedly she had been curious about Dimitris, and it was lucky she had studied the pictures in the magazine so intently because when she arrived in Richmond and drove past exclusive properties that backed onto the river she recognised his house, River Retreat.

She parked her car in the road and, out of habit, took her camera bag with her. Savannah hadn't made a plan of what she would do next. There was a good chance that Dimitris would refuse to speak to her. The gates were unlocked. Tension made her heart thud as she walked up the driveway to the front door and rang the bell.

A woman who seemed to be the housekeeper opened the door and glanced at her camera bag. 'You're here for the photoshoot,' she said before Savannah could introduce herself. 'Mr Kyriakou's kitchen studio is in the garden. Follow the path round to the back of the house and the studio is at the bottom of the lawn, next to the river.'

So far so easy. Savannah let out a soft sigh as she came round the corner of the house and took in the view of the sweeping green lawn bordered by flower beds filled with colourful blooms. Everywhere was immaculate and even the most determined weed would not dare poke through a gap in the patio stones, due no doubt to the vigilance of a full-time gardener.

She thought of the garden at Pond House that had been her mother's pride and joy. Evelyn no longer had the energy for gardening and the shrubs had gone wild. Savannah hoped that when the house was sold and she'd paid her father's creditors, there would be enough money left to buy an adapted bungalow for Evelyn and her carer to live in. But she would still need to earn a good income so that she could provide for her mum.

If word got around that the famous chef Dimitris Kyriakou had refused to work with her, people would think he was unimpressed with her photography, and it could have serious implications for her career. It was ironic that she and Dimitris had experienced a dramatic reversal of fortunes, Savannah thought. She had been brought up accustomed to wealth and privilege and it was deeply shocking to discover that her father had made his money from corrupt business dealings.

Her mother had been completely unaware of her husband's criminal activities. Growing up, Savannah's re-

lationship with her father had been difficult and she'd
tried to live up to his impossibly high standards. Since
his trial, when she'd learned the truth about him, she'd
felt as though the very fabric of her life and identity
had been ripped away.

When she'd first met Dimitris he had lived in a small
flat above his family's restaurant with his grandparents
and sister. Several years earlier, their parents had been
killed in a car accident and Eleni had sustained serious
injuries that meant she used a wheelchair. Eleni had
said she did not remember anything of the accident.
Savannah had asked Dimitris what had happened, but
he'd refused to talk about the tragedy. He hadn't told
her anything really about himself. His emotions had
been a closed book, but she was so wrapped up in being
in love with him she had convinced herself that he felt
the same way about her.

A trip down memory lane was not helpful right now,
Savannah told herself as she continued along the path
towards the timber and glass building that she recognised from Dimitris's cooking shows as his kitchen studio. His biography online stated that he had first been
taught to cook by his grandfather, a Greek immigrant
who had settled in London and opened a restaurant
that he'd named Hestia's after his wife.

Dimitris had gone to college and trained as a professional chef. He'd helped run the restaurant before he
and his grandparents and sister had suddenly moved
to Greece. In Rhodes he had been sous chef at a top
hotel. Later he'd moved to Paris, where he had become
the chef de cuisine at one of the city's most prestigious

restaurants. He had taken part in a cooking competition to find the best chef in Europe. The final had been broadcast live on television in England, and Dimitris had won and caught the attention of a TV producer who had given him his own televised cooking series.

An Adonis in the Kitchen had launched Dimitris's career as a celebrity chef and sex symbol in Europe and America, where he was hugely popular. Other series had followed. *Cooking with the Greek*, *Dinner with Dimitris* and *A Date with Dimitris* showcased his enthusiasm for cooking while his disarming personality and blatant sex appeal had earned him the nickname the Hot Chef.

Dimitris's impressive London house was proof that his single-minded determination to succeed had paid dividends. Savannah stood and watched the stately River Thames, so wide and blue and sparkling in the sunshine of what promised to be another glorious summer's day. A sleek motor cruiser moored next to the private jetty added to the sense of unobtrusive luxury.

'What are you doing trespassing on my property, Savannah?'

The gravelly voice from behind her made Savannah's heart lurch. She turned slowly, trying to prepare herself for the impact of seeing Dimitris again. But it was hopeless, and her breath rushed from her lungs as she met his sapphirine gaze.

CHAPTER THREE

THE STUDIO'S BI-FOLD doors were open, and Savannah wondered how long Dimitris had been standing there. He looked divine in faded jeans that hugged his lean hips and a white jersey top clinging to the defined ridges of his muscular torso.

'You shouldn't be here,' he said curtly. 'Someone at Philpot's was supposed to tell the agency to send a different photographer.'

'I wanted to talk to you...' She found herself talking to Dimitris's back when he swung round and strode across the studio.

Savannah followed him inside. The kitchen studio was a large, light-filled space with a glass roof and furnished with pale wood units against the bare brick walls. An island with a hob stood in the middle of the room and behind it were professional ovens, sinks and more worktops.

The heavenly smell of freshly baked bread filled the air. Her stomach grumbled when she saw rolls cooling on a rack. She hadn't had time for breakfast and had barely eaten anything when she'd been at the hotel with Matt. Her cheeks burned at the memory of the humiliating events of the previous evening.

'I'll call Philpot's to find out why my instructions were not followed.'

If he spoke to Tara Brown the PR manager would contact Bev to ask if a replacement photographer had been assigned to the shoot. Savannah knew that her visit to Dimitris's home would be highly embarrassing for her agent. Bev should not have broken the client's confidentiality and revealed that Dimitris was Philpot's new brand ambassador.

'I'm not here for the photoshoot. If you would let me explain…'

'I have nothing to say to you.'

His dismissive tone was the last straw. Anger rolled in a red mist through her. The hunger pangs in her stomach were vying with the ache in her heart. Dimitris's riverside studio in the grounds of his beautiful house emphasised how different their lives had become. Savannah did not resent his success, but she was scared of what losing Pond House would do to her mum's physical and emotional health.

Her job as a photographer gave her a vital source of income and some much-needed personal pride, but with one phone call Dimitris could ruin everything she cared about. His phone was on the counter. As he stretched his hand towards it Savannah shot past him and grabbed the phone.

'I don't want you to *say* anything,' she told him fiercely. 'I want you to *listen*.'

His eyes darkened to the blue-black of obsidian as he glowered down at her from his superior height. She inhaled the spicy scent of his aftershave, and something visceral twisted in her stomach that in turn made her furious for being so weak. She could not allow him to affect her the way he had when she'd been an impressionable teenager.

'I am not Matt Collier's mistress. I went on a couple of dates with him after he'd told me he was single. At the risk of repeating myself, I had no idea he was Eleni's fiancé. I don't know why I'm surprised that Matt lied,' Savannah said bitterly. 'I've never met a man yet who was capable of telling the truth.'

Dimitris's scowl deepened, but Savannah refused to be cowed. She had been lied to all her life—by her father, her ex-fiancé Hugo, Matt Collier, who had dented her pride but not her heart, she acknowledged honestly, and Dimitris, who she'd put on a pedestal years ago.

'It's none of your business, but I have never been married.'

Dimitris's expression was inscrutable. Savannah remembered that even when he'd been younger he had kept a tight control over his emotions. It had made his fierce passion all the more exciting, knowing she had broken through his barricades. 'I never lied to you,' he said brusquely.

She rolled her eyes. 'Oh, please. When you ended our relationship you said it was so that you could concentrate on your career. But I know my father gave you money to dump me. He told me that he had been suspicious of your motives and as a test he offered you two hundred and fifty thousand pounds to break up with me.'

Savannah's satisfaction that she'd finally had a

chance to confront Dimitris about what he had done was mixed with gut-wrenching disappointment when a startled look flickered on his handsome features. His guilty expression confirmed what her father had told her. Ten years ago Dimitris had chosen money over her.

'I'm not sure what I found more insulting. The fact that you used me for sex, or that you accepted a bribe to dump me,' she said sarcastically. 'Either way, you are no better than Matt Collier. I'm not defending him,' she insisted when Dimitris's jaw hardened. 'Matt lied to Eleni and to me. But you acted no better when you deceived me.'

'I never used you for sex. But, in hindsight, I realise I should not have got involved with you.' He frowned. 'You were young and ridiculously innocent, and not only because you were a virgin. You wanted a fairy tale that I couldn't give you.'

She felt her cheeks burn. 'When we made love it was amazing for both of us. You let me think we had a future.'

He shook his head. 'You wove a fantasy of happy ever after. But you were about to go to university and had your whole future in front of you. I had a failing restaurant to manage, and elderly grandparents and a disabled sister to take care of. I had nothing to offer you.' Dimitris hesitated. 'Did your father tell you anything else?'

'What do you mean?' Savannah grimaced as she thought of everything her father *hadn't* told her about his business empire that had been built on corruption and lies.

On the surface her family had appeared to be perfect, with her a spoiled only child whose father doted on her. But from a young age she had been aware that Richard O'Neal did not love her, despite all her attempts to please him and win his approval. She had wondered, and still did, if there was something wrong with her for her own father not to have cared about her. Dimitris's rejection had reinforced the feeling that she was somehow unlovable.

At his trial her father had been exposed as a serial fraudster. Savannah was angry that she had allowed him to dominate her life while she'd striven to be the perfect daughter. Now she was furious that another powerful man could influence her life, her career and, most importantly, her income that she badly needed so that she could look after her mum.

The tense silence in the studio shattered when Dimitris's phone rang. His expression was sardonic as he held out his hand for her to return his phone. She noticed the name Tara Brown on the screen. It had been a waste of time throwing herself on Dimitris's mercy, Savannah thought bitterly.

On the counter was a mixing bowl containing a thick, pale liquid that looked like pancake batter. Frustration bubbled up inside her, and without pausing to consider the consequences she dropped Dimitris's phone into the batter.

He swore. 'Why the hell did you do that?'

'I didn't want you to complain about me to Tara Brown,' Savannah muttered. 'I really needed the Philpot's assignment.' She had burned her bridges now. The awfulness of what she had done was sinking in faster than Dimitris's phone had sunk to the bottom of the bowl of gloop.

His jaw hardened and she sensed that he was containing his anger with an effort. His steely self-control made Savannah feel even more idiotic. She wanted to provoke a reaction from him, and if that reaction was blazing fury that matched her own, so much the better.

She gasped as Dimitris's arm shot out with the deadly speed of a cobra, and he captured her hand in his firm grip. A sensation like an electrical current shot from her fingertips, all the way up her arm and spread through her body. She prayed he did not notice that her nipples had hardened and were jutting through her tee shirt.

He pushed her hand down into the bowl of batter mixture. She curled her fingers around his phone and when she lifted it out of the bowl, blobs of batter dripped onto the worktop.

'I will expect you to reimburse me for the cost of a new phone.'

That was a joke. His phone was an exclusive and very expensive brand, but her savings were almost depleted and she could not afford to pay for a replacement device. The most sensible thing to do would be to apologise profusely to Dimitris and claim temporary insanity if he decided to prosecute her for wilfully damaging his property. But the word sorry stuck in Savannah's throat.

Anger burned inside her. She had been her father's dutiful daughter and Dimitris's devoted lover, but both men had betrayed her and rejected her love. All her life she had suppressed her emotions, mindful that her father would disapprove of any bad behaviour. She had wanted his approval, his *love*, so badly, just as she had longed for Dimitris to love her years ago. Now she discovered that rebelliousness was empowering.

Saying nothing, she lifted her hand and wiped the phone down the front of Dimitris's shirt, smearing him with batter mixture. His eyes narrowed and gleamed dangerously, but Savannah was past caring. Her reputation for professionalism was in tatters and things couldn't get any worse. She wiped his phone over his shirt a second time. It felt so good to be bad.

There was a warning glint in Dimitris's dark blue gaze as he snatched the phone out of her fingers and dropped it onto the counter. Savannah braced herself for his anger, but he merely raised his brows and his mouth curved into a mocking smile.

'If you are so desperate for me to take my shirt off, you only had to ask,' he drawled.

Savannah stopped breathing when he grasped the hem of his top and lifted it slowly over his head to reveal his bare bronzed chest, overlaid with black body hairs that arrowed down his taut abdomen and disappeared beneath the waistband of his jeans. She could not recall if she had moved or he had, but they were standing so close that she breathed in the spicy scent of his aftershave.

'I...' She wanted to deny his suggestion that she'd hoped he would remove his shirt, but her tongue had cleaved to the roof of her mouth, and all she could do was stare at him and drink in his male beauty with eyes that felt like they were stretched too wide. It was like staring at the sun, and she was dazzled by him. If she lowered her lashes she knew his image would be imprinted on her retinas.

He had haunted her dreams for a decade, but this was no fantasy. Dimitris was real. Compelled by a need she did not fully understand to evoke a response from him, she laid her hand on his naked chest and felt the erratic thud of his heart mimic her own frantic heartbeat.

'You should not have come here, Savannah,' he said harshly as he clamped his hand over hers where it lay on his chest and dragged it down. Embarrassed that she had touched him, she was about to move away. But with a curse he wrapped his arm around her waist and hauled her towards him so that her breasts were crushed against the hard wall of his ribcage. She lifted her stunned gaze and found his face so close to hers that she could have counted his eyelashes if her attention hadn't been fixated on his mouth.

Ten years ago their chemistry had sizzled if they had so much as looked at each other, but Savannah's inexperience meant she had not understood her feminine power. Last night, and again now, she recognised the hungry gleam of desire in Dimitris's eyes and her heart thudded as she waited in breathless anticipation for him to kiss her.

He lowered his head until his lips almost met hers. His warm breath whispered across her skin, and she could not repress a shiver of longing as she inhaled the subtle scent of sweat and desire on his skin. But then, shockingly, he reared back and set her away from him, dropping his arm down to his side abruptly, so that she swayed on her feet.

'*Theós!*' he bit out savagely. His breathing was laboured, and she sensed that his control was as balanced on a knife-edge as hers was.

His rejection lacerated her fragile emotions, and her brain urged her to flee from him as an injured animal might make a dash for safety to lick its wounds. But her feet seemed to be welded to the floor and she could not move. As they stared at each other she was conscious of an ache low in her pelvis and the slick warmth between her thighs added to her humiliation that he might detect the betraying musky scent of her arousal.

'Good morning.' A female voice came from the doorway. 'Oh! I apologise if I am interrupting...' the woman said as Savannah hastily stepped back from Dimitris.

'Good morning, Tara.' His tone was casual, and his features that seconds earlier had looked as though they were carved from granite took on a bland expression as he greeted the woman who had entered the studio. 'You are not interrupting anything. But if you had arrived a couple of minutes ago you would have seen me accidentally spill pancake batter everywhere. Miss O'Neal was helping to clear up the mess.'

'O'Neal?' A frown appeared on Tara Brown's perfectly made-up face. She was the epitome of elegance in a pale grey trouser suit and matching stiletto heels.

Savannah wished she'd worn heels instead of trainers. Out of habit she ran her fingers through her hair before remembering she'd tied it in a ponytail, which came loose so that blonde strands fell across her face. She thought she heard Dimitris make a rough noise in his throat.

'I just tried calling you to let you know that a problem has arisen with the photoshoot,' Tara Brown told him.

Savannah's heart sank as she waited for Dimitris to denounce her. But, to her surprise, he slipped his phone that still bore traces of batter mixture into the back pocket of his jeans.

'I dropped my phone earlier and it doesn't appear to be working,' he murmured. 'Give me a couple of minutes to change my shirt and then you can explain the situation.' He nodded to Tara and did not look at Savannah as he swung round and strode to the far end of the studio to disappear through a doorway.

The team of production assistants were arriving. Bright, confident professionals who were chatting and laughing as if they did not have a care in the world, Savannah thought enviously. She was certain that Dimitris would tell Tara Brown what she had done to his phone, and in all honesty she could not blame him. Her career as a food photographer was effectively over as a result of her stupid behaviour. No one wanted a diva on a photoshoot. Her common sense belatedly put in an appearance, and she decided to slink away and avoid an embarrassing conversation with Philpot's PR executive.

Dimitris slammed the door of his office that doubled up as a dressing room when his cooking programmes were filmed at the kitchen studio. He headed into the adjoining shower room, threw his shirt into the laundry basket and braced his hands on the vanity unit. Resting his forehead on the cool tiles above the sink, he dragged oxygen into his lungs.

Damn her.

The previous evening's unexpected encounter with Savannah had disturbed him sufficiently that he'd taken steps to prevent a second meeting today. But evidently she hadn't been informed by the photographic agency that she was not required for the photoshoot. When he'd spotted Savannah in the garden he had been dismayed by his body's reaction to her.

Among his friends it was a joke that the media had labelled him the Hot Chef. The nickname was a tongue-in-cheek reference to his sex appeal rather than his temperament. In fact he was renowned for his coolness under pressure. Nothing fazed him. Working in professional kitchens was a notoriously stressful environment, but Dimitris always remained calm. However, meeting Savannah again had evoked a primitive response in him.

He pictured her in slim-fitting black trousers and a stretchy tee shirt that showed off her toned figure and those firm breasts that he'd glimpsed rather more of last night when they had spilled out of the front of her dress. When he'd found Savannah in a hotel room with his would-be brother-in-law she had looked like a seductress in her sexy dress. Dimitris told himself he could not be blamed for his assumption that she was Matt Collier's mistress. But she had insisted that she hadn't known Collier was engaged to Eleni. Ten years ago Savannah had been fiercely honest.

'Maybe you don't love me, but you can't stop me feeling the way I do about you. I love you, Dimitris.'

Cursing the unwanted memories of his relationship with a teenage Savannah that Dimitris had known from the start was a mistake, he strode across to the wardrobe and took out a clean shirt. In truth, the real reason he had asked Philpot's to arrange for a different photographer was because he'd wanted to avoid the edgy feeling Savannah aroused in him.

It was not the only thing she aroused, he thought self-derisively. He had been uncomfortably hard from the moment he'd found her in the garden, looking entirely too beautiful and still with that air of vulnerability that tugged on his protective instincts. Unfortunately, those instincts had not been apparent when he'd almost kissed her.

Dimitris did not know what disturbed him most— that he'd been overwhelmed by an urgent desire to cover Savannah's mouth with his, or that he'd come to his senses in time and pulled back. The flare of disappointment in her hazel-green eyes had nearly tempted him to take her in his arms again, and to hell with the consequences.

But he'd had to deal with the consequences of his actions on that fateful car journey eighteen years ago. He bitterly regretted his hot-headedness when he had been a teenager. Emotions were dangerous, which was why he channelled his passion into cooking, and why he never allowed any woman too close.

'You are an empty shell,' one of his ex-lovers had

accused him, when inevitably he'd ended the relation-ship after a few weeks.

Women had fallen for him since he was a youth, and more so since he'd become wealthy, he acknowledged cynically. What would they say if he told them that he was toxic? He had killed his parents and ruined his sister's life. How would Savannah react if he admit-ted the truth? He had never told her anything about the car accident. He'd never spoken to anyone about what had happened and his belief that it had been his fault.

Dimitris's jaw clenched. He was unlikely to ever see Savannah again. For years she had hovered on the pe-riphery of his consciousness. He had convinced him-self that he remembered her because she was the only virgin he'd slept with. He preferred his lovers to be ex-perienced and his no-strings rule was non-negotiable.

He switched on his phone and cursed when the screen remained blank. Savannah's outrageous be-haviour when she'd dropped his phone into the batter mixture had fired his temper, and in those moments of heightened emotion a mixture of anger and desire had seen him pull her into his arms. Thank God he'd come to his senses before he had kissed her.

The young woman he had known years ago had been sweet and shy and had adored him with a puppy-like devotion that Dimitris had been bitterly aware he did not deserve. This new Savannah had an attitude and a temper. She was even more beautiful and decidedly sassier than she'd been at eighteen, and she tested his self-control like no other woman ever had.

Determinedly shoving the past back where it belonged, Dimitris returned to the studio and found his assistants and technicians setting up for the photoshoot. Philpot's PR executive Tara Brown looked tense.

'The agency sent another photographer instead of Savannah O'Neal, as you requested,' she explained. 'There seems to be some confusion about why Miss O'Neal came to the studio today. Unfortunately, her replacement was involved in an accident on his way here and has been taken to hospital. I am trying to arrange another photographer, but I'm afraid it means a delay to the start of the photoshoot. The alternative is to postpone until another day.'

Dimitris did not favour delaying the shoot. His sister had flown to Athens that morning, in need of sympathy from a friend who was to have been her chief bridesmaid. He was keen to return to Rhodes and break the news to his grandmother that the wedding was cancelled before Eleni arrived at the villa. *Yιαγιά* Hestia's well-meant fussing would be too much for his sister right now.

The solution to get back on track was obvious, but he was reluctant to suggest that Savannah could take the photographs. He had a curious feeling that his life was about to change for ever. Impatiently, he reminded himself that he was in control of his destiny. His reaction to Savannah, *that near-kiss*, had stemmed from his shock at seeing her again.

'Rather than delay the shoot, you could ask Miss O'Neal to take the photos for the magazine. I might have acted too hastily when I asked for a different photographer.' He correctly interpreted Tara Brown's confused expression. 'I've had a second look at Miss O'Neal's portfolio and decided that I like her style of photography.'

Tara did not hide her relief. 'I saw her leave the studio a few minutes ago. I'll go after her.'

'She can't have got far.' Dimitris glanced at his watch. 'The shoot is already behind schedule, and we need to make a start.'

He was puzzled by Savannah's claim that she needed the Philpot's assignment. It couldn't be for financial reasons. When she'd turned twenty-five she should have come into a great deal of money that had been held in a trust fund managed by her father.

He recalled, with a mixture of bitterness and distaste, the meeting he'd had with Savannah's father ten years ago. The offer of money as a bribe had been humiliating. But he'd been persuaded to break off his relationship with Savannah to protect her fortune after Richard O'Neal had threatened to remove her as a beneficiary of the trust fund and cut her off financially. Dimitris wasn't proud that he'd accepted the money, but he had done so to prevent Savannah learning the truth about Richard.

Fate had conspired to throw them together again, he brooded. But he only had to get through today, and thankfully his emotions were back under control. Although the uncomfortable throb in his groin when Savannah walked into the studio a few minutes later mocked his belief that he was unaffected by her.

CHAPTER FOUR

'MISS O'NEAL...'

Savannah heard a voice behind her and slowly turned around to see Philpot's PR executive hurrying down the driveway. She braced herself for a showdown, convinced that Dimitris must have made a formal complaint about her behaviour.

'Thank goodness you hadn't left. We want you to stay for the photoshoot after all.' Tara Brown sounded flustered. 'The other photographer sent by the agency can't make it. Apparently he fell down the escalator at the tube station and has a suspected broken wrist.'

'Mr Kyriakou won't want to work with me,' Savannah said with certainty. Not because she had stupidly damaged his phone, but because Dimitris had wanted to kiss her. The self-disgust in his eyes when he'd set her away from him had heaped more humiliation on her.

'It was Dimitris's idea to call you back.'

Savannah wondered if the replacement photographer had really been involved in an accident. Perhaps Dimitris had set her up to humiliate her publicly for her unprofessional behaviour. But if there was any chance she could salvage her career and professional reputation she would be a fool not to take it. Still she hesitated, reluctant to face Dimitris again. It would be safer on her emotions if she walked away.

'Miss O'Neal?' the PR woman prompted.

'Okay,' Savannah said quickly before she could change her mind. She needed the money, and all she had to do was work with Dimitris for one day. 'I'll stay for the shoot.'

Her heart thumped as she followed Tara Brown across the garden, and she took a deep breath before she stepped into the studio. The oxygen escaped from Savannah's lungs in a whoosh when the first person she saw, the only person she saw in fact, even though the room was full of people, was Dimitris.

Her gaze collided with his and she noticed that his eyes were the same shade of navy-blue as the shirt he'd changed into after she'd wiped batter over him. The top couple of buttons were undone to reveal a vee of olive-gold skin and a sprinkling of black chest hairs. He was lethally beautiful, and it occurred to her that she might not survive him a second time.

For a split-second she was tempted to run back to her car and break the speed limit driving away from Richmond. Food photography entailed working in close proximity to the creator of the dishes. She would have to stand beside Dimitris and photograph each stage of him preparing his recipes, but how on earth would she be able to hide her treacherous body's response to him?

'Miss O'Neal. Savannah. Welcome to River Retreat

studio,' Dimitris greeted her smoothly. He glanced around at his assistants, mostly young women who gazed at him like adoring concubines in the presence of their sultan. 'We have a busy day ahead, but before we get down to business I prepared breakfast for everyone. Help yourself to Greek style pancakes with honey and walnuts. I made a fresh batch of pancake batter,' he added drily when Savannah sent him a startled look.

She felt herself blush as an assistant pushed a serving plate across the counter towards her. The thick, fluffy pancakes drizzled with golden honey and sprinkled with crushed walnuts looked divine, but although she was hungry her stomach rebelled at the idea of putting food into it. She doubted she'd ever look at a pancake again without cringing with embarrassment.

She unpacked her camera equipment and read through the schedule of dishes that she would be photographing. The art director and food stylist introduced themselves and discussed ideas for props to be used in the shoot. Dimitris strolled over to join in the conversation and Savannah hoped he did not notice her stiffen as she struggled to ignore her awareness of him.

'Thank you for giving me the chance to prove the quality of my work,' she murmured after the stylist and director had walked away.

'It makes sense for you to do the photoshoot as you are already here. I don't have time for a delay.' Dimitris's jaw hardened. 'I must go to Greece to support my sister.'

Savannah remembered how caring and protective he had been of Eleni years ago. She had even felt envious that he loved his sister but not her. From his curt tone she guessed he still blamed her for Eleni's broken engagement. Her temper simmered. She couldn't work with Dimitris while she was conscious of his disapproval.

'Is Eleni very upset?'

'What do you think?'

'I think Matt Collier made a fool of us both, and I also think Eleni could do better than to marry a cheat and liar.'

Dimitris stared at her, and Savannah thought she saw an imperceptible softening of his hard features that gave her hope he was prepared to believe she had been duped by Matt to have a relationship with him.

'Tell me about your methods for photographing food,' he said, breaking the tense silence between them. 'I see you use a DSLR.'

'A digital single-lens reflex camera allows me to shoot a lot of pictures fast so that I can capture every detail of a dish as it is being created. I'll take literally hundreds of shots to achieve the perfect image. Speed is of the essence,' Savannah explained as she warmed to her theme. 'I've discovered that it only takes seconds before a bowl of pasta loses its glossiness and looks dry, and crisp lettuce leaves adorned with a creamy dressing soon wilt and appear unappealing.'

He nodded. 'I agree that food must look so real it almost leaps off the page. When readers look at photographs in a magazine, rather than see inanimate pictures I want their senses to be fired so that they imagine the aroma of spicy lamb koftas and the crispy texture of filo pastry.' He glanced at his watch. 'There is a lot to do. I hope you're prepared for a long day.'

She followed Dimitris over to the kitchen island and watched him assemble the ingredients for the first dish he would cook. He moved with an easy grace and once again she was struck by how incredibly handsome he was. It was no surprise that he was a sex symbol to his legions of female fans. But Savannah was determined to ignore her inconvenient attraction to him and concentrate on the job that gave her the means to financially support her mum and pay for the care Evelyn needed as her MS worsened.

Tears pricked her eyes. Her mum was the sweetest, kindest person. Gentle and unworldly, Evelyn had been an art therapist who had devoted her time to helping others until her illness had forced her to give up work and she was no longer able to paint. Savannah would do anything for her mum, even if it meant working with the man who had once broken her heart. After today she would not have to see Dimitris again, but meanwhile her camera felt comfortably familiar in her hands as she started to shoot.

Hours later Savannah stretched, her muscles tight from standing for long periods of time and aiming her camera. She hitched herself onto a stool in front of the counter and opened her laptop to download the last batch of photographs. It would take her a few days to edit the pictures before sending them to the team at Philpot's. The art director and Dimitris would have the final say on which photos would appear in the magazine.

The photoshoot had been fast-paced and hectic, and she'd discovered that Dimitris was a consummate professional. He was a talented and passionate chef, and his recipes were innovative yet unfussy. Savannah had worked with many chefs since she'd become a food photographer, including some who were full of their own self-importance and strutted around the kitchen like demi-gods, shouting orders at their hapless assistants.

Dimitris was relaxed and charming, and he'd worked tirelessly throughout the long day to produce twelve different dishes—most chefs would make four or five. He'd insisted that the production team took breaks to eat the food once it had been photographed, but Savannah had been too engrossed in her work and had only drunk a couple of cups of coffee all day.

The awkwardness she'd felt with Dimitris had disappeared while they'd worked together. He had been keen for her to take unusual shots—a close-up of a mussel, a garlic clove at the moment it was crushed beneath the blade of a knife, spaghetti sliding out of the pan and falling messily onto a plate.

'I'm looking for authenticity in the photos,' he explained. 'Food shouldn't be perfectly arranged on a plate. Real food is honest and sexy, and I want images that make people drool.'

The dishes he created were a feast for the senses, and his energy and enthusiasm made him the most exciting chef Savannah had ever worked with. The photographs she had taken were some of her best, even to her perfectionist eyes. Looking up from her laptop some while later, she discovered that she was alone. The production team had packed up the lighting equipment and props and the kitchen assistants had cleared away the mountain of pots and pans. The studio was peaceful, bathed in the golden sunlight of a summer's evening.

Dimitris emerged from his dressing room. Evidently he'd just showered, and his hair was still damp and curled rebelliously over his collar. He had changed his clothes again and was wearing a white silk shirt and narrow black trousers that from their superb tailoring were doubtless a designer brand. Everything about the way he looked spoke of a successful self-made multimillionaire who had reached the pinnacle of his career and was comfortable in his own skin.

He stood behind Savannah and looked over her shoulder at the photos on her laptop screen. 'These are very good.'

'They'll be better after I've edited them.' She breathed in the citrus and spice scent of his cologne and felt a tug deep in her pelvis. 'I hadn't noticed how late it is. I'm sure you want to rush back to Greece to comfort your sister. Eleni must be devastated that her marriage plans have been ruined.'

'At least she discovered that Matt Collier is an unreliable cheat before she married him,' Dimitris said evenly. 'Eleni called to say she is going to stay with friends in Santorini for a few days and I am not in a rush to return to Rhodes.'

'I expect you have plans for the evening.' The tabloids had recently been in a frenzy after Dimitris was spotted leaving a nightclub with an actress from a popular TV soap. Savannah felt a stab of jealousy. She was desperate to leave before he guessed how much he still affected her. She packed up her laptop and slid off the stool, but an agonising sensation of pins and needles in her foot made her legs buckle.

Dimitris caught hold of her arm as she stumbled. 'Are you all right?' He cursed. 'I'm not surprised that you almost fainted. You didn't eat anything all day.'

'I'm fine.' She prayed he did not notice the frantic thud of her pulse in her wrist.

He clearly wasn't convinced. 'You can't drive home while you are feeling lightheaded. You had better stay for dinner.'

Savannah bit her lip. Dimitris had sounded far from enthusiastic. 'Three's a crowd. I assumed you have a date tonight,' she mumbled when he raised an eyebrow.

'I don't,' he said drily.

She looked away from his enigmatic gaze and saw a white stain down the front of her black tee shirt. The likely culprit was yoghurt. A tub had been spilt over the worktop and must have transferred to her clothes when she'd leaned in to take a close-up shot of a dish of moussaka with a yoghurt and cheese topping.

'You can freshen up at the house. Besides, we still need to discuss what you intend to do about replacing my phone.' He picked up her camera bag. 'Can you walk, or do you still feel faint?'

'I'm fine. It was just a cramp in my foot.' Common sense told her to decline his offer of dinner, but the microwavable meal waiting for her at home did not hold much appeal, and the opportunity to see inside his home was irresistible.

'My housekeeper Mary and her husband John look after the house and garden,' Dimitris explained when they left the studio and walked along a path lined with lavender bushes and roses. The perfume of the flowers was intoxicating in the sultry air of the summer's evening. The recent heatwave was forecast to end with thunderstorms.

'John also drives me when I need a chauffeur. Did you park in the road?' Savannah nodded. 'Give me your keys and John will move your car onto the driveway.'

He ushered her through a set of French windows into an elegant drawing room with a parquet floor. 'When the previous owners renovated the house they kept many of the original Victorian features,' Dimitris explained, watching Savannah trace her fingers over the oak panels that lined the walls.

She followed him into a huge entrance hall with an exquisite tiled floor. 'You have a beautiful house and an amazingly successful career. Did you ever imagine when you lived in a flat above your grandfather's restaurant that you would be a famous chef and would own a property in an expensive part of London?'

'Yes.' His chiselled features showed no emotion. 'I was always ambitious and knew where I wanted to be. I never doubted I would be successful.'

Dimitris had put his pursuit of success above everything else—including her. Savannah had always known it, but his stark admission did not hurt any less. His determination to establish his career had been at the expense of their relationship, such as it had been. She supposed he had used the money her father had given him to open his first restaurant in Greece.

The truth was that at eighteen she had been too young to fall in love. She had been looking for affection that her father had denied her, and she'd mistaken her teenage fascination with Dimitris for a deeper emotion. It infuriated her that she hadn't forgotten him in ten years. But she was an adult now and meeting him again was an opportunity to realise that he was not a fairy tale prince but an ordinary man with flaws, and she hoped she would finally be able to get over him.

The woman who Savannah had met when she'd arrived at River Retreat that morning emerged from the kitchen. 'Ah, Mary,' Dimitris greeted her. 'Can you show Miss O'Neal to the guest cloakroom. She will be staying for dinner. We'll eat outside on the deck.'

A few minutes later Savannah groaned when she saw her reflection in the cloakroom mirror. Her ponytail had come loose, and she had panda eyes where her mascara had smudged in the heat of the studio lights. She ran her fingers through her choppy shoulder-length bob. When she had worked as a cosmetics model she'd been advised by a make-up artist to always keep in her handbag eyeliner and a rose-coloured lip gloss that doubled up as blusher, to highlight her cheekbones.

A voice came from the hall. 'Miss O'Neal, I've brought you something to wear.' Savannah opened the door and saw the housekeeper holding a pile of colourful silks. 'Dimitris often hosts pool parties, and these kaftan dresses are for female guests if they want to cover up after swimming,' Mary explained. 'He suggested you might want to get changed and I'll launder your clothes while you are having dinner.'

Savannah remembered in the magazine article about Dimitris there had been a photo of the swimming pool, which was a modern addition in the basement of the house. He had been pictured sprawled on a poolside lounger, surrounded by gorgeous women wearing tiny bikinis and not a kaftan in sight.

Back in the cloakroom, she stripped off her stained tee shirt and trousers. Sifting through the kaftans, she picked one made of pale gold silk. The flowing gown felt deliciously cool on her skin, and the golden threads woven through the material glimmered softly when she moved.

She tied the matching belt around her waist and slipped off her trainers, deciding to go barefoot. For a final touch she took her perfume spritzer from her handbag and sprayed her neck and wrists with her favourite fragrance. The scent evoked memories of her eighteenth birthday party.

It nearly hadn't happened after her parents had been delayed by a tropical cyclone in Asia and were unable to fly home in time for her birthday. Her mother had persuaded her father to allow the party to go ahead. The sense of freedom had been heady when Savannah had woken on the day she turned eighteen, an adult free to make her own choices. Her first attempt to be more independent when she'd got a job as a waitress at Dimitris's grandfather's restaurant had not won her father's approval as she'd hoped. He had said that Hestia's restaurant in a run-down area of London was not the kind of place he expected his daughter to work. Savannah had felt that she could never please her father.

The party that evening had been on the terrace next to the outdoor pool. The party organisers had set up a champagne bar in the pool house and the caterers had served canapés. Savannah remembered that she had laughed and danced and given the impression that she was having a wonderful time. But as the hours had passed and *he* hadn't arrived, she'd wanted to cry with disappointment.

'Dimitris is working this evening,' Eleni had told her when in a fiercely casual voice Savannah had asked if he was coming to the party. 'The private function was booked at the last minute. My grandfather said we need the money and Dimitris must cook tonight, even though Hestia's is usually closed on Sundays.'

Eleni had tired easily and needed to go home early. Savannah had wheeled her chair out to the car when her grandfather came to collect her. The party had palled after Eleni had left, and she'd been relieved when the other guests departed at eleven o'clock, leaving behind the debris of balloons and banners and birthday cake squashed onto the patio stones. She'd kicked off her high heels and sat on the side of the pool to dip her toes in the water when a deep voice over her shoulder caused her pulse to skyrocket...

'Happy birthday, Savannah.'

Dimitris emerged from the shadows, and she scrambled to her feet, staring at him with her heart in her eyes. 'You came,' she said breathlessly.

'I said I would.' He gave a wry smile. 'Better late than never.'

There was still an hour left of her birthday and Dimitris's arrival made it the best birthday ever. She smiled at him, and the low sound he made in his throat sent a quiver of excitement through her. It occurred to her that she'd only ever seen him at the restaurant when she answered the service bell or carried dirty plates to the sink. Her shy overtures and his playful flirting had taken place in a busy kitchen. This was the first time she'd been alone with him.

'I have never seen you look as beautiful as you do tonight.' Dimitris had only ever seen her wearing a waitress's uniform. Savannah had spent hours choosing a dress for the party, and she hoped the silver halter-neck gown would make him realise that she wasn't a foolish girl. She was a woman with needs that only he could fulfil.

'This is for you,' he said huskily. 'Your birthday present.'

She took the package he held out and ripped off the brightly coloured wrapping paper to reveal a bottle of perfume. Sensuelle, the new fragrance by a famous perfume house, was exorbitantly expensive.

'Thank you, but you shouldn't have…' she faltered, blushing at her clumsiness.

'I won't always be poor,' he drawled. There was steel beneath his soft tone. 'Allow me.' He unscrewed the lid on the bottle and tipped a few drops of perfume onto his fingertip. 'Move your hair.'

Mesmerised by him, she lifted her hair and he

pressed his finger to the sensitive spot behind her ear, transferring the exquisite fragrance to her skin. Her heart thudded as Dimitris trailed his fingers over her neck and collarbone, hovered over the pulse beating erratically at the base of her throat, before sliding down her décolletage to the vee between her breasts.

'You've driven me crazy for weeks.' His hoarse admission made her feel dizzy with desire and when he drew her into his arms she tilted her face up to his and parted her lips for his kiss. Dimitris's eyes were the inky blue of the night sky and gleamed as brightly as the stars. 'I want to make love to you, *mátia mou*.'

She pressed herself closer to him, eager to become a woman and give her body to the man who had captured her heart. 'I want you too.'

Swallowing hard, Savannah jerked her mind back to the present. Ten years ago she had been young and in love. She'd naively believed that Dimitris felt the same way about her—although he'd never actually said that he loved her, she thought with a heavy sigh.

When she stepped out of the cloakroom the housekeeper was waiting for her and led the way through the house and across the garden. Dimitris was standing on the deck, half turned towards the river. Savannah's heart missed a beat as she studied his proud profile. He was gorgeous—and unobtainable. She understood now what she'd refused to accept at eighteen, when her heart had been full of hope and her head full of dreams.

Anger seared her with the white heat of a lightning bolt. She was furious with herself for being so affected by Dimitris. How pathetic that she only wore the brand of perfume he had given her for a birthday present *ten years ago* as some kind of homage to him. She was twenty-eight and he was the only man she had slept with. She was mired in the past, trapped by the immature feelings she'd once had for Dimitris. It was time, way past time in fact, that she moved on and stopped being an idiot over a playboy who probably hadn't given her a second thought in years.

CHAPTER FIVE

DIMITRIS SENSED SAVANNAH'S presence behind him although she hadn't made a sound. The evocative fragrance she wore was carried towards him on the faint breeze, evoking memories he had never managed to forget and rousing his body to instant and urgent life.

There had been occasions in the past decade when he'd been in a nightclub or bar somewhere in the world and caught a hint of perfume that he recognised as Sensuelle, and had found himself transported back in time to a balmy summer's night in a north London suburb.

By the time he'd finished work at the restaurant he'd known that Savannah's party would have ended. If he'd had any sense he would not have jumped on his motorbike and ridden to her parents' mansion on the edge of Hampstead Heath. But then if he'd had any sense he would not have spent far more of his wages than he could afford on perfume for her birthday present.

All summer he had been enchanted by Savannah's shy smile. She'd made him think he could be a better person than he knew he was, and even that he might one day be able to forgive himself for destroying his family. It had been a difficult summer, with worries about his grandfather's failing health and his sister's latest round of surgery. Savannah had been a distraction from his responsibilities and the guilt that hung like a dark shadow over him.

His grandfather would have retired years before if Dimitris's father had been alive to take over the restaurant. Likewise, if the accident hadn't happened Eleni would have been able to go dancing, but instead she was stuck in a wheelchair while her schoolfriends had fun. Only Savannah hadn't abandoned her friend, and her loyalty had forged a strong bond between the two girls.

Dimitris had been aware of Savannah's fascination with him. It was not the first time it had happened, and previously with other young women he had gently but firmly made it clear that he wasn't interested. He should not have got involved with Savannah and he certainly should not have made love to her on a daybed in the pool house, especially after she'd confirmed his suspicion that she was a virgin.

Cursing beneath his breath, he jerked his mind away from the past. But there was danger in the present, he realised as he raked his gaze over Savannah and felt an urge to spear his fingers in her messily sexy blonde hair.

All day he had been supremely conscious of her standing close to him in the studio while she'd taken photos of the food he'd cooked. Her svelte figure revealed by her tight-fitting clothes had driven him to distraction. It should be a relief that she had changed into a loose kaftan that concealed rather than flaunted her feminine shape. But the shimmering silk skimmed her body and gave a hint of the delectable curves beneath it.

For years whenever Dimitris had detected the heady scent of dark red roses mixed with the sweetness of peonies and the smoky warmth of the exotic essential oil Oudh that a perfumier had combined to create Sensuelle, he had instinctively looked for Savannah and felt unsettled by his disappointment that she was not there. She was here now, and he was conscious of the heavy thud of his pulse when she came to stand beside him on the deck.

He pulled out a chair for her to sit down at the table and knew from the imperceptible stiffening of her body that she felt the electrical current that passed between them.

'Your car wouldn't start,' he told her as he moved round the table and sat opposite her. 'John thinks it might need a new battery. He'll arrange for the car to be towed to a garage in the morning so that it can be checked by a mechanic.' He uncorked the wine. 'At least you can have a drink. John will drive you home later.'

She seemed about to decline, but then gave a shrug. 'Why not. It's been quite a day.'

He poured the wine and lifted his glass towards her. 'To unexpected reunions,' he murmured drily.

Dimitris had chosen a robust red made from a variety of grapes called Xinomavro that were grown on the wine estates in northern Greece. There was an earthiness to the wine, yet it was surprisingly smooth. Savannah took a sip from her glass and gave a faint sigh as she visibly relaxed.

'This looks amazing,' she murmured, studying the platters of food on the table when Dimitris removed the covers.

There were colourful salads, dolmades—vine leaves stuffed with rice and herbs, meatballs with feta cheese, grilled Halloumi served with wedges of lemon and plump Kalamata olives.

'Mezze is my favourite kind of meal,' he admitted as he passed her various dishes. 'I think of it as honest food made from simple ingredients, but created with care and passion it becomes a feast. Sharing food with friends is one of life's fundamental pleasures.'

Cooking was much more than his career. It was an outlet for his creativity and allowed him to deal with emotions that he kept under tight control in every other area of his life and relationships.

Savannah tucked in enthusiastically. 'Everything is delicious,' she said as she tore off a piece of pitta bread, dipped it into a bowl of creamy hummus and popped the morsel into her mouth. 'And messy.' Her tongue darted out to lick hummus from her fingers. Catching Dimitris's gaze, she gave him an impish smile. 'I haven't discovered an elegant way to eat with my fingers.'

Elegant be damned. His blood roared in his ears. Earlier he had been reminded of how tactile Savannah was when he'd watched her stroke her fingers over the wooden panels in the drawing room. He had imagined her touching him and learning his body anew. Now he felt an overwhelming urge to stride around the table and pull her into his arms so that he could flick his tongue over the corner of her mouth and lick off the tiny smear of hummus. He wanted to taste the red wine that stained her lips. But overwhelmed was not a word in his vocabulary. It suggested a loss of control, and he never allowed that to happen.

He forced his mind from the carnal thoughts that he reminded himself were inappropriate when he'd already decided he would not see Savannah again after this evening. But he was curious about her and steered the conversation to safer topics.

'What made you decide to work behind a camera rather than in front of it?'

'I suppose you are referring to my brief modelling career.' This time her smile was self-deprecating. 'It wasn't something I set out to do. After university I got a job with a web design company.'

'I remember you had planned to study art at university.' It was disturbing that he had not forgotten anything about her, Dimitris brooded. Savannah had made an impact on him in a way that no other woman ever had.

'I switched to fine art photography. But I found working in web design didn't really interest me. When I was spotted by a modelling agency and won a contract to represent a cosmetics company it gave me a new direction and the opportunity to travel and meet some interesting people.'

'Why did you stop?'

'My mum fell ill, and I moved back home to help

look after her.' Savannah drank the rest of her wine, and Dimitris leaned across the table to refill her glass. 'When Mum was first diagnosed with multiple sclerosis she was still able to work in her garden that she loved so much. For fun I started playing around taking photos of the vegetables she'd grown and the meals we made from home produced ingredients. I put together a series of photographs for a calendar to raise funds for the MS charity. That led to my interest in food photography. Being a freelance photographer allows me to arrange my work so that I'm at home when Mum's carer has a day off.'

She sighed. 'The downside of being self-employed is that I don't earn a regular salary and it's taking a while to establish myself as a food photographer. I hope my car won't be too expensive to fix because I can't afford a big repair bill...or buy you a new phone.'

Dimitris was annoyed at the inconvenience of having to replace the phone that Savannah had destroyed, but he was even more irritated that she'd blatantly lied. 'You must have had a wild time for the last three years to have spent the substantial amount of money in your trust fund,' he drawled.

She looked puzzled. 'How do you know I was supposed to receive a lot of money when I turned twenty-five? When we knew each other ten years ago I was unaware that my father had created a trust fund and made me the beneficiary.'

Dimitris silently cursed his mistake in mentioning the trust fund that Richard O'Neal had spoken of when he'd blackmailed him to end his relationship with Savannah by threatening to cut off financial support for her. 'You said you were *supposed* to receive the money. Why didn't you?'

She lifted her glass and drank more wine before replying. 'Three years ago my father was suspected of financial impropriety. Following a lengthy police investigation he was charged and later convicted of serious fraud. His assets were seized, including money that he'd placed in a trust fund. I was meant to be the beneficiary, but my father, who was the sole trustee, had established the fund to launder money he'd acquired through his corrupt business dealings. Obviously I didn't have a legal right to the fund that was used to conceal my father's criminal activities.'

While they had been eating, dusk had fallen and the solar lamps on the deck cast long shadows. 'Two months ago my father died, owing several million pounds,' Savannah continued tonelessly. 'At the end of his trial he was found guilty and given a five-year prison sentence. His outstanding legal bill and other debts must be paid out of his estate, and there will be nothing left for my mum to live on.'

'*Theós!*' Dimitris was stunned by the news of Richard O'Neal's death, and the realisation that the other man had taken the details of their private conversation to his grave. He gathered that Richard hadn't told Savannah he was not in fact her father. From what Savannah had said, Dimitris guessed her mother had not explained the truth. It was not his place to reveal the secret that was likely to be devastating for Savannah, but he felt uncomfortable. 'What about Pond House?' he asked.

'It will have to be sold to pay back everything my father owed. I haven't had the heart to tell my mum how bad the situation really is. She loves Pond House. I would do anything to keep it, but I can't see a way. Mum doesn't have any money of her own and I've spent virtually all of my savings on the upkeep of the house and private nursing care for her.'

Savannah gave a hollow laugh. 'It's a pity I didn't marry Hugo Roxwell when I had the chance. At least I would have been entitled to the sizeable divorce settlement which was included in the prenuptial agreement Hugo had wanted me to sign.'

When Dimitris had seen a photo of Savannah smiling at her English aristocrat and showing off a diamond engagement ring he'd felt sick to his stomach. The newspaper had reported that the happy couple were planning a lavish wedding at the country estate of Hugo's father, Lord Roxwell.

For three days Dimitris had drunk himself into a stupor, but then he'd sobered up and focused on building his career, and if occasionally he'd imagined Savannah happily married and with a brood of children, he'd reminded himself that he did not deserve to have a wife and a family of his own. He wondered why she hadn't married.

'I take it that the path of true love did not run smoothly. You didn't waste any time after we had broken up, accepting a marriage proposal from your aristocrat boyfriend.'

She glared at him. 'I think I can be forgiven for being flattered by Hugo's attention after the way you treated me. You told me on the day I was flying to New York for a belated birthday trip with my parents that our relationship was over. When I arrived home four days later, the restaurant was boarded up and a neighbour told me that you had moved to Greece with your grandparents and sister.'

Her voice was unsteady. 'Eleni was my best friend, but I didn't get a chance to say goodbye to her. She sent a text saying that you had told her not to keep in contact with me. That was cruel. Even if you hated me, you had no right to spoil my friendship with Eleni.'

'I didn't hate you,' Dimitris muttered. He could not explain that Richard O'Neal had insisted on severing all ties. 'I suppose your father approved of your aristocrat.'

She nodded. 'My father had come from a poor background, and he was obsessed with status and climbing the social ladder. He put pressure on me to marry well. He'd invested money in an art gallery owned by Lord Roxwell and managed by Hugo. My father arranged for me to work as an assistant at the gallery and persuaded me to defer my place at university for a year.'

Savannah sighed. 'Hugo was charming and attentive. The truth is that I was on the rebound after you had dumped me, and I convinced myself that I had feelings for Hugo. But I realised that I wasn't ready for marriage. When I suggested to Hugo that we should wait for a year or two, he was furious. He admitted he'd wanted a rushed wedding because his grandmother's will stated that he had to be married before he could claim the inheritance she had left him. Hugo moaned that his father gave him a pittance for an allowance.'

Her hazel-green eyes glowed with angry fire. 'Hugo was only interested in money, and he wasn't in love with me. I seem to attract men who don't care about me. You didn't,' she said bitterly.

In fact he had begun to have feelings for Savannah ten years ago, Dimitris brooded. He'd been terrified that he could actually fall in love with her. Love was a responsibility he did not want. In his head he had still been a grief-stricken fourteen-year-old boy. Supposing he caused an accident and Savannah died, just as his parents had died? He could not bear to lose someone else he loved. He had decided when he was a teenager that it was safer not to allow love into his life, and it was a rule he'd kept for the past eighteen years. But he owed Savannah some sort of explanation.

'I accepted money from your father because my grandfather was seriously ill and desperate to return to Rhodes. My grandparents had spent what little money they had on caring for my sister and I after our parents were killed. The money allowed me to buy a house in the village where my grandfather had been born so that he and my grandmother could retire, and it was where he died two years later.'

Savannah stood up and walked to the edge of the deck. For a few moments she stared at the dark river before she turned and leaned against the rail. The moon had risen and in its silvery gleam she was mystical and insanely beautiful. Dimitris could not look away from her. In the distance came the rumble of thunder that warned of a gathering storm.

'You put a financial value on me when I was eighteen and made me feel worthless. You took my pride and my heart and trampled on them.'

His jaw clenched when he heard the pain in her voice. He felt guilty that he'd hurt her, but he could not explain that one reason he'd accepted money from Richard O'Neal had been to protect Savannah's financial security. It was ironic that despite his good intentions and his belief that he had acted in Savannah's best interest, she and her mother had been left penniless as a result of Richard's criminal activities.

'I can understand that you'd wanted to help your grandfather. It must have been an easy decision to accept money from my father because you never loved me,' she said, still in that brittle voice that felt like a knife in his chest. 'But there is something you want from me, isn't there, Dimitris?'

He wanted to deny it, but his heart gave a jolt when Savannah untied the belt of her kaftan. 'What are you doing?' he demanded.

She did not reply, and his breath hissed between his teeth as he watched her lift the gold silk gown over her head in a fluid movement and drop it onto the deck. Dimitris heard a harsh curse and realised it had come from him. Savannah's pale pink bra and knickers were not especially fancy, but somehow that made her even sexier.

'Put that goddamned thing back on.' He stared at the kaftan that was a pool of gold at her feet, not daring to look at a half-naked Savannah when he was imagining peeling her panties down her milky thighs. 'You are making a fool of yourself,' he bit out.

'I have been a fool over you for too long.' She walked back across the deck, a silver goddess dappled by moonlight.

Dimitris felt his blood thicken and head south to his sex as his eyes were drawn to the dark outline of her nipples visible beneath her lacy bra cups. He leaned back in his chair when she stood in front of him. For once she was taller than him and he had to look up at her face.

Theós! She was as exquisite as Aphrodite from ancient Greek legend. He felt a nerve flicker in his cheek as he fought to control his response to her. 'What do you think I want from you?'

She leaned towards him and placed her hands on his shoulders. Her breasts swung forwards and he clenched his fists to stop himself from cradling the plump mounds in his palms.

'This,' she whispered against his mouth.

And God help him, Dimitris could not deny it. But he *must* resist Savannah. She was the only woman to have ever breached his defences and he could not risk getting close to her again. But knowing the danger did not lessen his craving.

She was such a fool. She should have known that challenging the iceman would result in her humiliation. Dimitris's hands lay on his thighs, and he made no attempt to touch her. His mouth was a rigid line beneath her lips and his eyes had narrowed so that Savannah had no idea what he was thinking. Only the laboured rise and fall of his chest gave a clue that he was not as unaffected as he wanted her to believe.

Frantic to evoke a reaction from him, she nipped his lower lip with her teeth. His lashes flew open and the hard glittering desire in his eyes caused her heart to miss a beat. Dimitris swore and clamped his hand to the back of her head as he opened his mouth beneath hers and the kiss exploded between them. *Finally.*

Savannah's limbs turned to jelly. She had initiated the kiss, but Dimitris took charge of it, sliding his lips over hers with thrilling mastery. A sudden loud clap of thunder sent shockwaves through her and raindrops as big as pennies spattered against the deck and lashed her skin.

Without breaking the kiss, Dimitris levered himself out of his chair and wrapped his arm around her waist to steady her. He towered over her, and she arched her neck while he continued kissing her and kissing her with a hunger that made her wonder if he had missed her through the long years apart as much as she had missed him. Of course he hadn't, her common sense piped up. He was responding in the same way that any male in the prime of his life would when a woman had thrown herself at him.

The rain was falling harder, and Dimitris's black curls were plastered to his brow. He caught hold of her hand and pulled her after him across the sodden lawn towards the house. Lamps had been switched on in the drawing room and their harsh brightness was an unwelcome return to reality after the concealing darkness outside.

Savannah felt the beginning of a headache that was probably the result of the wine. She only occasionally drank alcohol, and the wine had loosened her tongue and her inhibitions. But then Dimitris drew her into his arms, and she was only aware of him. His hands burned her skin and she ached for him to kiss her again until they were both ablaze in the inferno.

His midnight-dark eyes were as unfathomable as the deepest ocean. 'What do you want from me, Savannah?'

'One night with you. No strings and afterwards we walk away with no regrets.'

Her voice was surprisingly steady considering her outrageous request. But she needed to do this. She was sure she remembered her very short affair with Dimitris through rose-coloured lenses. If she slept with him again she would realise that their relationship hadn't been the life-altering experience she'd let herself believe for all this time.

His expression was as enigmatic as always, but his hands gripped her waist harder, and she sensed his shock and something more primitive that made her heart kick in her chest. 'Why?'

'There is unfinished business between us. If you had stayed in London and we'd continued seeing each other perhaps our relationship would have petered out. But you left abruptly, and I couldn't forget you. You have been a splinter under my skin, and I want to be free of you.'

Dimitris raised an eyebrow. 'It's the first time I've been likened to a splinter.' His voice deepened and the hard glitter in his eyes sent a tremor through Savannah. 'But I agree we have unfinished business to resolve.' He stepped back from her and held out his hand. 'Come with me?'

Part of her wished he wasn't making it her choice. It would be easier if he swept her into his arms and carried her off to bed. But Savannah knew that this had to be her decision. When she put her fingers in his, the flare of hunger in Dimitris's eyes told her that beneath his coolness a fire raged. Without another word he tugged her after him out of the room and across the hall to the stairs.

She was breathless when they reached the second-floor landing, but from nervous excitement rather than exertion. His bedroom was overtly masculine with sleek, dark wood furnishings, a huge bed with a black leather headboard and, of all things, a mirror on the ceiling. Savannah tried not think of how many other women he must have made love to on the bed. Her face grew warm as she imagined herself and Dimitris lying on the satin sheets and looking up at the reflection of their naked bodies.

Anticipation and a sense of disbelief that this was happening and she was actually going to have sex with Dimitris made her feel strangely lightheaded.

'Savannah?' There was a question in his voice as if he thought she had changed her mind.

Keen to disabuse him of the idea, she put her hands on the front of his shirt and started to undo the buttons. Her fingers were shaking, and she took a deep breath. She didn't want Dimitris to guess that she was relatively inexperienced. 'You should get out of your wet clothes before you catch a chill.'

'There's not a chance of that happening. I'm burning up,' he said hoarsely when she spread his shirt open.

His skin felt like warm satin beneath her palms. The whorls of black hairs on his chest were thicker than she remembered. He had been handsome when he was younger, but now he was breathtaking, so big and male—and aroused, she discovered when he tumbled her down on the bed and lay beside her so that they were hip to hip. She felt the unmistakable bulge of his erection beneath his trousers.

Dimitris claimed her mouth in a kiss that was intensely erotic but also poignantly evocative of when they had been lovers all those years ago. Savannah couldn't stop shaking as she acknowledged the enormity of what she was about to do. Not to mention how enormous he was, she thought with slightly hysterical humour. Was she making a mistake?

Doubt swirled in the pit of her stomach. Should she tell him that she hadn't made love for ten years, and he was her only lover? But he might reject her if she admitted her inexperience. The whole point of sleeping with him was a form of exorcism to free herself from the hold that Dimitris had over her. She just needed to get on with it, Savannah told herself as she kissed him feverishly, pressing her pelvis closer to the tantalising length of his manhood.

'You *are* eager,' he drawled. 'And so am I. You are very beautiful, Savannah.'

He traced his hands over her trembling body and

stroked his fingertips up and down her spine, soothing her as if she were a restless colt and he was her master. Savannah's limbs felt heavy as she gradually relaxed. Her cheek was resting on Dimitris's chest, and the powerful beat of his heart made her feel safe in his arms while the storm raged.

This was wrong. Dimitris shoved away the thought that it felt incredibly right for Savannah to be in his bed. The glow from the lamps gave her skin a pearlescent sheen. Her hair was a cloud of spun gold on the pillow and her mouth was lush and tempting. He cupped her breast and felt the hard point of her nipple jutting beneath her bra. Desire kicked hard in his gut, and his erection pressed painfully against the zip on his trousers.

His conscience insisted that he should not have brought her to his room. He should have been stronger and resisted the urgent drumbeat of desire pounding in his veins. He couldn't remember the last time he had been so turned on by a woman that his self-control was threatened. It had been the same ten years ago, a voice in his head taunted him. On the night of Savannah's eighteenth birthday he'd been blown away by her transformation from a shy waitress to a beautiful, sexy woman.

The image she had projected that night had been an illusion, Dimitris brooded. Beneath her seductive party dress she'd been innocent and unworldly, and when he'd made love to her he had been grimly aware that she deserved a better man than him. He hadn't told her that he'd been to blame for his parents' deaths and Eleni's injuries. Selfishly, he had enjoyed Savannah's adoration, even though he'd known that the future she'd hoped for with him would never happen.

But she was different now, he assured himself. Older and more experienced. *Theós*, she had propositioned him and suggested they have sex with no strings attached. Unfinished business. He'd agreed because she had been in his mind for a decade, and he wanted to move on. The chemistry between them had always been white-hot and even though he'd been furious when he'd found her at a hotel with his sister's fiancé, his body had responded on a primitive level, and he'd felt a searing attraction to Savannah.

Why not take what she was offering? He wasn't a hormone-fuelled twenty-two-year-old. He'd had countless lovers and never lost control with any of the women he'd taken to bed. It would be no different with Savannah, he assured himself.

CHAPTER SIX

SAVANNAH OPENED HER eyes and saw herself. Her reflection in the mirror above the bed was shadowy in the pearly half-light created by moonbeams slanting through a chink in the closed curtains. Dimitris was lying on his stomach beside her. She could not see his face, and his dark head was pillowed on his forearms. Her eyes followed the long line of his spine down to the waistband of his grey sweatpants that sat low on his hips.

He was on top of the sheet, and when she peeped beneath it she discovered that she was still wearing her bra and knickers. Memories of the previous night returned, and she was mortified that *nothing* had happened. She must be the only woman in the world to proposition a man and fall asleep in his bed before the action had started. She'd achieved nothing except to make a fool of herself—again.

Shuffling up the bed, she leaned across to the bedside table and saw the illuminated numbers on the digital clock—two a.m. A touch as light as gossamer brushed across her shoulder. Her heart was in her throat when she turned her head and met Dimitris's unfathomable gaze.

'Did we…?' She needed to check.

He shifted onto his side and propped himself on his elbow. 'If you believe that I'm the kind of man who would take advantage of a young woman who had drunk more wine than was wise, why did you offer yourself to me?'

His voice was controlled, but Savannah realised he was very angry. 'I don't believe you took advantage of me,' she assured him quickly. She hadn't seen him for a decade, but people did not change fundamentally, and she had always felt safe with him.

'I'm glad to hear it.' His eyes narrowed, hiding his thoughts. 'If we had made love you would not need to ask.'

His arrogance should have appalled her but she envied his self-confidence, while hers had taken another battering. 'Wine tends to make me feel sleepy,' she admitted ruefully. 'But I wasn't drunk when I asked to spend the night with you. I knew what I was saying. I appreciate you might have been trying to spare me embarrassment with the excuse that I'd had too much alcohol. But making an idiot of myself is something I do really well, and it's fine to admit that you don't want to have sex with me.'

Dimitris moved so fast that before Savannah could blink she was lying flat on her back and he was on top of her. 'Does this feel like I don't want you?' he growled. The weight of his body pressed her into the mattress and the heat of his skin scorched her.

She caught her breath as she felt the hard length of his erection beneath his sweatpants. With slow deliberation he circled his hips against her pelvis, making her aware of just how aroused he was. The heat of her feminine arousal pooled between her thighs.

'I needed to be sure that you are sure,' he told her. 'If you have changed your mind…?'

She licked her dry lips and saw his gaze focus intently on her mouth. 'I haven't.'

'Good.' The satisfaction in Dimitris's voice sent a quiver of response through Savannah. He moved so that he was lying on his side next to her and skimmed his hand over her body, creating a path of fire from her collarbone down to her hips and back again. He paused to investigate the dip of her navel before moving up to her breast. Savannah sucked in a breath as he stroked his thumb across her nipple. It instantly puckered and jutted against the fine lace of her bra cup.

'You were always *so* responsive,' he growled.

Sensation arrowed down to her feminine core, and she could not restrain a gasp of pleasure when he put his mouth over her nipple and sucked hard. She needed more and groaned her approval when he peeled the damp scrap of lace away from her breast.

The air felt cool on her exposed nipple. He bent his head once again and she speared her fingers in his hair to hold him to his task of licking one taut peak and then its twin. Desire flooded through her, and she was molten between her legs and ready for his exploratory fingers when he moved his hand down and eased the panel of her panties aside.

Savannah was certain that Dimitris held the key to her freedom. She'd held back from making love with other men, even with Hugo during their brief engagement, because on a subconscious level she'd felt that her body belonged to Dimitris. After tonight she would be able to relegate him to the past and in the future she hoped to have new relationships where she could explore her sensuality and perhaps meet a man who would fall in love with her.

At least that was the plan. But when Dimitris brushed his thumb over her moist opening and gently parted her before easing a finger inside her, she was instantly lost to his magician's touch. He muttered something in Greek as he tugged her knickers off and spread her legs wider apart.

When he pushed his finger deeper, gently stretching her, she arched her hips towards his hand, desperate for more of the exquisite sensations he was arousing with his intimate caresses. She gave a little sob of disappointment when he withdrew his finger and rolled away from her.

'Patience,' he murmured in a hoarse tone that sent a shiver of anticipation through her. He had stripped off his sweatpants and the sight of his muscular, hugely aroused naked body made her feel hesitant for a few seconds, especially when she watched him roll a condom down his swollen length.

He positioned himself above her, supporting his upper body with his hands on either side of her head so that he wasn't quite touching her. She melted in the heat of him, and her feminine instincts took over so that she slid her arms around his back and urged him down onto her. The press of his manhood against her opening almost sent her over the edge, but it also felt like the first time, ten years ago, when she had been nervous and unsure.

Dimitris tensed. 'Do you want to stop?'

'No.' She couldn't stop now that she'd got this far. She wanted to spend tonight with him so that she could bury the past. Beneath Dimitris's passionate caresses she recognised that he was holding back from her, as he had done when they were younger. For him it had only been about sex. She understood that now, and she needed to prove to herself that she could sleep with him without her emotions being involved.

He covered her mouth with his and the kiss exploded between them, wild and urgent. Dimitris pushed his tongue between her lips as if he wanted to learn the taste of her again, or as if he'd never forgotten. While their mouths clung, he eased forwards and entered her slowly, filling her inch by inch and waiting while her internal muscles relaxed to accommodate his powerful erection.

It was mind-blowing. A million times better than she remembered, and with a flash of despair Savannah wondered if her outrageous plan had backfired. How could sex with anyone else be better than this?

It got worse, by which her dazed brain meant it got a whole lot better when Dimitris started to move. He rocked forwards and drew back, once, twice, setting a steady rhythm. She lifted her hips to meet each thrust, remembering the synchronised dance they had performed countless times during the eleven nights they'd spent together so long ago. It was as if nothing had changed and now, as then, they moved together in perfect harmony.

* * *

He was a fool. But Dimitris could not think about his failings while he was buried deep inside Savannah. He refused to listen to his brain when it pointed out that it had been a mistake to have sex with her—not when it felt so right. More disturbing was the possessiveness that pounded in his blood while he drove into her and took them both inexorably closer to the edge. *She is mine...she is mine.* The mingled scent of the perfume Savannah wore and her musky feminine fragrance heightened his desire, and he did not care that he'd vowed never to own or be owned by anyone.

One night, no strings. And afterwards he would be free from his memories, and the dreams he sometimes had that she was in bed beside him, but when he rolled over to pull her close she wasn't there and he felt an emptiness inside him—as if everything he'd achieved, his successful career and the money and fame, meant nothing.

One night, already half gone, to sate himself on Savannah's gorgeous body. He'd never expected to meet her again, let alone reacquaint himself with her silken skin and delicate curves. When he'd pushed his shaft into her, she had been so tight that he had almost lost control there and then. He wondered how many lovers she'd had in the past ten years. His instinct told him not many, and there was no reason why that should have pleased him.

Dimitris concentrated on giving Savannah pleasure. Her breasts were especially sensitive, and he loved the moans she made when he used his mouth on her nipples, licking and sucking the swollen peaks while she dug her nails into his shoulders. He slipped his hand between their joined bodies and discovered the hidden nub of her clitoris. She tensed as he rubbed his thumb across her feminine heart while he continued to thrust into her with long, deep strokes.

With a sense of shock he realised that he was about to come, and he gritted his teeth, desperate to hold back the tidal wave. It *never* happened to him. He enjoyed sex but he was always in control. He stilled, and made himself wait, dragging oxygen into his lungs as he stared down at Savannah.

She was so beautiful, her face flushed with passion and her lips reddened from his kisses. Her eyelashes lifted and her eyes were more green than hazel as she stared back at him in a silent communication that went beyond words. Something moved inside Dimitris then, and an emotion he dared not define squeezed his heart.

'Please,' she whispered, locking her legs around his hips as if she feared he would leave her.

'I will please you, *mátia mou*,' he rasped. It was a promise rather than a boast. He pulled back almost completely and gave a powerful thrust, claiming her utterly. She sobbed his name and tremors tore through her as she climaxed hard. Her internal muscles convulsed around him, velvet on steel, and it was too much. The wave crashed over him in an unstoppable, uncontrollable tsunami before throwing him onto the shore, and he was dazed to realise he had survived the storm. But as his heart-rate gradually slowed, his cool logic returned. Sex with Savannah had been amazing, but he hoped she understood that he could not offer her more than physical satisfaction.

* * *

Savannah's face was buried in the pillow and she was lying on her stomach. As she came fully awake, memories of the previous night made her feel hot all over. Dimitris had made love to her three times and the night had been a blur of incredible pleasure.

She turned her head cautiously, afraid to meet his too-knowing gaze. To her relief, he was sprawled on his back, his eyes were closed and the steady rise and fall of his chest indicated that he was deeply asleep. Thank goodness for small mercies. Sex with Dimitris had been amazing, beyond compare, although she did not have any other experiences to compare it with.

Still, it had just been sex. Emotion had played no part in their night of passion, she reminded herself. Even when they had lain in a tangle of limbs, breathless, their hearts racing after another shattering orgasm, she must have imagined a connection between them that had felt deeper than their physical compatibility.

At eighteen she had believed that Dimitris's devastating charm and flashes of tender affection were signs that he loved her. But she had witnessed his charisma when he hosted his cooking shows on TV or appeared on chat shows. He was charm personified, the handsome, sexy, hot chef. No wonder women fell in love with him in droves. No wonder she had been besotted with him as an impressionable girl.

It would be easy to fall in love with him again. She longed to waken him with a kiss and arouse his body with her hands and mouth until he took charge and rolled her beneath him or lifted her on top of him and the magic started all over again. But the deal she had made with him and herself had been for one night only. Now it was morning and the cage door was open, ready for her to fly.

Trying to ignore the hollow feeling in the pit of her stomach, she slid carefully across the bed, hoping he wouldn't stir, secretly praying that he would. She located her knickers but couldn't find her bra. The shirt Dimitris had worn at dinner was on the floor and was still damp from the rain, but it was better than nothing, and she slipped her arms through the sleeves.

The problem of getting herself home without her clothes or transport was resolved when she crept out of the bedroom and found her laundered trousers and tee shirt neatly folded on a chair on the landing. Her trainers were there with her handbag and laptop. She dressed quickly, and when she ran down the stairs she met the housekeeper's husband John in the entrance hall.

'I thought I'd try your car again this morning and, to my surprise, the engine started,' he said, handing her the key. 'It could be an intermittent fault with the ignition. I suggest you drive straight to a garage and have a mechanic check the car over.'

'Thanks, I'll do that.'

But as Savannah drove away from River Retreat she knew she couldn't afford to spend money on her car while her finances were in a precarious state. At least she would be paid by Philpot's for the photoshoot, but her conscience pricked that she should buy Dimitris a new phone to replace his that she'd ruined. She had the unsettling thought that he'd taken his revenge by giving her more pleasure last night than she'd known it was possible for her body to experience.

With a murmured excuse Dimitris moved away from the group of party guests he had been chatting to. It was not the first social occasion in the past six weeks where he'd struggled to make small talk, and his jaw ached from forcing a smile. The death of his grandmother a month ago partly explained his dark mood, but his grief for *Γιαγιά* Hestia, who had been nearly ninety after all, was not the only reason for his restlessness.

He walked over to the wall of windows that ran the length of the hospitality suite at Philpot's headquarters in central London. The views from the twenty-second floor were spectacular, especially at night when the illuminated city was spread out in front of him. But he barely noticed the blaze of twinkling lights and turned his gaze towards the door once more, hoping that Savannah would appear. Philpot's PR executive Tara Brown had told him that Savannah had accepted an invitation to the evening's event to mark Dimitris's appointment as the supermarket chain's brand ambassador, and publication of the magazine featuring his recipes and her photographs.

When he'd woken the morning after the incredible night he had spent with Savannah, he'd told himself he was relieved that she had gone. But over the past weeks he'd found himself thinking about her too often for his liking. He could have contacted her through the photographic agency, but he'd resisted. What would be the point? He would not risk having an affair with her. She had meant something to him ten years ago, but he'd hurt her. That was what he did. He damaged the people he cared about. *Theós*, his sister had spent years in a wheelchair because of him.

Dimitris scowled at his reflection in the glass. He'd flown to Rhodes the day after Savannah had left him in Richmond and had spent much of his time testing recipes for his new cookbook. But for once he'd been uninspired by his work, and he had not found solace in the peaceful solitude of his villa overlooking the turquoise Aegean Sea.

He glanced towards the door again, and his heart slammed into his ribs when Savannah walked into the room. She looked stunning in a black velvet cocktail dress that moulded her slender figure and those pert breasts that he had discovered fitted perfectly in his palms. Her hair was caught up in an elegant chignon, and he longed to remove the pins and thread his fingers through the blonde strands.

She gave no indication that she'd noticed him and smiled at a guy who Dimitris recognised had been a lighting technician on the photoshoot at the Richmond studio. He told himself that he was relieved there would not be an awkward situation following their night of no-strings sex. Savannah had evidently moved on, and so had he.

Some forty minutes later his patience had expired after he'd watched Savannah flirt with the men who crowded around her. She laughed often, causing heads to turn in her direction. It struck Dimitris that there was something different about her. A self-confidence she had not possessed at eighteen or even six weeks ago.

He strode towards her with a purposefulness that made her bevy of admirers move away. To his annoyance, his heart was pounding when he stood in front of her. 'You were so late to arrive this evening that I thought you were not coming to the party.' He managed to sound casual but inside he was fighting an urge to sweep her into his arms and carry her off, caveman style, to somewhere where they could be alone.

Her hazel-green eyes widened, and Dimitris felt a surge of satisfaction that she could not hide her reaction to him. 'I'm surprised you noticed me. You've been knee-deep in attractive women for most of the evening.' Her tart voice only made him want her more.

'You were attracting a lot of male attention.' He was appalled that he sounded jealous. It was an unfamiliar emotion.

Savannah gave him an enigmatic smile worthy of the Mona Lisa. 'I'm enjoying my freedom. I was late because my car broke down and I had to make the rest of the journey by bus.'

'I'll drive you home.'

'It's okay, Alex has already offered to give me a lift.'

'If Alex is the guy who has been trailing after you like a puppy dog, he has been drinking and is probably over the limit to get behind the wheel of a car.'

Savannah's eyes flashed. 'Alex doesn't act like a puppy.'

'Don't tell me he's your boyfriend.'

'I'm not telling you anything. It's no business of yours who I date.'

'*Theós!* Are you sleeping with him?'

'No.' The angry flush on her face made her even lovelier. 'You are the only man I've been to bed with, if you must know.'

He stared at her. 'Since we last slept together a few weeks ago, you mean?'

'I mean ever.' She spun away from him, but he was not going to let her go after that startling piece of information. It seemed impossible, yet he believed her. He felt a stab of guilt when he remembered her faint hesitancy before he'd taken her to bed. Slipping his hand beneath her elbow, he steered her out of the room.

'How is it that I am your only lover?' Dimitris demanded, wondering why he felt so good about it. Possessiveness was another alien emotion to him. 'You are a beautiful, independent woman and you caught the attention of every man at the party.'

'I told you why. I couldn't forget you. But now...'

'Now?' His tone was as dangerous as he felt.

'Now I'm finally free to have other relationships, other lovers. The night we spent together gave me a sense of perspective. The sex was great. Clearly I'm no expert, but I'm sure you will tell me that it wasn't out of the ordinary.'

'That's where you're wrong.' It had been the most amazing night of his life, but he wasn't about to admit it. 'We are highly sexually compatible.'

She shrugged. 'You must have slept with hundreds of women, thousands.'

'The tabloids are not a reliable source of information.'

Savannah pulled away from him and started to walk

quickly along the corridor. 'I don't want this, Dimitris. I don't want you.'

'Liar.' He fell into step beside her as she pulled her phone out of her handbag.

'I'm calling a taxi.'

'I told you I'll take you home.' The lift doors opened, and he followed her into the small space. She glared at him but must have realised that arguing was pointless. Minutes later they walked across the underground car park, and he opened the passenger door of his sleek black saloon. Savannah climbed into the car and her dress rode up, giving him a glimpse of her toned thigh. Desire shot through him, and he silently acknowledged that one night with her had not been enough to satisfy his hunger.

They were both silent on the journey across the city. Dimitris had deliberately not been back to the north London borough he'd left ten years ago, and he was surprised by how little had changed. The high street where his grandfather's restaurant had stood was as run-down as when he had grown up in the area known for its high crime rate. But only a few miles from Camden they drove through picturesque and affluent Hampstead Village, and further out towards the heath the houses were big and gracious with expensive cars on the driveways.

At first glance Pond House looked no different than he remembered. But the shrubs in the front garden were overgrown, the once shiny black gates had rusted and there was an air of decay about the place. He parked on the driveway and switched off the engine.

He felt dangerously on edge and agonisingly aware of Savannah in the close confines of the car. Her perfume teased his senses, and he wanted to press his mouth against the pale column of her neck and feel the erratic thud of her pulse.

'My grandmother died recently,' he said gruffly.

'I'm so sorry.' Her voice was soft with sympathy. 'I remember Hestia when I worked at the restaurant. She was tiny and fierce and kept the waitresses in order, but she was kind too, and devoted to your grandfather.'

Dimitris's throat felt constricted. 'My grandparents were amazing. They still worked in their eighties.' It had been his fault that his grandparents couldn't retire. 'My grandmother passed away peacefully in her sleep. I think she was glad to be reunited with my grandfather.' He drummed his fingers on the steering wheel, wondering what had made him open up to Savannah.

'Would you like to come in for coffee?'

'Sure.'

'The house has been sold,' Savannah explained as she opened the front door. Packing boxes were piled up in the hallway. 'Luckily the new owners are keeping a lot of the furniture, but there's still a ton of stuff to sort out.'

'Have you found somewhere for you and your mother to live?'

She looked away from him, but not before Dimitris glimpsed a sheen in her eyes. Something tugged in his chest. 'Mum has decided that due to her disabilities she needs to move permanently into a nursing home that can provide the support she needs. I've found a wonderful place in Windsor, near to where Mum's sister lives. She is going to move in next week. The nursing home is expensive, but I've calculated that there should be enough money left after paying my father's debts to cover the fees for a while. I'll have to earn a decent income as a freelance photographer so that I can continue to pay for Mum to live at Willow Grange.'

'What about you? Where will you live?'

'I don't know. My studio is at the top of the house, and I'll miss the space and light in the attic room. Finding a new place where I can work is my priority. Various friends have said I can sleep on their sofa.'

Dimitris turned his head when a door opened and a woman in a wheelchair appeared. Illness and worry had aged Savannah's mother and she looked frail.

'Mum, I thought you had gone to bed.' Savannah leaned down to kiss her mother. 'I had trouble with my car and Dimitris drove me home.' She looked at him. 'This is my mother, Evelyn.'

Dimitris stepped forwards. 'I'm pleased to meet you. When my family lived in London my sister went to some of your art classes at the rehabilitation unit.'

'I remember Eleni, of course. And I hear that you are an acclaimed chef now, Dimitris. Your parents would be proud of you.' Evelyn smiled gently. 'The accident when they lost their lives was a terrible tragedy.'

'Yes,' he said brusquely. It would never have happened if he hadn't behaved like a brat.

A woman who was evidently Evelyn's nurse came and helped her into another room. Savannah led the way to the kitchen and filled the kettle. 'There's only instant coffee. I can't afford to buy the proper stuff.'

'Instant is fine.' Dimitris prowled around the kitchen, unnerved by the grief that had hit him hard when Savannah's mother had spoken of his parents. He pictured his mother's proud smile when he'd grown so tall that he'd towered over her the last summer they had been a family. He remembered watching his father making *tsoureki*, a traditional Greek bread eaten at Easter. The dough was divided into three pieces and shaped into a braid to symbolise the Holy Trinity.

'The secret is to keep the braid tight to stop the dough expanding sideways while it bakes,' his father had told him.

Dimitris always remembered that golden rule when he made *tsoureki* every Easter.

His memories shifted to ten years ago, when he had been here at Pond House with Savannah while her parents were delayed abroad. Every evening, after the restaurant had closed, he'd ridden his motorbike at breakneck speed to be with her. For eleven nights they had slept together in her bed and made love endlessly. He'd cooked meals for them in this kitchen, and he had felt closer to her than to any other woman before or since.

But he had known it couldn't last. Nothing good ever did. Her parents had returned, and the same night her father had been waiting for him in the alley behind the restaurant when Dimitris had taken the rubbish out. It had been a fitting setting for the filthy deal he'd been forced to make with Richard O'Neal, he brooded. Richard had bluntly told him that his plans for Savannah did not include her getting involved with a nobody with nothing who was going nowhere. Dimitris had never forgotten Richard's opinion of him, and he'd been spurred to prove the other man wrong.

Ultimately, Savannah and her mother were victims of Richard's criminality as much as the people and organisations he had defrauded. Savannah had admitted that she was practically penniless and soon to be homeless. She was desperate to help her mother, just as Dimitris had been desperate to help his grandparents return to Greece.

There was no reason for him to get involved with Savannah's problems, he reminded himself. The disturbing effect she had on him was a very good reason to walk away. But he did not want to abandon her again. He'd felt bad that he'd hurt her even though he'd acted with the best intentions. He could never come to terms with his guilt about his parents, but at least he could help Savannah and her mother.

'I have a proposition I want to discuss with you,' he said abruptly.

'What kind of proposition?' She looked at him warily and his conscience pricked that the way he'd treated her years ago had made her untrusting.

'I need a photographer to work on my next cookery book. I'm offering you a job, Savannah.'

CHAPTER SEVEN

'No. I MEAN, thanks for the offer. It would be a great opportunity, but…' Savannah flushed when Dimitris gave her an enigmatic look.

'But what? You told me that you are trying to build your reputation as a food photographer. Working on my book will give you valuable exposure.'

It was true. Dimitris's cookery books sold millions of copies. He was one of the most successful non-fiction authors in England and North America and it would be a huge boost to her career to work with him. Common sense said she should accept his job offer, but her instinct for self-preservation warned Savannah of the potential pitfalls.

When she'd left him asleep six weeks ago and driven home she'd felt confident that she'd got him out of her system. Dimitris was a skilful lover and he'd taken her body to heights of pleasure she'd never experienced before. But it had just been great sex without emotional involvement.

Since then she had been busy sorting out her father's affairs and organising a nursing home for her mum, and she'd barely given Dimitris a thought during the days at least. Annoyingly, he had invaded her dreams every night. But this evening when she'd spotted him at the party her pulse had accelerated, and she'd avoided him while she'd sought to regain the composure that Dimitris had the power to destroy with one of his sexy smiles. She was dismayed by the effect he had on her and couldn't risk working with him while she was still in the process of relegating him to her past.

'Why do you need a photographer? I know that the acclaimed food photographer Ian Clarke took the photos for your previous books.' Savannah always looked on the back page of cookery books to see who had taken the pictures of the food.

'Ian retired after the last book we worked on together. My publisher agreed that I can choose a photographer who I believe will best showcase my food. Your photos are fun and a little bit quirky, like my recipes. When we worked together on the Philpot's shoot you seemed to instinctively know what I was trying to achieve.'

Dimitris drank his coffee and grimaced. 'I can promise you decent coffee. But seriously, you'll be paid an upfront amount for the commission, and a percentage of the royalties when the cookery book goes on sale. I'm planning a big book with over two hundred recipes and photographs. I've scheduled six weeks to capture all the images, and you will stay at my villa in Rhodes for the duration of the shoot.'

Savannah knew it was unusual for a food photographer to receive royalties. Her potential future earnings would be huge, and she would not have to worry about finding the fees for her mum's nursing home. Dimitris was offering her the chance of a lifetime, but she hesitated.

'I assumed the shoot would be at your studio in Richmond.'

'I like the photos to be taken in natural light, but the daylight will fade earlier in England as the days shorten in the autumn. The clarity of light in Rhodes will give the effect I want of lazy summer days and relaxed living. After all, the title for the cookery book is *A Mediterranean Love Affair with Dimitris*.' He looked amused by her startled expression.

Savannah bit her lip. 'I can't leave Mum and go to Greece.'

'I can wait for a week while you help your mother move into the nursing home. This is a business proposition, Savannah. Nothing more,' he said, as if he wanted to make it clear that he wasn't interested in her for any other reason.

Perhaps working with him and staying at his home in Rhodes would allow her to see the real Dimitris instead of the man of her girlish fantasies or his public image as a sex idol, Savannah thought. She would prove to herself that she was over him.

'I admit I have a personal reason for asking you to work with me.'

Her heart missed a beat at *personal*.

'I would like to help your mother,' Dimitris continued. 'Evelyn was an art therapist at the rehabilitation centre where my sister spent a considerable amount of time when she was a child, recovering from her injures after the car accident.' His voice revealed no emotion, but Savannah sensed that he found it difficult to talk about the life-altering injuries Eleni had sustained in the crash that had killed their parents.

'When I was friends with Eleni at school she told me that she had done some art classes with Mum.'

'Art therapy really helped Eleni to deal with her emotions. She had been a happy, sporty kid, but after the accident she was unable to walk, and she lost interest in everything. Evelyn was wonderful with her, and it is no exaggeration to say that your mother helped my sister to be happy again. Eleni developed her artistic talent and she went on to study jewellery design, and now makes bespoke jewellery for her clients.'

Dimitris looked intently at Savannah. 'I would offer to pay your mother's nursing home fees, but I have a feeling that you won't accept.'

'Mum is my responsibility.' Savannah did not want to be beholden to anyone, least of all Dimitris.

'In that case, I suggest you meet me in Rhodes next week with your camera.'

The following week Savannah fastened her seatbelt when the plane's warning light above her head flashed on. Through the window she could see the spearhead shape of the island of Rhodes, surrounded by a turquoise sea. The guidebook said that Rhodes was the largest of the Dodecanese islands. As the plane began its descent the land below was a chequerboard of green and brown fields, and the towns had white cube houses.

The ruins of several ancient landmarks were visible from the air.

Savannah gripped the armrests as the airport runway came into view, not because she was a nervous flier, but the doubts that had tormented her since the plane had left London felt as though butterflies had been set loose in her stomach. She had made the right decision to accept Dimitris's job offer, she tried to reassure herself. It had been difficult leaving her mum, but Evelyn was settling into Willow Grange nursing home and was benefiting from using the hydrotherapy pool. Savannah's priority was to earn enough money so that her mum could continue to receive the care she needed.

After the plane had landed and she'd collected her suitcase and cleared Customs, she walked into the arrivals hall. Dimitris had told her that someone would meet her, and she'd assumed he would send one of his staff. She hadn't expected to see him striding across the concourse.

Her stomach swooped as she stared at Dimitris. She wasn't alone in noticing him. Women of all ages turned their heads to watch him. He looked breathtaking, casually dressed in sun-bleached jeans and a navy-blue polo shirt. His designer shades were pushed onto his head, and he exuded a raw sex appeal that sent a coil of heat through Savannah.

Breathe, she ordered herself as she walked towards him.

'Savannah.' His deep voice with a husky accent sent a prickle of awareness through her. 'How was your flight?'

'Fine. Well…there was a two-hour delay. I'm sorry if you have been waiting at the airport for me.'

'I checked the flight details and saw that yours was delayed. You should have accepted my offer to charter a private jet for you.'

She bit her lip, unwilling to explain to Dimitris that she did not want anything from him other than the money she would earn from the photoshoot. They would have a professional working relationship for the next six weeks.

They exited the airport building and he led her over to a sleek red Ferrari. 'My new baby,' he told her as he opened the passenger door. 'Isn't she a beauty?'

'Beautiful, but not very practical,' she noted a few minutes later, after he had abandoned trying to fit her luggage in the small boot of the car and wedged her suitcase and camera bag onto the back seat.

'Maybe not. But she's the love of my life.' Dimitris's grin made him seem boyish and reminded her of the young man she'd been besotted with years ago. He was even more gorgeous now, Savannah thought ruefully, conscious that her pulse was racing. 'When I grew up in a rough London neighbourhood, all the kids dreamed of owning a car like this one,' he told her. 'I was determined to turn the dream into reality.'

Away from the busy roads around the airport the highway hugged the coast, and the views of golden sand beaches were spectacular. Dimitris put the electric sunroof down. The azure sky was cloudless, and the sea shimmered in the bright sunshine. Savannah gave a deep sigh.

'That's how I feel every time I return to Rhodes,' he murmured. 'I can breathe here. I imagine the past week was tough when you moved out of Pond House and took your mother to Windsor.'

'Yes.' Her voice was thick as emotions she had been suppressing for days caught in Savannah's throat. Pond House had been her childhood home, but she had mixed feelings about it since she'd learned that her father had bought the house with money from his criminal activities. She had looked up to her father and respected him for being a brilliant businessman. She'd trusted him even though she'd felt confused and hurt that he did not care about her. Now she was wary of trusting anyone. Her goal was to build her career so that she was financially independent and not reliant on anyone.

This was a new chapter in her life, but Savannah was aware that her mum's life might end prematurely because of her illness. She wiped away a tear and stiffened when Dimitris took his hand off the steering wheel and reached across to squeeze her fingers.

'Witnessing someone you love suffer is the hardest thing,' he said gruffly. Savannah guessed he was thinking of his sister.

'Thank you for arranging a private ambulance to take Mum to the nursing home.'

'Does your mother talk much about your father?'

'Mum has hardly mentioned him since he died. It was a shock at his trial to learn about my father's illegal business dealings.' She turned her head to stare out of the window. 'On the surface we were a happy family, but there were tensions, and however hard I tried at school I felt I was a disappointment to him.'

Dimitris frowned. 'Did you ever discuss your relationship with your father with your mother?'

'Mum was a dreamer, and wrapped up in her art. She made excuses for my father and said he worked hard to provide a good life for us. I had the best of everything, but I felt that I should be grateful to him. I was envious of my friends who had a close relationship with their fathers.'

Dimitris cleared his throat and seemed to be about to say something, but he gave a slight shake of his head and lapsed into a brooding silence for the rest of the journey.

His villa was a vast white-walled property standing in sprawling grounds on a clifftop with incredible views across the bay. Bougainvillea vines smothered with vivid pink flowers grew against the walls, and rosemary and jasmine planted in pots by the front door filled the air with their fragrance. He carried her suitcase and ushered her into the cool and airy entrance hall.

'Welcome to my home, Savannah.'

Home. A lump formed in Savannah's throat at the thought that she was currently homeless. She hadn't had time to look for a flat before she'd come to Rhodes, but she knew that rental properties around Windsor where she could be close to her mum were expensive. Staying with Dimitris for six weeks would give her a chance to look online for somewhere to live when she returned to England.

She did not understand why she'd told him about her difficult relationship with her father that she'd never spoken about to anyone else. From now on she would stick to the boundaries of their working relationship, she decided. She turned and found him standing beside her. The citrus and spice scent of his aftershave evoked an ache deep in her pelvis. Her gaze collided with his and her heart missed a beat when she saw desire glitter in his eyes. With a gasp she stepped away from him as a man walked across the hall towards them.

'This is my assistant, Stefanos,' Dimitris said coolly. His chiselled features were unreadable, and Savannah wondered if she had imagined those few seconds of sizzling sexual awareness between them. 'Stefanos will give you a tour of the villa and bring your luggage up to your room. Meet me downstairs when you are ready.'

The villa's décor was crisply stylish and everywhere was white with touches of grey. The few elegant sculptures and abstract artwork on the walls had probably been chosen by an interior designer. There was nothing to give a clue to the personality of the villa's owner.

The guest bedroom was charming, although Savannah thought that some colourful cushions would break up all the white. She gave a cry of delight when she stepped onto the balcony overlooking the garden and saw an infinity pool that appeared to flow over the cliff edge and into the sea. It had been raining when she'd left London, but in Rhodes in late September the temperature was still as hot as a midsummer's day in England. She thanked Stefanos for carrying her luggage to her room, and when he'd gone she unpacked and swapped her jeans and sweatshirt for a sleeveless linen dress.

Glancing out of the window, she saw Dimitris in the garden with a woman. His arm was draped around her shoulders, and their body language seemed to suggest they shared a close bond. Savannah could not see the woman's face, but she had long, curly dark hair and an enviably curvaceous figure.

Was the exotic brunette Dimitris's mistress? Jealousy burned like acid in her stomach. How could she bear to work with Dimitris every day, knowing that he spent his nights with his mistress? But she had no option. He had handed her a lifeline when he'd offered her the photo assignment and she was determined to ignore her attraction to him.

'Ah, Savannah, there you are,' he said when she walked across the garden a few minutes later. Her brittle smile turned to shock and delight when she recognised his attractive companion.

'Eleni?'

'Savannah, it's so good to see you. Dimitris told me that you are the photographer for his new book.' Eleni's vivacious face was even prettier than when she had been a teenager. She walked a little stiffly over to Savannah and flung her arms around her. 'You haven't changed a bit.'

'But you don't use a wheelchair.' Savannah hugged her school friend. 'I didn't recognise you.'

'I'm able to walk thanks to my brilliant surgeon in America.' Eleni sighed. 'It's bad timing that I'm flying to the Far East tomorrow to attend a series of jewellery fairs. But we have this evening to catch up on ten years of news.'

'I'll leave you girls to chat,' Dimitris said. 'We'll eat outside on the terrace in half an hour.'

Savannah waited until he'd strolled back to the villa and took a deep breath. 'Eleni, there is something I need to tell you. I went on a couple of dates with Matt Collier after he told me he was single. I had no idea he was engaged to you until Dimitris found us at a hotel. Please believe that nothing happened between me and Matt.'

'Dimitris explained the situation when he told me that you would be working with him on his book,' Eleni said ruefully. 'I still feel hurt and angry with Matt for lying to me. He lied to you too. I know you wouldn't have dated him if you had known he was engaged. We were best friends at school, Savannah, and I've never forgotten your kindness when I was bullied by some of the other girls.'

'Dimitris was furious.'

'My brother has always been very protective of me. Sometimes a bit too protective.' Eleni sighed. 'Dimitris seems to blame himself for the car accident when our parents were killed and I was badly injured.'

'How could it have been his fault?'

'I don't know. I think I told you before that I have no memory of what happened. I wish I could persuade Dimitris to talk about the crash. It must have been traumatic for him and I'm sure it's not good for him to bottle things up. He has been amazing in the way he has taken care of me, and he paid for the surgery that enabled me to walk again.'

Eleni led Savannah over to a terrace where a dining table stood beneath a pergola covered with vine leaves and bunches of plump red grapes. 'Tell me about yourself. You were engaged, weren't you? I remember that Dimitris was in a bad mood for days when he heard the news.' Eleni did not hide her curiosity. 'I knew that the two of you were dating when we lived in London. Dimitris won a lot of money with a lottery ticket and days later he took me and our grandparents to Rhodes, where he'd bought a house for us. The move was so sudden, and I wondered if something had happened between you and him to cause you to break up.'

Dimitris was not likely to have told his sister that he'd been able to afford to buy a house in Rhodes with money he'd accepted as a bribe from her father, Savannah thought grimly. A winning lottery ticket had been a perfect excuse. Her anger ignited when she remembered how miserable she'd been after he had abruptly ended their relationship. At eighteen she had been starved of affection from her father, and she'd wanted to believe that Dimitris loved her. She wondered now if he had shown an interest in her because her family had been wealthy.

She had been fixated with Dimitris, and she was dismayed that he could still affect her. When they had arrived at his villa and she'd sensed the chemistry between them, she'd acknowledged that sleeping with him hadn't got him out of her system as she'd hoped. But she knew that Dimitris would never love her the way she yearned to be loved—totally and unconditionally. She'd spent her childhood trying to win her father's love, and she was not going to waste any more of her emotions on Dimitris.

Perhaps she would sign up to a dating app that some of her friends used, and when she returned to London after the photoshoot she intended to socialise more. She couldn't let her bad experience with Matt Collier put her off. But, deep down, Savannah wondered if she was unlovable, and it was the reason her father and Dimitris had rejected her.

A sound from behind her alerted her to Dimitris's presence, and her treacherous body reacted instantly as each of her nerve-endings zinged and her nipples hardened so that her lacy bra scraped against the sensitive peaks. She fought the urge to cross her arms over her chest as her gaze was drawn to his face and she recognised the flare of desire in his dark blue eyes before he looked away from her.

It was a relief when Eleni's cheerful voice broke the tense silence. 'What are we having to eat? Mmm, *pastitsio*,' she said when Dimitris placed the serving platter he was holding on the table and removed the lid. 'It's the Greek version of lasagne,' she told Savannah.

'I know that *pastitsio* is your favourite dinner, *paidí mou*.' Dimitris spoke to his sister in an indulgent tone that Savannah had never heard him use before. Something twisted inside her that she was ashamed to admit was envy. Dimitris loved his sister and he had loved his grandparents. After he'd dumped her, she had told herself that he was heartless, but now she had evidence that it wasn't true. He just hadn't loved her.

Once again Savannah's feeling of insecurity, that stemmed from her father's indifference, surfaced. When she was a model, men had admired her for the way she looked. Ten years ago Dimitris had wanted to have sex with her, but he had trampled on her girlish dreams of romance and happy ever after. Now she was going to spend the next six weeks working with him and living in his home, but she would be on her guard against his potent charm.

Dimitris opened the bifold doors of his kitchen studio and took a deep breath of sea air. He loved the villa, and his favourite place was the studio that stood apart from the main house. Below the cliff was a secret beach, accessible by a set of steep steps carved into the rocks.

The studio was not just his workplace where he developed recipes and ran his business empire, it was his sanctuary. The views of the bay and the crystal-clear sea were stunning. His own piece of paradise. Not bad for a boy who had grown up in a rough part of London and failed most of his exams at school because he'd been too busy helping to run the restaurant and taking care of his grandparents and orphaned sister to have time to study.

He had money, two beautiful homes and a flashy car—all the trappings of success, but there was an emptiness inside him that material possessions could not fill, and guilt was a dark shadow over him. He'd distracted himself with sexual liaisons with women who understood that he wasn't in the market for a relationship. But since he'd slept with Savannah two months ago he'd felt restless. On the few occasions recently when he'd invited a woman to dinner his libido had taken a hike and at the end of the evening he'd driven them home rather than ask them to spend the night with him.

Things had been worse since Savannah had come to stay at the villa. His awareness of her was a constant throb in his groin and he felt like a teenager fired up with hormones. He told himself it was a normal response to a beautiful, sexy woman. In other circumstances Dimitris would have pursued his sexual interest and instigated an affair. But he held back from Savannah for the same reason that he had fought his growing feelings for her years ago.

For eleven magical nights her sweetly passionate response to him had aroused his body and touched his soul. She had made him forget what he had done, and that he did not deserve her love. But when Savannah's father had more or less forced him into a despicable deal, Dimitris had accepted money from Richard O'Neal because he felt responsible for his grandparents and sister. He acknowledged that it had given him an excuse to break up with Savannah before his fledgling feelings for her had deepened.

Dimitris raked his hand through his hair. Usually he was relaxed while he was working on a new book, but he felt edgy and unsettled. For the past two weeks he had spent hours every day with Savannah while she photographed each stage of the recipes he prepared.

He hadn't employed a food stylist or art director because he liked to keep things simple he'd explained on the first day of the shoot, when she'd asked about other members of the art team.

While Savannah was taking photos she often had to lean across him for a close-up shot of a dish, and Dimitris knew from the giveaway pulse thudding crazily at the base of her throat and the swift rise and fall of her breasts that she was aware of the sexual energy between them, and trying to ignore it, as much as he was.

There was a month remaining of the schedule to complete the cookery book and he hoped his self-control would last. It had to because he could not risk sleeping with her. He knew she was attracted to him, but he sensed that she would hope for more than sex if they had an affair. But sex was all he wanted. Physical satisfaction without commitment. He had hurt too many people in the past, including Savannah, and he didn't want anything else on his conscience. Knowing that he had caused his parents' deaths would haunt him for ever.

His nostrils flared as he watched her slide off the stool where she had been sitting at the counter and working on her laptop. Like him, she was wearing denim shorts. Hers were cut high up on her thighs, and her long legs had acquired a golden tan from the warm Greek sun. Her vest top moulded her breasts, and it was obvious that she wasn't wearing a bra.

Desire kicked in his gut as he imagined slipping his hands beneath her top and fondling her breasts. He watched them bounce when she walked towards him, and his jaw clenched. Her hair was caught in a high ponytail with blonde tendrils framing her face. She looked at once wholesome and sexy and she was sending him out of his mind.

'I'm ready when you are,' she said, hooking her camera bag over her shoulder. 'I'll admit that when you suggested cooking and photographing the seafood recipes down on the beach, I thought you were mad. But I've been looking at the mood board we created before we started shooting. All the other shots have been taken in the studio and although we have used different props it will be good to do something different.'

He nodded. 'It would be easy to take a picture of the sea or the beach and use it as a backdrop, but I want readers to almost smell the salty air and feel the sea breeze when they look at a photo of absolutely fresh prawns cooked with ouzo and a rich tomato sauce.'

Savannah grinned, and for once her diffidence with him slipped. 'You're making me feel hungry.'

You are having the same effect on me.

Dimitris gave a silent groan and turned away to pick up his backpack, which held the ingredients he would need plus cooking pans and a portable stove for outdoor cooking.

'The beach looks an awfully long way down,' she said minutes later when she stood beside him on the top of the cliff and looked over the edge.

'I'll go first. The steps are steep but take it slowly and you'll be fine.' Dimitris had climbed the steps hundreds of times. He paused halfway down and glanced over his shoulder at Savannah. She was pale and looked terrified.

'I'm not great with heights,' she admitted.

'*Theós*, why didn't you say so?'

'You planned to do the shoot on the beach, and it's my job as a professional to take the photographs that you want.'

He swore. 'Turn round and climb back up the steps. We'll think of another idea.'

'No.' She took a deep breath. 'I'm all right. Let's keep climbing down.'

Dimitris did not know whether to admire her determination or feel frustrated by her stubbornness. He walked up the steps to where she had frozen and held out his hand. 'Hold onto me and we'll go down together. I won't let you fall.'

She took his hand without hesitation, and he felt a mix of emotions at her trust in him. Would she have such blind faith if she knew that his stupid behaviour had been the reason his parents had died? He was at a loss to understand the urge that had come over him to tell Savannah about the accident. He had never admitted to anyone that he had been responsible, not even Eleni—especially Eleni. His sister's childhood and teenage years had been ruined and he was to blame. All he could do was ensure that Eleni's life was as good as he could make it.

While his mind was in the past, Dimitris had made a slow descent of the steps and guided Savannah down. She let out a shaky breath when they reached the bottom. Some colour had returned to her cheeks, but he couldn't forget how scared she had been.

'What a beautiful, secluded beach. It was worth the climb.' She kicked off her trainers and ran into the sea to paddle. 'The water is so warm. I wish I'd brought my swimsuit. Is it safe to swim here?'

'Yes, there aren't any strong currents.'

Dimitris set up the portable stove on some flat rocks and walked over to where Savannah had sat down on the sand. She was staring pensively at the waves that rippled against the shore. 'Why are you afraid of heights?' he asked, dropping down beside her.

'It's silly. An irrational fear from something that happened when I was younger.'

Dimitris thought of how his stomach cramped whenever he was driving and saw a lorry travelling in the opposite direction. He had to steel himself not to hit the brakes and trust that the lorry wouldn't collide with his car. 'Events in childhood can affect us when we are adults,' he said gruffly.

Savannah sighed. 'It was nothing really. I fell off my horse when I was thirteen. I wasn't a very confident rider, but my father insisted that I learned to ride because he said it was what posh people did. He spent a fortune on a thoroughbred horse, but Merlin was too big and strong, and I couldn't control him. I was competing in a gymkhana in front of a big crowd when my horse refused to jump over a fence. I was petrified,' she admitted. 'Merlin stopped dead and I was thrown over his head. I remember being in the air and looking down at the ground, knowing it was going to hurt when I landed.'

'Were you injured?'

'Not seriously, luckily. I was bruised and shaken. While I was lying on the ground and crying, my father stormed over and yelled at me for being stupid. He was furious that I'd made a fool of myself and him.' Savannah bit her lip. 'My father always made me feel that I was a disappointment to him. Needless to say, I never rode a horse again. When I was standing at the top of the cliff, I imagined myself falling.'

'I would not have suggested doing the photoshoot on the beach if I'd known about your fear of heights.' Dimitris frowned. 'When we knew each other before, I had the impression that you and Richard were close. You often spoke about how wonderful he was, and I believed you were a daddy's girl.'

'I pretended that he was the kind and loving father I wished he was. I think I hoped that if I imagined hard enough it would be true.' Savannah sent Dimitris a wry glance. 'I was good at make-believe. I fooled myself that you were in love with me because I was looking for affection that I didn't get from my father.'

Dimitris cursed silently. Richard O'Neal had told him a shocking secret, but it was not up to him to explain the truth to Savannah. Only her mother could do that, and perhaps Evelyn had her reasons for withholding information that Savannah had a right to be told.

'Now Richard is dead you might find it easier to talk to your mother about how you felt that he hadn't been a loving father,' he suggested.

Savannah shrugged. 'There's not much point now.

Mum is struggling to come to terms with the fact that my father was a criminal.'

Dimitris stood up and offered his hand to help her to her feet. Savannah's issues were not his business, he reminded himself. After the photoshoot she would return to her life in England, and they were unlikely to meet again. It was odd how his heart sank at the thought.

When Savannah put her fingers in his, he remembered how she had trusted him when they'd climbed down the cliff steps. She rose gracefully to stand beside him, and he tensed when he breathed in the seductive scent of her perfume. Her eyes widened and were more green than hazel. Dimitris was certain she felt the prickling awareness in the atmosphere between them. His heart was thudding, and he could not make himself move away from her. She was so beautiful. His brain told him to resist the hunger that heated his blood, but his gaze was riveted on her mouth as he lowered his head towards her.

One kiss. That was all he wanted. *Liar*, he mocked himself. He was desperate to pull her down onto the sand, remove her clothes and his, and make love to her. *Desperate* suggested a lack of control that Dimitris would not tolerate. He jerked away from Savannah, breathing hard. Her parted lips were a temptation he must resist. Colour spread over her face at his rejection, and he felt bad. But she'd just told him that she had yearned for affection from her father. Her vulnerability now made her off-limits.

'We should get on with the photoshoot while the daylight is still good,' he said, already striding up the beach.

The cookery book would give Savannah an income in royalties that would allow her to pay her mother's nursing home fees. Years ago, Evelyn had helped his sister and it was for that reason he'd asked Savannah to photograph his recipes, Dimitris reminded himself.

He cursed when he searched in the backpack and discovered he'd left a bottle of olive oil behind in the kitchen studio. 'I'll have to go back for the cooking oil while you start setting up your camera,' he told her.

But when he climbed the steps to the top of the cliff and looked down at the beach he saw that Savannah had taken advantage of his absence to pull off her shorts. She tugged her top over her head, baring her breasts. Dimitris's mouth ran dry as he watched her wade into the sea wearing just her knickers. *Theós!* She would tempt a saint, let alone someone as flawed and guilt-ridden as him. He did not deserve her, and Savannah deserved a much better man than him.

CHAPTER EIGHT

'MY NEW RESTAURANT in Crete opens tomorrow night. I'd like you to come to the launch party with me.'

Savannah looked up from her laptop screen as Dimitris strolled into the small sitting room off the villa's open-plan living area that she used for an office. Working in the evenings gave her an excuse to avoid him, which was vital after he had nearly kissed her on the beach a week ago.

Her face burned as she remembered how he'd stopped when his lips had been centimetres above hers. It was not the first time Dimitris had rejected her, but it would be the last, she vowed. Hence after they ate dinner together at the end of a long day working in the kitchen studio she always headed straight to her office. It was unfortunate that the window overlooked the pool where he swam most evenings. The sight of him wearing black swim briefs that left little to her imagination evoked an ache of longing low in her pelvis.

Dimitris had made it plain that he wasn't interested in her, and never again would she offer herself to him as she had done at his house in Richmond, she promised herself. Her plan to get him out of her system hadn't worked, Savannah acknowledged ruefully. But they were halfway through the photoshoot, and outside of working hours she just had to avoid him as much as possible for the next three weeks. That would be difficult if she accompanied him to a party.

'Surely you have a PR photographer to take pictures at the launch party.' Savannah turned her attention back to her screen. Dimitris looked gorgeous in jeans and a loose cream shirt with the top buttons undone, giving her a glimpse of his tanned skin and wiry black chest hairs. She prayed he couldn't see the betraying hard points of her nipples beneath her thin cotton dress.

'My public relations team will take promotional photos at the restaurant. I intend to use the event to promote my new cookery book and I'll give a couple of interviews to the media. I need you there to talk about how you photographed the recipes.'

He crossed the room noiselessly and Savannah snatched a breath when he spun her chair round so she was facing him. 'There's no need for you to work editing photos until late every evening,' he said with a frown. 'The schedule for the book is on track. The launch party of Hestia's Crete will be a good opportunity to raise your profile as a food photographer. The restaurant is the tenth in the Hestia's chain since I opened my first restaurant here in Rhodes.'

'Did you use the money you accepted from my father to fund your business?' She could not hide her bitterness. It was important to remember that Dimitris had broken her heart once before. Savannah sensed it would be easy to fall for his sexy charm again. When they worked together in the studio she'd discovered that he was clever and entertaining, and he had a sharp wit. He made her laugh with stories about the various kitchens he'd worked in when he'd been a junior chef. It was dangerous to like him, Savannah reminded herself.

'No,' Dimitris said heavily. 'I spent the money from your father on a house for my grandparents and to pay for some of my sister's medical treatment. Everything I have achieved in my career has been the result of the long hours I spent perfecting my cooking. I was lucky to be given some great opportunities and worked hard to get to where I am today.'

Savannah chewed her lower lip. 'I don't have anything to wear to the party.' It was the only excuse she could think of.

'Leave it to me. I'll organise a dress to be delivered to the villa tomorrow.'

'I don't…' She broke off when Dimitris gave her an impatient look.

'I expect you to accompany me to the party. It's not negotiable. Promoting the book is part of your job,' he said coolly before he strode over to the door. Savannah succumbed to the childish urge to stick her tongue out at his back as he left the room.

The next day, after working in the studio, Savannah went to her room and found a large flat box on the bed. Inside was a dress that she knew must have cost much more than she could afford. Hopefully, her credit card would take the strain. The money she'd earned from the Philpot's shoot had nearly all gone on her mum's nursing home fees.

She showered and blow-dried her hair before catching it in a loose chignon. The dress was a full-length silk sheath in olive-green with a low-cut bodice and narrow shoulder straps that meant she couldn't wear a bra. The dress fitted like a dream, and she had to admit that the colour and the simplicity of the style suited her slim figure. Another box contained a pair of silver stiletto heel sandals and a matching purse.

Would Dimitris think she looked good in the dress he had chosen for her? She wished she didn't care about his opinion, but her heart was thumping when she went to meet him.

He walked across the entrance hall while she was halfway down the stairs. When he saw her, his jaw firmed as an almost feral expression pulled his skin tightly over his hard cheekbones.

'You look stunning.' The flare of desire in his eyes lit a flame inside Savannah. But she was confused. After he hadn't kissed her on the beach she'd assumed that he'd suppressed any attraction he might have felt for her.

Dimitris looked breathtaking in a black tuxedo. His hair was more groomed than usual, although it still curled at his nape, and the dark stubble on his jaw was neatly trimmed. When Savannah reached the bottom of the stairs and walked towards him, the spicy scent of his cologne evoked a tug of longing in the pit of her stomach.

'Come into the sitting room. I have something for

you.' He ushered her into the room and handed her a slim velvet box. Inside was an exquisite peridot pendant on a gold chain and a pair of peridot and diamond earrings. Savannah closed the lid and gave a tiny sigh of regret as she held out the box to him.

'The jewellery is beautiful, but I can't afford it. The dress probably cost the earth.'

'I don't expect you to pay for the dress or the necklace,' Dimitris said coolly. 'I asked you to attend the party with me and I have simply provided you with an outfit to wear.'

Savannah bit her lip. The dress was one thing but... 'I can't accept the jewellery,' she insisted.

'Most of the women on the exclusive guest list at the launch party will be showing off their diamonds.' Dimitris opened the box and lifted the pendant from its velvet cushion. He moved behind Savannah and fastened the gold chain around her neck. She could not disguise a shiver of reaction when his fingers brushed across her skin. 'Wear the jewellery tonight, hmm?' he murmured. 'It's not a big deal, but if you want to you can return it to me after the party.'

She could hardly refuse. Savannah stepped in front of the mirror and fixed the earrings to her lobes. The peridot pendant nestled in the hollow between her breasts and when she turned around Dimitris's gaze lingered on the low-cut neckline of her dress. He moved away to collect her camera bag from the coffee table where she'd left it, and she released her breath. The simmering sexual attraction between her and Dimitris threatened her already shaky composure.

* * *

He had chartered a helicopter to fly them to Crete, the largest of the Greek islands and hugely popular with tourists. His new restaurant was located next to a pretty harbour full of fishing boats. When they arrived, the sun was a fireball sinking into the sea and staining the sky pink and gold. A steady stream of guests arrived in cars, boats and helicopters which landed on the helipad on the roof of the restaurant.

Dimitris had said the guest list was exclusive and Savannah recognised several international celebrities. During her short modelling career she'd attended many glamorous events, but nothing as grand as this. The paparazzi had gathered outside the front of the restaurant to snap pictures of the guests, who posed by the door before they stepped inside to enjoy a champagne reception.

She stiffened when Dimitris placed his hand on her waist to guide her to where they were to stand for the publicity shots. Intense media coverage of the opening night of the restaurant was important to attract customers to Hestia's Crete. Dimitris was the star of the evening, and he was relaxed and smiling and drop-dead sexy in front of the cameras.

'Smile,' he instructed as she stood tensely beside him. 'And try to relax. We have been working hard recently, and it's time to have some fun.'

Savannah's heart gave a jolt in response to the gleam in Dimitris's eyes. She was determined to ignore her fierce awareness of him when he kept his hand on her waist as they entered the restaurant. After he'd greeted his guests he led her over to a few journalists, who asked questions about the new cookery book and Savannah's role as the photographer. She coloured when Dimitris described her as one of the best food photographers in the business.

'Let me show you the kitchen,' he said, catching hold of her hand as he opened a door at the rear of the restaurant.

Unsurprisingly, the state-of-the-art kitchen was bustling and chaotic. The staff were clearly excited to see him. The head chef Kostas spoke English and explained to Savannah that several of the young chefs had received financial support during their training from Dimitris's charity which helped youths from underprivileged backgrounds.

It was obvious that Dimitris was revered by the staff, and he spoke to each of them, asked about the food they were preparing and joked with them while Savannah unpacked her camera and took photos of the dishes for the promotional campaign.

'All the youngsters want to be a famous chef like Dimitris,' Kostas told her. 'They are inspired by him. He devised the recipes on the menu when he came and spent days here in the kitchen. He asked for their ideas and suggestions and encouraged them. Dimitris is their hero. He made it to the top, but he never forgets that he started at the bottom.'

During the five-course dinner, which was superb, Savannah's thoughts returned to the past. She had been devastated when her father told her that Dimitris had accepted a bribe to dump her. 'I set your boyfriend a test,' Richard O'Neal had told her. 'If he genuinely had feelings for you he would have refused the money. But he took it, and it proves that he felt nothing for you.'

Dimitris had used the money to help his elderly grandparents to retire and he'd paid for his sister's medical care for the injuries she had received in a car accident that Eleni had suggested he somehow blamed himself for. He had worked hard to become successful. Unlike Savannah's father, who had made money from crime and who had left her mum destitute. She sighed. It would be so much easier if she could label Dimitris a villain and hate him for hurting her feelings when she'd been eighteen. But he was a complex man, and the truth was she had been searching for love that her father had withheld from her.

'Do you not like the food?' Dimitris murmured when Savannah toyed with her dessert. *Kataifi* was made with chopped walnuts and flavoured with cinnamon, wrapped in a crispy, buttery dough and drenched in a lemon-scented syrup.

'It's delicious, but I've eaten too much,' she said ruefully. 'I'll have to do some exercise to work off the pounds I'm sure to have gained.'

'You could swim in the pool instead of watching me from your office,' he said drily.

She gave him a startled look, mortified that he might think she had spied on him in the pool.

He quirked one eyebrow. 'I wondered if you were avoiding me.'

'We work together in the studio every day,' she muttered.

'But you prefer not to spend time with me after work?'

Savannah's temper flared as she wondered where he was going with the conversation. What did he want from her? 'I had the impression on the beach a week ago that you want us to be work colleagues and nothing more.'

His dark blue eyes were unfathomable, but she noticed a nerve flicker in his cheek. He sipped his wine before he said softly, 'Is that what you want, Savannah?'

She was about to assure him that of course it was. Anything other than a strictly work based relationship with Dimitris would be dangerous. But she was transfixed by his masculine beauty, and when he smiled she felt more alive than she'd done in ten years. 'I don't know,' she admitted huskily.

The band had been playing smooth jazz tunes during dinner, but now the guests had finished eating and the tempo of the music increased as people stepped onto the dance floor.

Dimitris pushed back his chair and stood up. He offered his hand to Savannah. 'Would you like to dance?'

Not a good idea, her brain cautioned. But if she refused it might arouse his suspicion that she was fighting her attraction to him. Taking a deep breath, she placed her fingers in his. He led her to the dance floor and placed his hands on her waist as they moved to the beat of the music. The brush of his thigh against hers made her insides melt. Savannah had only drunk one glass of champagne, but she felt intoxicated by the heat of his body and his male scent: spice, phero-mones—desire.

It was nearly midnight when the last guests left the restaurant. Dimitris called all the front of house and kitchen staff together and thanked them for their hard work making the opening night a success.

'The head chef told me that a percentage of the prof-its from your restaurants is paid to your charity and funds a training scheme to teach young people how to cook,' Savannah said after they had climbed into the helicopter, and it took off.

Dimitris nodded. 'I was lucky that my grandfather taught me how to cook, and I was able to develop my skills at catering college. Many kids are not given the chance to start a career, especially when Greece ex-perienced economic problems in the past years. I'm glad to put something back into the industry that has enabled me to be successful.'

'You must feel proud of everything you've achieved.'

'Must I?' His voice was strangely grim, and he looked away from Savannah and stared out of his win-dow. She didn't understand the reason for his change of mood. At the restaurant he had been charming and when they had danced together he'd flirted with her, and it had taken all her willpower not to fall under his spell.

They were both silent for the rest of the flight to Rhodes. Savannah had never flown in a helicopter at night. It was magical sitting in the cabin and looking out at the dark sky scattered with stars that seemed close enough to touch.

When the villa came into view she sensed that some of Dimitris's tension had eased. The helicopter landed and he jumped out and offered his hand to help her down the steps. They walked past the infinity pool that looked pretty, lit with multicoloured underwater lights. The water flowing over the edge disappeared into the darkness.

Savannah's pulse thudded as a memory of Dimitris standing at the edge of the pool before he dived in came into her mind. She pictured his broad, tanned chest covered with dark hairs that arrowed over his flat abdomen and disappeared beneath the waistband of his swim briefs, and heat coiled through her.

'How about that swim for the exercise you said you needed?' He grinned at her startled expression, and she felt herself blush as she wondered if he had somehow guessed that she'd had erotic thoughts about him.

'It's late and I think we should go straight to bed.' Horrified that he might think she had propositioned him, she said frantically, 'I mean alone, to our own beds, obviously.'

Dimitris halted and turned her towards him, cupping her chin between his fingers to tilt her face up to his. 'I think that might be what is known as a Freudian slip,' he murmured, amusement and something else in his eyes that sent a quiver of excitement through Savannah. He rubbed his thumb absently over her jaw and the unexpected tenderness in his caress chipped at her fragile defences.

'I want to make love to you, Savannah. And I think you want me too.' Beneath his almost casual tone was a rough note of sexual hunger that evoked a moist heat between her legs. But this man had wrecked her emotions when she had been young and vulnerable, and even though she was older and, hopefully, wiser she was afraid to give in to the desire running rampant through her body.

He lifted his other hand and ran his finger from the base of her throat, down her décolletage to the hollow between her breasts, where the peridot pendant gleamed in the moonlight. It was impossible to hide from him the jerky rise and fall of her chest as she fought the temptation to sink against his whipcord body. He captured her hand and carried it to his mouth to brush his lips over her palm and then the inside of her wrist, where her pulse was going crazy.

His other hand still cupped her jaw. He traced his fingers over her cheek and up to her ear. His touch was as light as gossamer and her resistance melted beneath his sweet seduction when he lowered his head and moved his lips over her cheek. The delicious abrasion of his stubbled jaw on her skin aroused her unbearably and the temptation to tip her head back so that he could claim her mouth with his own was overwhelming. His closeness and the glittering desire in his eyes when he lifted his head and stared down at her made her feel as weak as a kitten.

'One night was not enough for either of us, was it, Savannah?'

Dimitris's voice broke the spell he'd woven around her with his skilful seduction.

'How many nights would be enough?' she asked

tautly. 'Five, ten? There are twenty-two nights left until the photoshoot is finished. Will you have tired of me before then?' Savannah pulled away from him, desperate to hide the riot of her emotions.

His eyes narrowed. 'Is it necessary to quantify a time period that our relationship might last? We both want to be lovers, so why not take things one day at a time?'

'Relationship!' She huffed out a breath. 'You have said publicly in the media that a relationship and commitment are not what you want. But they are what I want. At least the possibility of something more meaningful than casual sex.'

Dimitris frowned and Savannah said quickly, 'I don't deny that I am attracted to you. I can't hide the way I react to you. But having sex to scratch an itch is not enough for me.'

'Theós!' he exploded. 'In what way have I acted as though I view making love to you as simply a way to satisfy my baser instincts? We have grown close in the past few weeks.'

'So we would be friends with benefits?' She bit her lip. 'Dimitris, you told me that your car is the love of your life. Yes, we have got on well while we've worked together, but you don't allow anyone to get too close, do you? Not emotionally, and certainly not me.'

'Is that what you want?' he gritted. 'For me to lay bare my deepest feelings?'

She gave him a wry look. 'Do you have any deep feelings?'

'How about my guilt, and self-loathing. Are they enough *feelings* for you?' He raked his hand through his hair. His jaw was clenched, and his eyes were al-most black with fury and something else. *Pain*, Savan-nah realised with a jolt of shock.

'Dimitris…you don't have to…' Too late, she realised she had opened Pandora's Box and she was desperate to close it again so that he would not look like he did right now…wrecked. He wasn't made of granite, he was a flesh and blood man, and he was hurting.

'You started this,' he told her harshly. 'You might as well hear all of it.'

'I killed my parents.' Dimitris heard Savannah's swift intake of breath and reminded himself that he deserved the look of shock and horror that flared in her hazel-green eyes. 'Not directly,' he said grimly, 'but I caused the accident in which they died, and my sister was so badly injured that it seemed impossible she would walk again.'

Do you have any deep feelings?

Savannah's question had opened the floodgates and he could not hold back the tidal wave of self-recrimi-nation from pouring out. He had more emotions than he could handle, and a long time ago he'd stopped try-ing and had locked his feelings away in a box labelled *Do Not Open*.

He had meaningless affairs with women who were too self-absorbed to wonder who he was beneath his public façade of a careless playboy. He was aware that his success was in part due to his sex appeal. Women wanted the Hot Chef, the Greek god in the kitchen, and no one had ever tried to discover the man he really was—except for Savannah.

She was looking at him with a mixture of curiosity and concern in those incredible eyes of hers. 'How could you have caused the accident? You were what? Fourteen or fifteen? You can't have been driving the car.'

Memories—*pain*—surged through him. 'My parents were taking Eleni to her ballet class,' he said heavily. 'I was supposed to have ridden my bike to football training, but I'd overslept and persuaded my mother to drop me at the sports centre.'

If only he'd woken earlier, his parents would not have died. The seeds of the accident had been sown when he'd forgotten to set his alarm. Dimitris could never forgive himself for his stupid mistake that had such tragic consequences.

'My mother was driving.' His voice rasped in a throat that felt like he'd swallowed broken glass. There was almost a sense of relief in opening up to Savannah, even though he was sure she would despise him once she knew the truth. He'd spent almost two decades fooling other people, fooling himself that he was fine. But he wasn't fine, and he was fairly certain that Savannah saw through him.

'I'd got in with a bad crowd at school, but that's no excuse. I was a brat.' His jaw clenched. 'An argument started about my attitude. I was unkind to my sister and Eleni started crying. My father turned around and told me to apologise, but I was rude to him. My mother took her eyes off the road and looked over her shoulder at me, in the back of the car.'

Dimitris tasted bile in his throat as he relived the moments before the crash. 'For those few seconds while my mother's attention was distracted, the car veered out of the lane. A lorry was travelling in the opposite direction. In the split second when I realised we were going to hit the lorry, I shouted a warning. I think my father grabbed the steering wheel. But it was too late, and it was a head-on collision.'

'Oh, God. It must have been horrific.' Savannah's voice was gentle. Dimitris did not understand why she hadn't recoiled from him in disgust. 'But you were not responsible for what happened.'

'Of course I was responsible,' he said savagely. 'I've explained how I had distracted my mother.'

The police had taken a statement from him as part of their investigation into the cause of the crash, and he'd told them that his mother had momentarily lost concentration. He'd later heard that the lorry driver had survived. For months afterwards Dimitris had expected to be arrested for causing the crash. But just because no one else blamed him did not mean that he was blameless. He knew what he had done, and now Savannah knew.

'The last words my mother spoke to me were that my family were concerned about me...and they loved me.'

'Oh, Dimitris. It was an accident. It wasn't your fault.' Savannah's eyes were fiercely bright, and tears clung to her lashes. With a jolt of shock he realised that she felt sympathy—for him.

'Don't you dare suggest that I wasn't to blame,' he said savagely. He *knew* it was his fault, and he couldn't understand why Savannah was not convinced of his guilt. 'Eleni spent years confined to a wheelchair because of my stupidity. How do you think she'd react if I told her how the accident happened?'

'I think you should talk to her about the crash. She told me she has tried to discuss it, but you clam up.'

'If I admitted to my sister what I had done she would have every right to hate me.' He turned away from Savannah while he struggled to bring himself under control. There was a hollowness in his chest as if his heart had been ripped out. *This* was why he avoided emotions. It was easier not to care about anything.

'Eleni was all I had left of my family. Of course I had my grandparents, but they were heartbroken to lose their only son and their grief added to my guilt. I couldn't bear that Eleni would blame me because she was an orphan and couldn't walk. I vowed to take care of her and work hard to provide for her and give her the best life I could.'

Savannah came to stand in front of him. 'I'm certain that Eleni wouldn't blame you. She adores you, and she would want you to stop blaming yourself.'

He shook his head. He'd carried his guilt for so long and despite what Savannah had said he knew there could be no absolution for him. He was furious with her for suggesting there could be. She put her hand on his arm and he flinched even as his damnable desire for her sparked into flame. His emotions—*Theós!* he hated that word—felt raw, and he couldn't handle the understanding in her eyes, he couldn't handle *her* when he felt a stupid urge to cry like a child.

'I need a drink.' He shrugged off her hand and strode towards the poolside bar. Her heels clipped against the tiled floor as she followed him, and he cursed and swung round to face her. 'Go to bed, Savannah.'

His control felt dangerously close to snapping. He wanted to take her right there on the tiled floor, shove her dress up to her waist and free his aching erection from his trousers to sink into her slick heat. He longed to make love to her until there was nothing in his head but her softness and heat and the scent of her perfume that he did not doubt would haunt him for as long as he lived.

'Go!' he bit out. 'You were right, I can't give you what you want.' He didn't wait for her to respond, and when he walked away and she did not follow he told himself he was glad.

CHAPTER NINE

SAVANNAH STOOD BY her bedroom window and watched Dimitris in the pool. He swam length after length without pausing, as if he wanted to push himself to his limits, or as if he was punishing himself. She sensed it was the latter.

It was her fault. Guilt was an arrow through her heart. His pain and his need to keep on swimming, up and down, up and down, was his way of dealing with his agonising emotions after she'd accused him of not having deep feelings. How wrong she had been. And how cruel. Because her instincts had told her that the real Dimitris was a far more complex man than the charming, sexy chef he presented to the world.

The truth was utterly heartbreaking. Since he was fourteen—an age when many teenagers were impressionable—he had believed that he was responsible for his parents' deaths and his sister's life-changing injuries. And for eighteen years he had not told anyone of his secret torment, until she'd challenged him to reveal the pain he'd carried inside him for so long.

But it had not brought him comfort to finally speak about the accident. She'd been unable to convince him that he was blameless, and he had rejected her sympathy—rejected her. Tonight he had admitted that he desired her, but she'd acted like the teenage girl of ten years ago who had yearned for a fairy tale. Dimitris was not a fantasy prince, he was a man with flaws, but there was much to admire. His kindness when he'd offered her a job so that she had enough money to take care of her mum, his patience and understanding when she'd told him why she had a fear of heights, and he had shown his philanthropy with his charity that helped train young chefs.

He was a flesh and blood man, and she had made him bleed. Savannah closed her eyes, hating herself for being so blind. Dimitris's self-containment was not because he did not have feelings, it was a defence to hide his guilt and grief.

Where did they go from here? For a start, she could admit that she wanted to make love with him again. She looked back at the pool and caught her breath as Dimitris hauled himself out of the water. Naked, he truly was a Greek god. His toned, tanned body was long and lean, with hard thighs and a broad, muscular chest. He stood under the poolside shower and the spray flattened the whorls of black hairs on his chest. Her gaze followed the arrowing of hairs over his abdomen and down to where they grew thick around the base of his manhood.

Heat unfurled low in her belly, a hunger she could not deny. Life was unpredictable and could be over in an instant in a collision of metal hitting metal. Life could be cruel, as her mum's diagnosis of a degenerative disease had proved. Life was for living *now*, not worrying about what would happen in the future. Dimitris did not want permanency, but she was prepared to accept an affair with him on his terms. After all, he couldn't break her heart if she did not give it to him.

His bedroom was on the same floor as hers, but at the front of the house overlooking the sea. She knew he must still be downstairs, and she did not hesitate before entering his room. The sight of the big bed sent a throb of nervous anticipation through her. Dimitris had given her a glimpse of the man behind the mask, and now it was her turn to let him see how badly she wanted him.

A breeze stirred the filmy curtain in front of the open door leading to the balcony. The sound of waves breaking onto the sand enticed Savannah outside. Twinkling lights lined the bay and the night sky was crowded with glittering stars. Minutes later she heard the click of the bedroom door and took a deep breath before she pushed the curtains aside and stepped into the room.

Dimitris froze and his eyes narrowed on her. He was wearing a towel knotted around his waist, and droplets of water clung to his chest hairs. He threw his clothes onto a chair before he spoke.

'What do you want, Savannah?'

'You.'

His lack of a reaction did not surprise her. No doubt he regretted revealing the emotions that he'd kept hidden for his entire adult life and he'd spent nearly an hour in the pool re-establishing his iron control over himself.

There was only one way to show him that she was serious. She slid the straps of her dress over her shoulders and shimmied out of the clingy sheath, slowly baring her breasts, her midriff and her hips. The green silk slithered to the floor, and she was left in just a black lace thong.

Still Dimitris said nothing, but his chest rose and fell as if it hurt him to breathe when she walked towards him.

'One night was not enough for me either,' she told him. 'I don't care how long we last.' She stretched out her hand and loosened the towel, but when she tried to pull it away he clamped his hand over hers.

'Are you offering pity sex?' he growled. 'For some reason you feel sorry for me and so you've decided to sleep with me?'

She shook her head, feeling her heart shatter a little when she thought of the burden of guilt he'd carried for so long. 'I don't pity you. I want to make love with you,' she said simply. She whipped the towel away and curled her fingers around his powerful erection. 'I'm pretty sure you want me too, but just to be sure…'

Her heart thudded as she sank to her knees in front of him. She had never done this before. But she needed to show him that she was his, utterly, for as long as the fire between them blazed.

'Savannah?' His voice was low and harsh, and he spoke her name like a warning—or a plea—when she ran her tongue over the tip of his manhood.

He muttered something in Greek and speared his fingers in her hair as if he intended to pull her head up and prevent her pleasuring him with her mouth. At least she hoped she was giving him pleasure. She was fascinated by the combination of steel and velvet against her tongue and was fairly sure that his ragged groan was of enjoyment, not because he wanted her to stop.

'What am I going to do with you, *mátia mou*?' The huskiness in Dimitris's voice made Savannah's heart contract.

She sat back on her heels and looked up at him. The hunger in his dark eyes intensified the ache between her legs and moist heat pooled there in readiness for him. How could this be wrong when it felt so gloriously right? She smiled. 'I hope you will think of something,' she said softly.

Theós! That smile. Impossibly, when Savannah smiled she was even more beautiful. Dimitris shuddered as she licked her tongue along his hard length. She was sending him out of his mind.

When he had discovered her in his room, his heart had crashed into his ribs. She was a goddess in her green silk dress that moulded every dip and curve of her body. He had told himself that ordering a dress for her to wear to the party was a reasonable thing to do. After all, she would be promoting his new cookery book. He'd bought the jewellery on a whim when he'd seen the gems displayed in a jeweller's window in Rhodes Town. The peridots reminded him of the mysterious green of Savannah's eyes.

But when he'd seen her glide down the stairs before the party, looking so beautiful that he'd felt a tug in his chest and his blood had surged into his groin, he'd realised that he was in trouble. He'd been unable to take his eyes off her all evening, and he had known that Savannah's prickliness had been her attempt to hide her awareness of him.

He did not understand how she could smile at him after what he'd told her. He *had* been responsible for the tragedy that had destroyed his family. His sister had spent years in a wheelchair because he'd been a stroppy, ungrateful teenager who hadn't deserved his parents love and he did not deserve to find love for the rest of his life.

Dimitris tensed. He could not think properly while Savannah was using her mouth on him so effectively that he realised he was seconds away from embarrassing himself and disappointing her. He never lost control. The truth was that no other woman had tested his control the way Savannah did. She made him feel things he was not ready to admit to himself, and so he shoved a lid on his emotions—he was good at that— and drew her to her feet, pulling her close so that her body was plastered against his.

Her stunning eyes, more green than hazel tonight, widened when she felt his erection jab between her thighs. 'I want you,' he told her rawly. He needed to lose himself in her sweetness and forget for a while who he really was, what he had done, and how he could never be good enough for her.

He lifted her into his arms and carried her over to

the bed. She was a lightweight, but his heart thudded painfully hard when she looped her arms around his neck so that her breasts pressed against his chest.

'Are you sure this is what you want?' he asked when he laid her on the bed. 'I can't give you…'

She silenced him by pressing her finger gently across his lips. 'All I want is to make love with you.'

He liked the shiver that ran through her when he removed the scrap of black lace from between her legs, and he liked even more the gasp she made when he pushed her thighs apart and lowered his head to lick his tongue over her moist opening. The scent of her feminine arousal made his gut clench and he wanted to simply drive his rock-hard erection into her to find the release he craved.

But this was all about Savannah and he told her so, not in words but with his hands and mouth and tongue as he gave her the most intimate caress of all while she gasped and squirmed and arched her hips towards him.

'Please, Dimitris. I want you *now*…'

He understood that her need was as fierce as his, and neither of them could wait any longer. Pausing to take a condom from the bedside drawer and sheath himself, he moved over her and slid his hands beneath her bottom, tilting her pelvis. And then he entered her with a hard thrust, and she gave a low cry and wrapped her legs around his hips. It was like a homecoming, and he almost came too soon.

He forced himself to take things slower and concentrate on her needs. He kissed her mouth, her throat, and trailed his lips over her breasts that were flushed rose-pink from the heat of her desire. Her nipples were dusky rose and swelled beneath his tongue when he sucked on them, and her guttural moans tested his control. Somehow he hung on and drove into her faster, harder, setting a rhythm that became increasingly urgent.

Savannah bucked beneath him and dug her fingernails into his buttocks. He held her there at the edge as he stared into her eyes, and he felt a connection that stunned him, a tenderness that terrified him. And then she smiled, and something inside him cracked. He felt the first ripples of her orgasm and withdrew a little way before he thrust deep into her molten heat. Her internal muscles tightened around his shaft and with a groan he let go and tumbled with her into the abyss.

Savannah opened her eyes to find the room bathed in the pearly light of dawn. She wasn't in her room. Memories of the previous night flooded her mind, and she turned her head and saw Dimitris, lying beside her. He was asleep and she studied his handsome face. His features were softer, and his long black lashes made crescents on his cheeks. The stubble on his jaw was thicker with a night's growth and his mouth…*his mouth*… Heat coiled through her as she remembered how skilfully he had used his mouth on every inch of her body to give her incredible pleasure.

With a sigh she acknowledged that she had jumped into the fire, but she didn't regret sleeping with him. She knew that great sex was all he would offer, and she accepted it. She hoped that if they were lovers for the few weeks remaining of the photoshoot, their chemistry would fizzle out and she would truly be over him.

Dimitris moved his head on the pillow. He was still asleep, but he made a low groan. He brought his arm across his face. '

'*No...no!*'

He sounded in such terrible torment that Savannah wanted to weep. Another groan was torn from his throat and sweat ran down his face.

'*Are my parents all right? And my sister? Are they alive? No...*'

'Dimitris.' Savannah touched his shoulder. 'Wake up. You were having a dream.'

His chest heaved, and he sat up and stared at her, but it was as though he did not see her. 'Eleni...?'

'It's okay, Dimitris. Let it go.'

He blinked and jerked fully awake. His mouth twisted as he shrugged Savannah's hand off him, and she tried not to feel hurt by his rejection of her sympathy. 'Let it go?' He laughed, a low, raw sound without humour. 'How can I let go of the memories of what I did? It was my fault.'

She realised he was still half trapped in his dream. 'Do you often have nightmares?'

He raked his hair off his brow, and Savannah noticed that his hand shook. 'A few bad dreams are nothing compared to what my sister suffered for years after the accident.'

'Talk to her. Perhaps you will be able to come to terms with the past if you stop holding back from your sister,' Savannah told him gently. 'I had a message from

Eleni, saying that her business in Asia will finish next week and she is to return to Rhodes for a few days before flying to America.'

'Eleni's trip to Boston is for her final check-up at the spinal injury hospital.' Dimitris's jaw clenched. 'I know I must explain what happened, but I can't expect her to forgive me any more than I can ever forgive myself.'

He threw back the sheet and stood up. 'I'm sorry I disturbed you, Savannah,' he said tonelessly, in control of his emotions once more. 'It's still early. I suggest you go to your room and get some more sleep.'

Dimitris's heart was hammering, and his mind was full of terrible images of the car—a tangled heap of metal and the front barely visible where it had come to rest beneath the lorry. It was a miracle that he'd been pulled from the wreckage almost unscathed, one of the medics at the scene had said. No one had told him then that his parents had died in the crash. His grandfather had broken the news to him later when his grandparents had returned from the hospital where they had been visiting Eleni in the intensive care unit.

How could he forget? How could he let go of his guilt? He stumbled into his bathroom and locked the door behind him, needing to be alone, yet a part of him longed for the comfort of Savannah's cool hand on his shoulder. He did not deserve her gentle sympathy, he reminded herself as he stood beneath the punishing cold spray that could never wash away his self-loathing.

Eventually he dried himself and walked back into the bedroom. He stopped dead at the sight of Savannah asleep in his bed. The sheet lay across her waist and her bare breasts were perfect creamy mounds tipped with dusky pink nipples. The early morning sunlight, slanting through the blinds, danced over her sexily messy blonde hair and her slender limbs that were tanned a pale honey colour.

She was so beautiful, inside and out. He felt an odd constriction in his chest when he remembered her fierce insistence that he had not been responsible for the accident that had destroyed his family.

The ache in certain areas of his body were a reminder that he had made love to her twice more last night. Both times had been less urgent than the first, but just as intense. When he moved inside her they fitted perfectly together as if they belonged. Fanciful nonsense of course, he assured himself. Good sex—it had been sublime—was still just sex.

Last night had been amazing, but now it was morning and he needed to re-establish boundaries that had been crossed when he'd opened up to Savannah in a way he'd never done with anyone else. There was three weeks remaining of the photoshoot for his cookery book, and immediately afterwards he had a trip arranged to Australia for a promotional tour. Whatever he felt for Savannah would have burned out by then, he assured himself.

He wasn't ready to face her while his emotions still felt raw and exposed, like an onion that had been peeled layer by layer. He left her sleeping and went downstairs to the kitchen. It was his assistant Stefanos's weekend off. Dimitris made a jug of coffee and loaded a tray with a bowl of thick Greek yogurt, honey and some plump figs.

He stepped outside to the garden and picked mint leaves to tear over the figs. God knew why he impulsively cut a long-stemmed pale pink rose and placed it on the tray. When he returned to the bedroom he found Savannah sitting up in bed. She watched him warily as he put the breakfast tray on the bedside table.

'Sorry, I must have fallen back to sleep. Are you... okay?'

'I'm fine.' Confession wasn't good for the soul, whatever anyone said. He regretted that she had seen him when he was weak. It wouldn't happen again.

'I meant to go to my room, but I was tired after...' She broke off and blushed.

Dimitris couldn't remember the last time he'd seen a woman blush. It was a reminder that Savannah was different, more vulnerable, than the lovers he'd had in the past, who'd had no expectations from him.

'I enjoyed last night, and I think you did too,' he drawled. He did not want her to think that taking her to bed had been about anything more than satisfying their mutual desire.

Her breathing quickened when he sat on the edge of the mattress and tugged the sheet away from her breasts. 'We should get up and start work in the studio,' she said huskily.

'Have you forgotten it's the weekend?' He pulled the sheet down, and hunger tore through him as his gaze lingered on the vee of blonde curls between her thighs. He wanted to make love to her and lose himself in the sweet solace of her body, to banish the shadows of his nightmare.

Dimitris stripped off his sweatpants and lay beside Savannah on the bed. His erection nudged between her thighs when he lifted himself over her and supported his weight on his elbows. 'Weekends are when we relax,' he murmured. His nostrils flared as she reached down and curled her fingers around his hard shaft.

'You don't feel very relaxed to me. Quite tense in fact,' she teased him softly.

'Witch.' He didn't know what to make of her. She made him laugh. *Theós*, she had almost made him cry. Savannah made him feel things he was afraid to define, and he told himself it was desire that caused his heart to pound when he entered her with a long, deep thrust and smothered her gasp with his mouth.

The kiss was wild and hot before it became slow and sensual, with an underlying tenderness that only Savannah had discovered lurked in the depths of his soul and which he could not hide from her. He moved inside her, and she matched his rhythm, lifting her hips each time he drove into her with steady strokes, taking them closer to the edge.

It couldn't last, and she gave a sharp cry as she shuddered beneath him, and he felt the exquisite tightening of her internal muscles around his shaft. Moments later he reached his own shattering climax, and afterwards a sweet lassitude swept over him and he rolled onto his back, taking her with him and holding her close.

Much later Dimitris unravelled from Savannah and

they balanced the tray on their knees while they feasted on tart yoghurt and juicy figs. She chased a tiny shred of mint leaf across her lips with her tongue and he couldn't resist using his own tongue to lick off a smear of honey from the corner of her mouth.

'Tell me about your father,' he said, propping himself against the headboard. 'It must have been a shock when he was accused of corruption.'

'It felt like a bad dream.' She bit her lip and glanced at him as if she was remembering how she'd woken him from his nightmare. 'Although I didn't have a close relationship with my father I respected him until I discovered that he was corrupt to his core. The stress of his trial accelerated Mum's illness, I'm sure.'

Dimitris searched her face for any sign that she knew the truth about Richard O'Neal. 'Were your parents happily married?'

She frowned. 'I never heard them argue. They had quite separate lives. My father was always working, and Mum was busy with her art. I don't think they were particularly close.'

Savannah hesitated. 'A few years ago I helped Mum sort out some old letters and paperwork she kept in her bureau. Tucked at the back of a drawer was a photo of a young man. She took it from me and got upset when I asked who he was. My father was still alive then. I wondered if she had been in love with the man, but something had happened, and she'd married my father.'

Dimitris slid out of bed and walked outside to his private balcony. Could the man in the photo be Savannah's real father? he brooded. He felt guilty that he was keeping a shocking secret from Savannah. But he could not reveal what Richard O'Neal had told him. The person who should tell her the truth was Savannah's mother.

'Dimitris?' Savannah's voice was soft with concern, and when she joined him on the balcony the gentle expression in her eyes chipped at the ice around Dimitris's heart. 'I know you are worried about telling Eleni everything you told me. But she has a right to know the details of the accident. And one day you might be able to put the past behind you.'

'Why do you care?' he asked gruffly. 'I hurt you in the past.'

'I wish you had confided in me ten years ago. But I was immature, and I wanted you to rescue me like the handsome prince from the fairy tales I'd read as a child. I wish I had tried to get you to talk about your parents.'

Dimitris felt an ache in his chest when he remembered her at eighteen, so beautiful and trusting. There was a wariness in her now that he guiltily acknowledged he was responsible for. He wished he were different and could give her the fairy tale. But at the end of the photoshoot he would let her go so that she could find her prince. He was stunned by how much he hated the prospect, and how bleak the future seemed without Savannah.

He pulled away from his thoughts and smiled. 'I thought that after breakfast I would take you out on my boat to visit some of the other islands around Rhodes. Symi and Halki are both pretty islands.'

'A boat trip sounds amazing.' She caught her breath

when he lifted her up so that her pelvis was flush to his and she felt his burgeoning erection. 'We've eaten breakfast,' she reminded him when he carried her inside and tumbled them onto the bed. 'So are we going on your boat now?'

'I didn't specify how long after breakfast we would go on a boat trip, *mátia mou*.' He grinned as he eased between her splayed thighs so that his swollen tip pressed against her moist opening. 'But I have a feeling it will be *much* later.'

CHAPTER TEN

DIMITRIS SHOVED HIS hands in his pockets and turned away from the window where he had been staring unseeingly at the beach. His sister looked up from her book. 'I wish you would sit down. You have been prowling around the room ever since I arrived.'

He walked over to Eleni and lowered his tall frame onto the sofa beside her. In his mind he heard Savannah's voice urging him to open up to his sister. 'I need to talk to you…about what happened in the accident.' He pulled in a breath. 'Or rather why it happened.'

'Actually, I know what happened.' Eleni closed her book and gave him her full attention.

He frowned. 'Did you speak to Savannah?'

'Not about the accident. But when I mentioned to her that I wished I knew the details, she suggested that there might be a police file or some documents about the accident. I don't know why I'd never thought of it. I did some research and found an old newspaper report. All I knew was that our car had been in a collision with a lorry. The report said that the lorry had a tyre blowout that caused the driver to swerve across the road and into the path of a car.' She blinked away a tear. 'Our parents were in the front seats and didn't stand a chance.'

'That's not how it was.' Dimitris jumped up and stared at his sister. He had never followed up about the accident or looked for reports because he hated to be reminded of the worst day of his life. Besides, he knew what had happened and the part he'd played. 'I was responsible for the crash. I distracted Mum, who was driving, and she took her eyes off the road. I was a vile teenager and I made you cry. It was my fault that our parents were killed, and you were injured.'

Eleni stood and walked stiffly towards him. 'The newspaper said there was an inquest, and the cause of the crash was recorded as an accident due to a tyre blowout. The lorry had been properly maintained before the crash, and no one was to blame. It was a tragic accident.' She put her hand on his arm. 'Maybe you did do something in the car and Mum was distracted. But you were not responsible for the crash.'

Dimitris shook his head. 'I was to blame.' His mind reran the seconds before the crash, when he'd seen the lorry heading towards the car. He'd believed that his mother had swerved across the road, but the truth was it had happened so quickly, and he couldn't be sure. If the lorry's tyre had burst and the driver had lost control of the vehicle perhaps it had contributed to the chain of events. It did not change things though. 'If I hadn't behaved like a brat, Mum would have been able to focus on driving,' he told his sister. 'You spent years in a wheelchair because of me.'

'I can walk again because of the pioneering surgery

you paid for.' Eleni put her arms around him. 'Dimitris, it's time to let go of the past. You don't need to feel guilty, and I certainly don't blame you. The truth is I barely remember our parents, but you have taken care of me and protected me since they died.'

Savannah rolled her shoulders that were aching after she'd spent too long sitting in front of her laptop. Editing photos was just as important as actually taking the shots and allowed her to make fine adjustments to lighting, tint balance and contrast to achieve perfect images.

Dimitris walked into the studio, and she felt a familiar flutter of excitement in her stomach when he stood behind her and slipped his arms around her waist. He looked over her shoulder at the screen. 'These pictures are excellent. It was a good idea of yours to serve the *souvlaki* on a bed of orzo salad. The chicken on skewers looked boring frankly, alone on the plate, but the red tomatoes, black olives mixed with the white orzo in the salad bring the whole dish to life.'

'I'm going to adjust the brightness a fraction more and then I'll be happy with the pictures.' Savannah couldn't hide the little tremor that ran through her when Dimitris nuzzled her neck before sliding his mouth up to the sensitive spot behind her ear.

'You are a perfectionist, and I admire your dedication to your work, *mátia mou*.' To her disappointment he moved away and raked his hand through his hair. 'I spoke to my sister.'

Savannah's eyes widened but she did not say anything as she waited for Dimitris to continue.

'Eleni took your advice and researched information about the accident. Even though it happened eighteen years ago, she found a newspaper report which stated that the cause of the crash was a tyre blowout on the lorry.' He exhaled heavily. 'I still believe that I was partly to blame for distracting my mother. But Eleni doesn't blame me.'

'She loves you very much,' Savannah said softly.

And so do I.

The words slipped into her head, and she felt as though her heart was being crushed in a vice. She was in love with Dimitris. In spite of her determination not to fall for him, he had dismantled her barricades one by one. But the way she felt was different to when she had been eighteen.

This overwhelming feeling wasn't a teenage crush, this was the real thing. She hadn't put Dimitris on a pedestal. She knew he wasn't perfect, but she loved the imperfect bits—his grouchiness first thing in the morning before he'd drunk two cups of strong coffee, his obsession with flashy sports cars and his habit of telling her what happened in a film if he'd seen it before, so that she wasn't disappointed with the ending, he said.

She was madly in love with his sexy grin and his way of looking at her when she was talking as if he was utterly fascinated by her. She loved his enthusiasm when he took her sightseeing around Rhodes and other islands nearby. Most of all she loved how he brought her body to life with his clever hands and mouth. When he made love to her and gave her more pleasure than she'd imagined it was possible to experience, she had to remind herself that it was just amazing sex. For Dimitris at least.

It was all he wanted, and he had never pretended otherwise or promised more. There was just over a week left of the photoshoot and then he was due to fly to Australia, and she would return to England and try to get on with her life. Her heart contracted at the prospect of their affair finishing. It was too late to try to protect herself from being hurt, but it was her fault, not his.

She decided to enjoy the short time she had left with him, and every night of the following week she told Dimitris with her body what she dared not reveal to him with words. Her insecurity from growing up believing that her father did not love her meant that she was wary of revealing her emotions in case she was rejected.

For his part Dimitris made love to her with a new urgency and wild abandon, as if he was aware of the days slipping past increasingly fast. The cookery book was ahead of schedule and when it was finished he'd suggested a trip on his boat to the island of Kos at the weekend.

The last chapter was Greek desserts. Savannah had spent all morning trying to achieve the perfect shot of a chocolate mascarpone baklava with coffee syrup, but the layers of filo pastry stacked on top of each other between layers of chocolate mascarpone had kept slipping and the dish looked a mess.

Dimitris had said it was because the coffee syrup was too thin, and he decided to make re-make the dessert from scratch. The atmosphere in the studio was unusually fraught, and Savannah had a new worry that made her tense and on edge. Her period was four days late. It had never happened before, and she was always as regular as clockwork.

It was probably a blip, she reassured herself, but when Dimitris had driven her to Rhodes Town earlier in the day, so she could buy souvenirs for her mum, she'd nipped into a chemist and bought a pregnancy test. She planned to do the test in the morning, but meanwhile she felt slightly sick after eating a large portion of the abandoned baklava and hoped the nauseous feeling was a sign that her period was about to start.

A sudden loud clatter followed by a curse drew Savannah's attention across the studio. Dimitris had dropped a baking tray onto the counter, and the dozen pastry baskets that he'd painstakingly assembled were in pieces. Her handbag that she'd left on the counter had been knocked onto the floor.

'That's why you should always wear an oven glove to take a metal tray out of a hot oven,' he growled. His annoyance quickly faded, and he gave her a rueful grin.

'Did you get burned?'

'It's not too bad. I'll run my hand under the cold tap after I've rescued your bag.' He crouched down to pick up the contents of her bag that were strewn over the floor.'

'I'll do it,' Savannah said quickly. But she was too late. Dimitris straightened up slowly and held out the pregnancy test kit.

'What the hell?' His smile had disappeared, and his eyes were as cold as black ice.

'I'm a few days late.' She bit her lip when he stared at her as if she'd grown a second head. 'It's probably nothing to worry about.'

Or it might be a baby. For the first time Savannah actually allowed herself to think about what that meant. She'd hoped to have a family one day, but she'd assumed she would meet the right man and marry him before children came along. Life rarely went to plan, and she might be pregnant with Dimitris's baby. The idea evoked an unexpected fierce tug of longing in her.

Dimitris was scowling as if an accidental pregnancy was her fault. Her temper flared. It took two people to create a child.

If there was a baby.

In an instant she'd gone from it being a possibility to believing it was true—because she would love to have Dimitris's baby. She had been falling in love with him over the weeks they had spent together, working, laughing, making love. But the fantasy she'd built up in her mind that he would come to love her was crumbling before her eyes.

'*Theós!*' He dropped the pregnancy test on the counter as if it had burned him. 'You had better go back to the villa and do the test.' His jaw clenched. 'I'll meet you in a few minutes, and if it's positive we'll have to discuss what to do.'

Discuss what to do? Savannah watched Dimitris stride over to the sink and shove his burned hand under the tap. She bit her lip so hard that she tasted blood. If she was pregnant she would have her baby, there was no question in her mind. Dimitris could do what he damned well liked. But his attitude told her that he wouldn't want to be involved with his child. He had looked appalled at the prospect of her having his baby.

With a low cry she ran out of the studio. He expected her to go to the villa to do the test, but she was certain she was pregnant. She had all the symptoms—sensitive breasts, nausea and a missed period. She couldn't face giving Dimitris the proof of her pregnancy that would make him furious. She wanted to be alone, but there was nowhere for her to go except down to the secret beach. Dimitris wouldn't look for her there.

Savannah tried not to look at the sheer drop over the cliff. She had climbed down to the beach with Dimitris a few times, but he always went first and guided her down the steps. Her fear of heights was irrational, and it had started when she was thrown from her horse. She was angry that the incident when she'd been a child still affected her.

She remembered how nervous she had been at the prospect of taking her horse over a set of jumps in the riding ring. But her father had been keen for her to compete, and unusually he had come to watch her. In her imagination she'd pictured herself making a clear round over the jumps and her father proudly applauding when she'd received a rosette. Instead she had lost control of her horse and when she'd been lying on the ground, humiliated and tearful, her father had yelled at her and told her she was a disappointment.

'Savannah, what the hell are you doing?'

She glanced over her shoulder and saw Dimitris at the top of the cliff. Her eyes were blurred with tears, and she missed her footing and found herself falling through the air. It happened so quickly that she didn't have time to scream. She had been two-thirds of the way down the cliff, and she banged against rocks before landing heavily, face down on the sandy beach.

'*Theós!* Savannah…' Dimitris sounded odd. She heard him run down the steps, but she was too winded to speak and tell him she was okay. She was aware that various places on her body hurt, and she kept her eyes closed while she tried to get over the shock of what had just happened.

'Savannah.' Strong arms gently turned her over and she opened her eyes and saw Dimitris's haggard face. He expelled a ragged breath. 'I thought…' He shook his head. 'Never mind what I thought. Are you hurt?'

She moved gingerly. 'My hip hurts. I must have knocked it against the rocks.'

He pushed her skirt up to her waist, and even though she'd bounced down the cliff Savannah felt a familiar curl of heat in her belly when he ran his hands over the tops of her legs. 'You have some nasty grazes on your hip and thigh, and more grazes on your arms and shoulder.'

He lifted her carefully into his arms. His face showed no emotion, but a nerve flickered in his cheek as he carried her up the steps. Dully, she thought that if there had been a baby there might not be one now because of her stupid behaviour.

Dimitris carried her all the way back to the villa and put her in the car. The hospital was a short distance away, and when they arrived he scooped her up and strode into the accident and emergency department.

She was glad that the doctor spoke English. He first checked that she wasn't suffering from concussion. 'Your grazes and bruising are not serious, but the pain in your hip might indicate a fractured bone and it will be necessary for you to have an X-ray.' He wrote a few notes and glanced at Savannah. 'I must ask if there is any possibility that you could be pregnant.'

She dared not look at Dimitris, standing next to her hospital bed. 'Yes.'

'In that case it will be best if you do a pregnancy test before we can continue with an X-ray. The chance of radiation affecting an unborn child is very small, but if you are pregnant there are extra safety measures we can take to minimise the risk.'

Dimitris stared out of the hospital window. His car was below in the car park, an attention-grabbing scarlet speed machine that was even better than the poster of a sports car he'd stuck on his bedroom wall when he was a boy growing up in a deprived part of London. He'd promised himself that one day he would make his fortune and own the car of his dreams.

He wouldn't be able to cart a baby around in the Ferrari, and the boot was too small to fit a pram in. *Theós!* He forced back a wild laugh. How could there be a baby? He had never considered having a child. A baby would require responsibility, commitment, and love—everything that Dimitris had successfully avoided all his adult life, with the one exception of his sister.

He guessed that the frantic thud of his heart was a sign that he was in shock. When he'd seen Savannah tumble down the cliff he'd experienced the same sickening terror that he'd felt in the car, seconds before it had ploughed headlong into the lorry. When he'd raced down the cliff steps he'd expected to find Savannah's crumpled and lifeless body on the beach, and his relief that her injuries appeared not to be serious had evoked a stinging sensation behind his eyes. He'd suppressed his emotions, something he was so good at, and focused on getting her to the hospital as quickly as possible.

Dimitris pinched the bridge of his nose as the emotions he'd felt on the beach pushed through his defences. When Savannah had told him that she might be pregnant it had felt like a bomb had exploded and his life would never be the same again. He hated the sense of not being in control, and of events happening that frankly scared the hell out of him.

He heard a slight noise behind him and swung round as Savannah walked into the room. His gut clenched at the sight of the large purple bruise on her shoulder and more bruises and grazes on her arms and legs. But it was the wounded expression in her eyes that hurt him the most because he knew he was responsible. To say he had not reacted well to her possible pregnancy would be an understatement.

'What is the result of the test?' he asked tautly.

'I had a blood test because pregnancy in the first weeks can be detected earlier than with a urine sample. We'll know the result in a few minutes.'

'I don't understand how it could have happened. We were always careful.'

'Don't worry, Dimitris. If I am pregnant you won't have to be involved.'

Her scathing tone scraped his raw emotions. 'If you are pregnant I am already involved. I won't shirk my responsibility for the child.'

'For God's sake!' she snapped. 'Your attitude is why I won't want you involved. I don't want my baby to grow up with a father who is only around out of a sense of duty. Children pick these things up. I always felt that my father didn't love me, and I used to think I'd done something wrong.'

Guilt kicked Dimitris in his gut when he thought of the secret that Richard O'Neal had told him. He had to somehow persuade Savannah to talk to her mother about her father.

After what felt like several lifetimes the door opened and the doctor walked into the room. 'The pregnancy test is negative,' he told Savannah. 'So we can proceed with the X-ray of your hip. The nurse will come to take you to the radiology department.'

'Well, that's that,' she muttered after the doctor had gone. 'I'm sure you must be relieved.'

'Aren't you?' In fact Dimitris did not feel elated as he'd expected. But why on earth would he feel deflated by the news that he was not going to be a father? A baby was the last thing he wanted, he reminded himself. 'An unplanned pregnancy would not have been ideal.'

'Not ideal at all.' She sounded brittle. Battered and bruised from her fall down the cliff, she looked infinitely fragile. He recalled her stricken expression when he'd challenged her about the pregnancy test that had fallen out of her bag. Shock had made him react badly.

He guessed she had climbed down the cliff because she'd wanted to hide from him as if he was an ogre. He blenched when he thought that she could have been badly injured or even killed and he would have been to blame. The guilt that had haunted him since he was fourteen reminded him that he destroyed everything good in his life. He wished he could put his arms around Savannah to comfort her and reassure himself that she was unharmed. But she was prickly and defensive.

She went with the nurse to be X-rayed, and an hour later she had been given the all-clear and insisted on walking to the car without help from Dimitris. They were both silent while he drove back to the villa. She spent the journey staring at her phone, and he wondered if it was a tactic to avoid conversation. A chasm had opened up between them and he did not know how to reach her, or if he should try. The truth, he had always known, was that she was safer away from him.

'Go and rest while I make you something to eat,' he told her when he ushered her into the villa. He could not help himself and ran his finger lightly down her pale cheek. A feeling of loss cramped in his gut when she flinched. 'You've had a nasty experience and you are bound to feel the effects of shock, *mátia mou*.'

'Stop.' Her eyes were luminous with tears, but she spoke in a cool voice that chilled him. 'I'm going to my room to pack. I've booked onto a flight to London tonight.'

'Is this because I didn't jump for joy about having a baby?' His jaw clenched. 'What did you expect?'

'I should have expected you to react the way you did,' she said flatly. 'You told me that you can't give me what I want. I guess I hadn't realised until I did the pregnancy test how much I want to have a family one day. These past few weeks that we have spent together were fun, but we both knew our affair had an end date.' She gave him a ghost of a smile. 'We want different things. Nothing has changed from ten years ago. I'm looking for love, the deep, everlasting kind.'

The kind of love that ripped your heart out when it ended abruptly, like when his parents had died. Dimitris didn't want to feel that intensity of pain ever again. He wished he could carry Savannah up to the bedroom they had shared for the past weeks and ignite the passion that always simmered between them. He wanted to show her how good they were together, without love and its associated emotions to create problems. But he couldn't make love to her while she was so fragile and looked achingly vulnerable.

They were compatible physically, and in so many other ways. If only she would see that what they had was enough. *Theós*, he had shared more of himself with her than with any other woman. What more did she want from him? Babies, he thought grimly as he watched her walk slowly up the stairs.

When a taxi pulled up in front of the villa half an hour later, Dimitris stood on his balcony and watched Stefanos carry Savannah's suitcase to the car. He fought the temptation to go after her and beg her not to leave.

He was used to his affairs being on his terms. Women did not leave him. Except for Savannah, who had left him twice, a voice in his head taunted him as the taxi drove away.

She'd gone because he wasn't enough for her. She wanted to be loved and it was not an unreasonable request. Her generosity of spirit and boundless compassion meant that she deserved to find love. But she deserved a better man than him. A man who was not afraid to admit his love for her openly and honestly, Dimitris thought bleakly.

CHAPTER ELEVEN

A MONTH LATER Dimitris acknowledged that he was not looking forward to the party at his publishers. His editorial team and the hierarchy of management were great people, the food was bound to be good, and the champagne would flow. But he did not have any enthusiasm for anything, not the party that would be the first of many during the festive period, nor Christmas, which he would be spending alone this year because Eleni had met a new boyfriend and was going to St Lucia with him. Dimitris had lost his zest for life and only his iron willpower stopped him numbing his pain with a bottle of single malt.

He stood next to the French windows in the drawing room of his house in Richmond. It was ironic that the house was called River Retreat when the river, swollen by the rain that had fallen relentlessly since he'd arrived in London three days ago, had breached the banks and flooded the lawn at the bottom of the garden.

The glorious weather on Australia's Gold Coast had failed to lift his dark mood, and his jaw had ached from forcing himself to smile for the audiences who had packed theatres to watch his cooking demonstrations.

At the end of the tour he had returned to Rhodes where the winters were mild. The sun had been shining in the blue sky, but the villa had been full of Savannah, although very much not full of Savannah. Memories of her were everywhere. Her collection of colourful cushions enlivened the neutral décor of the sitting room and her perfume lingered in his bedroom. He often woke in the middle of the night and reached for her, before he remembered that she'd gone.

He had tried to call her to check that there were no repercussions from when she'd fallen down the cliff, but her number had been unavailable. He knew he was fooling himself. What he really wanted to do was beg her to forgive him for behaving so badly when she'd thought she was pregnant and ask her if she could find it in her heart to love him. With a sickening lurch in the pit of his stomach Dimitris knew he was the greatest fool of all time.

He had come to England on a mission. Savannah had confided to him that her relationship with the man she'd believed was her father had been strained, and she'd felt unloved. Dimitris sensed that she was still affected by the rejection she'd experienced as a child. He hoped he could persuade Savannah's mother to tell her daughter the truth that she deserved to hear.

Savannah had encouraged him to open up about the accident to his sister, and now he was closer to Eleni than ever, and slowly beginning to forgive himself and accept that he could not change the past or predict the future, but a life without love was no life at all. He just hoped he hadn't left the discovery too late to stand a chance with Savannah.

* * *

November in England was grey. Grey skies and the dull gleam of rain on grey pavements mirrored Savannah's bleak mood. Christmas was still weeks away, but the shop windows were decorated with festive scenes and the gaudily coloured lights on every high street failed to lift the blanket of misery that had swamped her since she'd left Dimitris.

She couldn't contact him even if she'd wanted to. Somewhere on her journey from Rhodes to London she had lost her phone. It was an old device and because she hadn't backed up her contacts she did not have Dimitris's mobile number. She could probably reach him through his publisher if necessary. But why would she? It was over between them and the sooner she accepted it the better.

By now he would have finished his cooking tour in Australia and had probably returned to Greece, where the weather would be a lot better than in London. Savannah had spent the past weeks looking for somewhere to live and had finally moved into a tiny flat that cost a fortune to rent but was a ten-minute drive away from her mum's nursing home.

She parked her car in front of Willow Grange and ran through the rain to the entrance. She went to her mother's room and found her in bed. Evelyn looked fragile propped against the pillows.

'I'm sorry you had to come out in this awful weather.' To Savannah's consternation, tears filled her mother's eyes.

'Mum—what's wrong?'

'Dimitris came to see me yesterday.'

Dimitris? Shock and pain tore through Savannah. She missed him so much. 'What did he want?'

'He asked me to tell you something I should have told you a long time ago. A secret that I have kept from you for far too long.' Evelyn's voice shook. 'I couldn't tell you when Richard was alive because he had sworn me to secrecy. Since he died...well, I should have been honest with you, but I was afraid that you would hate me.'

'Nothing could make me hate you,' Savannah said gently. She could not imagine what secret her mother had kept from her. 'What do you want to tell me?'

'Richard wasn't your father.'

Too shocked to speak, Savannah stared at her mum. From as far back as she could remember, she'd sensed that her father had not loved her. Now finally she understood the reason why she hadn't felt a connection to Richard. She wasn't unlovable, as he had made her feel.

'Then who is my real father?' A memory came to her. 'Was he the man in the photo?'

Evelyn nodded. 'I'll try to explain. I married Richard only a few months after we had met because I was desperate to escape from my bullying stepfather. I was an assistant at an art gallery and Richard liked to boast to people that I worked for Fortescue's. He had come from a poor background and was obsessed with social position.'

She sighed. 'We tried for a baby for five years, but nothing happened. The marriage was strained and I... I fell in love with someone I'd met at the gallery. Johan was a Dutch artist. It was love at first sight for both of us, but I was married. We had a brief affair before Johan returned to Holland and died in a motorbike accident soon after.'

Evelyn wiped her eyes. 'I discovered I was pregnant and confessed to Richard that the baby wasn't his. I was sure he would throw me out. I had fallen out with my family and did not have any money. I was terrified that I would have to give my baby—you—up for adoption.'

'Oh, Mum.' Savannah handed her mother a tissue.

'Richard didn't want a divorce because he thought it would make him look a failure. He agreed to bring you up as his own daughter but made me promise that I would not tell you or anyone the truth. To the outside world we were the perfect family and Richard was a successful businessman. He was determined that you should marry into the aristocracy and encouraged you to accept a proposal from Lord Roxwell's son. But I knew you were not in love with Hugo, and I was glad when you broke off your engagement.'

Savannah's thoughts were reeling. 'You said Dimitris persuaded you to tell me the truth. How did he know that Richard wasn't my father?'

Evelyn shook her head. 'I didn't really understand what he meant. It was something to do with a financial deal that Richard had forced him to accept years ago. Dimitris told me he was worried that your self-confidence had been damaged because Richard hadn't shown you affection when you were growing up. Apparently there was a boyfriend recently who was not honest with you.'

She had nearly let Matt Collier push her into sleeping

with him, Savannah remembered. Dimitris was right to guess that she'd felt she had to put up with being treated badly by men because her father—Richard—had made her feel unworthy of being loved. Everything made sense now. At eighteen she'd had a crush on Dimitris even though he hadn't given any indication that he wanted a long-term relationship with her.

Evelyn was tired, and before Savannah left she hugged her mum and assured her that she understood why she'd kept the identity of her real father a secret.

'Richard threatened to stop his financial support for you, including your private school fees,' her mum said tearfully. 'He was manipulative. As the years passed I felt guilty for keeping such a huge secret from you. Dimitris said he felt sure you would be able to forgive me, and you had persuaded him to be honest with his sister.'

When Savannah returned to her car she sat for a few moments, trying to make sense of her whirling thoughts. Her main feeling was of relief that she could let go of her difficult childhood now she knew the truth. She realised that her mum had been in an impossible situation, but she didn't feel so forgiving of Dimitris who, from the sound of it, had been aware for years that Richard was not her father.

On impulse she turned her car towards Richmond. Dimitris had visited her mum the previous day and he might still be in London. The traffic was heavy, and by the time she drove along next to the river the car's engine was making a strange noise. Taking the car to a garage to be serviced was on her list of jobs that she hadn't got round to. Savannah gave a sigh of relief when she saw that the gates in front of River Retreat were open, and a black saloon was parked on the driveway. Dimitris must be here. Her car died just as she turned through the gates. She couldn't change her mind about seeing him now, she thought as she ran through the pouring rain up to the house.

'Savannah?'

She'd expected the housekeeper to open the front door, and her breath left her lungs in a rush when she stared at Dimitris. He looked gorgeous in black jeans and a storm-grey cashmere sweater. Her heart splintered as she studied his sculpted face that looked leaner, so that his cheekbones were sharp and his eyes held a bleakness that shocked her.

The rain had soaked through her sweatshirt and her hair was stuck to her scalp. She shivered, and he immediately opened the door wider. 'Come in. My housekeeper and her husband are in Canada visiting their daughter,' Dimitris explained as he stepped into the cloakroom and returned to hand Savannah a towel. 'You had better take your sweatshirt off, and it can dry in front of the fire.'

Savannah's teeth were chattering, and she felt self-conscious as she pulled her sweatshirt off and gave it to him. She hoped he would think it was the cold that had made her nipples harden so that they jutted through her silk blouse. She followed him into the sitting room, where a log fire was blazing. He waved her to an armchair, but she preferred to stand while she confronted him.

But her temper that had simmered while she'd driven to his house was replaced with fierce awareness of

Dimitris. He rested his arm on the mantelpiece, and she noticed that he'd lost weight. She knew he kept himself fit by working out regularly in the gym, but his whipcord body was leaner, and he looked weary as if he hadn't been sleeping.

'How was Australia?' She felt a sharp stab of jealousy as she imagined him lounging on a beach with a bevy of tanned, toned beauties. Maybe he'd lost weight from a lot of exercise between the sheets.

His dark eyes searched her face. 'I missed you,' he said in an oddly husky voice.

Her heart slammed into her ribs, but she told herself he didn't mean it. After all, he had made no attempt to stop her leaving him in Rhodes. 'I've just been to see Mum. She told me that Richard was not my real father.'

Dimitris exhaled slowly. 'Ah.'

Savannah's anger reignited. 'You *knew*. Why didn't you tell me? Surely I had a right to know?' She frowned as a memory of the previous time she had been at Dimitris's house in Richmond surfaced, and the conversation they'd had over dinner. 'How did you know about the trust fund that my fa… Richard had set up?' she demanded.

'He told me.' Dimitris sighed heavily. 'Richard threatened to prevent you from receiving a fortune that he said was held in trust until you were twenty-five if I did not break off my relationship with you.'

Seeing that Savannah was too shocked to speak, he continued, 'I had initially refused the money he'd offered me as a bribe. But he got nasty and said he wouldn't allow me to screw up his plans for you to marry into a titled family. I called his bluff and told him that I didn't believe he would cause financial harm to his own daughter. That was when he revealed that he wasn't your father. In his words, he had brought up another man's child and paid for your private education, and in repayment he expected you to marry well and increase his social standing.'

Savannah sank down onto the sofa, and Dimitris came and sat down next to her, although he kept a distance from her. 'Richard insisted that I accepted the bribe and never saw you again,' he told her, 'or he would cut off all financial support for you and your mother. You were used to a high standard of living and were about to go to university. I couldn't risk that Richard would carry out his threat.'

'He was a terrible man.' Anger and hurt poured through Savannah as she stared at Dimitris. 'When we met again after ten years you should have told me the truth. Richard was dead by then and couldn't harm Mum or me.'

'It was your mother's secret,' he said tautly. 'I couldn't reveal what I knew.'

She blinked away the tears that filled her eyes. 'I trusted you.' Everything she had believed they'd shared, friends as well as lovers, and a sense that they had grown closer while she had stayed at his villa, had been in her imagination.

Finally Savannah knew that Dimitris would never love her as she deserved to be loved. She had accepted second-best with her brief engagement to Hugo years ago, and with Matt Collier. Neither of them had cared about her. She had hidden her emotions because she'd been afraid of rejection, but there was no shame in loving someone, even if that person would never feel the same way about her.

'I fell in love with you,' she told Dimitris, lifting her chin so she could meet his gaze. 'But you are not the man for me. I want romance, love, a family of my own. I spent a night with you, hoping to free myself of my teenage crush on you. Now I truly am over you.' She stood up and walked over to the door. Her heart was breaking, but next time she would give her heart to a man who appreciated her.

'Savannah...don't go.' Dimitris's voice sounded as if he'd swallowed broken glass.

'There's nothing for me here and no reason to stay.' She was determined to stay strong and fight for the future, the love she wanted, whoever that might be with. She turned to look at him and her lungs felt as if they were being squeezed in a vice when she saw his tortured expression.

Dimitris walked towards her jerkily, with none of his usual grace. He looked like a man on the edge of hell. 'I love you.'

'Don't,' she whispered. 'Don't joke.'

He put his hands on her shoulders as if he wanted to physically stop her from leaving. His face twisted as if he were in pain when he saw her tears. 'Do you think I would make a joke about the way I feel about you?'

'You don't want a relationship, commitment.' She tried to step away from him, but his fingers tightened and he stared down at her, his eyes blazing with raw emotion that made Savannah's heart thud.

'I want you—*us*,' he told her in a strained voice. 'The weeks we spent together at the villa were the happiest of my life. The only other time I felt that happy was for eleven nights ten years ago, when I held you in my arms and imagined that we were the only two people in the universe and nothing could come between us.'

She shook her head. 'You went away...'

'Richard took a gamble when he told me he wasn't your father. He used emotional blackmail to get me to accept the bribe and never see you again, because he had guessed that I loved you and would do anything to protect your financial security.'

'So you decided it was better for me to have a trust fund rather than for us to be together.' Her voice shook. 'You knew I loved you.'

'Yes, I knew, but I was scared.' Dimitris's jaw tightened. 'I was afraid to admit to myself how I felt about you. I didn't want to love you because it was agony when my parents were killed. I promised myself that I would never care about anyone so deeply again, so that it couldn't hurt so terribly if I lost that person.'

Savannah felt as though she was standing on the edge of a precipice. She felt dizzy, but she was no longer scared of heights. Dare she believe the fierce emotion blazing in Dimitris's eyes?

He placed his hand under her chin and gently tilted her face up to his. 'I do love you, Savannah. No other woman has ever claimed my heart. It's yours for eternity and I will be committed to you for the rest of my life.'

He cradled her cheek in his palm and wiped away

the tears that trickled down her face. 'Don't cry, *agápi mou.*' His jaw clenched. 'You are the sweetest, kindest person and I know you would hate to hurt even me, who once hurt you so badly. If your tears are because you have to tell me that you don't feel the same way about me—' he swallowed '—that you don't love me, then do it quickly.'

She bit her lip. 'I just don't know…' Her words faded and her heart stopped when she saw that Dimitris's eyelashes were wet. And suddenly she did know, and she believed that, impossibly and incredibly, he loved her. It was there in the suspicious brightness in his eyes and the way he swallowed hard. It was there in the faint tremor of his mouth and his hand that shook when he smoothed her hair back from her face so tenderly, so lovingly.

'Oh, Dimitris, I love you too much to ever hurt you. And you love me.' There was wonder in her voice, but certainty too. He loved her and she thought her heart might explode with happiness.

His arms came around her and he pulled her into his heat and strength and held her close to his heart that was thundering in his chest. *S'agapó.* I love you,' he told her over and over again. He kissed her fiercely, and then lifted his head and stared down at her.

'I thought that if I avoided falling in love I would never be hurt. But when you left me I couldn't function, and I realised that denying my love for you was tearing me apart. I knew I had to find you and beg you to give me another chance to prove I can give you everything you want and deserve.'

She held his face in her hands and kissed him with all the love in her heart. 'Prove it now.'

He grinned as he swept her into his arms and carried her upstairs to his bedroom. 'If you insist, *kardiá mou*. I think you are going to be a very bossy wife.'

'Wife?'

Dimitris laid her on the bed and tugged the blouse over her head. He cupped her breasts in his palms and let out a ragged breath. '*Theós*, you are beautiful. Will you marry me, Savannah, and make me the happiest man in the world?'

Her smile was pure sunshine. 'I will. Now, will you please stop talking?'

She helped him remove his clothes and he set about rediscovering her body with hands that shook a little and a mouth that worshipped her breasts before he moved lower and pushed her thighs apart. When he entered her it was as if it was the first time, and there was wonder and joy in their lovemaking as they whispered words of love and reached the pinnacle together, before tumbling back down to earth to lie entwined while darkness fell and they were alone in their own private world.

'For ever,' Dimitris vowed. 'Just you and me and the children I hope we will have in the future. He kissed her tenderly. 'The future begins now, my love.'

* * * * *

BACK TO CLAIM
HIS ITALIAN HEIR

KATE HEWITT

MILLS & BOON

For Jenna, who has been with me all the way!
Love, K.

CHAPTER ONE

'I DO.'

The words ringing out through the church were not the ones Emma Dunnett expected. They weren't the ones *anyone* expected, because this was the part of the wedding ceremony where everybody was meant to stay deliberately, determinedly silent, without so much as a sneeze or a sigh. Someone, it seemed, hadn't got the memo.

Emma stared at her husband-to-be in alarmed confusion as an electric, expectant silence tautened the near-empty sanctuary and people in the congregation started turning their heads, craning their necks to catch a glimpse of the mystery speaker. Her groom was looking just as surprised as she was, his forehead crinkled as his uncertain gaze swept the church for the unknown speaker, lost in the shadows in the back.

'You...do?' This from the priest who was marrying them, who also looked confused—there was way too much confusion going on, clearly—peering through the shadowy sanctuary at whoever had spoken with such ringing certainty.

I do was not the answer anyone wanted to the question that had just been given: *'Does anyone have any objections to this marriage? Speak now or for ever hold your peace.'*

No, no one ever wanted to hear someone so much as clear their throat when it came to that particular question. Nobody was supposed to actually *answer* that, Emma thought with a blaze of panic, her mind a blur as she searched the darkened church for the speaker of those damning words. Asking the question was just a matter of form, a relic from a bygone age, even. A second's silence, a silent sigh of relief, a shaky smile, and then they moved on. They said their vows, they left the church, they were married, and everything could go on happily.

'Yes,' the voice from the back of the church called, his tone strident and certain, faintly tinged with an indefinable accent, tickling Emma's consciousness, making her stomach dip.

That voice...

'I most definitely do have objections. One in particular, as it happens.'

The priest was still peering among the pews, where only a handful of guests had gathered—mainly Will's family and a few friends, all of whom had been rather bemused—to put it mildly—at his willingness to marry a woman he'd met only a little over a month ago. They were all looking much more than bemused now, Emma realised as she caught sight of their faces—Will's mother was doing her best impression of a gorgon, stony-faced and sour. She'd never wanted her only son to marry someone she considered a shameless gold-digger, having said so to Emma's face, more than once. Well, so what? There were worse things to be called. Worse things to *be*.

Not that that was what she was. At least, not *exactly*. She was marrying Will for security, it was true, but he knew that and they'd become friends. It would be, she hoped, a good basis for marriage. For a family.

She glanced again at Will's mother and saw her lips twitch in something like satisfaction. Had she arranged this, a way to extricate her son from the so-called siren's seductive claws? Considering Emma had never even kissed Will, who wasn't interested in her that way anyway, being cast in the role of scheming seductress was a little ridiculous. Not that his mother would believe just how chaste their relationship was, especially considering Emma was fourteen weeks pregnant...with another man's child.

A sudden bubble of laughter rose in her throat, and she managed to swallow it down. Bursting into giggles at a moment such as this was definitely not something she wanted to do; the situation was clearly dire enough. She didn't want to make it worse, even if laughing had always been her deliberate, defiant default, her own brand of courage throughout a tumultuous childhood. Laugh instead of cry, show your sense of humour along with your spirit. It had served her well enough in the past, but now...when her life looked about to be derailed, *again*?

'Who are you?' Will called out, uncertain ire flashing in his pale blue eyes. Emma tried to give him an encouraging smile, although the truth was nothing about this situation felt remotely encouraging. Already she could feel her safe and certain future slipping from her fingertips, as it always seemed to.

Just when she'd settled into the latest foster home, got a decent job, managed to save a little bit...every time, something seemed to go wrong. And for someone who had always had to rely on her own wits and not much else, something going wrong could be disastrous. Hopefully that wasn't the case this time, because now she had someone else to consider. Someone tiny and precious and very, very vulnerable.

She straightened, one hand resting on her slight bump as she heard footsteps down the nave of the church, swift and solid.

'Sir?' the priest called, squinting as he tried to catch sight of the figure striding down the nave, each footfall more purposeful than the last, thuds that reverberated through Emma, echoed in her heart. 'What objections can you possibly have to this marriage?'

'What objections?' A shudder ran through her, like an icy finger down her spine, straight through her soul. She *knew* that voice. It was the voice that had haunted her dreams, when she'd woken up in tangled sheets, gasping with a potent mix of desire, hope and grief—a roughened thrum, shot through with a velvety softness, a hint of laughter lurking somewhere deep within the assured rumble, a voice that conjured so many memories, and too many regrets. A voice that had made her smile, even when she hadn't wanted it to.

Hold onto your senses, Emma. Head over heels is definitely not for you, even if you want it to be.

It was a voice she'd never, ever expected to hear again, because its owner was dead.

'My objection,' the owner of that silky, powerful voice continued, coming to the front of the church, a shaft of sunlight from the stained glass above gilding his dark hair in gold, 'is that the bride is already married. To me.'

Nico Santini turned blazing green eyes towards Emma, who felt as if she'd turned to stone. Or maybe ice, because, looking at the freezing fury in her husband's eyes, she suddenly felt very, very cold. Another shiver went through her, and she dropped her bouquet, white rose petals scattering across the stone floor of the church, releasing their heavy scent, making nausea rise up in her in a tidal wave of realisation as her head swam and her body continued to tremble.

'Nico…' His name came out in a croak. 'How…?' She found her mouth was too dry, her heart pounding too hard, for her to finish that improbable question. *How* could he be here? He was *dead*. Dead! He'd died nearly four months ago, just one week after they'd had a whirlwind romance and wedding, all within the space of a single month. And here she was about to have another one, and… *No.* He couldn't be here. He couldn't be alive. She'd seen the death certificate. They'd had a *funeral.* Or at least a memorial service, as his body had never been found. And then she'd been basically bundled out of the door and onto a plane before she'd barely got out of her mourning dress, as per, apparently, Nico's wishes.

So why was he here, in Los Angeles, looking so thunderous? She'd last seen him in Rome, about to travel to the Maldives, where she'd been so sure he'd been killed in a terrible accident, the engine failing on the small plane he'd hired to take him to one of Santini's world-famous luxury resorts.

A shudder went through her. She couldn't cope with the mix of emotions she felt: surprise, a wary, absurd joy, but most of all a creeping sense of dread. She'd never known this man, she understood that now, never mind that she'd married him in a haze of hope and happiness. She didn't want him here, back from the dead, looking absolutely furious, and understandably so, considering the nature of the situation.

Emma was suddenly, painfully conscious of her pale yellow wedding dress, the bouquet she'd just dropped on the ground, the short veil hiding her hair, and, most of all, the groom next to her, the man she'd been about to marry until her husband had walked through the door. Beyond all that, though, she was tinglingly aware of Nico's thunderous expression as he willed her to look at him, which she wouldn't. Couldn't. Not yet, anyway. What on earth was she meant to do?

'Sir?' the minister demanded, his tone turning slightly querulous.

She had no idea how to handle this situation besides running away, not that she'd get very far in this dress and heels. Nico, *here*. Nico, her *husband*. Except they'd barely known each other and, despite the blaze of happiness she'd felt when he'd taken her in his arms, she'd started to fear he'd been tiring of her anyway, the way everyone else had in her life. Every foster family, every friend, every person who took a kindly interest and then walked away. Her own mother, even. Why should Nico have been any different? His family had certainly seemed to think he hadn't been.

'Emma?' Will's voice was soft, hurt, and she turned to him, saw the wounded look on his face. What could she possibly say to him?

'Will... I... I'm so sorry... I can explain...' Except Emma knew she couldn't, not really. Out of the corner of her eye, she saw his mother swell up like a bullfrog, full of vindication as she turned to the woman on her left, some aunt or other. And then there was Nico...standing there like a dark angel, a determined warrior, fierce and furious and absolutely certain.

Her husband...back from the dead.

'Emma, what's going on?' Will asked, his voice rising a little. 'Who is this guy? Are you actually married to him?'

'I told you about Nico...' Emma began, in a whisper.

Will's face flashed with confusion. 'But he *died*—'

'Of course, she knows me,' Nico cut him off, his voice vibrating with icy contempt. 'And yes, she is married to me. I am her husband.' His gaze swung from Will back to Emma, pinning her in place. Eyes as green as moss, and she'd seen them soft with desire, smiling down at her before he'd lowered his lips towards hers for a long and lingering kiss. Now those eyes looked like chips of emerald, glinting hard and cold. Well, there was no love lost on her side, either, all things considered. There had been no love at all, because she hadn't known him. He hadn't known her. No matter what she'd tried to let herself believe.

'Emma?' Will said again. The priest cleared his throat. Nico stared at her, his cold gaze not wavering. This was hideous. Hideous and unimaginable and really rather terrifying, because Nico wasn't playing the besotted lover now. He looked as if he hated her, and maybe he did. Maybe he had before he left for the Maldives, or almost.

'Nico was already tiring of you, Emma. He said as much to me. The sooner you leave, the better.'

After a lifetime of being passed like a parcel, she knew when it was time to get out. When she wasn't wanted. She'd learned to read the signs—the flash of impatience in the eyes, the tightening of the lips, the weighted pauses and significant looks. And of course sometimes she didn't need to read them; they were spelled out in blazing big lights.

'Adopt Emma? Absolutely not.'

Her foster mother's voice, laced with incredulity, echoed painfully through her all these years later. Yes, Emma knew what rejection looked like, felt like, and so she hadn't waited around to face it again.

Now she opened her mouth. Closed it. Will let out a soft sound of distress, and the look of scorn on her husband's face was mixed with an arrogant, blazing satisfaction. He was clearly in control here, calling the shots just as he always had before. As happy as she'd let herself be, Emma had been under no illusions about who had had the control in their short-lived relationship—Nico. Always Nico.

He was the one who had set the parameters of their affair. *'A few weeks in New York, yes, I'll fly you to Rome, it will end when I say it does.'*

And then, to her shock, he'd asked her to marry him, and even though she should have known better, she'd agreed. She'd wanted the fairy tale, no matter how brief it turned out to be. It was no surprise at all that Nico had come to regret his uncharacteristically impulsive decision.

'I…' she began, and then found she couldn't go on. In addition to already feeling icy, incredulous and yes, terrified, she was also starting to feel dizzy. Very dizzy, because even as she stared at Nico standing there like an avenging angel her vision was starting to tunnel and she had a strange metallic taste in her mouth.

'Yes, Emma?' Nico drawled coldly.

'I…' She couldn't see to get past that one word. A whisper ran through the congregation like a lit fuse. The world was blacking at its edges, as if she were looking through a telescope, and Will was still gazing at her with a puppyish mixture of hurt and concern. She wasn't brave enough to look at Nico again.

Once more Emma tried to speak. No words came out. There were spots dancing in front of her eyes, and the sight of Nico was becoming smaller and smaller, like a pinpoint at the centre of her eye, shrinking into the distance. If only he would go away completely…

'Emma—' Will said, stepping towards her, but it was too late.

The last thing she saw before she crumpled to the floor was Nico's incredulous fury emblazoned on every taut line of his beautiful face.

Well, that certainly was one way for his errant wife to weasel out of a situation. Nico tamped down on his fury as he stepped forward to Emma's crumpled form. Her erstwhile groom was looking at her in dismay, fluttering his hands uselessly. What a waste of space, stuffed in a suit. He needed to be got rid of immediately, along with all these rubbernecking guests.

'Clear the way,' Nico commanded as he bent to pick up his wife. She smelled of the roses from her fallen bouquet along with the scent that was uniquely her, a scent he remembered, that he'd breathed in deeply. He'd once asked her what perfume it was, and she'd laughed, a gurgle of pure enjoyment.

'Just soap,' she'd told him, her golden eyes dancing, sparkling like bits of amber. 'Eau de Dollar Store.'

He'd laughed back and snatched her up in his arms, breathed in the sweet, soapy scent of her hair, revelling in her, in *them*. What a fool he'd been. What a naïve, deluded fool.

'Sir—' the groom began, and Nico silenced him with a single look, swift and blazing.

'Your part in this farce is over,' he told the man flatly. 'Emma Dunnett—Emma *Santini*—is my wife. I'll take over from here. You can see yourself out, along with all your guests. As quickly as possible, if you please.'

He drew Emma, lolling lifelessly in his arms, against his chest. She was light, her body lithe and slender, maybe even more than he remembered. Her golden-brown hair was wreathed in roses with a short veil, and she wore a simple ankle-length shift dress of pale yellow. At least she hadn't worn wedding white, he thought sardonically.

How could she have betrayed him like this?

And yet, why should he be surprised? He'd had betrayal in his life before, a string of deceptions that were still painful to acknowledge. His mother's affair, his father's remoteness, all based on the lie of who he was—and who he wasn't. If the people he'd loved most in the world had deceived him so utterly, another treacherous act should hardly shock him…and yet from her.

From her.

The priest, having sprung into motion, gestured for Nico to head to a small room off the sanctuary of the church. Nico deposited Emma on a small, worn sofa and stepped back.

'Sir,' the priest stammered, 'this is highly irregular…'

'We'll be out of your way in a few minutes,' Nico assured him, 'after my wife has regained her senses. Could you please leave Emma's things outside the door for my driver to retrieve?'

He had a car waiting outside, and no interest or intention in staying here for a single second longer than necessary.

'Please, if you could leave us alone,' he commanded, and with an unhappy look the priest scurried away. Nico heard the murmur of voices and click of heels before the door closed, and he knew the guests were leaving. Good.

As he gazed down at the supine form of his wife, he hoped, belatedly, that she hadn't injured herself, but then acknowledged that, despite her fall, Emma was clearly someone who always landed on her feet. She'd demonstrated that admirably today.

Her eyes fluttered open, and she caught sight of him—a gleam of awareness brightening her golden irises before her lids drifted shut again.

Lord help him, but she was beautiful. More beautiful than he'd even remembered. And he'd spent *months* remembering—months in a hospital bed, trying to remember his own name, her face feeling like the only thing his mind hadn't let him forget.

And that face was before him right now—heart-shaped and pale, her faintly snub nose scattered with golden freckles, her pink lips slightly parted. Her chest rose and fell in pants that were too agitated to be the deep and even breathing of someone rendered unconscious.

'Open your eyes, Emma,' Nico commanded flatly. 'I know you're awake.'

If anything her lids scrunched even more tightly shut. Nico let out a huff that would have been laughter if he'd been remotely amused. He wasn't, because he was too angry for that. And he was angry because that felt so much better than being hurt.

Just a little over three months he'd been gone. Three *months*.

'Emma.'

A breath shuddered out of her as she kept her eyes resolutely closed. 'I don't feel like opening them,' she confessed in a croaky whisper.

'Because you want me to just go away,' Nico surmised in a hard voice. 'I'm not surprised.'

Finally Emma cracked open a single eye, to gaze at him uncertainly. 'Aren't you?'

'No, why should I be, considering how quickly you were able to forget me?' he replied coolly. 'Two weddings in the space of three months has to be a record for just about anyone.'

'Three and a half months,' she corrected weakly, and this time Nico did let out a huff of laughter—hard, humourless laughter, because she was certainly showing her true colours now. How could he have ever been so deceived? Because he'd let himself, he knew. Because, after the revelation of his own birth, he'd wanted to belong to someone. Well, lesson learned. Abundantly. Don't go looking for love. Don't even believe it exists, because he had yet to see it in his own life, from his own father.

'I stand corrected,' he told her. 'Three and a half months from one wedding to the next...those two weeks make *all* the difference, clearly.'

She opened both eyes this time as she regarded him with a weary sort of apprehension. 'How is it that you are alive?'

'You sound so pleased that I am.' She didn't reply and he forced himself to continue, not to dwell on the truth that was staring him so bleakly in the face. She'd never cared about him at all. He'd just been a meal ticket, as his cousin

Antonio had told him, right from the beginning, incredulous that he'd been so foolhardy as to marry a woman after an acquaintance of a mere three weeks. Nico had scoffed at his cousin, determined to believe that he was acting only out of spite and jealousy; their relationship had become increasingly strained since his father's revelations, with Antonio embittered at not being handed the reins of Santini Enterprises.

And yet he, usually so pragmatic and resolute, had let himself, in a rare moment of weakness, be deluded by the most absurd fantasy. Well, no longer. Not for one second more. 'I'm alive,' he told her, 'because I survived the plane crash. Obviously.'

She shook her head slowly, eyes wide as she stared at him in dismay. Clearly she didn't relish the idea of living together as husband and wife again. Well, it wasn't all appealing to him either, but he'd be damned if he'd let her commit bigamy by marrying another man.

'But where have you been for the last three months?' she asked, her voice sounding thin and papery. She was lying on the sofa like some sort of Snow White, her hair spread about the cushion, the circlet of roses having been knocked askew. Her figure was elegant and lithe, reminding Nico of how he'd explored every inch of that body, every intriguing dip and lush curve, how he'd made them his own.

He clenched his hands into fists to keep from reaching for her, even now. 'Three and a half months, you mean,' he reminded her in a voice like a blade, cutting and quick. 'After the plane crashed into the Indian Ocean, I was rescued by a fishing boat, and then I was in a cottage hospital on a nearby island. After that I was transferred to a rehabilitation centre in Jakarta, before I returned to Rome last week. Any other questions?'

'Why didn't you let me know you were alive?' This came

out more stridently, a golden blaze in her eyes that reminded him of why he'd fallen in love with her, or at least thought he had. That spirit, that humour, the sparkle in her eye, the quirk of her lip. It had lightened something inside him, something that had desperately needed lightening, but of course it had all been false, a tissue of carefully constructed lies, because he'd never known her at all, not truly. That reality was staring him smack in the face right now.

'Because first I was in a coma,' he explained flatly, 'and then I couldn't remember my own name. I had no identification, no way of anyone knowing who I was. That had been destroyed in the crash.' His voice pulsed with a pain that he did his best to hide. Those months had been torturous in their own way, and yet in the midst of all the pain and uncertainty, he'd remembered her. He almost wished now that he hadn't.

Emma's golden eyes widened as she scooted up on the sofa. 'You were in a *coma*?'

'It's a little late to sound concerned.'

Her mouth dropped open, eyes flashing. 'Nico, you can't blame me for not knowing—'

'I can,' he informed her in a voice of silky, suppressed rage, 'blame you for marrying the next man who offered. I assume he was the next man?' He jerked his head towards the door to the sanctuary, which he sincerely hoped was now empty of guests—and groom. 'Not a very impressive specimen, all told. Really, you could have done better.'

'Don't insult Will,' she replied with quiet, dignified resignation. 'Or blame him. He's done nothing to you.'

True, but Nico felt a scorching flash of fury all the same. 'No,' he agreed when he trusted his tone to be pleasant. 'I don't blame him. Quite the contrary, my dear.' He bared his teeth in the semblance of a smile as he took a step closer to her, watched her shrink against the cushions of faded velvet. Was she pretending to be afraid of him, to add to the drama, appeal to some sort of sympathy? Damsel in distress was a role she knew how to play to the hilt, but it wouldn't work this time. Far from it. 'I don't blame your groom,' he told her with succinct, acid sweetness. 'I blame you.'

CHAPTER TWO

EMMA GAZED AT the fury simmering in her husband's eyes and felt everything in her shrink. She supposed she should expect him to be angry, but that sneering derision twisting his lips made her want to curl up in a ball, close her eyes again, and pretend he wasn't here. This was such a *mess*.

Their marriage had been a mistake. She was pretty sure Nico had already been coming to that conclusion, even if he liked to bask in his self-righteous rage now. Yes, she *had* been about to marry another man, mere months after she'd married him. And yes, he had been declared dead, but such a trifling consideration wouldn't bother Nico. He'd always seemed to her a man who understood right and wrong, saw it in stark, certain terms—unlike her, who'd had to bend the truth more than once just to survive. Who had learned not to trust in happily-ever-afters, even if she'd dared, ever so briefly, to wonder if she could have one with Nico.

Now Emma knew that their marriage never would have lasted past the honeymoon stage, and, with another person to consider, she wasn't about to jump into that shark tank again. Looking at Nico's furious expression, she doubted he wanted her to, either. So why was he here?

'Emma?' he prompted silkily. 'Care to make any explanation as to why you wanted to enter into matrimony with another man so soon after you had done so with me?'

'Because I needed to,' Emma replied bluntly. 'Something you could never understand.' She folded her arms and looked away, telling herself she could deal with his anger, because the truth was she preferred it. If he stayed angry, she wouldn't remember how kind he'd once been. How considerate and tender, in a way that had just begun to chip away at the carefully constructed walls she'd built around her heart, brick by necessary brick.

Don't trust anyone. Don't let people in. Definitely don't start to care, because then you'll get hurt. You'll be rejected by the people you'd come to trust, which hurts so much more.

Well, fortunately she hadn't started to care. Much. He'd died—or she'd thought he had—before her defences had been truly breached, and in the three and a half months since then she'd had plenty of time—and reason—to build them up again. He was angry? Well, so was she. His family had treated her abominably, and she'd had no reason to think Nico wouldn't have gone along with it, had he been alive. She had decided a long time ago that she would never stay somewhere she wasn't wanted, and Nico certainly didn't look as though he wanted her now.

But he doesn't know about the baby.

And how on earth was she supposed to tell him, when he was already so furious with her? The last thing she wanted was for Nico Santini to order her life around, all while in a self-righteous rage. She didn't deserve that, and her baby didn't, either.

'You needed to,' Nico repeated, his voice positively dripping with sarcasm. 'Really.' He towered above her, arms folded, biceps rippling, a vengeful god in a three-piece suit. Three months in a coma or hospital or wherever had not diminished his hotness one bit, Emma acknowledged sourly. It would have helped if it had. Why couldn't he look a little…anaemic? Injured, at least? The only sign that he'd been in a crash at all was a scar by his eyebrow, and in fact that livid little line just added to his sexiness, drat the man. The close-cropped ink-dark hair and vivid green eyes didn't help, either, along with the body that, despite being in a hospital bed for several months, looked every bit as powerfully muscular as it ever had. Everything about Nico Santini was potently virile, intoxicatingly male. And right now she really wished it weren't.

'Yes, really,' she replied with a shrug, as if it were a matter of indifference, as if her heart wasn't threatening to jackhammer through her chest. Nico would never understand what it was like to need something—security, safety, a roof over your head. He would never believe that she'd had a genuine friendship with Will, that she hadn't been taking him for a ride. She certainly wasn't about to explain any of it to him, only to be scoffed at. 'You were dead, Nico, or so I thought. I don't have to offer excuses, and you have no right to be angry.'

'No right!' He looked outraged, and a sudden laugh rose in her throat like a bubble. Thankfully she swallowed it down. She did not want to incite his rage any more than she already had.

'No right,' she repeated. 'We'd only been married a week. We barely knew each other. How long did you expect me to play the grieving widow?'

'Longer than you did, clearly,' he bit out, the skin around his mouth turning white before he swung away from her.

Emma was under no illusions that he was hurt by what she'd done. He hadn't loved her, after all. She'd always known that, deep down. Nico might have played the attentive lover for a while, but it had never been real. Their relationship had never been tested, had never had a chance to see if it would endure. And when he'd died—or at least she'd thought he had—his true colours had been revealed by his family.

No, he was angry because of his pride, she supposed. He'd always made it clear he would be the one who decided when their relationship ended. Well, she had been the one to end it, but then he'd been *dead*.

'So you have no excuses,' Nico stated flatly as he turned around, his expression now forbidding. 'Nothing to exonerate yourself.'

'I don't need to exonerate myself, and I really don't know what you expect me to say.' Emma glared up at him as she folded her arms, mainly to hide her very small bump, because she was pretty sure he didn't realise she was pregnant—with his child. And when he realised that…well, she had no idea what he might do. She doubted he wanted to continue their marriage, all things considered, but she would die before she let him take her child away from her, the only family she'd ever had. She had no intention of revealing anything more than she had to, not until she knew what Nico wanted. Not until she could trust him with the truth.

Yet looking at those glinting green eyes narrowed in anger, she still remembered—painfully, shamefully—how soft and mossy they'd seemed after she'd first met him, how he'd looked at her with something almost like love. Of course, it hadn't really been love, not even close. She knew that, of course she did, but still, it had felt…well, as close to love as she'd ever known, maybe, which was pretty pathetic, she acknowledged now, especially since Nico had made it clear at the start that he didn't love her.

She'd been fine with that, had accepted it, as she'd accepted it for her whole life. Something about her, she suspected, had always been fundamentally unlovable, if the foster families she'd cycled through were anything to go by. Whether it was indifference, weary kindness, or out-

right cruelty, they'd all abandoned her in the end. But now…
now she had to think differently, because now she had to
watch out for someone else, as well. Someone infinitely
important. Someone whose well-being mattered far, far
more than her own.

She'd been a waitress at a small Italian bistro in New York
when she'd met Nico just five months ago, the kind of hole-
in-the-wall place that billionaires weren't supposed to fre-
quent, and yet Nico had. He had a table in the window, his
paperwork spread out while he sipped a glass of Chianti,
and Emma walked by him, transfixed by the blade-like precision of his cheekbones, the fullness of his lips, the breadth
of his shoulders, the expensive fabric of his shirt stretching
tautly across them as he studied the papers before him with
a remarkable and focussed intensity.

He was utterly unaware of her, of course—that was, until
she breathed in the spicy scent of his cologne and, stupidly
overwhelmed by its heady fragrance assaulting her senses,
she tripped over her own feet and managed to dump an entire plate of spaghetti and meatballs right into his lap.

He jumped up, appalled and furious, accidentally knock-
ing his glass of wine over his papers in the process. He
snatched the glass to turn it upright, but of course it was
too late. He was covered in sauce and his papers were covered in wine. Total disaster.

And Emma, because it was all so awful, and she was
pretty sure she was going to get fired for causing it, laughed.
It was her default, her defence mechanism, a way to not let
herself be hurt by the casual cruelty, or, sometimes even
worse, pitying kindness she'd encountered throughout her
life. And, face it, a gorgeous man with a crotch full of spaghetti *was* funny. Sort of.

A horrified giggle escaped her in a bubble of sound, and

he swung his infuriated and incredulous gaze towards her before she clapped her hand over her mouth. Now was not the time to laugh, she told herself severely, not when this incredibly handsome and obviously powerful man had just had his dinner, his paperwork and his suit all ruined—by her. And she knew how powerful people liked to blame their underlings for just about everything. Not that she'd met anyone remotely as powerful and magnetic as the man in front of her, spaghetti and all.

'I'm so sorry,' she said, trying for a deeply contrite tone, even as another giggle escaped through her fingers.

Nico stared at her for an endless moment, and for the first time she got the full effect of his eyes—like emerald lasers—as well as his beauty. *Sculpted* was the word that came to mind, except that conjured an image of statues of white marble, lifeless and cold. Nico was very much alive, pulsing with disbelief and anger, and yes, beauty. He really was the most beautiful man. His eyelashes, Emma noted with a distant numbness, were ridiculously long. And curly. What kind of man had lashes like that and still looked formidably, potently male? Because he certainly did.

'Are you actually laughing?' he demanded, his voice a low rasp, lightly accented, and she forced her mind away from his eyelashes and shook her head, her hand still pressed to her mouth.

'No…' she managed, not all that convincingly.

Nico didn't have time to reply, because the manager and owner of the restaurant, Tony, swept down upon them, full of apologies—and fury for Emma.

'Signor Santini, I am so sorry! I cannot believe this has happened! This stupid, clumsy girl, she will be fired! Immediately.' Tony, who had been all paternal friendliness to Emma before now, glared at her. 'Get your things. You will leave at once.'

'It was an accident…' Emma whispered, rather feebly, because already she knew there was no point. She supposed she deserved to be fired, after such a mishap, and yet it still stung—and scared her. Jobs weren't easy to get without a reference, and she was living paycheque to paycheque as it was. She had maybe ten bucks in her purse and nothing to eat. She watched as Nico picked a strand of spaghetti from his trousers, and, with a rather wryly self-deprecating look, deposited it on the table.

'I'll go,' she told Tony, 'but you still owe me a week's wages.'

'The impertinence!' her boss huffed, flapping his hands at her. 'A week's wages, when you have insulted my best customer! Away with you.'

Even though she trembled inside, Emma forced herself to stand her ground. 'I'm very sorry about what happened,' she replied steadily, trying not to let a telltale tremor creep into her voice, 'but I have worked here all week and I am owed that money.' And she needed it. Desperately.

'Your wages,' Tony informed her coldly, 'will go towards reimbursing Signor Santini for his suit.'

'That won't be necessary,' Nico informed the ruffled restaurateur. He turned to Emma, his look wry but also knowingly magnanimous, as if he were being so very generous with this concession. 'But I imagine your wages might just about cover the dry-cleaning bill.'

What an absolute gentleman, Emma thought sarcastically, *being so generous.*

She knew his suit had probably cost hundreds, if not thousands, of dollars, and there was no way she could pay for it—or even the dry-cleaning. Both were well within his budget, though. *He* wasn't wondering how he'd pay the rent this week, or where his next meal was coming from. No one who hadn't lived on that knife edge could possibly understand how it felt, balancing precariously, always in danger of life slicing you right open.

'Fine,' she snapped out, because she had no choice and, even in her most desperate moments, she'd never let herself beg. Not even to a man as potently handsome as this. While Tony fumed and Signor Santini stared at her in bemusement, clearly having expected her to fall about in gratitude, she turned on her heel and stalked away. Her fingers trembled as she undid her apron strings, flung it on the pile of dirty laundry in the kitchen. One of the chefs gave her a sympathetic look.

'Tough one, Em.'

'Yeah.' She tilted her chin, gave him a smile of pure bravado. She might deserve it, but she didn't particularly want anyone's pity. She'd stood on her own two feet for too long to go courting that. She took her coat and left the bistro without a backward glance, even though she had no destination in mind. She owed the week's rent on the shabby room she rented in Hell's Kitchen, and now she didn't have it. She could grab her stuff, at least, but she knew her landlord, a guy with a beer belly and a wandering eye, would not allow her to sleep there with the rent unpaid. Not unless she offered him some *favours*, which she had no intention of doing.

So what would it be? A homeless shelter? Sleeping on the street? Oh, the options were *so* attractive. She didn't really have any friends in this city, not yet anyway. She'd only been here for a couple of months, trying to figure out her next move, as always, and barely one step ahead. A sigh escaped her as she continued to put one foot in front of the other, yet with no idea where she would go.

She was halfway down the street when Signor Santini caught up with her.

'Excuse me—miss?'

She turned to him, eyes narrowed in suspicion. Did he want her to pay for his suit, after all? As if she could. Or was he angling for something else, the way her landlord was? Although, Emma acknowledged, that might be flattering herself rather a bit too much.

'It occurred to me that you might have been treated a bit unfairly,' he told her quietly, surprising her, because *that* she really hadn't expected. 'It was an accident, after all.'

'Might have?' Emma repeated, with spirit, before she could control her tongue. 'A *bit*?' He raised his eyebrows and her momentary courage immediately deserted her. Here he was apologising and she still couldn't keep from coming out swinging. It tended to be her default, along with the laughter. Ways to fight when you had no other weapons. 'It *was* an accident, and I really am sorry,' she told him, because she supposed he deserved that much, no matter the man's arrogance. 'I really do hope your suit's not ruined and those papers weren't too, uh, important.'

'They were a crucial contract,' he replied, smiling a little, 'that has to be signed today.'

'Oh.' What was she supposed to say to that?

'Fortunately, I was thinking I needed a little more time to consider the matter, and now I have it.' He raised his eyebrows again, a smile lurking about his mouth, revealing a dimple. Suddenly this man—this incredibly handsome, powerful, glorious-looking man—seemed somewhat approachable. Kind, even. And Emma's deliberately hardened heart thawed the tiniest little bit.

That was when she should have turned around and walked away, Emma reflected as she gazed up at Nico standing above her now, filled with self-righteous fury. She should have run as fast as she could in the opposite direction, knowing it was always better to guard her heart and stay safe. Instead he'd asked her out to dinner, and she'd said yes, because she'd been hungry and she'd had nowhere to go, and also because he'd intrigued her, this man with so much power, and yet who had kind eyes and a dimple. That dinner had turned into an evening, into a weekend, into an affair she'd expected to end at any moment, when Nico said it would.

Instead, three weeks later, they'd been married.

What had he *expected* her to say?

Nico stared at Emma in incredulity, irritated beyond measure that his wife could be so utterly unrepentant. There was not a flicker of guilt in those golden eyes, although she did, he acknowledged, look tired. And pale—too pale. Now that he was looking at her properly, he realised how completely exhausted she seemed, with violet shadows under her eyes, and a drawn look about her mouth. Despite the curves he'd noticed earlier, there was a gauntness to her face and arms that alarmed him. This was not the Emma he remembered, the one he'd left in their marital bed, smiling sleepily up at him as he'd wound a tendril of curling golden-brown hair around one finger and drawn her towards him for one last kiss.

'I'll be back in a couple of days,' he'd told her, and she'd fallen back against the pillows, her heart-shaped face framed by navy satin, a smile of pure satisfaction curving her lips.

They'd spent the last hour in bed, and a very pleasant hour it had been. Although pleasant didn't even touch what he'd found with her—powerful was a more accurate word, explosive even better. When he touched Emma, his head reeled and his senses spun and his body ached. Their chemistry had shocked, thrilled and frightened him all at once, because he'd never, ever experienced it with anyone else. He'd never been in love, not even close, and he'd wondered if it was love with Emma. He'd almost wanted it to be, fool that he was. Good thing he'd come to his senses before it was too late, but their explosive chemistry was why he was reluctant to touch her now. He needed to keep his focus.

'So you have no explanation to offer,' he stated coldly, 'as to why you were willing to marry another man just three months—'

'Three and a half,' she reminded him with that cheeky smile he remembered from when they'd met. It was the same smile she'd given him right after she'd dumped a plate of spaghetti in his lap and then started to laugh—had that all been planned, an admittedly unorthodox way to arrange a meeting? How could she have possibly known how charmed he would have been by her honesty, her artlessness? When so much of his life had turned to lies, the family he'd considered his bedrock crumbling around him, he'd appreciated her unvarnished candour, her willingness to laugh at life, to take it as it came, unlike him, with the familial duty that had always weighed heavily on his shoulders, never more so when he'd discovered the deception at its base.

Too bad he'd been utterly wrong about it all. Ridiculously naïve, which stung even more, because he was smarter than that. He would never be so naïve again.

'Three and half,' he agreed tersely. 'Thank you so much for pointing that out.'

'You're welcome.'

Nico gritted his teeth, amazed and infuriated by her seeming insouciance. Even lying there, looking exhausted, she still had the same impish spirit that had first attracted him to her. But now was surely not the time to be cracking jokes. He wanted her humble, contrite, *begging* him to take her back, despite her betrayal. It would have gone some way to dampening down his anger.

'I would have thought,' he said through his teeth, 'that you might be a bit more regretful, all things considered.'

'I'm not sure why you would think that,' Emma returned, eyes flashing. 'You were declared dead. I was free to marry.'

'In indecent haste—'

'Says who?'

Nico stared at her, amazed at how she was continually coming up swinging—almost as if she were angry at him, or perhaps simply she didn't care at all. Yet something about it, he realised, didn't make sense, not if she was what Antonio had told him she was, what she'd shown herself to be—a shameless gold-digger only interested in cold, hard cash.

'She had her hand out before I'd even written the cheque,' had been his exact words. 'And she couldn't leave fast enough, Nico.'

Even with the strain that had developed between him and his cousin in recent months, Nico had believed him, and, in any case, Emma marrying the next man who offered paid proof to his cousin's words. Not that he should have been surprised. He'd married Emma in a moment of weakness; he'd only been intending an affair when his passion would spend itself and then they'd both go their separate ways, satisfied. It should have happened that way, but instead, reeling from the news he'd been given, he'd chosen to marry her, a woman unlike any other he'd encountered—and it was something he'd obviously had cause to regret. The three months' rehabilitation, where he'd clung to hazy memories and half-hoped-for dreams had put her on a pedestal. Well, she'd been knocked right off it now.

But he still couldn't quite believe her gall at seeming so angry at him. Why wasn't she, the shameless gold-digger she was meant to be, on her hands and knees, begging to come back? You didn't annoy the golden goose when it had made an unexpected reappearance, after all. You thanked your lucky stars and did your best to seem contrite and humble so you could keep gathering all those lovely eggs.

Emma was definitely *not* doing that. Why not? Why was she showing her true colours so unabashedly? Was it because he'd caught her in the act, about to marry some other sop? Or was something else going on, something he didn't know about, didn't understand?

'Perhaps you have not considered the implications of my survival,' he remarked coolly. 'I am not dead, and so you are, in fact, still legally married to me.'

The sudden vulnerable look in her eyes as she shrank back against the sofa made him realise, uncomfortably, that he didn't actually *want* her cowering or begging, although what he *did* want still remained to be seen.

'I assumed,' Emma said after a moment, her voice coming out in something close to a croak, 'that you wouldn't wish to be married to me any longer, all things considered.'

'All things considered? What things would those be, Emma?'

She looked away, her hands still folded across her middle. 'We only knew each other a couple of weeks, Nico. They were amazing weeks, it was true, but... I always expected you to regret our marriage.' She paused, biting her lip. 'If you hadn't been in that crash...'

She trailed off and he took a step towards her. 'If I hadn't been in that crash...?' he prompted softly.

Emma shrugged, still not looking at him. 'We would have divorced eventually, don't you think? Our marriage was clearly a mistake.'

'I can certainly see that now.' Although her saying it so plainly still stung, even as he acknowledged there was some truth in her words. They'd married in haste, as virtual strangers. Perhaps he would have regretted it.

'Why did you agree, then, just out of curiosity?'

She turned back to him, her eyes sparking golden defiance. 'Because...because I wanted to be happy, if only for a little while, and it was the best offer I'd had in a long time,' she told him bluntly, lifting her chin a little. 'Something else you could never understand.'

So she really was unabashed about it, Nico acknowledged dispassionately. Well, fine. At least he knew now, for certain.

'Now we know where we stand,' he told her, his smile a mere stretching of his lips. 'Considering the nature of our situation, I'm sure an annulment can be arranged, and, if not, then a divorce.' The words fell heavily from him; no matter what he felt right now, or in what haste he'd married this woman, he'd still intended to take his vows seriously. Unlike Emma.

Her face paled and something almost, almost like hurt flashed in her eyes before her chin tilted that little bit higher. 'If that's what you want.'

'Isn't it what you want?' he challenged mockingly. 'You're hardly tripping over yourself to win me back, Emma. Really, considering the state of my portfolio, I would have expected a *slightly* warmer welcome. After all, I have a feeling my bank balance is decidedly more impressive than the one of the guy out there you were willing to give yourself to.' His stomach cramped as he briefly imagined such an unsavoury scene. 'What was his name? Will something?'

'Will Trent,' she said quietly.

'Was he really the best you could find?' He shook his head in a parody of disappointment. 'At least you're not pretending to be the woebegone widow. I suppose you're pragmatic enough to realise it would be too hard to pull off.' Perhaps that was why she seemed so reluctant; she knew she'd already been rumbled. 'All in all,' he finished, 'this is probably the better play. Kudos for thinking of it.'

She closed her eyes as she shook her head, her face pale. 'This isn't a *play*.'

'No, I suppose not,' he acknowledged, unable to keep from jeering, 'considering you don't have an angle left, do you? No way to win me back. Too bad.'

'I don't want to win you back,' she flashed, her eyes opening, the anger in their depths jolting him. 'Why would I?'

The stark honesty he saw in her expression felt like a fist to his solar plexus. Clearly his bank balance wasn't enough of a draw, a fact that shouldn't have hurt, of course not, and yet somehow still did. 'Then at least we're in agreement,' he told her. 'Because I don't want you back, either.'

Emma let out a sound that Nico suspected was meant to be a laugh but came out more like a sob. 'Why did you even come here, Nico?'

'I suppose I needed to see for myself.' He hadn't wanted to believe his cousin. Hadn't wanted to believe Emma wasn't what she'd seemed, what he'd made her into during his three months' rehabilitation.

'Well, now you have,' she said wearily, and he gave one, terse nod.

'Now I have.' And yet he was, bizarrely, still reluctant to simply walk out on her. He could arrange an annulment or even a divorce without the need to see her again; why wasn't he doing just that? Why was he standing here, somehow unwilling even now to let her go? Emma, he acknowledged, had got right under his skin. Wormed her way into his—not his heart, no, never that, but his affections. As angry as he was with her—and he *was* angry—he also felt that old tug of desire, that fascination he'd felt when she'd dumped a plate of spaghetti on him and then laughed. He *couldn't* walk away, as much as he wanted to.

'Nico?' she prompted uncertainly. Clearly, she was expecting him to stalk out, just as he'd intended, but he still couldn't make himself do it. They were *married*, and although it had been in haste, he'd taken his vows seriously. Did he want to end their marriage as precipitously as he'd started it?

Did she?

'I'm thinking,' he said slowly, and Emma's eyes narrowed. Then her face went alarmingly pale and she clapped a hand over her mouth. Nico frowned, about to ask her if she was all right, but he wasn't given the chance.

'Sorry,' she gasped out, and then she scrambled off the sofa, rushed to the bathroom adjacent, and wretched loudly and comprehensively into the toilet.

CHAPTER THREE

SHE'D HOPED THE morning sickness was over, Emma reflected as she kneeled in front of the toilet, her cheek resting on the porcelain, her eyes closed. She had just completely voided the contents of her stomach, and Nico had heard it all, heaven help her.

What now?

She felt too worn and weary even to think. Her stomach, even though utterly empty, heaved again, but she managed to swallow it down. She heard his footsteps as he came into the bathroom. She breathed in the smell of his cologne—that same, woodsy scent—and her stomach swirled with nausea even as her heart ached with remembrance. Walking hand in hand, lying in bed, legs tangled together, too afraid and jaded to actually believe someone like her actually got a happily-ever-after, yet hoping still…

Well, obviously she didn't get one, considering the current situation. Except what even was the current situation? What was Nico *thinking* about? And could she really let him walk out of there without knowing about his baby? Yet the alternative felt worse…a loveless marriage with a cold, autocratic man who as good as despised her. Was that what she wanted for her child—the same thing she had, a father who had never really wanted her, who was only there on sufferance?

'You've been sick,' he remarked tonelessly.

'Oh, well done, Sherlock,' Emma returned on a huff of tired laughter. 'A-plus for your deduction skills.' She closed her eyes again, her cheek still pressed against the seat of the toilet, feeling utterly spent.

'Here.' To her surprise Nico crouched down and pressed a square of cloth into her hand—his handkerchief. Briefly she remembered teasing him about always carrying a hand-kerchief—*'What are you? Mr Darcy or something?'* He'd just smiled and shrugged. She was glad for it now, although she wasn't sure she could take his kindness, even one as small as that.

Slowly she eased up into a sitting position, her back against the wall. She dabbed her lips self-consciously and with a small, wry smile—how she remembered that smile!—Nico leaned over and flushed the toilet.

'Thanks,' she mumbled. 'I'll feel better in a few minutes.'

'Will you?' He cocked an eyebrow. 'Where did that come from? Has the shock of my reappearance made you lose your lunch, or are you suffering from a touch of the flu?'

Emma hesitated, and in that second's damning pause she saw suspicion flash across Nico's features, tightening his mouth. 'Emma?' he prompted silkily while she pressed the handkerchief to her mouth, now simply to stall for time.

She couldn't lie, she realised despondently, not about something as important as this. And yet how could she con-fess the truth? Considering what she'd seen of Nico today, she didn't know what he'd do. What he was capable of. Would he take her child away from her, the way she'd been taken from her own mother, determined to claim what was his? Or perhaps he'd agree to some 'marriage in name only' arrangement, install her in a flat or house somewhere out of the way… All in all, she supposed she could cope with that, as long as she had her baby, but she had no guarantees that Nico wouldn't cut her out of his life as ruthlessly as if wielding a pair of scissors, considering how angry he was with her. How little he thought he could trust her.

Or, Emma considered hopefully, maybe he'd let her go. Maybe he wouldn't even care about his own child. She didn't know him well enough to know, and yet she was afraid to trust him with the truth. She had too much hard experience not to handle things *very* carefully in this regard. Her own childhood had been loveless, miserable. She wanted so much more for her baby.

Yet could she even provide it without Nico? She thought of Will, with both regret and longing. Simple, safe Will, who would have been a good father, who would have given her and her baby a home. Was it wrong to want such basic things? To marry for them?

'Is it the flu, Emma?' Nico asked, his voice a low, velvety thrum, laced with danger.

'Could you help me up, please?' she asked, holding out one hand. 'I'd like a drink of water before I answer your questions.'

'I wouldn't think they would be so very difficult to answer,' he replied, extending a hand. 'Considering it's just the one. "Yes, I've been a bit under the weather" would do it.'

'Well, then, yes, I have been a bit under the weather,' Emma replied tartly, for that much was certainly true. She reached for his hand, jolting at the feel of it—dry and strong, long, tensile fingers clasping over hers as he hauled her to her feet. Remembering how that hand had touched every inch of her body, intimately, tenderly, with possession, making her feel so much pleasure, so much *love*. No, not that. Never that.

Breathless, she stumbled and nearly fell against him, managing to catch herself in the very nick of time. She didn't trust herself when in that much close contact with him, the hard, muscled wall of his chest. Just breathing in the scent of him was enough to have longing course through her, along with the dizziness and nausea, which thankfully was starting to subside.

But Nico still looked suspicious.

'Under the weather,' he repeated neutrally, his gaze tracking her as she made her way back to the sofa. The smell of candle wax and dust peculiar to old churches was adding to her nausea, she decided. She needed fresh air, freedom. And she wanted to stall for time, time to think about how she could handle this, although she had a feeling time wasn't going to help her all that much.

'Could we go somewhere else to have this discussion?' she asked, a bit desperately. 'Somewhere public?' She'd feel safer then, more in control. Maybe then she'd know what to do.

'Of course, my car is waiting,' Nico replied without missing a beat. 'I'll text my driver.' Before Emma could formulate a response, he had thumbed a quick text and then stepped over to her, his hand under her elbow, and was guiding her towards the door.

'I don't want to go in your car,' she protested helplessly, for he was propelling her inexorably towards the church doors, so she had no choice but to walk with him. The sanctuary was abandoned, the only evidence that a wedding had been meant to take place were a few white rose petals still scattered across the floor, now curling and brown.

'Where else would you go?' Nico replied. 'Besides, you said you wanted a drink of water, and you look like you need a good meal. We'll go somewhere quiet and private to eat, drink.' He let a weighty pause settle between them. 'And talk.'

Oh, yes, *talk*. And what was she supposed to say? She didn't think she could actually keep the truth of his own child from him, Emma realised afresh, as much as that might be the wise thing to do, considering how hostile he was being. It felt smart, but it didn't feel right.

They'd stepped out of the church into a balmy California evening, the sky a stream of pink and lavender, the air holding the salt-tinged scent of the sea along with the choking smell of LA's usual car pollution. An SUV with blacked-out windows was idling by the kerb. A blank-faced chauffeur emerged from the driver's seat and opened the door for them to climb in the back.

As Nico continued to propel her towards the car, Emma finally balked. 'You can't frogmarch me in there,' she declared, digging her heels—all three inches of them—into the pavement. Typical of him to take total control.

Nico's breath came out in a quick, irritated rush. 'I'm not *frogmarching* you anywhere. I'm taking you to a restaurant in my car, so we can talk in a civilised manner.'

'What is there to talk about?' Emma challenged. She heard the desperation in her voice, and she knew Nico heard it, as well.

'Plenty, it seems,' he said grimly, and, without further ado, he took her elbow again and once more propelled her towards the car.

'If that wasn't frogmarching,' Emma tossed at him as she scrambled across the seat, 'I don't know what was.'

Nico let out a huff of hard laughter. 'You haven't lost your spirit, I see,' he said as the driver closed the door. Emma couldn't tell if it was a compliment.

She still amused him, Nico acknowledged reluctantly as Emma scooted as far away from him as she could, arms folded as she avoided his gaze, looking determinedly out of the window. Amused and aggravated him in equal measure, but still. He was, rather perversely, glad that she hadn't lost her spirit, that cheekiness that had made him laugh, what felt like a million years ago but was, in fact, only three months.

Three and a *half* months. He wasn't about to forget that. And why should he think she had lost such a quality, simply because he'd lost his? She'd been cartwheeling through life, it seemed, from one husband to another, while he had been struggling to hold onto his memories, and then regretting it when he did…

Nico pushed such useless thoughts away. As much as he regretted the past, he had to think of the future now, and how he was going to handle his errant wife, and he still didn't have a good answer to that, no matter what he'd suggested to her earlier in a fit of pique.

He'd come to Los Angeles on something between a vendetta and a whim, needing to see her for himself. He hadn't wanted to believe his cousin, Antonio, when he'd told her Emma had moved on immediately after the memorial service, had left for California while still wearing her widow's black. When Antonio had admitted that he'd kept tabs on her and knew she was seeing someone else, Nico had been shocked—and devastated, trying to hide the depth of his feeling from the rather cool gaze of his cousin.

'I'm sorry, Nico,' he'd said, with the slightest of grimaces. 'But at least now you know what she's really like. A ruthless schemer, after your money, just as I'd said. I'm glad her true colours were revealed before too much time had passed. After all, it hardly befits the CEO of Santini Enterprises to have such a…questionable wife.'

And Antonio would rather he was CEO himself, Nico suspected. In any case, time *had* passed, three whole months where he'd stupidly lived for her memory, pinned all his hopes on their joyful reunion. What a joke. He hadn't been able to make himself reply to his cousin's scathing assessment of Emma, but he'd got on the next plane to LA, to see her for himself. And because she was his *wife*, and he wasn't about to let her marry someone else.

But did he still want to be married to her himself? Live out their years together? Divorce didn't sit well with him, but neither did marriage, not when he knew what she was really like. Although, he told himself, perhaps that was a plus. No dishonesty, no prevarications…just honest desire. Because she still desired him, that much he knew. He'd felt the tremble in her slender body as he'd caught her in his arms. Felt the roar of response in himself. That kind of physical attraction wasn't, he reflected, to be dismissed out of hand. Maybe it was actually better this way…no love lost, after all. And he'd never meant to love her, anyway, because after all the deceptions of his childhood he wasn't all that interested in chasing that ephemeral emotion.

'Where are we going?' Emma asked, turning from the window to give him a bleakly challenging look.

'A small trattoria I know of,' he replied, and she rolled her eyes, a small huff of laughter escaping her.

'Of course, you know all the best Italian places, don't you?'

That first night they'd met, when he'd taken her to dinner to make it up to her—and because she'd fascinated him— she'd asked him why he'd been in such a hole-in-the-wall place as the bistro where she'd formerly worked. He'd told her it had the most authentic Italian food in New York, and that he made a point of finding all the best restaurants across the world—not the glitziest or most expensive, but the ones that offered the best and most authentic food.

She'd cocked her head, her amber eyes sweeping over him thoughtfully, and he felt as if he'd somehow gone up in her estimation, and the notion had pleased him.

Well, Felix Trattoria in Venice was the best Italian restaurant in Los Angeles, but he didn't care what she thought of it—or him—any more. No matter what the nature of their relationship turned out to be, that kind of emotion was definitely off the table.

They didn't talk for the rest of the short journey to the trattoria in one of LA's most bohemian and laid-back neighbourhoods, the restaurant just a few blocks from the beach and boardwalk.

After the driver opened their door, Nico helped Emma out of the car and into the restaurant, to the private table he'd already reserved in the back, a quick call made by his driver on the way over.

'Here we are.'

Emma eyed the table for two set in the secluded alcove askance, and again Nico wondered why she was so reluctant to be in his company. If he'd let himself think about it—and he'd been reeling too much to give it much thought on the twelve-hour plane journey over here—he would have expected her to have some explanation, no matter how absurd, as to why she'd been willing to marry again so quickly. He would have thought she'd try to get him to take her back, crawl on her hands and knees, metaphorically speaking—or maybe not—to get back on the gravy train.

Why wasn't she? What did he not know or understand that would make this situation make sense? Maybe he needed to start with Will, her erstwhile groom.

'Did you love him?' he asked baldly as they sat down, and a discreet waiter laid heavy linen napkins in their laps.

Emma threw him a swift, startled look. 'Love him…'

'Your groom.' He couldn't make himself say his name.

A small sigh escaped her and she looked down at her lap. 'No.'

'So he was just another meal ticket?'

She looked up quickly, her eyes flashing gold at his

sneering tone. 'He wasn't, as it happens, but is there something wrong with that?'

'Marrying someone for money? I would say so, yes.'

'Says someone who has never been hungry.' She pressed her lips together and picked up the menu, her stony gaze flicking down its offerings.

Nico found himself in the irritating position of having to backtrack slightly. 'I admit, there is no shame in marrying for money if you are clear that is why you're doing it,' he allowed. 'A marriage of convenience can be a very sensible thing, I'm sure.' Perhaps they would indeed come to a similar arrangement, in time. 'But pretending to care when you don't is reprehensible.' Feeling as if he'd already revealed too much, he picked up his menu.

'And that's what I had with Will,' Emma told him, her tone turning both quiet and fierce. 'We were completely honest with each other from the start. I didn't love him, and he didn't love me, and that was fine. We were just friends, good friends, and it suited us both.' She put down her menu. 'So perhaps you should stop with your assumptions.'

He hadn't been talking about Will, but that was something he was certainly not going to point out. 'Have you decided what you'd like to eat?' he asked instead.

'I'm not hungry.'

'Emma, don't be childish.'

'I'm not being childish,' she replied, her voice rising. 'I'm actually not hungry.' She glanced away. 'I haven't had much of an appetite lately, as it happens.' She bit her lip, as if she regretted saying that much, and his gaze narrowed.

'More of the flu?' he surmised as he lowered his menu and sat back, his gaze sweeping slowly over her, noting the rush of colour into her cheeks, the way she wouldn't look at him. Every sense prickled with suspicion. What was she hiding? 'Emma?'

A sound escaped her, something between a sigh and a sob. She bowed her head, and the suspicion prickling along the back of his neck sharpened into alarm. Was this the missing piece, the thing he didn't understand? 'Emma,' he said again, this time not a question, but more of a promise, although what he was even promising, he didn't know.

He leaned across the table, brushing her hand with his own. Her skin was so soft and so cold, and he had a sudden urge to wrap his fingers around her own, draw her to him, imbue her with his warmth. The anger he'd been feeling melted in an instant, replaced by a sudden, deep, pervading concern. 'Emma, tell me. Are you ill? Seriously, I mean?' He pictured hospital scenes, shock diagnoses, the secret she'd felt compelled to keep. 'I can arrange the best medical treatment—'

'No, I'm not ill,' she cut across him, 'not unless you count it as an illness.' Her voice was small and sad and defeated, but as she finally looked up at him her eyes still contained that old spark. 'Oh, Nico…the truth is, I'm pregnant.'

CHAPTER FOUR

EMMA LET OUT a laugh at the look of utter and complete shock on Nico's face. It wasn't remotely funny, of course, but laughter had always been her defence, and, in any case, she didn't think she'd ever seen him look so blindsided, so completely pole-axed, as if she'd just hit him over the head with a two-by-four. She shook her head, pressing her hand to her mouth.

'You should see the look on your face,' she told him, and his look of blatant incredulity morphed into a scowl.

'I can well imagine,' he bit out tersely. *'Pregnant.'* He shook his head slowly and Emma dropped her hand from her mouth with a sigh. No, not funny at all, especially when he looked far from pleased, just as she'd feared. Why had she told him? And yet how could she not have?

She knew she'd just taken a huge risk, that this could change everything. Nico, in all his arrogance and pride, would be certain to want to call all the shots about her life, her baby's life. So why *had* she told him? Because, she supposed, she had a core of honour just as he did, even if he would never believe it of her. And, she acknowledged, because she'd never known her father, and she was reluctant to have her baby not know theirs. And yet…what if that would have been the better choice? The safer one?

Telling him she was pregnant might have been just about

the stupidest thing she'd ever done, and yet she couldn't quite make herself regret it.

'So this is why you were marrying that man,' he stated, his gaze sweeping slowly over her.

'Will?' Emma asked, surprised he was making that jump. He hadn't reacted very much to the news he was going to be a father, she acknowledged with a flash of bitterness. 'Yes. I knew I couldn't provide for this baby on my own. I've barely been able to provide for myself.' She lifted her chin, daring him to challenge her. 'Will knew about the baby,' she added. 'He was absolutely fine with it.'

'And yet,' Nico returned scathingly, 'he was willing to walk away quickly enough when he discovered you were married to me. What sort of man does that?'

The condemnation in his voice annoyed her. He was blaming *Will* in this whole fiasco? 'You didn't actually give him much choice,' she pointed out. 'Since you told him to leave. And why wouldn't he? What else was he supposed to do, when we obviously couldn't marry, after all, since I was already married to you?' She would have to text Will and explain, she realised, dreading that conversation, even over the phone. Poor Will. He'd been so kind to her, and this was a horrible way to repay him. She would have to find some way to explain.

'I would think,' Nico returned coolly, 'or at least hope, that a man would have more regard for his own child.'

She stared at him—those cool green eyes, now narrowed; the full, sculpted lips pressed together in censure—and realised the assumption he'd made. He thought *Will* was the father, and although his presumption absolutely infuriated her, she recognised, reluctantly, that it was not an entirely unfounded conclusion to draw. She knew she wasn't showing very much yet; the obstetrician had said she was small for fourteen weeks, mainly because of the debilitating morning sickness she'd had since the beginning.

Staring at Nico, knowing what he now believed, she was tempted, treacherously, to let him go on believing it. Why shouldn't she, after all? He was controlling, suspicious, and right now he seemed as if he hated her—hardly the kind of father she wanted for her baby, or, for that matter, husband for herself. Why not walk away if she could?

Nico, Emma knew, had just given her the only out she could possibly take. If he believed she was pregnant with another man's child, he would almost definitely divorce her, as he'd already said he intended to do. Wasn't that really the best thing for both of them? He was never going to love or trust her again, not that she even wanted him to, of course, and she didn't love or trust him, anyway. Not any more. That kind of suspicion was hardly the best basis for a marriage, a family, and, anyway, she knew she'd always done better on her own. She'd stayed strong, safe, smart. She should walk away now, for the sake of her baby. *Their* baby...which was why she closed her eyes, let out a long, defeated sigh.

'Nico...the baby isn't Will's.' She parted with each word reluctantly, wondering even as she spoke if she was making a huge mistake. Another one. She was used to being tough, taking it on the chin, and looking out for herself, so why she was breaking all her rules now, she had no idea. Maybe because she'd never known her own father. She couldn't do the same to her own child...or to Nico. Even if it would be smarter to.

'Another man, then?' His nostrils flared and his mouth tightened. 'You do work fast, Emma. Faster even than I realised, it seems.' His voice vibrated with anger, and suddenly Emma found herself matching his fury. *That* was where he went with this? Yet another man? They'd been at it non-stop for their whole affair, why would it not occur to him that he, her *husband*, was the father?

'You really are remarkably insulting,' she snapped. 'I have to say, it's a real talent, along with making assumptions, which is what you've done since you marched into my wedding—'

He leaned across the table, his eyes flashing jade. 'A wedding that never should have happened!'

'You were *dead*!' The words seemed to echo through the restaurant, followed by the loud and obvious sound of someone clearing his throat. Emma glanced over and saw a white-jacketed server waiting to take their order, struggling to keep a bland look on his face. An unruly laugh escaped her and she put her hand over her mouth while Nico glared first at her, and then the waiter.

'We'll both have the *strangulet*,' he bit out. 'And mineral water, please.'

'I told you, I'm not hungry,' Emma protested, although now that her stomach was empty, she actually did think she could manage some food. She knew she should eat for the sake of her baby, yet she couldn't bring herself to bow to Nico's wishes yet again, even about something so small.

'You need to eat,' he returned with a quelling look. 'And the *strangulet* is the best thing on the menu. Besides, it's not too rich or spicy, so it should be appropriate.'

The waiter silently took their menus as Emma leaned back in her chair. Even when he was being thoughtful, Nico made assumptions. Acted arrogantly. The man really was impossible. She would be well rid of him.

He'd been like that before, she remembered, calling all the shots, although considering the luxury he'd showered her with, she hadn't minded too much. That first night he'd wined and dined her, and then, as it had been so late, he'd insisted she stay the night. A gentleman, he hadn't touched her then, but, looking back, Emma saw he'd still acted with the arrogance that that moment would surely come—when he said it would.

When they had begun their affair, he'd made it clear it was a temporary arrangement; she was only there at his behest, for as long as he decided it would last. He'd arranged everything—their accommodation, travel, even what she wore, ate, drank, did. She'd been, Emma acknowledged bitterly, like a doll he could dress up and play with, and she hadn't minded because the world he'd introduced her to had been so glamorous and intoxicating, unlike anything she'd ever known. She'd just been along for the wondrous ride, caught up in the fairy tale even as she tried to caution herself that, like everything else in her life, it wouldn't last.

Their whole relationship—the single month of it—had been out of time, away from reality. First in New York, staying in the most opulent hotel Emma could have ever imagined, and then in Rome, at his palatial penthouse flat. She hadn't even had a passport before she'd met him. She hadn't been anywhere, done anything, besides simply try to survive, and yet he'd opened worlds to her, with the travel, the luxury, the amazing food, the attention.

So many worlds…including the intoxicating one of passion. But she really could not let herself be distracted by the memories of *that* right now.

'So this Will was amenable to marrying you even though you were pregnant with another man's child,' Nico surmised, shaking his head, clearly finding the notion incredible, and, no doubt, repellent.

'Yes, he was.' She was too angry to bother correcting Nico right now, and in her fury she wasn't even sure that she should. The assumptions he made were really beyond the pale.

The waiter came back to fill their water glasses, and

Emma took a much-needed sip. Her throat felt terribly dry, and her heart was hammering. She took a steadying breath. 'He didn't want to marry anyone at all, wasn't interested in a romantic relationship, but his mother kept pressuring him, pretty unbearably. He's a shy, mild sort of guy, and he couldn't take it. So this was the solution.' And it had worked—or at least it *would* have worked—admirably for both of them. 'It was an amicable arrangement, based on companionship, nothing more,' she told Nico. 'Like I said, it suited us both.' And she would need to talk to Will and explain everything as soon as she could. He deserved that much, at the very least.

Nico didn't look particularly impressed by her words. Emma had a feeling that right now Nico wouldn't believe her if she told him the sky was blue. It was a wearying thought.

'And what of the child?' he asked. 'He was willing to raise it as his own, act as its father?'

Emma swallowed, nodded. All right, she'd been too angry to correct Nico, it was true, but this was starting to feel uncomfortably like lying. She really needed to tell him the truth, or at least decide for herself whether she was going to tell him. The longer she strung this out, the more furious he would be at her seeming deception…if he ever found out. And he would find out, because she really didn't think she could keep such a huge secret from him. Besides, she was terrible at lying. But as she considered all she stood to lose the words wouldn't come. 'Yes, he was,' she managed finally. 'Like I said, he's a good man.'

She'd met Will at a party she'd been hired to waitress for; he'd been at the bar, drinking steadily, and had, in something of a stupor, told her all about his controlling mother and the desire to simply live his life without her relentless interference. He was utterly committed to his work as a software engineer, and wasn't interested in any romantic relationships, although he thought he wouldn't mind having children one day.

Emma, having just discovered, to her great shock, that she was pregnant, had been wondering how on earth she was going to manage. She'd been living in a bedsit, enduring the usual hand-to-mouth existence, trying to eke out the money Nico's cousin had given her before she'd left. And yet despite all that she'd known, absolutely, that she wanted this baby. She wanted someone to love, someone to be hers. A family, at last, like she'd never, ever known. The family she'd always longed for.

She'd joked to Will that they should marry—and yes, it *had* been a joke, if a somewhat desperate one. To her utter surprise, Will had taken her at her word. He'd given her his card and asked for her number, and Emma had assumed that would be that—a drunken conversation, nothing more—when he'd texted her the next day.

Are you serious?

And she realised she had been. She'd had to be, because she didn't have any other options, and now she had someone else to think about. Someone so very important.

They'd spent a couple of weeks getting to know each other, and Will had been a reassuringly open book, a workaholic with a few, simple pleasures, happy to chat but generally enjoying his own company. He'd asked for a prenup, which had made sense, and told her she could redecorate his apartment in Santa Monica if she liked, as long as she left his study alone. He'd liked the idea of a baby, and had even come along to her first scan two weeks ago. They had never been going to have a great passion, or any passion, but that had been fine. After Nico, Emma wasn't ready to deal with that kind of explosive chemistry again, or any kind of chemistry, and Will really was happy in his own company. Emma had her baby to think about, and that had felt like enough. More than enough. Their marriage would have been simple and unexciting and *safe*.

And now it was over. The future she'd so carefully tried to construct blasted into smithereens…by the man sitting across from her.

'You look so sad,' Nico remarked mockingly. 'Are you missing him?'

'He's a kind man, and as you said, he was willing to take on another man's child,' Emma returned tartly, 'so yes, I am. He was a good friend.'

'And the father?' Nico asked. 'Another man who was your mark, I suppose?'

Her *mark*? What did he think she was, Mata Hari? She let out a disbelieving huff of laughter as she shook her head. 'I'd find your cynicism amusing,' she told him before she could think better of it, 'if it wasn't so pathetic.'

Anger flashed in his eyes and the skin around his mouth went rather alarmingly white. 'Don't test me, Emma.'

She shouldn't be so flippant or foolhardy, Emma knew. As tender as Nico had seemed during their whirlwind courtship and marriage, he was also a man who was known to be ruthless in business, who knew what he wanted and how to get it—and discard it, if he so chose. She'd looked him up, after the crash, and seen the trail of affairs and broken hearts he'd left behind him, a string of casual affairs that had made headlines. She hadn't been surprised, but it hardly inspired confidence now.

'How far along are you?' he asked, sitting back in his seat, his arms folded. 'Out of interest?'

She hesitated, her mind racing between viable options. Lie, and protect herself and her baby. Tell the truth…and take the consequences, whatever they might be. It felt, she thought despairingly, no choice at all.

'Well?' Nico prompted.

'Not...' She swallowed hard. 'Not very far along.'

Not very far along? Why didn't she know? Had there been that many men? No matter what he'd learned of her, Nico couldn't quite make himself believe that. When he'd taken her in his arms for the first time, she'd seemed remarkably innocent, and so very sweet. So very different from the women he usually took to his bed, who were as pragmatic as he was when it came to matters of the heart. He remembered the moment with Emma perfectly—it had been three days after they'd met. She had confessed she'd had nowhere to go and so Nico had told her she could stay in his hotel suite. He hadn't been leaving New York for a week, after all, and he'd felt badly for, admittedly indirectly, causing her to lose her job. He'd been determined to be the perfect gentleman and he had been, even as his attraction for Emma had threatened to overwhelm him.

Her whimsical guilelessness or *seeming* guilelessness— he knew better now—had won him over. After the lies of his childhood, his mother's damning silence, his father's painful coldness, here was someone simple and innocent and pure. Ha! As if. Had Emma actually been orchestrating their first encounter, when she'd stood on her tiptoes and brushed a kiss across his mouth? Had she just been pretending when he'd looked down at her, his heart starting to hammer in expectation, and she'd smiled so softly, so tremulously?

And when he'd asked, his voice already raw with wanting, throbbing with need, 'Are you sure?' she'd exhaled on a small sigh of surrender.

'Yes...'

Had that all been faked? And yet what had happened after hadn't been. He knew that absolutely. He remembered the feel of her beneath him, open and pliant, writhing and wanting. The explosion when they came together had rocked them both to the core, left them gasping and clutching each other as if they were the last bits of wreckage on a drowning sea. And when he'd looked down at her, smiling in a sort of wry disbelief, she'd laughed, a sound of pure joy.

'*Wow...*' she'd breathed, and he'd grinned, rolling onto his back, taking her with him, his arms clasped around her, sexual satiation combined with a soul-deep contentment.

No, Nico decided, some things could *not* be faked.

And yet right now Emma was definitely looking shifty. She kept her gaze lowered as she took little sips of water, her fingers trembling around her glass. What more could she possibly be hiding? Who *was* the father?

In one sudden, swift movement, Nico leaned forward, and captured her wrist in his hand, removing the glass with the other. 'What is it that you're keeping from me, Emma?' he asked in a low voice. 'Because it's obviously something. I've never seen you look so...so *scared* before.' He'd never seen her look scared at all. He'd always admired her spirit, her strength. Where had it gone? What had spooked her? Or was this too some sort of act?

He'd thought, for a few wondrous seconds, when she'd first told him she was pregnant, that she'd meant *he* was the father, and his heart had leapt with a wild mix of elation and amazement. A child of his own. It had been an unlikely notion, he knew, because she didn't look pregnant, and she'd have to be at least three months along—three and a *half* months—for him to be the father. Besides, they'd used protection assiduously. He'd made sure of that.

Then he'd realised, in the space of a single heartbeat, by the resigned look on her face, that of course he wasn't. She hadn't wanted to tell him about her pregnancy, he'd realised, because carrying another man's child would make her less attractive to him, understandably so. The disappointment that had thudded through him he'd pushed away resolutely. No need to feel that, all things considered.

And, he realised, it now all made an awful sort of sense—pregnant with another man's child, she'd known all along that he wouldn't want her back. No wonder she'd seemed reluctant, and yes, even scared that he'd returned. *That* was the secret she'd been keeping...but now that he knew, why did she still look fearful? Could there be more?

Emma glanced down at his fingers encircling her wrist, her face pale and drawn. He could feel her pulse fluttering beneath his thumb, and, without even thinking about what he was doing, he stroked the silky skin there, letting his thumb linger on her cool, soft flesh. A shudder escaped her, her expression turning dazed, and desire ignited low in his belly. One tiny, treacherous touch, and already he felt lost with wanting her. Remembering how it had been between them, overwhelming his senses, making him forget everything else. His mother's betrayal. His father's indifference. The sense of spinning in emptiness that he'd felt, not knowing who he was, where he came from or where he belonged. The world he'd wanted to walk away from as he'd forged a new one with her.

Lies, so many painful lies, but right now all he could remember was how her arms had felt around him, her body pliant and sweetly yielding beneath his as she'd gasped out his name...

'Please let me go,' she whispered.

After another heated beat he released her wrist and sat back. Emma cradled her arm against her chest, as if he'd hurt her. He knew he hadn't; he could see from her dilated pupils and flushed face that such a simple touch had affected her, too, the way it had him. She remembered how it had been between them, as well. The chemistry between them was just as strong even now, after she'd told him she was pregnant with another man's child. The realisation was both shaming and infuriating.

And yet…there were worse things, far worse, to build a marriage on than chemistry.

He let the possibility linger in his mind, just as it had before. Yes, admittedly the child was a complication he hadn't foreseen, and he, of all people, knew how difficult it was to take on another man's child, yet also, perhaps, potentially rewarding? Here, possibly, was a way to redeem the past… He could love this child the way he never had been. He could give it a hope and a future. Was he strong enough to do that? Did he want to?

His mind raced with new possibilities—Emma as his wife, in all senses of the word, or almost. Love, obviously, would not be part of this complicated equation. And her child—*his* child, or would be. He'd adopt it, naturally, as soon as possible. Treat it like his own in every way…if he could.

'Why are you looking at me like that?' Emma asked shakily, and Nico refocussed his gaze on her. The colour had receded from her cheeks, leaving her pale and drawn again, and she was still cradling her arm against her chest.

'I am considering our future,' he told her matter-of-factly.

'Our future? And what are you considering, exactly?' she asked, clearly trying to sound braver than she felt. She released her arm, resting her slender hand on the table, fingers spread as if to anchor herself.

'I didn't expect the child,' he admitted frankly. 'It has, to put it mildly, put a spanner in the works.'

She let out a choked sound, something not quite a laugh, but at least not a sob. 'A spanner in what works, Nico?'

'Our marriage.' He frowned, considering the ramifications. Could he really take on another man's child? He knew the pain and heartache that could cause, on both sides, and in truth he wasn't completely sure if he could love another man's child the way he would love his own. Shaming to admit, especially considering his own birth, but he knew he needed to be honest with himself. The last thing he wanted to do was act as his father had—be cold to the child entrusted to him, give it less than he or she deserved simply because of an accident of biology, of blood. The way he had been, although he knew he couldn't actually fault his father for excluding him. He'd included him in the family business—grudgingly, reluctantly, but he had. But Nico had always still felt the loss, the confusion at not understanding why his father could barely endure his presence...until his mother had, on her deathbed, hurled a grenade into their family, causing an explosion that still ricocheted through him to this day.

'What about our marriage?' Emma asked.

'Whether it continues.' His frown deepened as he realised fully that he couldn't walk away from his wife, even when she was pregnant with another man's child. He didn't even want to. 'The father,' he asked. 'Does he know about the child? Did you tell him? Why did he not take responsibility?' The man was clearly either in the dark or a complete cad.

'I...' Emma didn't have a chance to reply, for the waiter came with their meals then—two steaming plates of *strangulet*, tube-like pasta with fresh tomato, basil and garlic. They were both silent as he set the plates down before them and then, with a murmur of thanks, left them alone.

Emma's head was bent as she picked up her fork and toyed with the pasta on her plate, her brow furrowed.

'Well?' Nico prompted. 'Did you tell him?'

'I never had the opportunity,' she half mumbled, her head still bent over the plate.

'Never? Why not?'

'He...disappeared before I could.'

She sounded mortified, as if each word were painful to say, and so it would be, when he considered what she was confessing. A one-night stand, just about as soon as he'd been declared dead? He'd been missing for how long by then? A few weeks? A month? He swallowed down his anger.

'I see.'

Emma let out a wavery laugh. 'You really don't.'

'So tell me, then.' Nico heard the anger thrumming in his voice, and he knew Emma did, as well. 'And *look* at me, for heaven's sake, Emma. Or are you so embarrassed about your own behaviour you can't bear to look me in the eye?'

'I'm not embarrassed,' Emma retorted, looking up so he could see the golden flash of her eyes, 'although perhaps *you* should be, at your absurdly high-handed manner, making all these judgments and assumptions about me. If I'd known just how absurdly arrogant you were, I wouldn't have married you in the first place!'

He reared back, her response only adding to his anger. 'Oh, really? I'm just trying to find answers. Answers you seem suspiciously reluctant to give—'

'Oh, Nico.' Emma let out a laugh that definitely sounded more like a sob as she dropped her head into her hands. 'For heaven's *sake*. I cannot continue this ridiculous pretence any longer. I don't know why I even tried, except...' She trailed off, swallowing, and he tensed, annoyance flaring within him along with the anger, although he wasn't even sure what exactly to be annoyed about. 'Why don't you just tell me straight, for once, then?' he demanded.

She looked up again, bleakly this time, her eyes full of weary resignation. 'Nico, there isn't another man. Not Will, not some stranger or whoever you are imagining in your unending cynicism. *You're* the father of this baby.'

CHAPTER FIVE

AND SO THE die was cast. Amidst the fear and uncertainty, Emma felt a flicker of relief. She really had never been good at lying, which had certainly got her into trouble as a kid. She couldn't pretend she hadn't stolen food, or cheated on her homework, or done whatever she'd had to, to keep body and soul together. The result had been she'd been labelled a troublemaker from the get-go, which was not great when you were being cycled through the foster system, one family after another, each one passing you on like a parcel they didn't want. And probably not so great here, considering she'd just handed Nico all the cards, do with them what he would.

But what else could she have done? She'd tried—sort of—to go along with his assumption that there was another man, but it had been too hard—and too insulting. She'd seen the way his nostrils had flared and his lips had tightened at the thought of her sleeping around, never mind his own colourful past. He could have a dozen or more casual affairs, it seemed, but heaven forbid if she did. In any case, it seemed her husband had no trouble believing all manner of things about her—well, what else was new? Nico Santini was just showing he was like everybody else. She'd lived the fairy tale for a month, but it was now well and truly over.

Except she was still married to Nico…and he now knew

he was the father of her baby. Another fairy tale might be starting, of the Brothers Grimm variety, scary ending included. Emma's stomach tightened with anxiety.

'Mine?' Nico repeated, his voice filled with icy disbelief. 'Impossible.'

So now that she'd told him, he was going to deny it? 'Impossible?' she repeated, letting a huff of hard laughter. 'Not if you know about the birds and the bees, which I'm pretty sure you do.'

Annoyance flashed across his features. 'Don't be facetious, Emma—'

'Trust me, I'm not.' She shook her head slowly, wondering why he found it so hard to believe, when they'd been together for a whole month. Yes, he'd used protection, but everyone knew protection could fail, and there had been more than a few times when they'd both been in an eager rush, fumbling in their passionate haste, as she remembered all too well. Even now just a memory of such an encounter had heat blooming low in her belly, between her thighs. Unhelpful at this particular moment. *Very* unhelpful.

And yet all he really had to do, she reflected bitterly, was the maths. Did he really distrust her that much?

'Nico,' she said wearily, 'you are definitely the father, I promise. There hasn't been another man since you, so, really, you are absolutely the only candidate.' Make of that what he would, although from the blatant scepticism on his face, he was struggling to believe that, as well, and Emma wished she hadn't told him quite so much. She was feeling vulnerable enough already, even if he couldn't see it.

'I'm the father,' he stated incredulously, as if daring her to throw her hands up and admit she was lying.

Jokes! You're actually not. Fooled you for a second, though, didn't I?

'Yes, the father,' she repeated, rolling her eyes, an edge

to her voice, because he was really milking this whole incredulity thing just a little too much. 'I don't know why you're *quite* so sceptical. The dates do match up—'

He shook his head, determined to believe the absolute worst of her, it seemed. Well, most people did, but for some reason, stupidly, with Nico it hurt more. 'You said you weren't far along—'

'I'm fourteen weeks.'

His dark brow came together in a scowl as realisation dawned, a blazing light in his eyes, a tautening of his mouth. 'So what you actually mean is, you lied earlier.'

'I didn't lie,' she protested, knowing she was now on shaky ground. 'I was just...sparing with the truth.' Very sparing, but only for about half an hour. She couldn't have managed much more, she knew, as much as she might have wanted to.

'But why?' He slapped his palm against the table, startling her with the loud crack of sound, as colour slashed those magnificent cheekbones. He was, she realised, trembling inwardly, truly angry. Angrier, even, than when he'd stormed into her wedding, as she'd tried to marry another man. Was this about pride—or something else? It reminded her, painfully, that she really didn't know him at all, and once again she wondered if she'd just made a big, big mistake, trusting him with the truth of their child.

'Why would you lie about that?' he demanded. 'What purpose would it possibly serve?'

'You jumped to conclusions,' Emma replied, trying to rally. She was not entirely at fault here, for the misunderstanding. 'First thinking it was Will's, and then some... some stranger's! Thanks, by the way, for assuming I really get around. And that's not even considering the sexism of it being okay for *you* to get around but not me.'

'We're not talking about me right now, and what was I

supposed to think, when you did not correct me?' he returned, his voice rising. 'And you married within three months of—'

'Three and a half months,' Emma interjected with biting, saccharine sweetness. He was angry? Well, so was she.

'Enough!' he commanded in a freezing tone. 'If the child is mine, I assumed you would have told me right at the start, not prevaricated in order to keep the truth from me. The fact that you didn't made me assume it was not, which, I believe, is entirely and unfortunately understandable.' His eyes narrowed, his mouth thinning. 'Indeed, I am still sceptical, all things considered. Why *wouldn't* you tell me, Emma, for heaven's sake?'

'Oh, good *grief*.' She shook her head as she threw her napkin on top of the table, too weary to keep going around in circles, trying to convince him. 'I've had enough of this.'

'Emma—'

'I'm leaving,' she stated, stalking from the table on unsteady legs. Tears blurred her eyes and she blinked them back. It was ridiculous to feel so hurt. Nico didn't trust her? Well, she didn't trust him. A perfect match, then. As if.

'Emma, stop.'

She heard Nico push back his chair as she kept walking, towards the front of the restaurant. Not, she realised belatedly, that she had anywhere to go. She was supposed to be staying with Will tonight; he'd moved all her stuff—which admittedly was only a couple of suitcases—to his apartment yesterday. She supposed she could go there and throw herself on his mercy, but it felt presumptuous, considering all that had happened. But where else could she go?

'Emma, wait.'

She was at the front door when Nico grabbed her arm, turned her around to face him. 'Don't storm out of here in a huff—'

'I'm not in a *huff*,' she snapped. 'I'm just really tired of you doubting me constantly. And I'm tired full stop, because, you know, I'm *pregnant*, and I want to go somewhere and sleep, so can you please just leave me alone?' She tried to shake off his arm, but he wouldn't let her.

'I'm not leaving you alone,' Nico gritted as he steered her out of the front door, away from the prying eyes of the other diners. They were creating quite a scene. 'You're my *wife*.'

They stood on the sidewalk outside the trattoria, a balmy breeze from the ocean buffeting them, Nico still holding her arm. Emma closed her eyes as a wave of fatigue crashed over her. She was so not up for this. She'd been through the emotional wringer today, and, as much as she prided herself on quick thinking and good survival skills, right now she felt completely tapped out. She couldn't summon her usual insouciance, that determined, daredevil laugh, the eyebrow arched in challenge. She just couldn't.

'What do you want from me, Nico?' she asked wearily, her eyes still closed. 'Just tell me that, at least. What do you want from me right now?'

'I...' He sounded surprised by the question, baffled even, and she opened her eyes to find him staring at her, so clearly at a loss. 'Look,' he said finally, 'you're obviously exhausted, and you need somewhere to stay. Let's go back to my hotel. We can have these conversations later.'

As if on cue, his car glided up to the kerb and the driver hopped out. Emma hesitated, because she didn't really want to roll over and let Nico call all the shots *again*, but she knew she needed a break from the intensity, as well as some sleep, and it was getting late. Maybe tomorrow she'd stumble on a solution she couldn't seem to find now. She'd figure out a way to have this all make sense.

'All right,' she agreed, not all that graciously.

The driver opened the back door of the car and Nico

helped her inside. Emma leaned her back against the sumptuous leather as Nico settled himself next to her and the driver closed the door.

'Where are you staying?' she asked, and he named one of the city's most modern and luxurious hotels, in Beverly Hills, of course. Emma had walked by it a couple of times, awed by its tinted windows and sweeping arcs of glass and chrome, a testament to innovation. Nico had always had a taste for culture, a preference for the best. Some things, it seemed, hadn't changed.

It was the last thought that flickered through Emma's mind before, thanks to the soft leather seat and the smooth rolling of the car, she fell gratefully into a doze, the cares slipping from her for a few blessed moments.

Nico stared at Emma, now curled on her side, her head drooping towards her knees, already deeply asleep after just a few minutes in the car. He felt a sudden and surprisingly strong flare of protectiveness for her, looking so tired and so vulnerable. Was she really telling the truth about this child? She seemed to be, but still he was wary. He knew he had good reason to be, considering the situation. And, he acknowledged, reasons that had nothing to do with Emma and that she wouldn't understand. Reasons that still hurt to think about too deeply, when he considered the yawning abyss of knowledge of his own parentage. Now, with his mother dead, he would never know.

But his own child would.

He'd make sure of that.

He should, he supposed, make this simple, and order a paternity test. There was no reason not to, although he wondered if Emma would balk at such a request. But if she was being honest, then surely she wouldn't? And if the child really *was* his...

He realised that flare of protectiveness he felt was not just for Emma, his wife, but for his child.

His child.

A sense of incredulity, of wonder and hope, flooded through him, buoyed his soul. His own flesh and blood, unlike any other. Someone to love, to protect, to cherish. For ever.

If Emma was telling the truth...

Was he wrong, to doubt her so much? He thought of his cousin dismissing her as a gold-digger, with the cold, hard proof, after all, that she'd insisted on leaving, had taken the money Antonio had offered. And, all right, maybe she *had* married him for money, back then; she certainly didn't seem to be denying it now. But that, in itself, was a certain kind of honesty, and besides, she surely had to know that he could order a paternity test and sort this out in a matter of days. Why would she keep lying?

'Signor?'

Nico was startled from his thoughts by the driver, who had pulled up to the front of the hotel without him even realising.

'Thank you, Paulo.'

'The *signora*?' he asked, nodding towards Emma, still curled up on the back seat.

'I'll take care of her,' Nico replied, realising he meant it in every sense of the word. He got out of the car without Emma so much as stirring, and then, as gently as he could, scooped her up into his arms. She was light—so light!—and she curled into him unthinkingly, her head nestled against his chest. He breathed her in, smiling when he realised she still smelled of soap. Eau de Dollar Store, indeed. It was a heady fragrance.

'I can walk...' she mumbled sleepily, without moving, and Nico's arms tightened around her.

'It's fine,' he said gruffly. In truth, it was more than fine. She was a delectable armful, curled into him, her breasts pressed against his chest, his hands skimming her curves as he hoisted her securely against him. Desire stirred, a persistent ache in his groin, forcing him to shift his tempting bundle. He was not about to complicate things with that element, as wonderful as it had been. Not yet, anyway.

He strode through the ultra-modern foyer, all marble and glass, causing a few raised eyebrows and curious stares, and into the private lift that soared up eighteen flights, directly to the penthouse suite, which took up the entire top floor.

Stepping inside, he deposited Emma gently on one of the cream leather sofas scattered across the black marble floor of the soaring living space, floor-to-ceiling windows giving views of the city in every direction, so it almost felt like being suspended in mid-air.

As he stepped back she lifted her head, blinking the room into focus.

'Wow.' Slowly she looked around, taking in the mahogany bar, the grand piano, the priceless modern sculpture scattered about, and, most of all, the three-hundred-and-sixty-degree view. 'Some place.'

'Do you want to go to bed?' He'd meant the question innocently, but heat flooded his face—and his groin—at the mere mention of those evocative words. Seeing Emma sitting there, tousle-haired and sleepy-eyed, was firing his blood. Everywhere. 'I mean,' he corrected tautly, 'do you want to go to sleep.'

A small, playful smile curved Emma's mouth as she glanced at him from underneath her lashes, golden eyes glinting, before the smile dropped and she sighed. 'I know what you meant. And actually, in all honesty, what I'd really like is a bath. I'm assuming this place has some ridiculously huge, sunken tub? Marble, with jets?' She raised her eyebrows impishly and he found himself smiling back, even laughing a little.

'Of course it does.'

'Excellent.' She stretched, her yellow dress pulling taut across her breasts, making him ache all the more, before she stood up. 'Bring it on, then.'

Nico did his best to keep things matter-of-fact as he showed her the master bath, attached to the bedroom with its tempting, king-sized bed. The only bed in the suite as it happened, but they'd cross that rather interesting bridge when they came to it.

The bathroom was fitted out just as Emma had hoped—with a huge sunken tub of black marble and many jets. 'There's a dressing gown on the door,' he told her. 'And plenty of toiletries there, on the shelf. If there's anything else you need…'

'My stuff, I suppose,' she replied. 'I don't actually have any clothes with me besides this dress.'

'Where are your things?'

'At Will's apartment, in Santa Monica.'

He kept his expression neutral although he realised he hated the thought of her belongings there, *her* there. She would have been right now, as the man's wife, if he hadn't come into the church and disrupted the wedding. The thought was enough to make him grit his teeth, but he forced himself to relax. It hadn't happened. She was here, with him, and it was their future he had to focus on. Their child.

'If you give me the address,' he told her, 'I'll have Paulo fetch them for you and bring them here.'

She hesitated, and then nodded once, seemingly reluctantly. 'All right. Thank you.'

'Do you want to get them yourself?' he surmised, a bit sharply, and she sighed.

'No, Nico, not particularly, but I do feel I owe Will an explanation. He is a good, kind man, and I basically dumped him in it, deserting him at the altar.'

'With good cause.'

'Still, he deserves a conversation. I should call him tonight.' She glanced around, her eyes widening in sudden realisation. 'I just remembered, I left my bag at the church, with my phone and wallet—'

'Paulo retrieved your belongings from the church earlier. They're in the car. I'll have them brought up to you.'

She hesitated, seeming as if she wanted to argue the point, and then she nodded. 'Thank you.'

He paused and then said quietly, 'I know I've been angry, Emma, but I'm not some kind of monster here. I am trying to be reasonable about all this.' As hard as that was. He supposed he could ease up, a little.

'I know,' she said quietly, but she didn't sound particularly convinced, and he had the sense that it was as hard for her to trust him as it was for him to trust her. Yet had he really ever given her any reason to doubt him?

'Enjoy your bath,' he said, and then left, closing the door behind him. He heard her turn the lock with an audible click.

Out in the living area, Nico poured himself a healthy measure of whisky from the decanter on the bar and then stepped outside to the wraparound balcony, the glittering lights of Los Angeles spread all around him, the ocean a blanket of darkness in the distance. He breathed in deeply and let it out in a rush as the events of the last few days caught up with him, leaving him wrung out and just about as exhausted as Emma.

Less than a week ago he'd been in Jakarta, his memory coming back to him over the course of a difficult month, first in vague fragments and confusing pieces, and then with more clarity and precision. He'd remembered Emma first; when the rest of his life had remained cloudy and un-focussed, she had stood out like a beacon of hope, a shining angel.

He was embarrassed now to recall just how much he had clung to her memory, how he'd felt it had helped him to recover. When he'd been struggling to walk, to focus, to so much as think clearly, he'd pictured their future together, their joyous reunion, her incredulous wonder at finding out he was alive, and it had compelled him onward.

The fact that reality had been so far removed from his absurd fairy-tale fantasy had made him, he realised, a bit angrier and more accusing with her than he might have been otherwise. Than perhaps he should have been. Still, the discovery of her wedding, her betrayal, her shameless admission of marrying him for money…it all stung, still.

Two weeks ago he'd finally been in touch with his cousin, Antonio, who had been shocked to hear of his survival, and then, belatedly, pleased. Nico knew there was no love lost between them; Antonio would always be angry that his father had chosen him, the cuckoo in the nest, over his own blood, even if he'd only done it to save himself the humiliation of admitting to the world his wife had betrayed him.

When he'd returned to Italy, he'd received the news, from a rather smugly certain Antonio, of what really had happened after his alleged death. How Emma had demanded money from him immediately after the memorial service. How she hadn't wanted to be in touch, hadn't wanted anything to do with his family at all, just the cold, hard cash. Antonio had given her ten thousand dollars, a paltry amount really, but Nico supposed he understood his cousin's reluctance to offer more to someone who had clearly revealed herself as nothing more than a shameless gold-digger…just as he'd said she was.

And yet Emma had taken it, so Antonio had indicated, and gladly, considering the prenup he'd had her sign before their whirlwind wedding—the one spot of sense in his dazed unreality. She would have been entitled to more than ten grand, though, he realised, so sloping off with that relatively paltry amount of money, he mused now, was hardly the action of a gold-digger, at least not a very ambitious one—something he hadn't considered in his anger and hurt, when he'd learned from Antonio that she was marrying again. So what was really going on? Or maybe ten grand had seemed like a pretty good deal to her. He really didn't know.

What this all showed him, he thought as he tossed back the last of his whisky, was that he really didn't know his wife at all. And whether he could trust her remained to be seen. But if she was having his child, he would have to remedy both those situations as soon as he possibly could.

CHAPTER SIX

EMMA LEANED HER head back against the cool marble of the sunken tub and closed her eyes, enjoying the sensation of the hot, bubbly, rose-scented water frothing about her, her muscles starting to relax, her bones to melt. This was, she acknowledged ruefully, about as close to heaven as she could get right now. If only she could stay in this lovely warm bath for ever and forget the world—and the man—awaiting her on the other side of the bathroom door.

Unfortunately she couldn't. Her temples throbbed even as her body relaxed, and she wondered—again—whether she'd made a mistake in telling Nico about the baby. Well, she told herself, doing her best to be pragmatic as she opened her eyes and gazed about the opulent bathroom with its black marble and gold fixtures, the reality was, mistake it might be, but she'd made it. She'd told Nico he was the father of her child, whether he believed her or not, and she now had to deal with the fallout. Would Nico come round or would he stay suspicious? Would he keep her in his life so they could attempt to be some sort of family? Was that something she even wanted to risk?

A shudder of apprehension went through her, and she tipped her head back against the tub and closed her eyes once more. She couldn't think about all that just yet. One day at a time, one minute at a time, was the most she could manage if she wanted to hold onto her sanity. Eventually she would formulate a plan, a way forward she could live with. Hopefully. Right now, though, she was too tired, and all out of ideas.

Her hand crept to the slight, reassuring swell of her middle. 'I'm trying to keep you safe, little one,' she murmured. 'I really am.' Unfortunately, she still had to figure out just how to do that, with Nico now in the picture.

What, she wondered with a bittersweet pang, would have happened if he hadn't been in that plane crash? Would they have continued in their idyllic, time-out-of-reality way for much longer? Surely that fairy tale couldn't have lasted for ever. For the month she'd been with him she'd been sure it would end at any moment, that Nico would glance at her with a resigned sort of smile and say, *It was fun, but...*

Instead he'd asked her to marry him. She remembered the moment perfectly, as if it were engraved in her mind with crystalline clarity—she'd been on the balcony of his palatial apartment in Rome, gazing out at the ancient city streets, the Forum in the distance twinkling with its own lights. She'd had to pinch herself, quite literally, because she couldn't believe she was standing there, in such luxurious circumstances, with a man who made her head spin and her heart beat hard. Not, of course, that she'd had any intention of falling in love with him. She knew better than that. And yet...she'd been close, alarmingly close, simply because he'd been so kind to her.

Since she'd met him—well, truthfully, fifteen minutes after—Nico Santini had showered her with attention, care, interest and compassion. For someone who had learned to live life on her own a long time ago, it had been a much-needed, and rather frightening, balm to her soul. So she'd stood on the balcony and cautioned herself to be careful, to stay cautious.

Then Nico had walked onto the balcony, taken her into his arms, and murmured against her hair, 'Emma, marry me.'

Emma had stiffened in his embrace, utterly shocked. She'd never, not for one moment, not for one *second*, thought their fling was actually going anywhere. Nico Santini, hot billionaire, was amusing himself with the likes of her for a little while, and that was fine. *Fine.* She was of the take-what-you-can-get school of thinking. She'd had to be.

As Nico's arms had tightened around her, she'd eased back to gaze up into his face, searching his intent expression for clues.

'You aren't serious.'

'I am.'

He'd sounded so heartfelt. She'd been completely confused. 'Why?' she'd asked, meaning the question genuinely. Utterly.

'We've had fun these last few weeks, haven't we?'

'Yes, but...' That was all it had been. *Fun.* You didn't get married because you'd had *fun.* A man like Nico—wealthy, powerful, sexy as all get-out—didn't actually *marry* someone like her. He just didn't. Emma had known that. She'd understood it, accepted it, and she'd thought Nico had, as well. And yet there he was, holding her in his arms, asking her *that* question.

'Marry me, Emma,' he'd said again, sounding so much as if he'd really meant it, and even though she couldn't understand why he'd want to, the second time he'd asked she hadn't been able to resist. Even if it had made sense to be cautious. Even if it had been smart to guard her heart. How could a girl like her, who'd had to fight her way off the street, have said no to the best offer she'd ever had, was ever likely to have? The closest thing to a fairy tale that she could have hoped for?

A girl like her didn't say no, not to something like that. Even if she hadn't really known why he was asking. Even if she'd been scared of falling in love. Even if she'd been determined not to.

And so she'd said it. Simply, sweetly, on something between a sigh and a laugh. 'Yes. *Yes!*'

And Nico had taken her in his arms, and kissed her senseless, and for a few seconds—a whole week, even—it had seemed easy. They'd married in a small civil ceremony in Rome, a couple of his employees as their witnesses. She'd signed a prenuptial agreement and hadn't minded the understandable precaution.

He'd messaged his father and cousin, but she hadn't met them, not till the memorial service. She'd stayed in his flat pretty much for their entire marriage, save for the occasional outing for a coffee. Nico had either worked or taken her to bed, with not much else in between. She hadn't met his family, his friends, anyone. He'd never had to introduce her as his wife.

If any of it had rung alarm bells, Emma hadn't let it, because she'd wanted the fairy tale to be real, if only for a little while. Deep down she'd always known it would end one day, the way everything ended, because why wouldn't it? Why would a man like Nico—rich, powerful, unbearably attractive—stay married to someone like her? Maybe he'd needed to get her out of his system, slum it for a while before he moved on. Emma had told herself she was under no illusions…but part of her had still hoped.

Then, a week later, he'd left, and, while still at his apartment in Rome, she'd heard from a coldly drawling Antonio about the crash. She couldn't think about him, the way his mouth had pulled down and his dark eyes had tracked her, without her stomach cramping.

'Absolutely no survivors,' he'd said shortly. 'And as

you've only been married a week, and Nico was tiring of you anyway...'

She hadn't wanted to believe that last part, and yet she had, because people *always* tired of her. The foster families who hadn't wanted to keep her, who had moved her on because she wasn't lovable enough...even the one that she'd let herself love back.

'Emma? No, absolutely not...'

The certainty in her foster mother's voice, a woman she'd dared to love, who she'd begun to think loved her, rejecting her out of hand, with such certainty. It was a memory she couldn't bear to think about, not even all these years later.

In any case, Antonio had made the situation abundantly clear. 'You are not part of this family, and never will be. I'll give you ten thousand dollars, merely as a gesture of goodwill, with the assurance that you will never come sniffing around here again. Is that clear?'

By that time she'd been desperate to get away, stinging from his contempt, from the knowledge that if he'd been around, it would have been Nico, not Antonio, sending her on her way with such a disdainful expression. And so, as she'd clung to the last remnants of her pride, she'd nodded.

'Yes, absolutely clear,' she'd told him, making herself sound mocking, even though her heart had felt as if it were in pieces.

It wasn't. She wouldn't let it be, because she didn't let herself love anyone, not any more. Not even Nico. Especially not Nico.

And yet where did that leave her—*them*—now?

As exhausted as she'd been earlier, Emma knew she wouldn't be able to sleep until she'd spoken to Nico. She wouldn't rest until she knew what he intended for her, for their baby. And if she decided he couldn't be trusted? That he'd take away her child? Well, she knew how to run—far and fast.

But first she needed to explain everything to Will. She certainly owed him that much.

She reached over and pulled out the plug, watched the water swirl down the drain in rose-scented suds. Then she got out of the tub and wrapped herself in the thickest, fluffiest dressing gown she'd ever seen, combing her fingers through her hair and making good use of the hotel's luxury lotions. With nothing more to distract or delay her, she squared her shoulders, lifted her chin, and headed out of the bathroom.

Her bag was just outside the door, and Emma reached in it for her phone, heading to the privacy of the bedroom to make the dreaded call.

'Emma?' Will answered after the first ring. 'Are you okay? I've been worried—'

'Oh, Will. I'm so sorry.'

'So that man is your husband?'

'I thought he was dead. But…he wasn't.'

'He didn't seem that thrilled to see you,' Will remarked, and Emma let out a trembling laugh.

'No, but…we'll work it out.' At least she would try. She hoped Nico would, too.

'Well, you know I'm here for you,' Will said after a moment, and Emma's eyes stung. Even though she'd only known him a short while, Will was a good friend, and she was grateful for him.

'Thank you,' she whispered.

'You will keep in touch?'

'I'll try.' Right now it felt like the most she could offer.

The call finished, Emma knew there was nothing to keep her from seeking out Nico. The marble floor was cold and slick beneath her bare feet as she walked into the massive living area, a vast open space, looking for him. It took her a few minutes to find him, standing on the wraparound balcony, gazing out at the city lights.

Emma took a deep breath and then slid open the sliding glass and stepped out onto the balcony, the balmy evening air rushing over her skin, heated from the bath.

'Hello, Nico,' she said quietly.

Nico turned around, jolted by the soft sound of Emma's voice. He'd been so lost in his thoughts he hadn't heard the door slide back, or realised she'd come out here to join him. He glanced at her now, her face flushed from the bath, her hair curling about her shoulders in damp tendrils. The dressing gown enveloped her and yet still offered a tantalising peek of the shadowy vee between her breasts, a hidden valley whose delights he remembered all too well.

The dressing gown stopped just above her knees, and he could see the shapely curve of her golden legs. Everything about her made him ache to touch her, his palms itching with the need. A simple tug and the sash of her dressing gown would fall away; she'd shrug out of it and step towards him, naked and perfect. He'd take her in his arms as he had before...

With an enormous amount of effort, Nico forced the tempting vision away. He could not complicate matters with sex right now. 'Did you have a nice bath?' he asked in his most solicitous tone.

'Yes, it was amazing.' She offered him a small, wry smile that felt like a truce. 'I forgot how easy it was to get used to this kind of living.'

Presumably she hadn't had it, then, in the three and a half months since his alleged death, which had to have been part of the reason she'd gone for this Will. 'What did you do, after the plane crash?' he asked. He realised he was curious. He'd already determined he needed to know more about her, to figure out if he could trust her. Now seemed to be as good a time as any to start finding the answers he needed, assuming she would tell him the truth. He didn't yet know if that was a reasonable assumption to make.

'After your memorial service, you mean?' She let out a sigh as she turned back to the suite. 'Do you mind if we sit down? My feet are absolutely aching.'

'Are they?' He couldn't keep from sounding concerned, and she let out a little laugh as she walked back inside.

'Three-inch heels and pregnancy do not go together, as it turns out.' She sat on one of the sofas, tucking her legs up underneath her. 'What did I do?' she resumed, her expression turning thoughtful, guarded. 'First let me ask you what you did.'

It was clearly a prevarication, but one he decided he was willing to run with. For now. 'I told you, I was in hospital.'

'Yes, but…' She shook her head slowly, her eyes wide and golden. 'I can't get my head around the fact that you survived a plane crash. That must have been…' she blew out a breath '…terrifying.'

'I don't remember it, actually.' He glanced down, finding it weirdly vulnerable to admit even that much. It felt like a deficiency, a weakness, that his brain had these blanks.

Emma drew her brows together as she studied him. 'You don't?'

'No,' he admitted, settling back into the sofa, his hands splayed on his thighs. 'The crash itself is a complete blank. I don't even remember being on the plane, or any of it. The last thing I can remember comprehensively is—' *kissing you goodbye* '—a bit before,' he finished after a second's pause. 'Apparently, it's common for the brain to block out that kind of trauma. Sometimes the memories come back, sometimes they don't.' He smiled a bit crookedly. 'Or so the doctors told me.'

'Oh, Nico.' Her face softened with sympathy and caused a rush of—something—to course through him. A longing, deeper than desire, stirred in him. This woman had touched him in ways he never had been before. At least, he'd convinced himself of that, when he'd been lying in a hospital bed, with the memory of Emma the only thing he could hold onto. Whether it was a mirage or not hadn't mattered, not then.

But it mattered now. Love was most certainly not going to feature in their future at all, not in any shape or form. He'd learned better now. Wised up, thankfully.

'All I remember is waking up in a hospital bed,' he stated matter-of-factly. 'Staring around and having no idea where I was, or even who I was. Everything was a complete blank—just this whiteness. In my head.' He shook his head slowly as the memory of it filtered through him. 'It was terrifying,' he admitted, 'as well as completely disorientating.'

'I can't even imagine,' Emma exclaimed softly. 'How long was that for? When did your memories come back?'

He shrugged, again feeling that flash of vulnerability at admitting his ignorance. 'It's all a blur, frankly, and it didn't happen all at once. Bits and pieces…like pieces of a puzzle, except I didn't know how they fitted together, or what the whole picture was. For a month I was in a coma, and then another month of not knowing who I was, although I had random memories come and go, like flashes of lightning.' He remembered searching his empty mind, the vacuum of his memory, for much-needed clues, snatching at fragments of memory that drifted through his mind like ghosts, hazy and ephemeral.

'Then I started to remember more things—events, people, and as I got stronger I remembered more and more. Eventually I knew enough to contact my cousin, Antonio.' Who had hardly been overjoyed to hear from him, Nico recalled wryly. Had his cousin been hoping to step into his shoes as CEO of Santini Enterprises? Undoubtedly. Nico's return from the dead must have been a disappointment, although Antonio had at least pretended to be pleased.

'Antonio,' Emma repeated. 'You remembered him first, then?'

No, he'd remembered Emma first. Emma, lying in his bed, smiling up at him, her hair in a curly golden halo about her flushed face. Emma, tilting her chin as she gave him that impish smile, making his heart sing. *Emma.* 'Yes, and my father,' he repeated, and now his tone was just as neutral as hers. He'd remembered his father eventually—and the last conversation they'd had, when the man who had raised him had stared at him stonily before turning away in complete and utter dismissal. He would acknowledge Nico in public, but not in private, not as his son. He would never regard him with anything close to affection, and lying in a hospital bed, as the memories had filtered through him like shards of glass, lacerating his shredded conscience and drawing blood, he'd remembered the reason he'd walked away from his family—and into Emma's arms.

'And me?' she asked softly, glancing down. 'You...you must have remembered me?'

Nico looked away, his jaw bunching. He'd meant to deal simply in facts, but the emotions came chasing behind, galloping up on him, taking him by surprise. 'Yes,' he managed tautly. 'I remembered you.'

The silence that poured over them felt like honey, a golden web of memory weaving them together.

Yes, Nico could not keep from thinking, every thought like an ache deep inside him, *I remembered you. I remembered the exact shade of your eyes, how they glint when you laugh. I remembered precisely how you felt in my arms, how your breasts filled my hands. I remembered the squeal*

*of your laughter as I kissed my way down your body, as
the laughter became sighs and then gasps... I remembered
it all.*

He swallowed hard. Shifted in his seat, and forced his
mind onwards, out of the honeyed trap of the past. 'Anyway,' he said, apropos of nothing.

'Have you remembered everything now?' Emma asked,
and now she sounded cautious, wary rather than sympathetic. 'Besides being on the plane, I mean? There aren't
any more...gaps?'

'No, at least, I don't think there are. I suppose it's hard
to know what you can't remember, if you don't remember
it.' Sometimes he felt a nagging sensation that he'd forgotten something important, some conversation or piece of
information, like a tickle at the back of his brain, but the
doctors had assured him that was normal with amnesiac
patients. He'd learned, for the most part, to ignore it. To
focus on what he did remember...like Emma, until he'd
learned she'd been the one to forget him. Maybe he would
have been better forgetting, too, except not if there was a
baby involved. His baby.

'That all must have been incredibly difficult,' Emma
said quietly.

'It was.' He turned to face her again. Her hair was drying in curls, her face still flushed from the bath, and her
dressing gown had slipped off one smooth, golden shoulder. She was utterly delectable, and he could not deny how
much he wanted her. Still. Now. His heated blood was racing
through his veins, his hands itching to touch her. To draw
her to him, onto his lap, his lips on hers, his hands...and
they could both forget everything that had happened since
then; to catapult back to when it had been easy, the two of
them in bed, making each other's bodies sing.

He took a steadying breath. 'Tell me your side of the

story, Emma. What happened after you learned I had died? What did you do?'

The soft look of compassion on her face fell away in an instant, replaced by something far more guarded. 'I went to LA,' she said after a moment. 'As you know.'

'Yes, but why?' He leaned forward, wondering if this, perhaps, was the nub of it, the thing he didn't understand, or maybe he just didn't want to understand. Didn't want to accept she was exactly what Antonio had said she was from the beginning—only in it for the money. 'My family would have provided for you, you know, as my wife. I know we hadn't been married long, but—'

'No, they wouldn't have.' She cut across him, the words quiet and so very sure. 'As it happened, they didn't. They refused, not that I even asked, because it was obvious enough already.'

Nico frowned. 'Antonio said he offered you ten thousand dollars—'

'Yes, that's true, as a gesture of his goodwill.' Her mouth twisted as she made air quotes with her hands. 'Which I took, because I didn't have so much as a penny to my name, and I was desperate. I'm not ashamed to admit that.' Up went her chin, along with the golden flash of her eyes. 'But there was no suggestion of me staying with your family, Nico.' She paused, as if she were going to say something more, and then decided not to. 'I can't really begrudge your cousin or father that, though, considering the circumstances. You'd only known me a month. Antonio didn't know me at all. And I did take the money he offered, so I suppose he thought that proved whatever it was he thought about me.'

Nico stared at her in dismayed surprise, because this was definitely not how his cousin had framed the events. Antonio had insisted Emma had wanted to leave, had demanded the money he'd reluctantly given, and then gone on her merry way, shaking the dust from her shoes. Who was he to believe?

Looking at the lines of bitter hurt etched into Emma's face, he felt compelled to believe her version, even as he resisted such a notion, because what did it say about his cousin? His family? And yet should he really be surprised, considering how hard-nosed his father had been? How cynical his cousin? 'Antonio said you couldn't wait to leave,' he said slowly.

'That much is true,' she admitted. She glanced away, as if to hide her expression. 'I knew I wasn't wanted, so I chose to leave.'

He sat back, his mind whirling, his stomach tightening. This was definitely not the story he'd been sold, although he realised he wasn't really surprised. Why would his father be interested in his wife, when he hadn't been interested in *him*? And Antonio had always been pragmatic to the point of ruthlessness. Nico could still recall the way Antonio had grimaced when he'd told him he was marrying her.

'Keep her as your mistress, for heaven's sake, Nico, but don't actually marry the girl!'

And Nico, in a fit of pique, and a deeper hurt at the widening fissure between him and his cousin, had ignored that advice. Maybe he shouldn't have, he acknowledged grimly, but it was too late now. But why had he let himself believe Antonio's version of events upon his return? Was it because he'd been so wounded by Emma's apparent betrayal, by marrying again? Anger always felt like the stronger option.

'Do you believe me?' Emma asked, a vulnerable note creeping into her voice, making him ache.

'Yes,' he admitted, shaken by the truth of his words—and hers. 'I do.'

Suddenly the last three months—three and a half—took on a whole new, uncomfortable complexion. If Emma had left his family, knowing she wasn't welcomed…if she'd discovered she was pregnant with so very few resources… and if Will had offered to marry and provide for her…why wouldn't she say yes? For the sake of her—their—child?

Was it really fair to judge her for any of that? To be angry about it?

'Nico?' Emma asked softly, breaking into his thoughts. 'What are you thinking?'

I'm thinking that I wish things were simple and straight-forward, but they never are. I want to trust you even now, but I won't let myself because I've had to learn not to trust people.

His mother, who had lied to him his whole life. His father, who had rejected him. Antonio, the cousin who had been like a brother, until he'd discovered he wasn't. No, he wasn't about to be that honest, not with Emma, not with anyone. 'I'm sorry you had to face that,' he said, his voice roughening to hide his emotion. 'That would not have been my intention…or my wish, for you to have been cast out in such a way without any resources, financial or otherwise.'

She shrugged, glancing down as a tendril of her golden-brown hair fell in front of her face, obscuring her expression. 'I don't blame your cousin for that, to be honest. He barely knew me. *You* barely knew me.' She looked up then, and Nico was taken aback by the challenge in her eyes.

No, he realised, he hadn't really known her, but he'd thought he had. Was that his fault? For being so willing to believe, to jump with both feet, simply because he'd wanted to, so much, in a moment of weakness and wanting, when his own father had turned away from him?

'Still,' he said, 'it must have been very difficult for you.'

She shrugged, managed one of her old, insouciant smiles that still had the power to lighten his heart, even though he saw it didn't reach her eyes. 'Hey, ten grand is ten grand. It bought me an economy-class ticket to LA, and two months' food and rent until I found a job, got on my feet.'

And that was presumably when she'd run out of options—and met Will. It was all starting to make a terrible sort of sense. And, Nico realised, he was starting to believe—and even trust—his wife, at least in terms of this part of her story. Or at least want to, he supposed.

His heart, he knew, was another matter entirely.

CHAPTER SEVEN

EMMA SNUGGLED DEEPER under the covers, sleepily enjoying the luxuriously smooth feel of the silken sheets, the comfortingly heavy duvet. Her bones felt as if they were melting into the soft mattress, every muscle wonderfully relaxed for the first time in ages. Her eyes closed, her mind in a pleasant haze of sleep, she stretched like a starfish—and encountered a hard chest. A hard, warm, very *male* chest, muscles tensing and flexing under her questing palm.

She should have jerked her hand away. Even in her sleep-hazed state, some part of her knew this, absolutely. For her own health and safety, her own *sanity*, not to mention her battered heart, she should yank her hand back, jump out of bed and keep things very, very clear, at least in *that* regard. But in her sleepily befuddled state, she didn't. For a second, no more, she flattened her palm against that hair-roughened chest, enjoying the tickle of the crisp hairs underneath her palm, the flexing muscles, the warm, burnished skin.

Then a strong male hand captured her own, whether to still it or simply keep it there, she didn't know. Her breath caught in her chest and although she was still asleep—*mostly*—she moved out of instinct, out of need, unable to think past the blooming warmth and want deep in her belly. She rolled right into all that potent male warmth next to her in the bed, letting it engulf her, swallow her whole. At least that was what it felt like, as if she were being wonderfully subsumed.

In the next moment, the hand that had held her own had moved to the dip of her waist, slipping under her T-shirt and spanning her warm, welcoming flesh, covering it, owning it. Her hips came into contact with the very male part of Nico, nestling perfectly against him and sending a shockwave of sensation buzzing through her. *Now* she was awake. Very awake.

And now her mind was in an entirely different sort of haze—one of overwhelming, intoxicating desire. It thudded through her, made every sense blaze and yearn and strive, consequences be damned. Without being able to stop herself, not even wanting to, she pressed into him, sending fiery arrows of pleasure sizzling through her as his arousal pulsed between her thighs. Nico let out a muttered groan and, with his hands on her waist, he fastened her hips more securely against his, pressing against her, into her, so need flared deeper, hotter as his mouth captured her own in a plundering kiss and she remembered just how explosive it had been between them. How completely wonderful, shocking in its intensity, exciting in its passion, overwhelming her with both.

His touch was a tornado that caught her up in its heady whirl, as his mouth ravaged her own with a tender, velvety persistence and her mind blurred with longing. She grabbed his shoulders, anchoring herself to him as his hand slid from her waist to between her thighs, touching her with such clever, knowing intimacy that had her gasping aloud, pressing into him, yearning for more. She'd forgotten how good this was between them, how he made her come alive in a way she never, ever had before.

And Nico must have felt just as much as she did, for his

breathing was ragged and fast as he fumbled with the over-large T-shirt she'd worn as pyjamas, desperate to press his heated flesh against hers, just as Emma was...

Yet somehow, in the blur of desire, the blaze of need, sanity asserted itself, that still, small voice telling her this was really *not* a good idea, all things considered. Somehow she managed to hold onto that faintest shred of common sense even though everything in her was longing for more. So much more.

'Wait.' Emma pushed at his chest, which felt like an immovable wall, and to his credit Nico stilled instantly, his body pressed to hers, his *hand*...

'Emma?' His voice came out in a throaty rasp, his lips inches from hers, his forehead sheened with sweat as he held himself back.

'We shouldn't...' She hitched her breath as longing coursed through her. *Be smart, Emma. Stay safe.* 'I'm sorry, but I'm not... I'm not ready for this.'

Even if right in this moment she felt ready, more than ready. She was *yearning*. But if she gave herself to him, Emma knew, she'd lose her focus to stay strong. Smart. Safe. She might even lose herself.

She needed to figure out what their future was, before she let him into her bed, because as smart as she was trying to be, it was only a hop, skip and a jump from bed to heart, and she was not going to make that leap. Not now, and maybe not ever. She'd told herself she could separate the two before, and she might do it again, but right now she felt too vulnerable to even attempt to make that division.

Slowly Nico withdrew from her, and it felt like a loss. 'I apologise,' he said stiffly as he rolled up into a seated position, driving his fingers through his dark hair as a shuddery breath went through him.

'You don't need to…' she began helplessly, and then, not really knowing how to finish that sentence, she pressed back against the pillows and closed her eyes. Her heart was thudding, her body tingling everywhere with awakened, unanswered desire. Was she being really stupid? It wasn't as if they hadn't slept together before. Playing the prude when she was pregnant with his baby was kind of ridiculous, wasn't it?

And yet…she felt vulnerable enough already, and that was an emotion she didn't like. She wasn't about to become even more so.

'I'm the one who should be sorry,' she whispered. 'I didn't mean to…well, it all just sort of happened, I guess.'

'Well, I know it.'

He sounded wry, and Emma cracked open an eye, surprised he wasn't doing the whole coldly furious thing with her. He smiled down at her, definitely looking rueful, colour slashing his cheeks, his green eyes glinting, and she found herself smiling back. A laugh escaped her like a bubble, the last thing she expected right now, but she was glad for it. This side of Nico, playful and wry, was so much nicer than the arrogant, autocratic man she'd encountered last night. She was glad for it, for him.

'Come on,' he said, hauling her up by the hand. 'We have a doctor's appointment this morning.'

'We do?' Last night, after their conversation, she'd crashed into bed, too exhausted to as much as stir when Nico had obviously come in to sleep on the other side. She hadn't been aware he was there until morning, when she'd stretched and come into contact with him, in all his male glory.

'Yes, I arranged it last night, after you went to bed, with an obstetrician.'

He rose from the bed, wearing nothing but a pair of navy silk boxer shorts, looking utterly magnificent, his skin like burnished satin over bunched muscle, making her long to touch him again. Slide her hand along that warm, satiny skin.

Stop it, Emma.

'I had a scan two weeks ago,' she told him. 'Everything was fine with the baby then. I don't think I need another—'

'Well, I want to see for myself,' Nico replied, his tone firm as he headed towards the bathroom. 'And then, of course, there's the matter of a paternity test.'

Oh. Emma stared at his retreating back, watched as he closed the bathroom door with a firm click. Right, a paternity test. Because he still didn't trust that he was the father. Still thought she might be lying to his face, and about something so important.

Well, maybe stopping things before they got out of hand *had* been a good idea, then. She told herself she shouldn't feel hurt that Nico was being thorough; after all, they'd known each other for such a short time, and raising a child was a big deal. She told herself that, but Emma knew it didn't make much difference. She *was* hurt, and she was annoyed at herself for being so.

A lifetime of living on the sidelines of other people's lives had taught her not to care, and definitely not to love or try to be loved. That had never worked out, starting with her mother, from whom she'd been taken away when she was just six months old, and then following with the foster families she'd tried so desperately to belong to. Some had been kind, some not so much, some downright cruel, but not one of them had ever actually *wanted* her. Chosen her, even the one she thought might. The one she'd let herself love.

Emma? Absolutely not.

She'd never forget those words, that tone, spoken over

the phone by the foster mum she'd come to love, when she'd thought she wasn't listening. She had been, in hope, knowing the social worker would be calling, thinking her foster mum might finally say the words she'd been waiting to hear her whole life.

Emma. Yes. Of course.

After that she'd made the decision, at ten years old, not to let anybody in ever again. It had been a conscious choice, one she'd always stood by.

Work hard, act tough, be funny, make like you don't care and then you won't.

She could not let Nico Santini get under those defences... even if she was married to him. She'd resolved it before, and she would do so again.

Yes, it was a very good thing things hadn't progressed farther this morning. And they wouldn't do so again, not until she'd figured out how she was going to navigate this whole situation. Unfortunately a restful night's sleep had not presented her with a solution. The fact remained she was still married to Nico, pregnant with his child, and un-sure what their living situation could possibly look like.

The bathroom door opened, and Nico strode out, a towel slung low around his hips, his hair damp and spiky from the shower.

Emma watched, her mouth drying, as he reached for a pair of boxers from the suitcase open on a luggage rack. He dropped the towel and she hastily averted her eyes.

'Nico,' she protested weakly.

'What?' He sounded utterly unrepentant as he slid on a pair of boxers. Yes, she'd peeked from the corner of her eye, unable to resist the sight of the fabric sliding over his taut, muscled flesh. 'It's not as if you haven't seen it before, and we *are* married.'

A far cry from the man who had said they would divorce just yesterday. How could she possibly trust him—not just with her own life, but with that of their child? 'We might be married but not like that,' Emma replied, determined not to let him befuddle her with his body.

'Almost like that,' Nico replied, his voice lowering to a silken purr, making her blush. 'Very almost, as of this morning.' He reached for a crisp blue shirt from the wardrobe and slid his arms into it.

'Yes, about that,' Emma said, hugging her knees to her chest. 'I thought you'd sleep on the sofa or something.'

'The sofas aren't that comfortable, and besides, the bed was plenty big enough.' He turned around to face her, his long, lean fingers buttoning up the shirt, hiding his magnificent chest. The chest she remembered exploring with her fingertips just moments earlier.

'Not that big,' Emma pointed out. 'Seriously, Nico…we have to come to some sort of agreement, about what happens now.'

'What happens now?' His eyebrows rose as he straightened the cuffs of his shirt. 'It seems quite simple to me. You're my wife, I'm your husband, and that—' he nodded towards her middle '—is our baby.'

'You didn't seem so sure about that when you booked a paternity test this morning,' Emma retorted, and Nico looked startled.

'Emma, be reasonable. I have to be sure.'

Yes, because he couldn't trust her.

And you can't trust him.

And what was a marriage without trust? What was a *family*?

'Emma, surely you can see that?' he pressed, his voice so very reasonable.

Yes, she thought reluctantly, she supposed she could, all things considered, and yet it still stung, a *lot*, and it made her wonder how on earth this marriage of theirs was ever supposed to work, on any level. What did Nico even want—for her to fall in with his plans, pop out his baby, warm his bed?

Would that even be so bad?

Emma had always been a pragmatist; she'd had to be. Nico would always provide for her, she knew, and she could finally live without fear of where her next meal was coming from, or whether there would be a roof over her head. She'd never wanted to be loved, had chosen not to, and yet...

What if he walked away from their child, the way her mother had walked away from her? Could she subject her baby to such a risk?

Did she have a choice?

Nico couldn't tell what was bothering Emma, at least not exactly. He eyed her as they rode to the appointment he'd booked at one of the city's most exclusive obstetrics clinics in Beverly Hills, noting her narrowed eyes and pursed lips, the way she angled her head away from him. She'd been prickly since they'd woken up this morning...and what a way to wake up!

Was what had happened in bed between them this morning annoying her? As exciting as that delicious little interlude had been, it had also been unexpected, both of them caught up in the throes of their passion before they'd so much as blinked the sleep from their eyes. Not that he'd minded. At all. But, he acknowledged, it wasn't something they had discussed or planned, and maybe Emma hadn't been ready for it.

Or, he wondered, was it the fact he'd made this appointment? She'd seemed surprised and maybe even a little annoyed that he'd made it in the first place. Yet surely Emma could see the unfortunate necessity of a paternity test? It wasn't meant to be an insult on her character, simply a sensible precaution. Although, he realised uncomfortably, he supposed it *could* seem as though he didn't trust her.

Yet how was he meant to trust her when he'd walked in on her wedding to another man? Besides, considering his own parentage, he knew he needed to be absolutely certain that he was this baby's father. The test, he knew, was as much about him as it was about her…not that he intended to explain to her about that.

In any case, he decided, he'd get to the bottom of it after the doctor's appointment. Lay it all on the table, make everything clear. And tell her exactly what he expected from their marriage.

He glanced at her again, noticing the way she held herself, as if she were all sharp angles and edges, her expression both resolute and resigned. Nico found he didn't like her looking like that. He liked seeing her laugh, giving as good as she got, but since he'd told her they were going to the doctor's, all he'd got from her were monosyllables.

Last night—and this morning—had clarified things for him. Assuming the baby was his—and maybe even if it wasn't—he knew now he wanted a proper marriage with Emma. They had too much chemistry to ignore, and even when she was infuriating him, she made him smile. He enjoyed her company and he genuinely liked her. All good reasons, he thought, for her to be a proper wife, and for them to be a proper family. This time he wouldn't entertain fantastical notions of love, but he would enjoy all the other benefits of their union—from their time in bed to being a father.

As for Emma…she would have the same enjoyments.

Surely she couldn't argue against that? She'd been willing to marry that mopey software engineer for money, why not him? He was, Nico reflected, offering a *much* better deal. So why was she looking so annoyed right now?

Perhaps, he mused, he needed to be clearer what he was offering. How much. She'd only had a taste of the wealth and luxury at his disposal before the crash; now he would give her the full measure of it. He'd enjoy pampering her, he realised. Although she'd been sparing with the details of her childhood, she'd made it clear that she had no family, and her circumstances when he'd met her had seemed dire indeed. He'd enjoyed pampering her before, and he would do so even more now. He looked forward to giving her all the things she hadn't had before—travel, clothes, jewellery, evenings out…really, she had it made. She just didn't realise it yet. He couldn't wait to tell her.

The obstetrician's clinic was just a short ride away, off Rodeo Drive, a discreet brick building with a gold-plated plaque. Nico kept his hand on the small of her back as he ushered her into the comfortable waiting room, and gave their names to the receptionist at the front desk. Glancing at Emma, he saw how closed and pinched her expression was, her arms folded across her middle as she seemed to be doing her damnedest not to meet his eye.

Within a few minutes they were called, and Nico accompanied her into the examining room, as much to support her as to hear the information himself. The obstetrician, a kindly faced woman with curly grey hair, smiled at them both, a slight query in her brown eyes as she looked between them.

'Signora Santini?' she asked, looking directly at Emma. 'How can I help you today?'

Emma shot Nico an uncertain glance before replying in a half-mumble, 'I just need a check-up, I suppose.'

'Of course.'

'And a paternity test,' Nico filled in, only to feel as if the temperature in the room had taken a sudden nosedive. Emma was staring down at her lap and the obstetrician was giving him a coldly bland look.

'I see,' she said.

'That is possible, is it not?' Nico pressed. 'The receptionist assured me—'

'It is possible,' the obstetrician agreed, in a tone that matched her decidedly cool expression. 'Now, if you don't mind, I will examine Signora Santini in private.'

'But—'

The obstetrician pointed to the door. 'You can wait outside. Thank you, *signor.*'

Nico stared at her, flummoxed, before realising he had no choice but to exit the examining room.

'Very well,' he said, and with a glance at Emma, who seemed determined not to look at him, he left the room.

Outside he paced the waiting room, unable to stand still, wondering why he'd been excluded from the appointment, and fuming that he had. The whole point of this exercise had been to be more involved, not less. To build trust. Instead he'd been shown the door as if he shouldn't have been there in the first place.

And all right, he understood that this was women's stuff, and maybe Emma would like some privacy if the OB was going to poke and prod. But he still didn't like being cut out, and it left him feeling distinctly edgy and irritable to be kept in the dark. Neither sensation abated when, half an hour later, Emma emerged from the office, pale-faced but composed, and still not looking at him.

'Well?' he asked, and she just gave a little shrug, folding her arms and looking away.

'The results of the tests will be available tomorrow,' the OB told him in that same cool voice she'd used before. 'Emma has agreed to share any medical information with you, so I'll email a full work-up of her blood tests, in addition to the matter of paternity.'

He supposed he should be satisfied with that, but he was still left with the feeling he'd done something wrong. 'Thank you,' Nico bit out, and then, taking Emma's arm, he ushered her outside to the waiting car.

CHAPTER EIGHT

WELL, THAT HAD been absolutely humiliating, on far too many fronts. Emma scooted to the far side of the car as Nico slid in next to her. She turned her face to the window, unable to bear even looking at him. She was trying not to feel so hurt, heaven knew, but it was hard. Very hard.

'I've booked The Ivy for lunch,' Nico informed her as the driver closed the door and they started off.

'I'd rather not,' Emma squeezed out through a throat that felt too tight. 'I'd rather just return to the hotel.'

'You need to eat.'

Which was true enough, as the obstetrician had told her, among other things, that she was more than a bit underweight. Emma had explained about the morning sickness, and the doctor had been sympathetic, but also stern, more so than the doctor at the free clinic she'd gone to before, who had barely looked at her medical files.

'Think about the baby,' she'd told her, and Emma had, for a few seconds, felt like bursting into either tears or hysterical laughter.

I am, she'd wanted to say. *Trust me, I am.*

'I'll get room service, then,' she said. 'And you can watch me eat it, if you're so worried. But I don't need to swank about The Ivy.'

'Swank about? Is that what we'd be doing?' Nico sounded caught between amusement and annoyance.

'Whatever.' She hunched a shoulder, keeping her gaze away from him.

'I also thought we could do some shopping,' Nico remarked mildly. 'For some new clothes. You only had a few things in your suitcase, and they did not seem entirely suitable.'

'I only had a few things, period.' He'd arranged to have her things brought from Will's last night, and, going through them, Emma had realised just how shabby they were— a couple of pairs of jeans and some T-shirts. She hadn't wanted to ask Will to pay for anything before they were married.

'What happened to the things I bought you?' Nico asked, his voice mild, yet with an undercurrent of steel. Before his accident, he'd taken her shopping in Rome, and she'd cautiously picked out a few things, hardly daring to believe he'd let her, not wanting to press her luck.

'I left them in Rome,' she told him, her gaze still on the window. 'There wasn't the opportunity to take them with me.'

'You mean because of Antonio?' Nico asked, and now his voice held a thrum of anger, although this time not for her, thankfully. She hoped, anyway.

'Pretty much,' Emma replied shortly. 'He showed me the door and didn't give me the option of going back for anything, so I didn't.'

'I'm sorry about that,' Nico said after a moment, his voice terse. 'But surely there's all the more reason to shop for new, then,' he added. He had the deliberately mild voice of someone who was determined to be patient but finding it trying. Well, her patience had been tried all morning. Excessively.

'Maybe later,' she forced out. 'No need to buy me clothes if the baby's not yours, after all, and we won't find that out until tomorrow.' She turned to him and bared her teeth in a saccharine smile. 'Best to wait, don't you think?'

Nico's breath came out in a rush as his eyes narrowed. 'Is *that* why you're in a snit...?'

Emma stiffened. 'I'm not in a *snit*.'

'Annoyed, then. In a mood. Whatever.' His words came out in short, sharp bursts. 'I told you, the paternity test was simply a precaution. The test results will be returned within twenty-four hours, and in the meantime—'

'Fine, then. Like I said, I can wait till then for some new clothes.' She turned back to the window, more so Nico couldn't see the tears that had stupidly sprung to her eyes.

'Emma—'

'I mean it, Nico.' She didn't think she could take any more of this pointless arguing, not when she felt so raw. So *flayed*. Everything about that appointment had been excruciating, from having Nico demand the paternity test, to the OB asking her all sorts of personal questions, including ones about the more difficult aspects of her childhood spent in care, making her feel like some sort of pathetic freak. The last thing she wanted to do was dine and shop like the gold-digger Nico still seemed to think she was. 'Please just take me back to the hotel.'

'Fine.' He rapped on the glass that separated them from the driver and then issued terse instructions to return to the hotel. They didn't speak for the rest of the journey.

Emma was out of the door as soon as the car had pulled up to the kerb, and she marched towards the hotel without waiting for Nico to catch up with her. All she wanted was to barricade herself in the bedroom, or wherever she could find some modicum of privacy. Unfortunately, he had the key card to work the lift, so she had to stand in front of the doors, silently fuming, while she waited for him to stroll up.

'This tantrum of yours is most unbecoming,' he remarked, and she swung around, fists bunched, ready to punch him—or maybe burst into tears.

'My *tantrum*? Haven't you insulted me enough for one day? Or do you have some kind of quota you have to fill?' Unfortunately the words of angry challenge were belied by the catch in her voice. Emma saw Nico's expression change from irritation to confusion before she looked away, blinking as fast as she could to keep the tears at bay. Stupid, *stupid* pregnancy hormones. That was all this had to be, because normally she was so much tougher than this. She'd had to be.

The lift door opened and Emma marched inside, turning away from Nico. He remained silent as the lift soared upwards, the seconds ticking onward endlessly. Did it normally take this long? Eighteen floors wasn't *that* many.

Then, finally, the doors opened and Emma hurried into the penthouse, ready to barricade herself in the bathroom, or wherever she could get the space to cry in private, because she realised that was what she was going to do, whether she wanted to or not. The tears were coming, blinking be damned, and she was afraid it wasn't just because of hormones.

'Emma.' Nico's voice was quiet. Gentle, which didn't help. Now she was really going to blub.

'Please,' she whispered, and found she couldn't manage any more.

'Please tell me what's going on,' he stated quietly. 'I've upset you, I realise, and I want to know why.'

'If you don't know why, then you're an idiot,' she retorted, her voice muffled with the effort of holding back her tears. One slipped down her cheek and she dashed it away as discreetly as she could.

'Then I'm an idiot. Let's talk this through, please.' Although his tone was still gentle, it was one that didn't brook argument. Autocratic even in this. Although, Emma realised, she didn't even want to argue, at least not entirely. In twenty-four hours, Nico was going to discover he was the father of her baby, which meant he was either going to want to stay married, at least in some shape or form, or demand custodial rights and do what she feared most—take her baby away from her.

She had to make sure they worked things out, for better or worse, for the sake of their child.

'Fine.' She dropped her bag onto a chair by the lift doors and then walked to one of the leather sofas and curled up in the corner, letting her hair swing down to hide her face. She needed *some* kind of armour. 'Let's talk.'

Nico stared at her for a moment. 'First, I'll order some food. You need to eat.'

'So you're always telling me.' She waited for him to make the call, but he handed her the menu first.

'What would you like?'

'You're not going to tell me what the best thing on the menu is?' she retorted, before she could rein in her temper. Now was not the time to score petty points, but maybe that was all part of it. His arrogance. His authority. For a month, when she'd felt as if she'd fallen into a fairy tale, it had been more or less okay. But for the rest of her life? *For her baby's life?*

'I think you can decide for yourself what you want to eat.' The smile he gave her was wry, and it calmed her a bit, because it showed he was learning, if just a little. He could change, at least in this small way, or at least act as if he could change. It was small comfort, but it *was* still comfort, and she'd take that where she could find it.

'I'll have the soup and salad, please.' She handed him back the menu and he made the call, ordering a steak and salad for himself. With that out of the way, there was nothing for them to do but stare at each other and wait for one or the other to begin.

Nico sat on the sofa opposite her, loose-limbed and attentive, his green gaze steady on her. Even now she couldn't help but marvel at how breathtakingly attractive he was. That jaw. Those eyes. The hooded brows, the dark hair, the smell of his aftershave…

Focus, Emma.

'All right,' Nico said. 'Now, will you please tell me what has upset you?'

Emma took a deep breath and let it out slowly. She angled her head up to stare at the ceiling because looking at him suddenly felt too hard, and it might keep the tears from slipping down her cheeks. They were definitely pooling in her eyes, so blinking was clearly not an option.

'Nico, do you have any idea,' she began slowly, 'can you even imagine, how absolutely humiliating it is for the father of your baby to inform an obstetrician that he's there for a paternity test? *He* is, clearly not both of you, because he is the only one with the doubts about who you slept with. And then to face a whole bunch of questions after you'd left the room, to make sure I hadn't been coerced into the marriage, or was being abused, or anything like that.'

As well as questions she wasn't going to tell him about, about how she'd been treated as a child, why she had signs of malnutrition, of broken bones that hadn't been healed. Emma had explained as quickly as she could about being in care, about how some families weren't as nice as others.

And even the nice ones let you down.

'Well?' Emma asked when Nico was silent for a long moment. She couldn't risk taking her gaze from the ceiling, although she realised she was curious—and more than a little apprehensive—to know what his expression was. The silence felt ominous the longer it ticked on. What was he thinking, and, if she dared to look at him, would she be able to tell from those hooded eyes, that still face?

'Framed like that,' he answered at last, his voice low and level, 'it seems like it would be more humiliating for me than for you. Or at least more revealing. I'm not exactly thrilled that the OB thought I might be some kind of abuser.'

Emma let out a huff of humourless laughter. 'Yet I'm the one who had to answer all those questions, and who felt like some—some floozy who has lost track of the men she's slept with.' Among other things. The pity in the doctor's eyes when she'd explained about her childhood still made her cringe.

'Emma, you're not some *floozy*. I know that.'

'Then why did you insist on the test?' She lowered her gaze to look at him, anger thankfully taking the place of hurt, so the tears didn't fall.

He hesitated, before answering carefully, 'Considering I walked into your wedding, is it not at least a little understandable why I might need some tangible proof?'

She blew out a breath. 'I explained about Will and me,' she reminded him, trying to sound as reasonable as he was. 'How we were friends. I didn't have a ton of options, you know, Nico—'

'I do know that.' A weary sigh escaped him as he rubbed a hand over his face. 'Emma, trust me, I do know. At least, I understand. I had no idea my cousin acted the way he did until you told me about it, and he certainly didn't give that impression to me, but I believe you. I'm… I'm not judging you, for wanting to marry Will, all things considered.'

Her eyebrows arched as she stared at him in disbelief. 'Really? Because you certainly seemed to be right up until this very—'

'I apologise.' He spoke stiffly as he dropped his hand from his face. Now he didn't look angry or annoyed, but weary. Vulnerable, even, although Emma tried to steel herself against feeling too much sympathy. Softer emotions were not for her, pregnancy hormones or not. 'The truth is,' Nico said, his voice a low rumble, 'this paternity test was as much about me, as it was about you, if not...if not more so.'

'What?' Emma stared at him blankly. She had no idea what that was supposed to mean.

'I felt that I have to be absolutely sure I'm the father of this baby,' he continued, 'because...' He paused, took a breath, and then continued resolutely, 'Because my father wasn't sure about me.'

Emma gaped at him, shocked into silence. She had not been expecting *that*. 'What...?' she finally said, not even sure what question she was trying to ask.

'My father questioned my paternity,' Nico explained tonelessly, not quite looking at her. 'Although I only discovered that recently. He learned that he wasn't actually my biological father fairly recently, as well, but as I said he always had his suspicions...and he made it known, in his own way, all through my childhood.'

Nico glanced away from the stunned look on Emma's face, wishing he hadn't admitted so much, and yet knowing he'd had to, for her sake. He couldn't let her go on believing this had simply been about him not trusting her. It was himself he didn't trust, if she could ever even understand that. He might have masked it as a distrust of her, it was true, but at its root this was about him. His vulnerability and insecurity, something he'd never wanted to admit to her, to anyone, yet for her sake he had to.

'I didn't know that,' Emma said quietly, and somehow Nico managed to dredge up a wry smile.

'I know you didn't, because I never told you before.'

'I suppose,' she said slowly, 'there are a lot of things we don't know about each other.'

'We only knew each other a month,' he agreed, which was another reason for the paternity test, although not nearly as pressing as the doubts that clamoured inside himself. He never wanted his own child to feel the way he had. He never wanted to have the doubts his father had had, although he hoped he would be a better man and not show it the way his father had, in a thousand tiny, cutting ways, over and over again through the years.

'Why...?' Emma asked slowly. 'Why did your father have such doubts about you?'

'Because my mother had an affair around the time I was conceived.' He swallowed hard, fighting the urge to shift in his seat, because none of this was easy. Saying it all aloud brought back all of the painful memories, made him remember just how much they had hurt. His mother's halting admission, on her deathbed, so he'd felt as if he were losing her in more ways than one. How she'd always suspected but never told him, never helped him to understand why his father had been cold to him his whole life. He remembered his father's icily disdainful expression, his utter refusal to be moved. 'I didn't know about it until recently, as it happened,' he told Emma. 'I believe I told you my mother had died shortly before I met you?'

'Yes, a few months before.' Emma's face was already softening in sympathy, and Nico found he had to look away.

'She told me on her deathbed,' he forced out. 'She wanted to make it right somehow, but in some ways, I wish she'd never said a word, or maybe she'd told me a lot sooner, to help me to understand. I confronted my father, who admitted he had always had his doubts. I insisted we have a paternity test done as soon as possible, and so we did.' He swallowed. 'The results were conclusive. I was the product of an affair.'

He struggled not to close his eyes against the onslaught of that painful memory—his father's hardened expression, the way he'd turned away, dismissing him utterly. *I've always known, really.*

'Oh, Nico.' The gentle sorrow in her voice was nearly his undoing. 'I'm so sorry.'

He shrugged. 'In the end, it didn't change very much. Considering the situation, I offered to step aside as CEO of Santini Enterprises. Antonio is his blood relation and he would be just as good at the job, and I have my own business interests as it is. It seemed logical, but my father refused.' He let out a long, low breath. 'He said he didn't want to encourage speculation, which would be humiliating for him.' It had always, Nico had realised then, been about his father's pride. Not about him. Not even about Antonio, who had fumed at being passed over.

'And your relationship?' Emma asked after a moment. 'With your father? Did that…?'

Nico shrugged. 'It is what it is, what it has always been. Distant to the point of being non-existent, if I'm perfectly honest.' He paused, wondering whether to admit more, then deciding Emma deserved it. 'I tried to win his love when I was younger, did everything I could, but none of it was ever enough.' Getting good grades, always on his best behaviour, waiting by the window for his father to come home… and then later, as an adult, working all hours God gave him to prove himself, without ever understanding that it was a Sisyphean task. That he would never, ever be able to prove himself to his father. 'I stopped a long time ago,' he told Emma, although it hadn't been long enough. And even when he'd stopped trying, the feeling had persisted—that he wasn't good enough, he wasn't worthy of love. No, he wasn't about to make those kinds of admissions to Emma right now. There was being honest, and then there was being stupid. Pathetic.

He'd told himself that at least he now knew why his father had always acted as if he didn't love him. Surely that was better than always wondering, always trying and failing, again and again.

'And your cousin?' Emma asked after a moment, her tone turning probing yet cautious. 'What about your relationship with him?'

Nico shrugged. 'We were close when we were younger, as we're both only children, and we were raised almost as brothers. Antonio is my father's sister's son, and she died when he was a teenager, so he came into our family.' And his father loved Antonio more than he loved him, Nico knew. Antonio had Santini blood in his veins while he did not. Something else that shouldn't hurt any more, all things considered, but it did. 'Later, though, we grew apart, and more so when my paternity was revealed. Antonio wanted to step in as CEO, and my father refused.'

He turned to Emma, who was frowning, seeming lost in thought, her arms wrapped around her knees. 'Why are you asking?' he asked, because she was looking strangely hesitant and uncertain, as if she wanted to say more but wasn't sure she dared. In response to his question, she only nibbled her lip. Didn't speak. Unease deepened inside him, churning his gut. 'Emma?'

'It's…' She hesitated, and Nico had that tickling sensation he'd had before, at the back of his brain, when he'd been trying to remember something that had been eluding him. Was it about Emma? *Emma and Antonio?* But she'd only met him after his alleged death, and Antonio had sent her off. Hadn't he? Why was his mind spiralling out of control, into suspicion? What had he forgotten?

No, he needed to stop jumping to conclusions, fearing the worst because it had happened with his father. Not everyone was so untrustworthy, so unloving, and yet Emma…

Could he really trust her?

'Emma, what is it?' he demanded roughly.

A sigh escaped and she rested her forehead on her knees. Nico felt as if his stomach were suddenly coated in ice, his lungs frozen so it hurt to breathe. What on earth was she finding it so difficult to tell him? What more could there be?

'It's about Antonio,' she said at last. 'Something he said.'

'Something he said? What can you possibly mean? What happened between you and Antonio?' His tone came out cold, to hide his fear, and Emma lifted her head, glaring at him even as she let out one of her old, irrepressible laughs.

'Please tell me you are not actually thinking there was something going on between me and Antonio?' she demanded. 'Because that would, frankly, be completely paranoid and weird, not to mention totally absurd.'

Even though he was still feeling icy inside, Nico managed a laugh. 'Point taken.'

Emma shook her head slowly. 'Why don't you trust me, Nico?'

He shifted in his seat, feeling skewered by her soft, wounded gaze. 'I told you, this is as much about me as it is about you.'

'Is it?' She sighed, clearly not convinced. 'Well, as it happens, I haven't been sure I can trust you. Because of what your cousin said to me at your memorial service.'

'What Antonio said?' He sat up straight, frowning as he searched her resolute yet resigned expression. 'Something more than you've already told me, you mean?'

She took a deep breath, let it out slowly. 'He said he didn't want me sticking around because you'd told him that you'd been tiring of me already. That you'd looked into an annulment or divorce before you'd headed to the Maldives, and if I knew what was good for me, I'd take the money he offered me gratefully and never come sniffing round him or any of the other Santinis again, because I certainly wouldn't get anything more out of any of you.'

'He said…' Nico's mind was spinning. 'He said I was tiring of you?'

'Yes.' She tilted her chin at that stubbornly determined angle. 'And frankly there was no real reason for me not to believe it. We'd only been married a week, you worked for much of that time, and kept me stuck in your flat without introducing me to anyone, or even telling people you were married, as far as I could see.'

Nico blinked, because he certainly hadn't looked at it that way before. 'It was early days—'

'Sometimes I wondered if you were ashamed of me,' she confessed quietly. 'To be honest, I wouldn't blame you if you were. I was never going to fit into your crowd. But you asked me to marry you so suddenly… I wondered if you'd had cause to regret such an impulsive decision.'

'I had not been looking into either an annulment or divorce,' he stated flatly. He might not remember everything, but he was sure of that.

'But did you regret it?' she challenged. 'Honestly, I wouldn't blame you if you had.'

Expelling a shaky breath, Nico passed a hand over his eyes. He felt pain throb at his temples, like a jungle beat, promising the arrival of a migraine. He strove to keep it at bay. 'I don't know exactly what I thought before I left for the Maldives,' he admitted. 'I can't remember.'

'So you might have been considering a divorce—'

'No, I'm sure of that.' He spoke firmly, while Emma just looked at him, shaking her head slowly.

'Nico, how could you possibly be sure, if you can't remember?'

'Because…because when I woke up from the coma, you were the first face I saw in my mind's eye. The first person I remembered.' He looked away, embarrassed by the admission. He'd never meant to tell her that, to admit to such weakness—that he'd been fixated on a fairy tale while she'd viewed the whole world—and him—with clear-eyed pragmatism.

Emma was silent for a long moment, and he turned back to her, waiting for her response. 'I'm not sure that makes much difference,' she said at last, her voice small and sad. 'What you thought you remembered isn't the same as what really happened.'

'But if we don't know what really happened—'

'Nico, I meant what I said before,' she cut across him quietly, 'that we barely know each other. We only had a month together before the plane crash, and it was a month out of time, out of reality. You don't really know me, know my past, where I've been, what I've done, or even what I'm capable of, and I don't really know any of that about you. With that in mind, I can understand why you didn't trust me, why you would want a paternity test…but can't you understand why I find it hard to trust you?'

Nico stared at her for a long moment, her heartfelt words thudding through him. His head was really starting to ache now, as it often had since the accident, that strange, tickling sensation at the back of his brain worse than ever. Even as he acknowledged the truth of her sentiments, he had a niggling feeling that this would all make more sense if he could just remember…

Remember what?

'Nico?' Emma prompted softly.

'Yes, of course,' he allowed, forcing his mind back to

what she'd said, even as his head continued to ache and throb. 'All things considered, I understand what you mean. Our marriage was, it's true, a bit…rushed and abrupt, and we might have both had regrets, but that doesn't change the reality now.'

A small smile played with her mouth, although her eyes were still filled with worry and sorrow. 'Why *did* you marry me, so suddenly, as it happens? I might not know you very well, but it still seems out of character, and you'd made it clear at the beginning that we were only having an affair.'

Yes, he'd set those parameters as he always did, to guard his heart. Too bad it hadn't worked. 'Well.' He cleared his throat. 'I suppose it *was* something of an impulse decision.'

'Yes, clearly, but why?'

Why not be honest about this, as he had been before? Clearly there had been too many secrets in their short-lived relationship, and truth was needed for trust. 'I asked you right after I found out that I wasn't my father's son,' he confessed. 'It was a shock, even though in retrospect it shouldn't have been. And I suppose I wanted to feel…connected…with someone. To be part of a family again, in some way.'

Her eyes widened and her mouth parted softly in surprise. Nico looked away. Why had he said so much? It made him sound completely pathetic, as if he'd been begging for affection wherever he could find it.

'That phone call…before you came out on the balcony, when you asked me…that was your father? Telling you—'

'Yes, he was giving me the results of the paternity test.' His chest felt tight, and his head was aching abominably now, a thundering in his temples he longed to assuage. He needed to lie down in a dark room, preferably with a cold cloth over his eyes, but first he needed to finish this conversation. He knew how important it was. 'He said it wasn't a surprise, that he'd always been sure, deep down, that I wasn't his, and it didn't change anything for him—meaning, unfortunately, that he had no interest in having a relationship with me.'

'And that was why…' she whispered, shaking her head.

'The next day, before we married, I went to see him. I told him I'd resign, and that was when he refused. We were married that afternoon.' Put like that, it sounded strangely stark, and Emma seemed to think so too, judging by her bleak expression.

She let out a soft laugh, but the sound only held sadness as she looked down at her lap. 'None of it was about me at all, was it?' she surmised quietly. 'I shouldn't be surprised, of course, and I'm not, not really, but…you were right, Nico, when you said this was about you more than it was about me. I just didn't realise quite how much.'

And even though he'd meant that as a reassurance, he saw it wasn't now. She only looked hurt, that his marriage proposal hadn't been because she'd bowled him over, but because he'd been lashing out in his pain. And yet she had affected him more than any other woman…

'Emma…' He pressed his hands to his temples, trying to relieve the pressure that was building there. His stomach churned and his vision was starting to tunnel.

'It's okay, Nico. At least now we know where we were, as well as where we are now. Or,' she corrected with a crooked smile, 'you will when you get the results of the paternity test tomorrow.'

Nico swore softly as he dropped his hands from his head. 'I don't need the results. Not any more.'

'Don't you?'

Yes, damn it, he did, but for *his* sake. Couldn't she see that? Why did it feel as if he was damned one way, condemned another? There was no winning.

'This can be a fresh start,' he insisted, gritting his teeth against the pain in his head. 'For both of us.'

'A fresh start?' She laughed again, once more without humour, but at least it had more life in it, more spirit. 'And what will that look like, exactly?'

'We can decide together.' That was important to him. 'But as to how it will look…' Hell if he knew, he realised. They were still virtual strangers. How were they supposed to figure this out? And his *head*…

He sat back, letting out a breath as his temples continued to throb. He'd been hoping to stave off the migraine, but it was galloping towards him now, pulling him under. He had a few minutes, maybe only a few seconds, before it engulfed him completely. 'We'll figure it out,' he managed, 'and I promise you, I will always promise you, I will provide for you. I will keep you safe—' He stopped as the pain took over and he felt himself sagging forward onto the floor. He tried to hold himself upright, but the pain was too much, his vision going black, and the last thing he heard was Emma's startled cry.

CHAPTER NINE

'NICO.'

Emma dropped to her knees in front of Nico's prone body as his eyelids fluttered closed. Why hadn't she realised he was in pain? She could see it now, in the greyness of his skin, the beads of sweat on his forehead, the way he was clenching his jaw. She'd been reeling from everything he'd told her, all the implications tumbling through her mind, and so she hadn't seen what was right in front of her face. There was a lesson in that, surely, but right now she didn't have time to ponder it.

'Are you hurt?' she demanded, smoothing his hair back from his damp forehead. He forced his eyes open to gaze at her blearily. 'Can you tell me what's wrong?'

'Migraine,' he forced out through pale lips. He grimaced as his eyes closed again. 'I'm sorry, but I think… I think I might be sick.'

Emma scrambled up and ran to the kitchen that was along one wall of the open space. Flinging open cupboards, she found a bowl and brought it back just in time for Nico to retch helplessly into it.

'This is bonding, isn't it?' she told him on a shaky laugh, determined to see the bright side of things. 'First, I was the one who was sick, and now you are. I suppose it will be my turn again next. Where's your handkerchief when you need it?'

'In…my right-hand pocket,' he managed in a croaky whisper.

She laughed again, softly, and reached for the small square of cotton, dabbing his lips with it. He smiled faintly and her heart twisted, a sharp pain beneath her breastbone.

Don't start now, Emma, she cautioned herself. *Don't start falling for him again, just because he smiles at you.*

After the emotional whirlwind of the last twenty-four hours, that was the last thing she needed. She had to keep a cool head. Her heart, too.

'Are you going to be sick again?' she asked gently, and he shook his head.

'I don't think so…thankfully.'

'Do you have any painkillers or medication?'

He nodded and then managed, 'It's in my washbag, in the bathroom. A brown bottle.'

'I'll get it.'

She found it easily enough, noting the prescription was to be taken as needed, in the case of migraines. Back in the living room, Nico had tried to ease himself into a sitting position, only to slump back down again, with a grimace. He had to hate being seen as so weak, Emma realised with a wry pang. She might not know a lot about him, but she knew he was a proud man, and he'd admitted a lot to her today. A lot of weakness and vulnerability. She realised it made him more appealing to her, not less, as he might have thought. As to their future…well, she couldn't think about that just yet.

'Let me help you to bed.'

'I can do it—'

'No,' she replied with a laugh and a shake of her head,

'you really can't. Not unless you want to crawl there on your hands and knees. Let me help you, Nico.'

With no real choice but to acquiesce, he nodded, and she was able to help him to his feet as he struggled to manage as much as he could on his own, even though his face was taut with pain, his whole body tense. Somehow, with one arm around his shoulders and another around his waist, Emma managed to help him stumble to bed. He collapsed on top of the sheets with a groan as she took off his shoes, unbuttoned his shirt and trousers while he gazed up at her through half-closed lids.

'Are you ravishing me, Signora Santini?' he asked, his voice slightly slurred from the pain, as well as, no doubt, the heavy medication he'd been given that was now kicking in.

She laughed as she slid his trousers from his legs, admittedly enjoying the feeling of his powerful thighs and taut calves under her hands. He had a beautiful, powerful body, even if he seemed weak as a kitten now. 'I'd certainly have to be the one to ravish you rather than the other way round, considering the state of you right now,' she teased as she dropped his trousers onto the floor.

He gazed up at her through half-closed lids, wearing only his boxers and unbuttoned shirt, his tautly muscled chest visible through the parted fabric. He looked as sexy as a male centrefold, Emma acknowledged, even with his grey, pain-filled face.

'You could let me try, at least...' he mumbled, reaching one hand up to her before it fell slackly to his side.

'Some try, Casanova.' Emma brushed a lock of hair from his forehead, disarmed by his obvious vulnerability and even more dismayed by her own reaction to it—a sudden, surprising welling up of tenderness. It had been better, she realised, when he'd been arrogant and angry, because it had been much easier to keep her distance. Or even when she'd worried she couldn't trust him—because she knew she did now. She trusted him and she *liked* him, and she knew she really couldn't afford to feel that way. Not now, and not ever. Letting someone in was too risky. She knew that, and so, it seemed, did Nico. They'd both, in their own ways, been hurt by their families, by the love they'd offered but hadn't had accepted. She didn't think either of them wanted to risk in the same way again. If they were going to stay married, it was going to have to be one strictly of convenience, no tender emotions involved.

Which was a much-needed reminder in this particular moment.

'You should sleep,' she said as she pulled the duvet up over him and, with his eyes fluttering closed once more, he reached out to her, encircling her wrist with his fingers, the touch enough to cause a shower of sparks racing all the way up her arm, a swift blaze of yearning to start in her centre. Maybe she would ravish him after all…

'Stay with me?' he asked, his voice low and rough, and her desire melted into something deeper. Something dangerous that she kept trying to steel herself against.

'But you need to sleep…'

'Please?'

It was the please that did it, the unabashed yearning in his voice. 'Yes, all right,' she said, and he pulled her towards him until she fitted against him, her head on his shoulder, the steady thud of his heart beneath her cheek, her body curled into his. They'd lain like this during their one month together, she remembered, and every time it had been bittersweet.

Bitter, because she'd tried to caution herself against feeling too much, trusting too much, and sweet because he'd made her feel safe and wanted and even loved. There hadn't been love involved, not really, she *knew* that, and, more importantly, there wouldn't be this time, either.

But could they forge some kind of future together, for the sake of their child? Could they learn to get along, to like one another, to be a family? Could she trust him with her child, if not her heart?

Maybe she could, she thought sleepily, her eyes fluttering closed as she snuggled closer to Nico. Maybe, if they both kept their heads—and definitely their hearts—this could work out. It could work out wonderfully.

Nico lowered his phone as he stared out at the hazy blue sky, the city shimmering under the late morning sunlight.

'Your wife is really rather unwell, Signor Santini. Something simply must be done.'

The OB's words, spoken so censoriously, still rang in his ears. She hadn't added *and that's your fault*, but she might as well have done. He certainly felt it was.

What had he been thinking, dragging Emma around the city, forcing pointless confrontations, when she was pregnant, tired and emotionally overwrought? And, as the OB had told him, underweight, seriously anaemic, and with high blood pressure. He'd thought she'd looked a little pale and gaunt when he'd first seen her, but he'd had no idea of the seriousness of the situation. And now he needed to rectify it. Immediately.

He took a deep breath and squared his shoulders, doing his best to banish the remnants of yesterday's headache that still lingered at his temples. He'd slept for sixteen hours straight, right around the clock, waking this morning to an empty bed and the phone ringing—the OB telling him what she'd learned about Emma, all of it alarming and even disturbing. He'd had no idea about so much…and, he realised, he still didn't, at least not entirely. Not enough. But he wanted to.

He ran a hand through his shower-damp hair and turned to the bedroom door, needing to find Emma.

'You're finally up,' she said from her seat at the breakfast bar. She'd been flicking through one of the designer magazines the hotel provided but she pushed it aside now, smiling tentatively as he came into the room. For a second, a memory of sleepy warmth, her body snugly next to his, had lingered in his mind like the vestiges of a dream. Had she slept in the bed with him, cuddled up together? She might have, but he couldn't really remember; the medication had knocked him out.

Right now what he could remember, all too clearly, was how she'd seen him—weak, sick, *being* sick, stumbling to bed. Hardly his best self, and yet somehow she was still smiling as she looked at him, and things between them felt easier. Less tense, even though the OB's warning words still weighed heavily in his gut.

'I'm sorry I slept so long,' he said as he went to the kitchen area to pour himself some coffee. Emma twisted around in her seat to track him with her gaze.

'I'm glad you did,' she said. 'You needed it, clearly.'

'You need your sleep, too.' He turned to face her, leaning against the counter as he cradled his coffee cup. She looked fresh-faced and artless this morning, her hair piled on top of her head in a messy bun, wearing a long, loose sundress with a button-down shirt open over it, yet he still saw how pale she seemed, and how thin, her wrists poking out from the cuffs of her shirt. 'The OB called me just now,' he told her.

'She did?' Emma's sunny, open expression immediately turned guarded, alert, in a way that made him feel both guilty and sad. 'Why did she call you, and not me?'

'Because she wanted to yell at me, I think.' He smiled wryly and her expression lightened, just a little, which made him glad. 'She's emailing you the results of all the tests, as she said she would yesterday.'

'There's only one test that really matters though, isn't there?' She didn't speak with any rancour or bitterness, but Nico felt it all the same. No matter how he'd explained how demanding the paternity test really had been about him, he knew it had hurt her, just as he knew he was sorry for that. Sorrier than he'd expected to be, considering what he'd just learned.

'That test was conclusive,' he replied quietly. 'I am the baby's father, as you told me, and as I really knew all along.' He might have jumped to conclusions because it had felt easier, or at least stronger, to be angry rather than hurt, but the reality was, he knew, that he'd never truly doubted Emma. 'I'm sorry for questioning you,' he told her.

She let out one of her irrepressible laughs, her mouth twitching. 'An apology! I'm so honoured.'

He frowned, because she made it sound as if he never said sorry, and he did, surely... 'I apologise when I'm in the wrong,' he told her, although it came out just a little bit like a question.

'Which obviously isn't very often, then,' Emma returned tartly, even though she was still smiling. 'I think that's the first one I've heard.'

'Is it?' He blinked at her, surprised, and she laughed again.

'Perhaps this is the time for a bit of self-awareness, then,' she teased. 'You do have the habit of being a bit...autocratic. Dare I say it...arrogant?' She bit her lip, widening her eyes, and while he knew she was just teasing—sort of—there was more than a sting of truth in her words.

He really had been riding a wave of self-righteous fury,

Nico acknowledged, ever since he'd walked into her wedding—or maybe, he realised with a jolt, even before that. When he'd taken her away from that restaurant, swept her up into his own privileged world, he'd felt like her rescuer. He'd liked showering her with attention and gifts, having her look up to him, dependent on him, even a little bit in awe. He certainly hadn't treated her like an equal partner in their short-lived marriage—as Emma had pointed out, he hadn't introduced her to anyone, hadn't tried to really include her in his life. Hadn't even thought of it.

The knowledge was uncomfortable, shaming. Maybe it was a result of a childhood of never feeling as if he could do or be enough to his father, but he'd definitely enjoyed being Emma's everything, for a little while. Making himself the centre of her world, because he'd never been that before. But was that how any relationship, never mind a marriage, was really supposed to be?

'Nico?' she prompted. 'You are frowning pretty ferociously. You know I was kidding, right? Well.' Her smile widened. 'Sort of, anyway.'

'Right.' He was frowning, Nico knew, because having these realisations about himself really wasn't comfortable, even if it was necessary. 'Well, then, I'm sorry I haven't been willing to admit when I'm wrong,' he told her. 'There—that's two sorrys in the space of a few minutes, so consider yourself doubly honoured.'

She grinned at him, eyes dancing. 'Must be a record.'

'Must be.' He took a sip of his coffee, trying to order his thoughts for the conversation he knew they needed to have. He'd marched in here, about to tell Emma his plans—that he was taking her away, taking care of her as she so clearly needed, and all without her having so much as a say in it. Suddenly that didn't seem like such a good idea.

'The OB mentioned a few other things,' he told her at

last, choosing his words with care. 'She'll tell the same to you, but she told me because she felt I should do something about it.'

'I did tell her she could share my medical records with you,' Emma replied with a defiant shrug, although her expression had turned wary. 'I had nothing to hide.'

'I know.' Nothing to hide, but there were still things she hadn't told him. Hadn't wanted to tell him, perhaps, because like him she didn't like sharing what seemed to be weaknesses. Admitting vulnerability.

'So, do something about what?' Emma straightened in her chair, her gaze serious.

'Your health.' He came to sit next to her at the table, regarding her sombrely. 'You're worryingly underweight, apparently, as well as anaemic. And the OB believes you've been stressed, which isn't good for the baby, obviously.' And there were other things she'd told him too, things from her childhood that made him ache. Made him want to protect Emma with everything he had. Everything he was.

'Oh. Wow.' Emma folded her arms, hunching her shoulders. 'Well, I knew I was a little bit underweight from when I went to the clinic a couple of weeks ago, because of the morning sickness, but that is getting better, now that I'm starting the second trimester.' She sounded defensive, a little hurt, and that made him ache all the more.

'The OB wasn't blaming you, Emma, and I'm not, either.' He realised that was where she was going with this, and it was not the takeaway he intended at all. 'If anything, I'm blaming myself. I marched in here and dragged you around and didn't think about your condition—'

'You didn't know about my condition at first, and, in any case, it's only been a couple of days. I was underweight and I guess anaemic before you came on the scene, Nico, so you don't need to blame yourself.' She rallied, cocking her head as she gave him a teasing smile even though she still looked worried. 'That's the other side of arrogance—you think everything is your fault.' She tapped his chest playfully. 'The world does not revolve around you, you know.'

'I know.' But he'd wanted it to, he realised. Was that why he'd been so determined to be with Emma, to marry her? Because after his parents' revelations, he'd wanted to be the centre of someone's world, and he'd known from the start that she was alone and vulnerable. It hardly put him in an admirable light, but at least he was aware of it now. He could choose to be different; he could choose for their relationship to be different. Instead of being the centre of Emma's world, she could be the centre of his. Emma and their child. Nothing else, he knew, was as important as they were.

'The main thing now,' he told her, 'is to get you healthy again. Give you time to rest, relax, eat good food and grow our baby.' And recover in ways he hadn't realised she'd needed to.

Her pupils flared and a small smile touched her mouth. 'You sound rather protective all of a sudden.'

'I feel protective.' She had no idea of just how much.

'All right, then.' She shrugged. 'I promise I'll eat better. Where's my prenatal vitamin?'

She was teasing, but he was utterly serious. 'They're being delivered this morning, along with some iron pills for the anaemia. But I was thinking of taking a few more proactive steps, Emma.'

She raised her eyebrows, looking uncertain and trying to hide it with her usual spirited insouciance. 'Such as?'

He hesitated, and then admitted, 'I have a villa on a private island in the Mediterranean. It's a very peaceful place, completely secluded. I thought we could go there for a few weeks. You could rest and recover, and so could I, for that matter. As you saw yesterday, I'm not completely over the effects of the accident.'

'How is your head?' she asked, reaching one hand out as if to touch him but then dropping it before she did. He wished she hadn't; he welcomed her touch.

'It's a lot better than it was yesterday, but I think we could both use a bit of a break. And…it could be a chance to get to know one another properly. Because even though we're married, you were right when you said we barely knew each other. That month we had together was a bit surreal, wasn't it?' He smiled crookedly. Surreal, yes, but also wonderful, in its own way. Now, however, was the time for reality… however that looked. However it felt.

She smiled uncertainly, her gaze scanning his face, as if looking for clues. 'Okay, so we stay on your island for a few weeks. Then what?'

Then what, indeed. 'That's up for discussion,' Nico answered slowly, although he knew now what he wanted. 'We're married, and we're going to be a family. How that looks is up to both of us.'

'Wow, have you been taking a class or something?' Emma teased, and Nico shook his head, smiling.

'No, but you've been schooling me, I guess.'

'Ha.' She shook her head back at him as they smiled at each other, and it felt both silly and rather wonderful. Nico eased back, determined to stay logical. Pragmatic. He wanted to do this right, and that meant not engaging his emotions too much.

'Well.' Emma looked down at the floor, a tendril of wavy golden-brown hair falling in front of her face, obscuring her expression from his view. 'I suppose I don't really know the answer to that.' She glanced up, peeping at him from behind her hair. 'What do *you* want it to look like?'

Nico sat back, considering the question. 'Santini Enterprises is based in Rome, so I'll need to be there for work on occasion, but once the baby comes, I suppose we'd want more space than a flat in the city.'

'Even though that flat is palatial,' she teased.

'Maybe you want to be involved in choosing our home,' Nico suggested. 'We could buy somewhere new, something you've picked yourself.' He liked the idea. A fresh start, away from his family, the memories, everything. A fresh start for the two of them, whatever that ended up looking like.

'I could pick?' She sounded so incredulous that Nico glanced at her, frowning.

'Well, we'd pick together, I suppose, but why not?'

She shook her head slowly. 'It's just… I've never…' She let out a rather wobbly laugh. 'I've never had my own home before.'

'You haven't?' His frown deepened as he realised again how little he actually knew about her, although he was starting to understand, or at least to guess, with the glimmers of knowledge both the doctor and Emma herself had given him about the lack in her childhood—lack of love and, it seemed, lack of even basic care. Evidence of cruelty too, which infuriated and saddened him in equal measure. But, he reminded himself, things could be different now. For Emma, for him, for them. And a few weeks on a private island together would give them abundant opportunity to get to know each other—in every way possible.

CHAPTER TEN

ONCE AGAIN, just as she had when she'd first met—and married—Nico Santini, Emma felt the need to pinch herself. To scrunch her eyes shut and then open them wide again, to make sure this wasn't all a glorious dream that was going to evaporate as soon as she looked at it too closely.

'Make yourself comfortable,' Nico said as he strolled into the main cabin area of the Santini private jet. He'd told her he usually travelled business class for environmental reasons, but he'd used Santini Enterprises' private plane to get to Los Angeles as quickly as possible, and now they needed to take it back again, to Rome. To her new life.

A shiver of both excitement and apprehension rippled through her at the thought. Everything had moved so quickly, it was hard to believe it was only forty-eight hours since Nico had interrupted her wedding, twenty-four since he had done something of an about-turn, becoming consideration itself, kindness personified...just as he'd been when they'd first met.

Back then she'd told herself to be cautious, even as she'd ridden the wave of luxury and pleasure, let herself enjoy it all because it had been so utterly different from the rest of her life, and she'd been sure it would end eventually... which it had. Second time round she fully intended to be more cautious, more careful. Things could change on a dime, and yet...

It was hard not to buy into the fantasy, the fairy tale, at least a little. Hard not to want something she'd never had, and yet she knew she needed to keep herself from it, if she could. Stay smart and safe, because while Nico seemed intent on building a new life together, Emma intended to remain guarded, at least a little. Guard her heart, if she could, because she knew how much it hurt when you tried to love someone and they let you down. Time and time again, from her mother when she was a baby to the foster mum who turned away to the man, years ago, when she'd been reeling from leaving care—they'd all walked away without a backward glance while you were left gasping and shattered.

'Emma? No, absolutely not. Sorry...that was never going to be a possibility.'

Her foster mother's words, and her firm and certain tone, still haunted her in her weaker moments, when she remembered how much she'd hoped, *believed*... And for nothing. Always for nothing.

It had been the same with Eric, the man she'd convinced herself she loved simply because she'd wanted to *be* loved. A brief fling, and he'd left her without a thought. She'd tried to act as if she hadn't cared, hoping that maybe then she wouldn't.

All those painful experiences had taught her a hard yet necessary lesson, and she knew now that she most definitely wasn't ever going to open herself up to that kind of pain again. Since Nico didn't seem to want to either, she hoped they really could make this work. Or so she kept telling herself.

'This plane is amazing,' she remarked, running her hand over the buttery leather of a built-in sofa on one side of the main cabin, facing another sofa, a low coffee table between them, with a bowl of exotic-looking fruit its centrepiece.

'I'll give you the full tour before we take off.' He smiled

at her, and she tried to ignore the fizzing sensation in her stomach the mere curve of his lips caused. *That* was an aspect of their marriage she was both looking forward to and feeling extremely apprehensive about, because she knew when Nico touched her she forgot everything, especially how to guard her heart, and she needed to stay careful. Controlled. As soon as he touched her, all her resolutions could be blown to smithereens, and where would that leave her?

Nowhere she wanted to be.

'Sure,' she told him, smiling back, trying to ignore that fizzing, the way his jade gaze lingered on her, making her body heat, her blood surge, and her mind remember how it had been between them before. 'That would be great.'

'Come on, then.' He kept one hand on the small of her back—his palm searing her through the thin material of her T-shirt—as he guided her to the back of the plane. 'This is the study,' he said, opening a door to a room with a large desk and a couple of leather club chairs, a wall lined with bookshelves.

'I feel like I'm on Air Force One,' she told him, not altogether joking. The private plane was really like nothing she'd ever seen before, nothing she could even imagine. She'd had a month of living in Nico's luxurious world, but it had never felt as real and permanent as it did now, on their way to his private island. A whole island, to himself. Even after the luxury hotels and flats from before, this was definitely next level.

'It's convenient for work,' he replied with a shrug.

'Do you know, I don't even know what you really do for Santini Enterprises.' She turned from her perusal of the shelves, mostly books on economics and business, with a few classics of literature thrown in. 'You said your father said you were the face of the operation, but what does that mean, exactly?'

Nico propped one powerful shoulder against the door-frame as he folded his arms. 'I handle all the deals, basically,' he told her. 'Santini Enterprises has a lot of different interests—resorts, like the one in the Maldives I was going to see, as well as hotels, tech companies, a few other things. My father loves to acquire businesses, sell the ones he doesn't need, and buy more. I manage the negotiations.'

'Do you enjoy it?'

He looked startled, as if the question had never occurred to him. 'I don't know if I do or not,' he replied slowly. 'I like closing a deal, I suppose, but I never really thought about doing anything else. Working for Santini Enterprises was always going to be in my future. I was never given the choice to consider any other options.' He grimaced slightly. 'Even though my father resented the fact that he suspected I wasn't his son, he still wanted me to take over the family business. Sometimes I've wondered why, if it was just a point of pride.'

'Pride can be a very powerful thing.' After all, Nico was a proud man. Had it been pride that had taken him all the way to California in search of her, or something more? Emma wasn't sure, and she wasn't brave enough to ask. 'And if you had been,' she asked instead, 'what would you do? Your dream job. What would that be?'

He let out a little laugh, the sound one of uncertainty that made Emma's heart both ache and melt in a way she wasn't entirely comfortable with but couldn't keep herself from. As wealthy and privileged as he'd been his whole life, she realised, Nico's experiences oddly mirrored her own. A lack of choice. A fear, even an inability, perhaps, to let yourself dream. She hadn't expected such a point of similarity.

'I suppose,' he answered slowly, his arms folded as he leaned his head back against the door, 'I'd like to do something similar, but on my own, and for smaller companies that don't usually get a look-in. A venture capitalist, of a sort, but for grass-roots operations, home-grown businesses who need the opportunity.'

She smiled, envisaging the kind of businesses he meant—companies that started in someone's garage, a stay-at-home mum turning her kitchen into a bakery, a high-school geek making his tech ideas into millions. 'I like the sound of that.'

'Do you?'

He lifted his head so his jade-green gaze blazed into hers, both searching and finding, and her breath caught in her chest as her heart started to race. A moment of friendly solidarity morphed, in an instant, into something else. Something more.

'I like the idea of looking after the little guys,' she replied a bit unsteadily, 'since I've always been one.'

'Is that how you've felt? Like a little guy?'

She shrugged. 'If a little guy is someone who never has the power or opportunity or choice? Yes. Pretty much. But I haven't always been great about making opportunities for myself. That can be scary, on your own, which is why I think it would be great if you helped people like that along. Partnered with them.' She hadn't meant to reveal quite so much, and so she continued, a bit hurriedly, 'I think you'd be good at that, too, actually. Giving people the courage as well as the opportunity to raise the bar...' She trailed off because her mind was hopelessly buzzing and he was looking at her with such heat, such blatant need. When had anyone, anyone other than Nico, looked at her like that? Made her feel like this—important and, most of all, wanted? Very wanted.

'Emma...' He took a step towards her and she held her breath, waiting for his touch. Craving it, because she knew how it made her feel. How his hand skimming along her skin could create sparks, a raging fire. And how that fire could consume her, burn away all her good intentions to guard her heart...

But she couldn't think about any of that now. She could only think about him, coming closer, about to touch her, consume her. They hadn't touched since that sleepy fumble in bed that had awakened her body, made her remember all too well how he felt. How he made her feel—and wanted to feel again.

Last night, exhausted by everything, she'd gone to bed early while Nico had stayed up making preparations for their trip, and Emma had wondered when—not if, not any more—they would come together again. They would make this marriage real for a second time, even better than before.

He took another step towards her, reaching for her hand, lacing his fingers through hers as he tugged her gently towards him. 'I'm glad you're here,' he said softly, and she gave a little, unsteady laugh.

'So am I.' Although she was still afraid. Afraid of falling for this man who was doing everything right—something she knew not to trust.

'We can make this work,' Nico murmured as he drew her ever closer, so her hips bumped his and heat flared deep inside, along with an almost unbearable yearning. 'Can't we?'

'I'd...like to think so.' Although she was having trouble thinking right now, with Nico's body so close to hers, the scent of his cologne—of him—in her nostrils, making her dizzy. His fingers skimmed her cheek, tucking a tendril of hair behind her ear, and leaving a fiery trail of longing in its wake. Emma's lips parted soundlessly. Nico dipped his head. Her heart tripped, caught, tripped again. He was going to kiss her...

'Signor Santini?' The flight attendant's discreet cough

had Nico dropping his hand and Emma springing away, her heart now juddering. 'We're ready to take off.'

'Thank you, Enrico.' Nico's voice was calm although Emma saw the spots of colour high on his cheekbones. He had been as affected as she was by their almost-kiss, and the realisation was wonderfully thrilling. She, who had never had anyone care about her enough to be affected by anything she did, could make this man's breathing ragged and his face heat with desire.

But you can't make him love you, so don't even try.

The reminder was painful but necessary. As long as she kept everything in perspective, Emma told herself, she'd be okay. She'd be safe—from the dangerous treacheries of her own heart.

'Pity I didn't get to show you the bedroom,' Nico murmured as he stepped closer to her, his breath tickling her ear. 'But I will later.'

Was that a promise? Before she could reply, he continued, his voice low, 'That part of our relationship is not in doubt, Emma, but we'll resume it only when you're ready to. You can be assured of that. I have no interest in pressuring you in that way.'

More consideration and kindness. Tears stung her eyes, even as her body still tingled. She was on emotional overload, and it was dangerous. Frightening. Emma drew a steadying breath.

'Thank you,' she said, and he let his fingers skim her cheek one last time, so she struggled not to close her eyes, lean into the caress.

'Although I must admit I hope it's sooner rather than later,' he told her, his voice a wry rumble. 'Because you're just about killing me here.'

She let out another unsteady laugh and then followed him out of the study to the main cabin, where they took their seats.

* * *

Nico gazed out of the window of the plane at the stretch of azure sky and felt a glow of satisfaction deep inside— as well as a very much *unsatisfied* ache of longing. That would be dealt with in time, he was sure, and very pleasurably so. He had no doubts about that. He just needed to wait for Emma to feel as ready as he was.

He had come to realise a few things about his wife over the last few days, as well as remembering their month together from before. Things that, taken individually, hadn't struck him overmuch, but now which were starting to come together to form a whole, surprising picture.

Yesterday the OB had told him that Emma had not had many of her childhood vaccinations, and her check-up had revealed a few worrying details—a wrist broken as a small child that hadn't been set properly and so had healed at a slightly awkward angle, something he noticed now as she sat across from him, one elbow propped on the arm rest, her gaze distant and thoughtful. There was a bump where her wrist met her hand, small and virtually unnoticeable, unless you were looking for it, which he was.

'I'm telling you these things, first of all, because Emma herself gave me permission to share her medical details with you,' the OB had said. 'Otherwise, of course, I would not be saying a single word. But also because she has clearly not had proper medical care for long stretches of time in her life, and I want to make sure she gets that care now.'

'She will, absolutely,' Nico had replied, his voice gruff, his mind reeling from other things the OB had said—that Emma had shown signs of childhood malnourishment; that there were scars on her leg that could be cigarette burns.

'She didn't use the word abuse,' the OB had said, 'when

she was talking to me, but clearly there were elements of it in her childhood. I trust she will be safe with you.'

'On my life,' Nico had promised. 'On my *life*.'

Now he turned from his view of the sky to Emma, curled up across from him. 'It's eleven hours from here to Rome,' he said, 'so this might be as good a time as any to get to know one another.'

The look Emma gave as she turned to him was definitely wary. Just like him, she didn't enjoy talking about her childhood, herself, and he was starting to understand why. Nico relaxed back into his seat. 'But first let me get you something to drink, eat.'

A small smile quirked her mouth. 'You're always feeding me, it seems.'

'I like feeding you, and you need fattening up.' He pressed a discreet button in the armrest of his seat and Enrico came swiftly into the main cabin.

'Signor Santini?'

Nico glanced at Emma. 'What would you like?'

She shrugged, laughing. 'I don't even know. Umm… some crackers?'

'That's it?' Nico couldn't keep from sounding disapproving, and she rolled her eyes.

'And some cheese.'

'What kind?'

'What kind do you have?'

'This plane is well stocked, Emma. We pretty much have whatever you want.'

She laughed softly. 'It's going to take me a while to get used to this. Okay, I'll have some Cheddar then, please.' She glanced at Enrico. 'Thank you.'

'My pleasure, Signora Santini.'

He left the room while Emma shook her head slowly. 'Signora Santini. I'm going to have to get used to that.'

'You were Signora Santini before,' Nico pointed out.

'Yes, but no one ever really called me that. I barely saw anyone in the week we were married.'

Nico frowned. 'I don't think I quite realised that at the time. I don't entirely remember…'

'It's okay, Nico.' She leaned over to brush the back of his hand with the tips of her fingers. 'It wasn't just about you. It was me, too. I know we were married, we *are* married, but I think part of me was always bracing myself for you to change your mind…which was why I believed Antonio when he said I was already on the way out.'

A blaze of anger fired through him. He would definitely need to have words with his cousin. 'But why were you? Bracing yourself, I mean?'

She shrugged. 'Because it happened so fast. Because you're rich and powerful and attractive as all get-out, and I'm…' she trailed off with a shrug before finishing with one of her old laughs '…not.'

'Rich and powerful, perhaps not, but attractive as—what did you say? All get-out?'

A playful smile quirked her mouth. 'Mm-hmm.'

'You are definitely that.' He leaned over to tuck a tendril of hair behind her ear, letting his fingers linger on her cheek, her skin soft and cool beneath his touch. Her eyes fluttered closed briefly and Nico ran his thumb along her lips as a shudder escaped her.

'Nico…'

'I can't keep from touching you,' he admitted as he traced the outline of her lips. 'Do you mind?'

'Mind?' She let out an unsteady laugh, her breath hitching. 'No.'

'Good.' He leaned forward, just as the door to the cabin opened.

'Signora Santini? Your cheese and crackers.'

Nico smiled wryly even as his heart thudded in response to that simple touch. 'It seems we are always being interrupted,' he told Emma sotto voce, and she smiled back, her face flushed, her breathing still unsteady.

'Thank you, Enrico,' she said, and the attendant withdrew again, leaving them alone.

'So,' Nico said, determined not to be distracted again—although what a lovely distraction it was—'we were going to get to know one another.'

'Is that what you were doing?' she teased, eyebrows raised, as she piled Cheddar on top of a cracker and took a large bite.

'I suppose there are different ways of accomplishing that goal,' he agreed wryly. And some were more pleasurable than others. 'But for now, considering the likelihood of us being interrupted yet again, we'll keep it to conversation.'

Her eyes danced as she brushed crumbs from her lips. 'Pity.'

Indeed it was a pity, and he was glad—very glad—she thought so as well. It made his blood sing to think they would remedy that situation one day—or night—soon. Very soon, he hoped. 'Indeed,' he managed, shifting in his seat to ease the persistent ache in his groin. 'But as for now, tell me about yourself. Where did you grow up?'

It seemed an innocuous enough question, but it was as if a veil had dropped down over Emma's face, behind her eyes. Her expression stilled and she put down the rest of her cracker, brushing her hands before tucking them under her thighs. 'Mainly in upstate New York,' she said, her tone as cautious and careful as the expression on her face. 'But I moved around a bit.'

'Yes, I think you mentioned as much before.' But not much else, and he hadn't asked. He hadn't wanted to delve into the past, either hers or his, back then. He'd simply wanted to revel in the moment, to blot out anything else.

Now he felt differently. Now he wanted—needed—to know.

'How come you moved around?'

She shrugged. 'That's just the way it was.'

He leaned forward, lowering his voice, trying to keep his tone gentle. 'You sound as if you don't want to talk about it.'

She sighed and looked out of the window at the blaze of bright blue sky. 'I don't, not particularly, but I suppose you should know at least the basics.' She took a deep breath, squared her shoulders, and then turned back to look at him. 'I was taken away from my mother when I was six months old, due to neglect. She tried to get me back a year later and failed.' She hesitated and then admitted quietly, 'That was part of my fear, initially, and why I was reluctant to tell you about the baby. Our baby. Because I was scared you might take him or her away from me.'

'Away from you?' Nico sat back, his mouth agape, unable to keep the horror from his face, his voice. 'Emma, I would never do that.'

'I think I know that now,' she admitted a bit shakily, 'but considering what happened to my own mother... I was scared.'

He frowned. 'But your mother neglected you?'

'So they said. I don't actually know. The case files reveal very little. And trust me, when you've gone through the foster system, you see how, despite the best intentions, good people sometimes get taken advantage of and bad people can get a free pass.' She shrugged, and he knew she must have seen that in her own life. The broken wrist, the burns. How much had Emma suffered?

'Whether that happened to my mother or not, I don't know. She died when I was two, a car accident. And I never knew my father—so I suppose we have that in common.' The smile she gave him was wry, determined, and made him ache because it felt so brave. 'I was bounced around from foster family to foster family until I was thirteen, when I was considered too old and frankly too much of a handful for families, and so I ended up in a care home. They're not as bad as you might think,' she added quickly, before he could say anything. 'In some ways, they're better. You can stop trying so hard, to get a family to like you. Want to keep you.'

They had that in common too, he realised. Trying to win people's love. All in all, it sounded like an absolutely wretched childhood. 'And what happened then?' he asked quietly.

'I aged out of the system at eighteen.' She shrugged. 'Again, not as bad as you think. They give you some support, they don't just dump you in it, although by that time it's usually not enough. Most of us feel a little lost. I know I did. But I enrolled in a catering course—I've always liked cooking. I had dreams of opening my own restaurant one day.' She ducked her head a bit, as if this was revealing too much. 'But as it happens, I dropped out after a year.'

'Why?'

'This is starting to feel a bit like an interrogation.' He thought she was trying to sound playful and not quite managing it.

'I don't mean it to be. You can ask me questions too, you know.'

She arched an eyebrow. 'Suddenly you're an open book?'

He shrugged, determined to keep going. Keep trying. 'I'll try to be.'

She let out another breath as she turned to the window. 'I don't even know what to ask.'

'Anything,' he replied, hoping he meant it.

She turned to face him. 'Have you ever been in love?'

Nico tried to keep his expression interested but bland as her question jolted through him. *Had he?* He thought of the affairs he'd had in the past, meaningless flings he'd never even tried to go deeper with, because he hadn't wanted to take that risk, and in any case none of the women had seemed worth it. And as for Emma…well, he'd tried to convince himself he was in love with her, had let that notion carry him through his rehabilitation…but he knew now that you couldn't love someone if you didn't know them. What he'd felt had been infatuation, maybe even obsession, but not love, no matter how much he'd tried to convince himself otherwise. 'No,' he said, and knew he was speaking the truth. 'Have you?'

'No, definitely not.' She spoke decisively. 'All right, another question. Do you want to be in love? Fall in love?'

She clearly wasn't pulling her punches. Nico hesitated, determined to be honest, even if it was risky. 'Considering you're married to me,' he remarked lightly, 'is the question you're really asking, do I want to fall in love with you?'

A startled look passed across Emma's face, like a bird taking flight. 'I suppose,' she finally answered slowly.

And how was he meant to answer that? Nico wondered, realising the trap he'd neatly laid for himself. He'd started out on this venture determined not to fall in love with Emma—the Emma he'd thought he'd known, that he couldn't trust. He'd wanted the kind of arrangement where he reaped all the benefits and yet risked nothing, certainly not his heart. Right now that seemed like a poor exchange, indeed, especially when he was realising Emma wasn't anything like the heartless gold-digger of his imagination. But was he ready to admit to her what—and how much—he did want? He wasn't even sure he could admit it to himself.

He wasn't sure he knew…although he thought he might be beginning to suspect.

'I'll answer first,' Emma said, before he could formulate a reply, 'since you seem to be thinking about it. I'm not interested in falling in love, *being* in love, at all. You might as well know I dropped out of that catering course because of a guy. No one important, really, but after I'd aged out of the system I was feeling a little lost, like I said, and I pinned all my hopes on him. Clearly a mistake.' Her mouth twisted. 'But it was more than that, really. The truth was, I was scared of failing. Better to quit than to fail—that, unfortunately, has been my motto for a lot of my life. But in terms of the guy… Eric…' She took a steadying breath, let it out slowly. 'I didn't love him, not really, but I tried to convince myself I did, and unfortunately, he ended up being just like everybody else.'

'Like everybody else?' Nico probed, wondering just what that meant.

'Not interested in sticking around for the long haul.' She hunched her shoulders, tilted her chin, a heartbreaking combination of courage and hurt. 'But even before that, I'd pretty much made my mind up about that sort of thing. I basically grew up on my own, and I've liked it that way. I don't want to…need people like that. Emotionally, I mean. I choose not to, because…well, because it's easier. There was one family who I thought…' She stopped, shaking her head. 'Anyway. That's how I've lived my life, and that's how I want to keep on living it. Friendship, affection, trust… all good.' She gave him a determined smile. 'But love, no.'

Which he could, unfortunately, understand. Hadn't he been a bit similar—choosing not to try to win his father's love because he realised he could never earn it? But it had been a hard and hopeless way to live, and he wasn't sure he wanted it now, or in the future.

'Don't you have anything to say?' Emma challenged.

'I suppose I understand why you would feel that way,' Nico replied after a moment.

'And that's okay with you?' she pressed. 'I mean, considering your own background, I sort of assumed it would be. That you're not interested in…that kind of thing, either.' She glanced at him, her amber eyes filled with uncertainty, but also, Nico thought, a wary sort of hope. But what was she hoping for? That he agreed with her—or that he didn't?

'Emma,' he said finally, 'we're just getting to know each other now. It all feels a bit precipitous to put limits on our relationship, but certainly, I see your point. We've both been hurt before. It's understandable that we'd both want to take measures to make sure that doesn't happen again.'

She bit her lip, her uncertain gaze scanning his face. Nico kept his expression deliberately bland. 'So it's okay with you?' she pressed again, and he nodded.

'Yes, of course,' he told her, because what else could he say? This was the only thing she wanted to hear, and he didn't know his own heart yet. 'It's okay with me,' he reassured her, and Emma nodded. As she sat back against her seat, Nico couldn't decide if she looked disappointed—or relieved.

CHAPTER ELEVEN

THIS PLACE WAS, Emma thought, far from the first time, utterly amazing. She stood on the terrace off her sumptuous bedroom in Nico's villa as she watched the sun set over the tranquil, aquamarine waters of the Mediterranean Sea lapping the white sand beach at the bottom of the villa's landscaped gardens.

They had arrived at his private island yesterday, after the overnight flight to Rome, where they'd left the Santini private jet and boarded a small hire plane to fly directly to the island, a few miles from Capri, near the Bay of Naples. By the time they'd arrived, Emma had been too jet-lagged and exhausted to do much but look around blearily and collapse into the bed Nico's housekeeper Maria had shown her—a huge, soft king-sized one with views of the sea. His bedroom was adjoining, but the door between the rooms had stayed firmly closed, and after nearly fourteen hours of sleep she'd felt much refreshed and ready to explore.

They'd breakfasted together on yogurt, fresh fruit, and pastries, and then Nico had offered to give her a tour of the island, which Emma had accepted with enthusiasm. After their conversation on the plane the day before, she'd felt reassured they were on the same page when it came to the nature of their relationship. They could be friends, they could even be lovers, but they wouldn't be *in* love. It was an important and necessary distinction, and one Emma was glad she'd made, even as she castigated herself for seeming so arrogant—as arrogant as Nico once had been!—to think he would actually fall in love with her.

Of course he wouldn't, she'd scolded herself when she'd gone to rest in the private jet's sumptuous bedroom during the flight to Rome, and Nico had stayed in the main cabin to work. The reminder had been more for her than for him, not that she'd had any intention of telling him as much. But a man like Nico Santini—rich, powerful, and yes, attractive as all get-out, just as she'd told him—wasn't about to fall headlong in love with someone like her, a gutter rat who'd been bounced around so much because no one had ever wanted her enough to keep her. That much was obvious, and it was clear Nico hadn't needed the warning, which was a good thing. Of course it was.

Or so she'd told herself as they'd spent a very pleasant few hours wandering around the island, among the twisted trunks of an ancient olive grove, through the villa's gardens with its climbing bougainvillea and tinkling fountains, down to the sweep of white sand where Nico's private yacht was moored. He'd kept the conversation light and easy, and Emma had relaxed into the chat and banter, grateful that they could enjoy each other's company without having another intense 'getting to know you' talk that she knew she wasn't ready for.

It had been hard, admitting as much as she had, the day before on the plane. She wasn't used to being so vulnerable and tended not to talk about her childhood, the conveyor belt of foster families she'd rotated through, never spending anywhere very long. Except, of course, the last family…she'd spent a whole year with them, in some ways the happiest year of her life…or so she'd thought.

But she definitely hadn't wanted to go into all that with

Nico, although perhaps she would one day. In any case, he hadn't asked any invasive questions and she hadn't either, and it had been enough simply to enjoy each other's company, learning little things about him that she hadn't known before—that he liked chess, was scared—or slightly wary, as he'd put it—of spiders, that he'd had a dog growing up and would like one again.

And she'd told him bits and pieces about her own interests—that she loved cooking although she'd rarely got the chance to cook much of anything, living in bedsits, that fantasy novels had been her escape of choice as a teen, and she'd never had a pet but thought she might want one one day, although perhaps she'd start small, with a fish or a lizard.

'A lizard!' Nico had exclaimed, laughing. 'They're not very cuddly.'

She'd shrugged, smiling, not wanting to admit that she was a bit nervous to be wholly responsible for a pet. It hardly seemed like a good thing to admit to the father of the baby you were carrying, after all.

'How about a dog and a cat?' Nico had suggested, his arm around her as they'd strolled back up to the villa for lunch. 'We could teach them to get along.'

'Maybe.' She was still getting used to the whole idea of that *we*; that she and Nico were going to build their lives together. He seemed to have got on board with it remarkably quickly, but Emma knew she needed time to catch up. How could she, who had never known her parents or what it meant to be in a family, build one? *Be* one?

After lunch, Nico excused himself to catch up on work and Emma spent a few hours exploring the villa itself, wandering through its many comfortable rooms, all with views of the sea, and ending up in the cheerful, red-tiled kitchen with the housekeeper, Maria.

'Of course, you must do as you like with the kitchen and

food,' Maria assured her while Emma glanced around at the bright copper pans hanging from the ceiling, the bowl of oranges on the table, the ropes of onions and garlic and bunches of herbs hanging from a wooden rafter. 'A woman must always be in charge of her own kitchen.'

'Thank you, that's very kind.' Emma wasn't sure she was confident enough to take charge of a kitchen like this, as much as she liked cooking. Maria seemed more than capable, and she couldn't imagine more or less elbowing her out of the way so she could have a go.

Perhaps she just needed more time, she told herself as she headed upstairs to her bedroom to get ready for dinner. During their walk Nico had encouraged her to think of the villa as her own, and yet she struggled not to feel like a guest, and a temporary one at that. Nico talked about buying houses and getting pets and she still wondered when he was going to turn around, frown regretfully, and say, *Actually, Emma, this isn't going to work.*

The way everyone else in her life had.

Would she ever get over that deep-seated fear? she wondered as she changed into a pale pink sundress with spaghetti straps. Nico had thoughtfully had an entire wardrobe of clothes shipped to the villa for their arrival, and he'd insisted she keep what she liked and returned what she didn't.

'And I'll need to go to Rome on business soon, so perhaps you can accompany me, and we'll make a shopping trip of it, as well.'

Emma had stammered her thanks, even as the question had hammered through her head: *Why are you being so good to me?* She'd thought it before, and when she'd believed he'd died in that crash, it had almost been as if she'd been expecting it, or something close to it, because when had anything in her life gone right?

And yet now something was. Wonderfully. She really just had to trust it. Lean into it. Let it happen.

It had only been a few days, she reminded herself, and they had weeks, months, maybe even years to get used to each other, to grow. She needed to stop second-guessing herself and enjoy what was right in front of her—Nico included.

Her stomach dipped as she remembered how he'd held her hand as they'd walked through the olive grove, their fingers loosely entwined. How, when he'd helped her over a piece of driftwood on the beach, his hand had spanned her waist and his gaze had briefly, blazingly, met hers. Emma knew Nico meant what he said—he would wait for her to be ready; the ball was firmly in her court when it came to that aspect of their relationship.

And maybe that was the missing piece that would help her feel settled. That would build trust as well as intimacy. That would remind her of how wanted this man made her feel, and how safe.

As long as she kept guarding her heart...

'There you are.' Nico came out onto the terrace, smiling, looking relaxed and rather wonderful in a pale green button-down shirt and dark trousers, his feet bare, his teeth gleaming in his tanned face.

'I was just enjoying the sunset.' She glanced back at the ribbons of lavender and orange that were streaming across the sky as the sun sank towards the placid surface of the sea. 'This feels like paradise.'

'I'm glad.' He brushed her cheek with his fingers. 'You deserve a little paradise.'

Instinctively she tensed at the note in his voice, something she feared might be a bit too close to pity. 'Don't feel sorry for me, Nico,' she warned quietly. 'Because of my childhood or whatever.' She didn't think she could take his pity, not when all she'd ever had was her own strength. She needed to keep it; she couldn't bear for him to feel sorry for her. They wouldn't be equals then; they couldn't be partners.

He raised his eyebrows, his fingers still lingering on her cheek, making it hard to think. To stay strong. 'Do you feel sorry for me?' he asked. 'Because of my childhood… or whatever?'

'Am I supposed to?' she returned tartly, but smiling too, glad he'd flipped it back on her rather than giving her assurances she wasn't sure she could believe.

'No. Definitely not.' He ran his hand from her cheek to her shoulder and down her arm, twining his fingers with hers. 'If anything, I admire you, Emma, for overcoming so much.' He paused. 'The OB told me some of the things you must have been through.'

She felt a blush heat her cheeks as she imagined what some of those things must have been, the more painful parts of her childhood she'd tried to forget. Why had she agreed, in a moment of defiance, to let her share her medical records with him? 'What kind of things?' she asked, although she wasn't sure she actually wanted him to say it aloud. Still, she wanted to know how much he knew.

'That you'd been malnourished as a child. And that you must have broken your wrist at some point and it didn't heal properly, probably because it hadn't been seen to.' He paused and then added, his voice so achingly gentle, 'And that there were scars on your legs that looked like cigarette burns.'

A lump was forming in her throat, making it hard to speak. Her eyes blurred so the world was just colour—the orange and violet of the sunset, the blue of the sea, the green of Nico's kind, far too kind, gaze. She hadn't expected him to say so much, to know so much. How much had that doctor been able to guess from her determinedly brief answers? 'Well, some of those foster families weren't so great,' she managed in a half-mumble. 'One in particular was pretty bad. But, you know, some were really good…' The ones that hadn't wanted her.

'Oh, Emma.' She couldn't see what he was doing because of her blurred vision, but she felt him. His arms came around her and he drew her softly against him, so her cheek was pressed against his warm, solid chest and she could breathe in the wonderful scent of his aftershave, of *him*. She closed her eyes and a tear slipped down.

'Please don't feel sorry for me, Nico. Really. I don't want you to.'

His hand was warm and steady on her back, moving in slow, comforting circles. 'I told you, I don't. Do you think I should?'

'No, it's just I couldn't stand your pity. I've always tried to be strong—'

'You are strong, Emma. Stronger than you even know.' He eased back, framing her face with his hands, using his thumbs to gently wipe away her tears. 'Stronger than I ever realised.'

'It's hard enough to feel like your equal,' she confessed unsteadily. Maybe that was part of her trust issues—she wondered why he'd want her long-term, when nobody else had. 'I just don't want to feel even more…inferior.'

'Inferior?' His eyebrows rose, his fingers stilling on her face. 'You are far, far from that, in absolutely every way,' he told her, his voice a low, steady thrum, 'I promise you. And I also promise you, as I did before, that I will be there for you in a way those foster families never were. I'll always keep you safe, Emma, I promise.'

His voice throbbed with sincerity as Emma gazed up at him, wondering if she could believe him, longing to yet still struggling—not because of him, she knew, as much as herself. The doubts she still felt. And yet…it was so tempting to believe. She might not want to court the dangers of loving Nico, but living with him as his equal, his friend, and yes, his lover? She realised she wanted that. Desperately.

'Do you believe me?' he asked, and she managed a smile, small and tremulous, but there.

'I'm trying to.'

'How can I convince you?'

As he looked down at her with such tenderness, his hands still framing her face, Emma realised she knew exactly what she wanted—and needed—right now. Not more probing questions or well-intentioned reassurances, which only fed into her doubts and fears, but rather tangible proof—proof that this could work, that *they* could, in the most fundamental and elemental way possible.

'*Well...*' Her smile deepened as she let out an unsteady laugh and let her gaze drop to his mouth before looking up again, a gasp caught in her throat at the gentleness in Nico's eyes darkened with desire. His gaze scanned her face, searching for answers, and she gave them as she lifted her face up for his kiss.

'Are you sure...?' he asked, and she nodded.

'Yes.' Of this, absolutely. There was still so much she was unsure and afraid of—trusting Nico with her heart, whether they could be a family together, whether she could trust herself.

And yet this? Them, together, as one? Yes. She was sure of that. To prove it, she stood on her tiptoes and brushed a kiss across the velvet of his mouth, revelling in the touch and taste of him.

It only lasted a few seconds, but that was all it took. Nico clasped her to him, plundering her mouth with a savage sweetness that thrilled her to her core. Oh, how she'd missed this. She'd let herself forget how good it had been, because it had been easier not to remember, not to miss what she'd had with him, so very briefly.

Although, she acknowledged dazedly, as he blizzarded kisses along her cheek and jaw down to her throat, his mouth moving everywhere with delicious intent, it was even better now, because their relationship was already so much deeper. Built on trust, growing in affection, not some out-of-time fantasy that never would have gone the distance. This, she hoped, would…if she could let herself believe in it.

Somehow they stumbled off the terrace, and into her bedroom. Emma turned to him, her heart hammering with expectation and just a little fear, because her body was different now and, even though everything so far had been absolutely explosive, she still felt unsure. What if he didn't like the changes pregnancy had wrought? She knew she was too thin in some places and she had a very small baby bump, and maybe Nico wouldn't…

That thought was obliterated as he reached for her, pulling the sash of her sundress loose, sliding the skinny straps off her shoulders. Breathlessly, she wriggled free as his own breathing turned ragged.

'You're so beautiful,' he told her softly and Emma let out a nervous little laugh.

'I don't feel beautiful,' she confessed, because she'd never thought of herself as all that special, and it still amazed her that Nico desired her as much as she knew he did.

'Then let me show you.' He reached out and unclasped her bra, letting the garment fall from her shoulders so she could shrug out of it. Another shrug and the dress, which had caught around her hips, fell to the floor in a puddle of colourful cotton. Nervously, she kicked it away. She was naked save for a pair of bikini briefs, and Nico was still fully dressed. This was feeling a little unequal.

'Feel,' Nico said, and he drew her hand to his chest, so she could feel the thundering beat of his heat under her palm. 'You see what you do to me?' He drew her hand to the buttons of his shirt. 'Will you undress me?'

The question, asked in a rasp of desire, held a vulnerable note that made her ache. It thrilled and amazed her, humbled her too, that he could want her. That he wanted to show her how much. Carefully, her fingers trembling just a little, she unbuttoned his shirt and then spread the fabric apart with her hands, revelling in the feel of his pectoral muscles, perfectly sculpted.

Emma let her hands dance and slide across his chest, exploring every beautiful, burnished inch of him before she dropped her hands to the waistband of his trousers, thrilling even more to the feel of him, yet also suddenly shy.

'You're not going to chicken out, are you?' he teased softly and laughter gurgled in her throat.

'No. Definitely not.' No way was she a chicken, and in truth she was looking forward to this. To all of it. With a flick of her finger she undid the button of his trousers, and then drew down the zip over the impressive, pulsing length of him. A soft groan escaped him as her fingers trailed along his arousal before she pushed his trousers off his hips and he kicked them away, pulling her into his arms to kiss her again, both of them blinded by need.

They half walked, half stumbled, to the bed, limbs entwined, bodies clasped together. Emma didn't think she could ever get enough of him, the feel of him against her, the sense of being both desired and cherished, possessed and protected.

Her head hit the pillow as Nico braced himself on top of her, giving her one blazing look of possession before he bent his head to her breasts. Emma's eyes fluttered closed as he slowly kissed his way down her body, taking his time, enjoying every moment, his hands following the fiery trail of his lips, laughing softly against her skin as a moan escaped her and she arched upwards, silently begging for more, which he gave—and gave.

She didn't think she'd ever get enough, she thought dazedly as she fisted her hands in the dark crispness of his hair and his lips trailed from her navel to even lower as he spread her thighs with his hands and tasted her deeply, making her arch and moan and cry out because it was all so intense, and intimate, and also somehow new. She'd never felt this way before, not even with Nico, and she didn't think anyone else could ever make her feel as much again.

'Nico...' she managed in a half-sob, desperate for release, and he raised his head to brace himself above her as, in one smooth stroke, he entered her at last.

At last. Nico pressed his forehead to Emma's as he buried himself deep inside her, revelling in the velvety squeeze of her body as she enveloped him, wrapping her legs around his waist to draw him even deeper, so they were completely united, husband and wife—one union, one flesh. He'd never felt this way before—not with any other woman, not even with Emma. This, he realised dazedly, was new.

'Nico...' she said again, a promise, a plea, as she wrapped her arms around him, his whole body pressed to her as if they could fuse their flesh even more together and he began to move, long, assured strokes, each one stoking the flames of his desire higher and brighter, bringing him even closer to her, if such a thing were possible.

Emma met him thrust for thrust, pushing upwards and then drawing him in—higher, faster, hotter, brighter, until, at last, she cried out, convulsing around him as he spent himself, their bodies emptied and yet replete. Nico closed his eyes, overwhelmed not just by the pleasure, intense as it had been, but by the intimacy. What had happened had been profound in a way he could not articulate yet, not even to himself.

He thought—he *hoped*—Emma might feel the same for she didn't speak, no irrepressible laugh or insouciant smile this time. She just put her arms even more tightly around him and pressed her face into his shoulder as the last ripples of their shared climax shuddered through them.

Eventually, Nico didn't know after how long, he rolled over onto his back and Emma snuggled into him, her breathing slowing so he almost wondered if she was asleep. He slid his hand down her body and she let out a little sigh of contentment. Not asleep, then. Just sated, as he was.

As his palm skimmed her navel, he registered what he hadn't before, in the throes of their lovemaking—the slight swell of her pregnancy. *Their baby.* A thrill ran through him and he kept his hand there, spreading his fingers wide across the bump.

A little bubble of laughter escaped her. 'Is it strange?' she asked, and with his other arm he nestled her more closely against him.

'It's wonderful.'

'Are you…?' She paused, as if choosing her words with care. 'Are you nervous about being a father?'

He considered the question, sensing the hesitation behind it. 'No more than any man, I hope,' he said at last. 'What about you? Are you nervous about being a mother?'

'Yes, kind of.' Her voice sounded small, and he squeezed her shoulders gently in silent reassurance. 'As I told you, I never knew my own mother,' she continued quietly. 'And I didn't really have many examples of good mothers. There was one foster mother…' She stopped, and Nico glanced down at her.

'One?' he prompted gently.

'She was kind,' Emma allowed. 'But…it didn't last.' He

sensed there was more to the story, but she clearly didn't want to share it now. 'I just hope I'll know what to do. How to be.'

'We've both had parents who disappointed or failed us,' Nico told her after a moment, feeling his way through the words. 'But that doesn't have to define us. We can see it as opportunity—opportunity to be the kind of mother or father we never had. A chance to do it better than before, to get it right.'

She was silent for a long moment, weighing his words. 'But what if I can't get it right?' she asked at last, and the fear in her voice made him ache.

'The fact that you're even asking that question tells me you'll try your hardest,' he told her, 'and so will I. And, at the end of the day, that's all either of us can do.'

A little bubble of laughter escaped her. 'You're very wise, you know,' she told him as she tilted her face up to his. 'Don't let that make you any more arrogant than you are, though.'

'I'll try,' Nico promised, and there was laughter in his voice, too. 'Although I am compiling quite a list—rich, powerful, attractive as all get-out, and now wise…'

She punched his shoulder, laughing. 'All right, smarty-pants—'

'Is there anything else you want to add to that list?' Nico asked as he flipped her onto her back and pressed his lips to her throat before moving tantalisingly lower. Emma's eyes fluttered closed as her body became loose-limbed and pliant beneath his touch. He could spend hours exploring every inch of her, he thought as he kissed his way down towards her navel. Days… 'Fantastic lover, perhaps?' he murmured against her skin, and inched lower.

A breathy moan escaped her as her hands raked through his hair, anchoring him to her. 'I think you know that one already,' she managed unsteadily, and then neither of them spoke for a long time.

CHAPTER TWELVE

EMMA TILTED HER head up to the warm, benevolent sunshine, closing her eyes in pleasure even as her heart fluttered with anticipatory nerves. They'd been cruising up the coast in Nico's private yacht for the last three wonderfully relaxing days, and would be arriving in Civitavecchia that afternoon before heading to his flat in Rome—and real life.

They'd spent the last four weeks on his island, and Emma was reluctant to leave its comfort and safety and face the rest of the world—Nico's family included. No, she acknowledged as she opened her eyes and squinted up at the sun, she wasn't just *reluctant*. She was pretty much terrified. She'd complained that Nico hadn't introduced her to his friends before, but now that he was, she realised she didn't relish the prospect of meeting them, or any of the other guests at the charity gala she and Nico would be attending tomorrow night.

She'd never been to that kind of high-profile event before; in their first month-long relationship, she and Nico had kept to hotels and private restaurants, seeing no one. She'd never had to wear a fancy dress, or mingle with important guests, or act as though she fitted in when she never had before. Why did she think she would be able to now? Why did Nico?

Just thinking about it all made her feel as if an icy pit

had opened in her stomach, hollowed her right out. On the island, away from reality, she'd been able—mostly—to keep her old insecurities at bay. Now, as Rome drew ever nearer, they rose in full, clamouring force.

She was a fraud. Nico couldn't possibly want to spend the rest of his life with her. He'd walk away from her, just as everyone else she'd ever cared about had, when he realised what a dud she was.

Not that she wanted to admit any of that to Nico. And not, she knew, that he would give it any credence. But what Nico felt about her away from the rest of the world was surely different from when he had to parade her in public. She'd never been on the kind of display that she would be at this gala, and she was afraid—deeply so—that she wouldn't be up to the challenge. And even more worryingly, that Nico would see that—and agree. Tomorrow night felt like a test, and one she was desperately afraid she would fail.

The last four weeks had been, Emma acknowledged with a pang of nostalgia for what already felt in the past, incredible. It was the same amount of time she'd spent with Nico before the crash, but this time had been, she knew, different in every way. Their previous relationship had been, she realised now, nothing more than a figment, a fantasy, little more than snatched moments in bed in between Nico working, with her always waiting for him to tire of her and the whole thing to end. She'd never shared herself with him, not truly, and he hadn't with her. In comparison, the weeks they'd shared on the island had felt real and total.

They'd spent hours talking, chatting, laughing, sharing, as they'd explored the island, lounged in the garden, or swum in the sea; in the evenings they'd read books, or watched movies, or, more often than not, gone to bed where the pleasures there had continued unabated and deeper and more wonderful still.

Nico had taught her to play chess, and after the first week, Emma had worked up her courage to experiment in the kitchen, whipping up various meals. Nico had delighted in making sure she had whatever ingredients she required for the recipes she wanted to try, whether it was black truffles from France or sun-dried tomatoes from a farm in Sicily.

It had been fun and even exciting to make the meals they ate together, a form of caring that felt practical, tangible, a way to show him she cared without having to admit it to him—or even herself. And while it was true that not every meal had been a roaring success, Nico hadn't minded, and neither had she, both of them able to laugh at the unmitigated disaster that had been a very crisp sea bass with far too much lemon and garlic. Emma had been glad to return to her love of cooking, yet another avenue of her life that she'd turned away from, all because she'd been afraid to fail.

She'd learned a lot about herself over the last few weeks, and while it had been good, it had also been uncomfortable. Painful, even, to realise her own flaws and failures. In getting to know Nico, and having him get to know her, she'd begun to see the patterns she'd fallen into both as a child and an adult, mainly to guard her own heart. She'd never truly tried at anything, she'd realised, because she'd been so afraid to fail, both with relationships and in life, and she hoped she could be different now. She knew, with Nico, she wanted to be. She just didn't know whether wanting, or even trying, would be enough.

'Enjoying the sun?' Nico asked as he strolled onto the deck from the yacht's main cabin. He was dressed in loose trousers and a white open-neck shirt that made his skin look even more deeply bronzed. The weeks in the sun had only made him more beautiful, his eyes like bits of jade in his tanned face, his white teeth gleaming, and his hair as black as ever.

'I am,' Emma replied, shading her eyes with her hand. She enjoyed seeing him looking so relaxed, so far from the tense, suspicious man who had strode into her wedding. These weeks, she hoped, had been as healing for him as they had been for her. 'How long until we get to Civitavecchia?'

'Another hour, I think.' He smiled wryly as he sat on the deck chair next to her. 'Don't look so thrilled,' he teased.

'I'm nervous,' Emma admitted, although that wasn't even the half of it.

'About seeing my cousin? Trust me, I fully intend to have words with him about how you were treated.'

'I don't want you to fall out with your family,' Emma protested, and Nico shook his head.

'That, I'm afraid, has already happened. Things were tense with Antonio before you even came onto the scene.'

'Well, in any case, it's not that. At least not just that.'

Nico frowned. 'What, then?'

How could she explain it to him? Emma wondered helplessly. How could she make him understand her fear that once they were out in the real world, it would be different? That he would be different, that she would. And the relationship they'd been building would fall apart. Again.

'Whatever it is, Emma,' Nico said, reaching for her hand, 'we'll deal with it… Together.' His smile turned playful as he squeezed her fingers. 'And I hope we'll have fun while we're at it. After a month on a remote island, aren't you looking forward at least a little to getting back to civilisation?'

Emma managed a half-hearted smile back. 'Yes, of course,' she said, although the truth was she'd have been happy to stay tucked away in their own private idyll for ever. But beyond the charity gala, she also had a doctor's appointment and another scan this afternoon, and so the city—and real life—beckoned, whether she was ready for it or not. Whether they were.

An hour later, having changed into a simple tunic-style dress that left room for her ever-expanding bump, Emma disembarked from the yacht with Nico, to the SUV waiting to drive them into Rome for her appointment and scan that afternoon. A week of sun, sleep and good food, as well as plenty of prenatal vitamins and iron had, she hoped, put her back on the road to health both in terms of her weight and her anaemia. She hoped she wouldn't disappoint Nico in that regard, even if tomorrow night's gala turned out to be a disaster.

'I've arranged for you to have some beauty treatments to-morrow,' Nico told her as they drove through the city, a mix of modern buildings, ancient ruins, and pleasant piazzas.

Emma stiffened slightly, although she tried not to show her alarm at such a seemingly innocuous suggestion. 'You have?'

'Yes, I thought you'd enjoy them.' He glanced at her, be-mused. Clearly she wasn't doing a good enough job hiding her unease. 'Most women do, don't they? Hair, nails, facials, that sort of thing? I thought it would be a treat for you.'

'Yes, I suppose.' What else could she say? He'd already told her there would be an array of gowns to choose from, brought directly to the hotel, for the gala. She knew she should revel in playing Cinderella for a day, fairy godmother included, but she only felt afraid. Yet another test to try to pass, to fail.

During their whirlwind relationship, she'd always been expecting it to end; even after they married, Emma had wondered how long their relationship could really last. She hadn't let herself get invested, but now, she knew, it was too late.

She might not love Nico—and that was simply because she wouldn't let herself—but she still cared. Too much. She knew she'd be hurt—devastated, frankly—if he changed his mind about her after seeing her fail here in Rome.

And hasn't everyone changed their mind about you?

Why would Nico—rich, powerful, attractive, *amazing* Nico—be any different?

She tried her best to banish that mocking inner voice and give Nico a smile of gratitude, which he surely deserved. 'Thank you. That's very kind of you.'

His lips twitched. 'Why do I think you had to force yourself to say that?'

He knew her too well, already. 'I'm just not used to any of this,' Emma replied, something of an apology.

He touched her cheek, his smile turning tender, making her eyes sting. No, she really wasn't used to any of this. 'Then this will help you become accustomed,' he told her gently, 'which you'd better—this is the rest of your life, Signora Santini.'

Was that a promise? Emma smiled and tried to believe it, but even as Nico leaned over to kiss her, she knew she couldn't. Not entirely. Life had taught her differently, too many times already.

Nico glanced in the mirror as he twitched the bow tie of his tuxedo, a frown settling between his brows. As much as he'd told Emma he was looking forward to this return to civilisation, the truth was he would have rather stayed on the island, alone with her, lost in a wonderful world of their own making—both in bed and out of it.

As much as he'd enjoyed the earthly delights they'd shared, he'd also found a surprising sweetness in simply spending time with her, whether it was walking, chatting, laughing, or cooking together; he'd jokingly referred to himself as her sous chef, happy to chop or grate while she studied the recipes she was trying with an endearing intensity. He'd loved watching her come alive—the excitement and enthusiasm that brightened her eyes and curved her mouth, the deep laugh that gurgled up when he teased her, far more genuine, he realised, than anything he'd heard from her before. She'd blossomed these last four weeks, he believed, and he was both glad and grateful.

He'd had his own kind of flowering as well, Nico knew, or at least a certain sort of unbending. After being a workaholic for most of his adult life, eschewing serious relationships in order to win his father's approval, he had, for the last four weeks, put his working life more or less on hold in order to spend time with Emma. He'd done the minimum to keep the current business deals with Santini Enterprises going; after his being away for the months after the crash, his father and Antonio had both easily got used to working without him, and Nico found that he actually didn't mind. He had his own private business interests to consider, as well; the investments he'd made with his own money that would, one day he hoped, provide the foundation for an independent business, separate from his family, his past.

After Emma had asked him on the plane what he'd really like to do if he had a choice, he'd realised that of course he *did* have a choice. His father's lack of love and fidelity gave him a freedom he hadn't fully appreciated before, but he realised now that he had no need to stay with Santini Enterprises, that he did not owe his father, or his father's business, any loyalty...

It gave him room to think. To dream, in a way he never had before.

But even with those intriguing possibilities on the horizon, he wanted to focus on Emma, and the life they were building together. The appointment at the OB yesterday afternoon had been as different in every way from the last one as Nico ever could have hoped; he'd sat in on it, for a start, and the doctor had been encouraging about Emma's weight gains and increased iron levels. Best of all, they'd seen the baby kicking and moving on the scan—a truly wondrous sight. He had the printout in his breast pocket; he didn't think he'd ever tire of looking at that blurry form, their baby. Everything had looked healthy and hopeful, and for that Nico was incredibly grateful. No matter what troubles and tragedies surrounded their separate pasts, Emma and his child were the future. Their future.

Smiling at the thought, he went in search of Emma. He found her in the drawing room downstairs, gazing out of the long, sashed window at the view of St Peter's Square. She turned as he approached, and his breath caught in his chest at the sheer loveliness of her. She had, despite her nervousness, enjoyed the beauty treatments—or at least she'd said she had—and the result was that she now looked utterly luminous. Her hair was piled loosely on top of her head, and her skin, dusted with bronzer, glowed with both beauty and health. She lowered her gaze as he walked towards her, a faint blush touching her cheeks.

'I feel like Cinderella,' she told him. 'After the fairy godmother did her "Bibbidi-Bobbidi-Boo" bit.'

'You look like Athena,' Nico replied as he walked across the room and took her hands in his. 'Utterly stunning.' The gown she'd chosen, one of a dozen he'd had ferried over, was an off-the-shoulder piece in bronze satin, its draped folds lovingly nestling her small bump before flaring out around her calves and ankles. 'But there is one thing missing.'

She glanced up at him, amber eyes glowing like embers underneath her dark lashes. 'Missing…?'

'These.' He withdrew a pair of diamond chandelier earrings from his pocket, the stones sparkling in the light; he'd seen them at a jeweller's yesterday and thought they were perfect.

Emma's eyes widened as she took in the magnificent earrings. 'Tell me those are fake.'

'Fake?' Nico raised his eyebrows, smiling. 'You insult me.'

'I can't…'

'You can.' Sometimes he wondered how he could have ever thought she'd only wanted his money. She hardly seemed to use it, always protesting when he lavished her with gifts—clothes, jewellery, anything. Now he helped fasten the earrings, letting his fingers linger on the delicate lobes of her ears.

'You look beautiful.'

'I'm scared I'll do something stupid,' Emma blurted. 'Trip or say something silly… I don't even know.'

'All I want,' Nico assured her, 'is for you to be yourself.'

She shook her head slowly, the earrings nearly brushing her shoulders, her gaze wide and a little panicked. 'This isn't my world, Nico.'

'And I'm glad of it. I like you just as you are, Emma. I don't want you to be some fawning fashionista or boring socialite, whatever it is you have in your head that you think I'm expecting. I want you to be you.' Because, he knew, he was starting to care—very much—about the *you* she was. If only Emma would let him. Would believe him.

At his words, her lips trembled and her eyes filled. 'I suppose I have trouble believing that,' she told him shakily, 'because no one has ever wanted me to be me before.'

Gently Nico drew her into a hug, resting his chin on top of her head as she pressed her cheek against him. 'We've both had to overcome issues around trust,' he said. Heaven knew he'd had his own. 'But you can believe me, I promise.'

'I know that, really.' With her smile still seeming shaky, she eased out of his embrace. 'I don't want to get make-up on your jacket,' she explained as she turned away. 'And we shouldn't be late.'

'No,' Nico agreed, although he wished he felt more confident that he'd convinced her. He had so much more to say, to proclaim, yet he knew now was not the right time.

Twenty minutes later they were stepping into the ballroom of one of Rome's grandest hotels, its floor-to-ceiling windows providing a panoramic view of the city, its elegant confines filled with well-dressed guests. Next to him Emma took a gulping sort of breath and Nico turned to give her a reassuring smile, but she wasn't looking at him.

'It will be fine,' he murmured, and she nodded, tilting her chin and throwing back her shoulders, filling him with pride.

'Right.'

And it was fine, more than fine, Nico realised as they circulated among the guests. Emma was quiet at first, but then someone asked her something, he didn't even know what, and within minutes she was in an animated conversation with someone about a cooking show, of all things. It made Nico smile.

He looked forward to teasing her about it later. *What did you have to be worried about?* he'd say, and she would give one of her irrepressible laughs and roll her eyes before he took her to bed…

Yes, he was looking forward to that very much. He stood slightly on the sidelines as Emma continued to chat and circulate, enjoying watching her shine. Loving that she was able to be the woman she'd always been meant to be.

Loving her.

The realisation jolted through him. He'd been telling

himself all along that what they had worked because they didn't love each other, but now he realised what an absurd fantasy that was. Of *course* he loved her; what was loving, after all, but doing the things he'd done? Feeling the way he felt? Wanting more for her than he wanted for himself? It wasn't some ephemeral will o' the wisp that he could guard against, ward off if he just steeled himself; it was this. Her. Now.

And, he realised as he watched Emma shine, the prospect of loving her, the reality of it, didn't scare him at all. On the contrary, it filled him with hope—and joy. This was what he wanted. And he would tell her, he vowed, at the first opportunity.

CHAPTER THIRTEEN

THIS WASN'T SO BAD, Emma thought as she sipped her drink and smiled and nodded at her new acquaintance—a woman who was as addicted to the Food Network as she was. Her new friend might be worth millions, have a career as a human rights lawyer and a billionaire entrepreneur as a husband, but when it came to rating the best chefs on television, they were equals. A laugh escaped her at the thought, and she clapped her hand over her mouth before she realised she would smudge her lipstick.

As she lowered her hand, her gaze snagged on Nico's— he'd stepped back a bit, content, it seemed, simply to watch, although he was about as far from a wallflower as one could get. Now a faint smile quirked his lips and he raised his champagne glass in a silent, approving toast. To her.

How she loved this man, Emma thought, only to freeze, her mouth dropping open, appalled at the thought. The realisation that was thudding through her, because she'd tried so hard not to love him. Not to love anyone.

The woman she'd been chatting to had moved away, and Emma took a few steps to the side of the ballroom, her mind spinning with what she'd inadvertently revealed to her own wary heart.

She loved him.

She'd tried to stop it, resist it in every way, stay safe and smart…but he'd breached her defences anyway. With his kindness. And his tenderness. And his willingness to be vulnerable himself. And, she thought as another laugh bubbled up, his being attractive as all get-out—put together, it was an irresistible combination, and her battered heart hadn't been able to stand firm.

Still, she felt incredulous that he'd slipped through her defences without her realising. Torn down her barricades without her realising she was basically handing him the bricks. How had this happened, and how had she let it? And more importantly, far more importantly, what would she do now?

Emma knew her instinct was, as it always had been, to walk away. Run, even.

Don't fail; quit first.

She'd told Nico that had been her unofficial motto, uninspiring as it was, but it was hard not to protect yourself. Not to not want to get hurt. To walk away before someone else did the walking.

And yet…

Did she really want to run away from Nico? Nico, who had shown her so much kindness and passion, tenderness and care? Nico, the father of her child, the guardian of her heart?

No, and that was the scariest thought of all. She *didn't* want to walk away. She wanted—or least was willing—to risk her heart for once, to take this leap into the terrifying unknown. To let herself be as vulnerable as it was possible to be, by telling him she loved him, that she was choosing to believe in the fairy tale they were creating for themselves, moment by precious, tender moment.

But how? When…?

'Didn't you land on your feet?'

The cold, drawling voice had her twanging with tension

as Emma slowly turned around. Nico's cousin, Antonio, stood in front of her, looking every bit as derisively mocking as he had the last time she'd laid eyes on him, at Nico's memorial service.

She glanced around the ballroom a bit desperately, hoping for Nico to come to her rescue, but even though she'd only seen him seconds ago he'd somehow disappeared. Where had he gone? Why?

'Hello, Antonio,' she forced out coolly, doing her best not to let her voice tremble. Chin, tilt. Eyes, flash. Face this man down as who he was, cruel and louche. Nothing like Nico.

Are you sure about that?

'So how,' Antonio mused, 'did you manage to snare him a second time? Was it the brat?' He nodded, rather crudely, towards her modest bump. 'Clever, that, especially when he must have been using protection. Nico isn't stupid, after all.'

Emma straightened, stiffening her spine. 'I don't need to talk to you,' she declared in as firm a voice as she could manage, which, she feared, was not firm enough. Not firm at all.

'Do you really think he'll stay with you?' Antonio challenged, his voice turning silky soft. 'For the long term? Oh, I admit he's besotted, it's ridiculous. But do you actually think that will last? Do you think someone like you could actually hold the attention of a man like Nico for all but a nanosecond?' He let out a laugh—high, cruel, utterly derisive. Someone near them glanced over, frowning.

Emma felt a blush scorch her cheeks, but she forced herself to keep Antonio's gaze.

'I feel sorry for you,' she declared. 'You obviously have never been in love.'

'And you think Nico is in love?' Antonio asked incredulously. 'With *you*?'

The question, asked with such blatant, mocking disbelief,

caught her on the raw. Opened up all those old, wounded insecurities until she felt as if she were bleeding out. 'Why do you care?' Emma demanded shakily. 'What does it have to do with you?'

He took a step closer to her, looming menacingly close. 'I don't,' he told her bluntly, his scornful gaze raking her from head to toe. 'In fact, I couldn't care less. But I thought you might appreciate some plain speaking. There won't be ten grand for you this time.' He turned away without another word, while Emma was left shaken and reeling.

There wasn't a speck of truth in his statements, she told herself as she tottered on wobbly legs to the ladies' powder room. He was just a callous, cynical, *cruel* man who liked to tear people down for the fun of it. She'd known people like that before, all through her life.

And yet his words *hurt*. They exposed the vulnerability she was still trying so hard to hide, the fear that she wouldn't be good enough, that just as before, *always* before, Nico would change his mind, because everyone changed their mind about her...

'Emma? Absolutely not.'

The memory rushed through, scalding her with its shame. If people she'd let herself love, who had loved her, or seemed to, could be so certain about turning their backs on her, why should Nico be any different?

'It's not true,' Emma said aloud, but her voice sounded feeble to her own ears. It sounded doubtful—because she knew she did doubt. As much as she wanted to believe, to *hope*, she couldn't keep herself from fearing the worst—again. Because in the past the worst had always happened to her.

Taking a shuddering breath, Emma dabbed at her eyes and then repaired her make-up, determined not to let Antonio or anyone else see how he'd affected her. Then, with another breath, she straightened, squaring her shoulders, tilting her chin, and heading back out to the party—and the real world.

She'd barely made it a few steps past the powder room when Nico appeared, smiling easily, although a frown settled between his brows as he took in her undoubtedly still stricken expression.

'There you are.'

'Yes.' Emma did her best to smile, but she felt it wobble and slide off her face.

'Emma?' He touched her arm. 'Are you all right?'

'Yes, just tired.' She gave a slight grimace. 'Being on my feet for so long…all this socialising… I'm used to quieter island life now, I suppose!' She tried for a laugh and felt it ring false.

'Do you want to go home?'

Desperately.

'If…if you don't mind.'

His frown deepened, his gaze scanning her face. 'Of course not. Let me just make my apologies.'

Emma nodded woodenly as Nico turned to head back into the party. The sooner she got out of here, she told herself, the better. And yet she was afraid leaving the party wouldn't change the doubts that now clamoured in her own heart.

Nico weaved his way through the guests, intending only to speak to the host of the gala, to make their apologies. He hoped Emma really only was tired; she'd looked so pale and forlorn, even as she'd tried to smile. Perhaps coming to Rome had been a bad idea. Too much rushing about…

'You haven't said hello, cousin.'

Nico halted mid-stride and turned to see his cousin, Antonio, smiling at him pleasantly, although Nico noted that his eyes looked hard. Besides their brief meeting when he'd returned from Jakarta, before haring off to Los Angeles, he hadn't seen his cousin since the accident. Considering how he'd treated Emma, as well as the latent tension that had been simmering between them since his paternity had become known, he hadn't particularly wanted to.

Now Nico inclined his head. 'Antonio.'

'How's your recovery?' Antonio asked, and Nico thought his tone was rather cool. 'Get your memory back?'

'Of the crash? No.' Antonio had asked him how much he'd remembered from that day, and Nico had confessed it was all a blank. Now, as he took in his cousin's assessing look, he wondered why he was seeming even more distant and guarded. Was it because of Emma, or something else? Something more?

He wasn't about to broach that whole topic now; he needed to get back to her. 'I'll be back in Rome next week,' he said instead. 'To catch up on all that has happened in my absence.' And to tender his resignation so he could start his own company, but he had no intention of talking about that with his cousin, either.

'Of course.' Antonio's lips twisted. 'I've no doubt you're eager to be back at the helm.'

His cousin's sardonic tone gave him pause, and again, more unrelentingly than ever, he felt that odd, tickling sensation at the back of his head, as if everything would make sense if he could just *remember*…

'Nico?' Antonio frowned, his eyes narrowing. 'Why are you looking at me like that?'

'I…'

A memory was slamming into him as he stared at his cousin.

The pilot of the plane, a panicked look on his face, a parachute on his back. *'I'm sorry, signor.'*

Him, alone in the sabotaged plane, no parachute, no idea what to do. The fuel had been let out of the tank…he was flying low over the ocean…

He blinked Antonio back into focus. 'Sorry,' he said stiffly. 'I just…' He could think of no excuse. 'I'll see you next week.'

Antonio nodded tersely and Nico strode away, his mind reeling. *Antonio*… Could it be possible? Was he remembering things correctly? Antonio, his own cousin, had arranged the accident, hired the pilot to sabotage the plane? Had tried to *kill* him?

'Nico?' Emma's soft voice startled him out of his spinning thoughts. 'Are you okay?'

'Yes.' He bit the word off tersely; he could not tell her his concerns—his fears—now. He would not burden her with them, not until he was sure he could trust his memories, not until he knew what to do—and did it. Of this he would be in control. Completely.

They rode in silence back to his town house, Nico barely aware of Emma sitting so quietly next to him, her face turned to the window. When they arrived back home, Emma murmured something about having a bath, and Nico nodded his approval before closeting himself in his study to make some much-needed calls.

Two hours later, he was staring out at the dark night, his face cast into stark relief by a pale sliver of moonlight as the truth thudded through him. This, he realised, changed everything.

CHAPTER FOURTEEN

IT HAD BEEN two days since they'd returned from Rome via Nico's yacht, and what a miserable two days it had been. The journey had been as swift as possible, and Nico had claimed he had pressing business to attend to, leaving Emma alone. Since their return she had moped around the villa while Nico had made himself scarce in his study, intensely occupied, almost seeming to avoid her. No, she realised, bleakly, not almost. Definitely.

He'd skipped dinner both nights, even though she'd made something specially, and come to bed late, after she'd fallen into a restless, unhappy sleep. When she'd dared to ask him if everything was all right, he'd assured her it was—while not meeting her eye. They'd barely spoken since the gala, and Emma was afraid she knew why.

He'd tired of her, just as she always knew he would. And why wouldn't he, when she obviously hadn't managed the gala very well? She'd seen him talking to Antonio right before they'd left—had his cousin been dripping yet more poison into his ear? Poison that had obviously convinced Nico, since he was determined to keep her at arm's length.

Yet what could she do about any of it? In the past, Emma would have cut and run. She'd long ago learned not to wait around to be given the boot. Leave before someone made you, that had been her *modus operandi*, and it was her instinct to do the same now—an instinct she resisted.

She'd *changed*, hadn't she? She'd learned and grown and fallen in love. It seemed almost absurd that she'd realised she loved Nico just as he was realising the opposite about her, and yet even now, when her heart felt as if it were being rent in two, Emma knew it was true. She loved him. And if she truly loved him, she wouldn't run away as soon as things got a little dicey. A little tough.

No, what she'd do instead was confront him. Tell him how she felt. The prospect, which had already been terrifying, felt even more so in light of Nico's coolness towards her, and yet perhaps that made it all the more necessary. She'd stand her ground this time, Emma told herself even as she quaked at the thought. She'd fight for the hope of their family, of them. For love.

It took another endless, miserable day of Nico avoiding her before she managed to tiptoe up to the door of his study where he'd been closeted since early that morning, hand poised to knock. Her heart was thundering in her chest but before she summoned the courage to tap at the door, she heard Nico's voice. He must be talking on the phone, she realised.

'I want it done immediately,' he said, sounding more tersely clipped than she had ever heard him before. 'Immediately, do you understand? Absolutely no delays.'

No delays to *what*? Her hand hovered by the door as she strained to hear.

'Emma?' The surprise in Nico's voice made her tense. 'No, absolutely not. Absolutely *not*.'

Emma stumbled back as his words reverberated through her—the same words she'd heard a lifetime ago, when she'd been only ten years old, listening at the door of the kitchen as her foster mum had spoken on the phone to her care worker. Back then Emma had felt as if her heart had broken, but it was nothing to how she felt now. *Shattered*. Completely and utterly shattered, her heart nothing more than a handful of broken bits.

Blindly, without even knowing where she was going, she whirled around. Headed up to her bedroom and pulled out a duffel bag from the cupboard, started stuffing things into it. None of the clothes Nico had bought her, no, she'd take nothing of his. Just her own things, shabby as they were.

You're back where you started, Emma, are you really surprised?

Yes, she was, and that was the hardest thing. She'd given up on her own principles of staying smart and safe by falling in love—and look where it had landed her.

Dashing the tears from her eyes with an angry hand, she hurried out of the bedroom, and then slipped down the stairs and out of the front door. As she'd packed, she'd considered her plan—how to get off this island without Nico knowing, because she knew she couldn't bear to face him. Whether it was pity or contempt, she didn't want to see it on his face. She just wanted to go.

She'd get the groundskeeper, Maria's husband, Stefano, to take her in Nico's boat—not the yacht they'd taken to Rome, but the little motorboat he used to get supplies from Capri or the mainland. She'd come up with an excuse, or maybe she'd just beg, but somehow she'd get away.

Of course, it wasn't as easy as that. First she had to find Stefano, who was in the gardens, and then stammer out some story about how she wanted to go to Naples for some ingredients for dinner, and would Stefano take her? She knew it was at least an hour's trip, and before she'd finished her plea Stefano was frowning and shaking his head.

'I do not know, *signora*. It is a long way to go, and the waters, they are very choppy.' He smiled kindly. 'What ingredients do you need? I am happy to get them for you.'

'I want to go myself,' Emma insisted as tears started in

her eyes, knowing she sounded like a child. 'Please,' she whispered, and Stefano patted her hand.

'If it is so important to you, okay. I will go. Just let me get my things.'

Relief coursed through her. 'I'll meet you down by the boat.'

He nodded, and she hurried down to the dock, her heart still thundering. Just a few more minutes and then she'd be away. Why did that prospect make her feel worse than ever?

For a second Emma hesitated. She could go back to Nico, ask, even demand, what he'd meant. After everything they'd shared, surely she deserved an honest answer? And yet even as she considered such an option, Emma knew she didn't have the strength to go through with it. She couldn't bear to hear from Nico's lips how he didn't love her, didn't want her. It had been bad enough hearing it on the phone. Remembering how discarded she'd felt, how utterly rejected…

Again.

Emma glanced up at the path that wound from the dock to the villa, squinting in the hope of seeing Stefano coming back, ready to go. But as a distant figure came ever closer, she felt as if her once thundering heart was now suspended in her chest. For it wasn't Stefano coming back with the keys, but Nico, walking towards her with long-legged, purposeful strides—and he looked furious.

When Stefano told him that Emma was asking to go to Naples, Nico was both surprised and alarmed. After spending the better part of three days in a state of high tension, with a migraine constantly threatening to swoop down on him, this was the last thing he needed.

He needed Emma to stay on the island, safe and protected, until the matter of Antonio was completely settled.

He rose from his desk, trying to moderate his voice as Stefano gazed at him unhappily.

'I thought it was okay, *signor*?' he asked, twisting his hands together. 'The *signora*, she can go where she pleases?'

'Yes, of course she can. But not today. I'll explain it to her, Stefano.'

'She—she had a bag with her,' Stefano ventured nervously, and Nico frowned at him.

'A bag?'

'With…with clothes.' The groundskeeper hung his head, as if he wished he could take back the words.

It took Nico a few stunned seconds to realise what the man meant. Emma had been planning to *leave* him.

The first thing he felt was hurt, a deep, deep abiding pain in his chest, in his heart, but his old instinct rose to the fore and he pushed it away. No, he wasn't hurt. He was angry. Angry that after everything they'd had together, she was going to creep away like a thief in the night? How dared she? Had he been wrong about her after all, all this time?

'I'll take care of it,' he snapped, and Stefano nodded before hurrying away. Nico made his way down to the dock, his anger building with every second. Why would Emma leave him like this? How could she treat him this way, sneaking off without so much as a word?

Why are you surprised? She was willing to marry the next man just months after your supposed death.

No, he told himself, he wasn't going to think like that. Not any more. And yet it was hard not to, when the evidence was there right in front of him, Emma cowering with a duffel bag stuffed with her clothes, before she tilted her chin and glared at him.

'I'm going, and you can't stop me.'

Nico came to a halt on the dock and folded his arms. 'You

didn't think you could at least inform me that you were leaving?' he asked in a silky voice that belied his anger, his hurt.

'Why should I?' she threw at him in challenge, with all of her old spirit and courage. 'I'm just saving you the time, Nico.'

Nico stared at her—noticing how tightly she clutched her bag, her wide, frightened eyes, the way she bit her lips. No, she hadn't said that with her old, feisty spirit, only the fading façade of it. He took a step towards her and then stopped, because she seemed so wild, so desperate. Why?

'Saving me time?' he enquired. 'How so?'

'You…you know how.'

He shook his head. 'I really don't.'

'Why are you making me say it?' she cried. 'It was bad enough to hear it on the phone—'

'On the phone?' He frowned as he realised she must have heard him talking—did she realise what Antonio had done? Was she blaming him somehow? 'Emma, whatever you heard—'

'What I heard is you wanting to divorce me as soon as possible. With no *delays*.'

'What?' Nico couldn't keep from goggling at her. 'Emma—'

'Look, I've been left a lot in my life, okay? I know when things are starting to go south, and I try not to stick around. So spare me the post-mortem and I'll be on my way—'

'No, absolutely not.'

'That's what you said!' she exclaimed, her tone turning shrill, desperate. '"Emma? Absolutely not." I *heard* you, Nico.' Her voice broke on his name and everything in him ached with remorse.

'You might have heard those words, Emma,' Nico said as gently as he could, 'but you came to conclusions that were, I promise you, entirely wrong.' He glanced at the boat, the wind picking up that was ruffling the water, and then reached for her arm.

She jerked away. 'Don't—'

'Please, let's talk about this rationally, back in the house.' He longed to take her in his arms, but he kept himself from it, at least for now, when she would only resist. 'I can explain everything, Emma, I promise.'

She stared at him, tears filling her eyes, one slipping down her cheek and making his heart break. He'd caused this. He'd fed into her insecurities because he'd been too proud to explain everything properly, to admit how he'd failed, by not remembering. By not keeping her safe, as he'd vowed. By not wanting to admit that his family had turned on him utterly, rejected him more than he'd ever imagined. He'd been arrogant and autocratic, he realised, just as she'd teasingly accused all those weeks ago, and all to hide his own pain—a pain he should have shared with her, instead of trying to handle it on his own.

'Emma,' he said softly. 'Please.'

'I trusted you, Nico.' Her voice was soft and sad. 'I—'

She stopped abruptly, and, with a thrill of hope, he wondered if she'd been going to say she loved him—as he loved her. How he'd wanted to tell her, and yet this business with Antonio had completely taken him over, body and soul. He hadn't wanted to say the words to her until he could be sure he could keep her safe. Until their futures were secure.

Until he had no weakness to admit.

He'd told himself it made sense, but he knew now it had been nothing more than pride. Pride—just as his father had clung to his pride. Not wanting to be humiliated, to be seen as weak, the object of pity, because his own cousin had tried to kill him and was still walking free.

Gently he reached for her arm again. 'Please, can we talk?'

After what felt like an age but was only a few seconds,

Emma bit her lip and nodded. 'All right,' she whispered. 'We can talk.'

He clasped her hand in his as they walked back to the villa in a silence that felt more resigned, at least on Emma's part, than tense or angry. He wondered if he could convince her. He knew he needed to.

'So what is there really to say?' she asked without preamble when they were both in the villa's drawing room, its French windows open to the terrace that looked out to the sea.

'There is a lot to say, as it happens.' He took a steadying breath, determined to stay reasonable. Understanding. 'But it would help first if you'd tell me what you thought I said, on the phone. What you thought I meant.'

Her eyes filled with tears again and she blinked them back angrily. 'Wasn't it obvious?'

'Not to me.'

'You were going to divorce me. Or send me away. Or— something.' She hunched her shoulders, folding her arms, as if she could keep out the whole world.

Nico's heart ached for the woman before him, who had been rejected so many times she didn't trust love when it was staring her in the face. And why should she, when he hadn't been humble and brave enough to tell her?

'I wasn't, Emma,' he said gently. 'I had no intention of doing any of those things, because I—I love you.'

Her eyes widened and her lips parted but she said nothing, just stared at him, and so he continued, 'I should have told you before. I wanted to, but—events overwhelmed me. Events I'll explain in a minute. But the important thing is, the only thing really is, I love you. I realised it at the gala, watching you shine. Seeing you be the woman I've known you could be, the woman at my side whom I love, the woman who makes me the man I want to be. Or at least, to try. I realised it then, at the gala,' he amended, 'but I fell in love with you before. Not in a single moment, but over time—time that I spent with you. And I know we agreed that love was off the table, but what is love, if not this?' His voice rose in challenge. 'You and me together, enjoying each other's company, caring about the other person, wanting the best for them, no matter what it is? Isn't that love? Not some ephemeral fairy-tale feeling, but reality. Action. Fact.'

A tiny, incredulous smile quirked her mouth. 'That was quite a speech.'

He let out a shaky laugh, because the truth was he felt incredibly vulnerable for admitting for so much, when she hadn't said she loved him yet. Considering her actions today, maybe she wouldn't. 'Thank you,' he managed. 'I meant every word.'

Emma stared at him, unfortunately looking far from convinced. 'Why have you ignored me for the last few days?' she asked. 'Shut me out, ever since the gala? And what were you talking about on the phone, if not that?'

'I didn't mean to ignore you,' Nico told her. 'Although I accept that is how it looked and felt. I was very much consumed with—a business matter.' Some business matter, he thought, and yet even now he was reluctant to admit to her what had happened. How he had been betrayed.

Her eyebrows rose. 'A *business* matter?'

'At the gala,' Nico confessed slowly, 'my memory came back. From the crash.' Emma's eyes widened once more and he continued more resolutely, knowing he needed to be honest, 'I remembered being on the plane. It had been deliberately sabotaged. The pilot emptied the fuel tank and then parachuted out. I confronted him before he jumped— he told me he was sorry, and that…that Antonio, my cousin, had arranged it all.'

'What…?' The word came out in an incredulous breath. 'Nico, is that true? I'm so sorry.'

'I shouldn't have been as surprised as I was, perhaps. I always knew Antonio was rather ruthless, just as he was with you. And knowing he was truly a Santini and I wasn't, yet my father was still keeping me on as CEO… I knew it had hit him hard. Very hard, to plot my murder.' He tried to smile wryly but didn't manage it. Even though there had quite clearly been no love lost between him and his cousin, yet another betrayal had been hard to bear. Still was.

And isn't that at least part of the reason you didn't tell Emma?

Because he'd been ashamed, how comprehensively his family had rejected him. Because it had made him feel unlovable…just as she had felt for so long.

'That phone call was me talking to the private investigator, telling him I didn't want you to have to be involved or called as a witness in any way. I wanted to keep you out of it for your own sake, but… I shouldn't have made that decision unilaterally, and I certainly shouldn't have shut you out the way I did. I'm sorry, Emma,' Nico told her, meaning it utterly. 'I should have told you about it all. I shouldn't have kept so much from you for so long. I just…' He spread his hands helplessly. 'I wanted to handle it by myself. And I didn't want to admit I hadn't been able to. Or that my family had turned on me so thoroughly.'

'Oh, Nico.' She took a step towards him, her face softened with compassion. 'I, of all people, can understand that. The reason your phone call hit me so hard was because you used the exact words my foster mother did, when I was ten years old.' She took a careful breath. 'I told you there was one family above all the others that I cared about but I didn't tell you exactly what happened. I'd been there for a year…what felt like the happiest year of my life. They were so kind, and they really treated me as one of the family. Proper, you know? Real.' She bit her lip and then continued quietly, 'My case worker hinted that they might adopt me. In retrospect she shouldn't have said as much, but I think she wanted to give me some hope, and maybe she thought it was a sure thing. But I overheard my foster mum on the phone with her, and when she suggested adoption my foster mum said, "Emma? Absolutely not."'

She gulped a little, and Nico knew how much this still had to hurt.

'She was so certain, you know? And so...so scandalised. Like she never would have entertained the prospect for so much as a second. Well, I started acting out after that, I know I did, and I was gone within a couple of weeks. I never told her I'd overheard. I never asked why.'

'Oh, Emma.' He reached for her then, and she came into his arms with a small, unhappy sigh.

'When I heard you saying the same thing, it was like I'd gone back in time. I guess I went a little crazy,' she admitted unsteadily. 'All I could think about was how it had been before, and not having that happen again. Funnily enough...' She eased back, tilting up her face to look at him. 'I was coming to the study to confront you. To ask you why you were keeping your distance, and to tell you I loved you.'

Nico's grip tightened on her as his heart leapt. 'You were?'

'Yes. I realised it the night of the gala, as well. Maybe it was seeing you with so many other people... I realised how much.' She smiled shyly. 'I felt we belonged together.'

'We do.' His voice was fervent, and her smile turned playful.

'You're sure?'

'More sure of that than anything else in my life.'

Her expression turned serious as her arms tightened around his waist. 'And Antonio? What...what will happen with him?'

'It's being dealt with,' Nico told her soberly. 'It's what I've been dealing with for the last few days—hiring an investigator, getting evidence. He's being taken in for questioning today.'

'Oh, Nico. Your own cousin…'

'I know.' He swallowed, still finding it hard to bear, to believe, even after several days of thinking of little else. 'I knew he was ruthless, but I never thought him capable of such a thing. I… I loved him.' He bowed his head. 'And I suppose that was part of why I didn't tell you. I felt… ashamed, somehow, I suppose…that someone I loved would do that to me.'

'I know how that feels,' she whispered, and then gave him an impish smile. 'Although not the killing part.' Her expression grew serious again. 'But feeling rejected by the people you care about, who you thought cared about you?' she asked quietly. 'Yes.'

He knew she did, and he was grateful for her understanding and compassion. Nico pressed his lips to her forehead, closing his eyes as he silently thanked providence for bringing her into his life. 'We have more in common than we could have ever known,' he murmured.

'Definitely more in common,' she teased, placing his hand over her bump. 'Feel.'

To his amazement and joy, he felt a flutter against his palm—a tiny foot or hand kicking against him. He laughed aloud, and then so did Emma.

Nico gathered her into his arms, kissing her thoroughly. 'We have the future ahead of us,' he told her. 'All of it to look forward to, together.' He paused to kiss her again, smiling down at her, full of gratitude and joy. 'The three of us.'

EPILOGUE

One year later

'YOUR DAUGHTER HAS a strong pair of lungs.'

Nico came into the kitchen with a six-month-old baby on his hip, with a head of black curls and golden, long-lashed eyes. And she was screaming at the top of her lungs.

'Our daughter, you mean?' Emma teased as she took the baby from him and gave her a smacking kiss on the cheek. 'Thea just knows what she wants.'

'And right now she wants her mama,' Nico replied ruefully as Thea settled right down.

Emma laughed and leaned over to kiss him on the cheek, as well. 'She just wants her nap. I'll put her down now before I finish this.'

'You look like you're in the middle of something,' he remarked, glancing around at the pots and pans bubbling away on the stovetop.

'Nothing that can't wait.' Three months ago Emma had, with capital from Nico's new business, started her own private catering company. Based in the country house they'd bought in Tuscany, she provided meals for dinner parties and private occasions. She'd only had a few bookings so far, which was fine, since Thea was so young, but the business looked set to grow, just as Nico's did.

The last year had been one of beginnings—learning to

be husband and wife, and then to be parents. Learning to let go of the family they'd lost—Antonio was in prison, and Nico was no longer in contact with his father—and finding their new support system. Maria and Stefano had moved from the island to Tuscany with them, and served as honorary grandparents, emergency babysitters, and much-valued friends.

All in all, it was a life Emma never would have dared dream for herself—a life of love, of happiness, of warmth and sharing and joy. Not that it had all been easy; the old insecurities sometimes rose to the fore for both of them, and it took patience and honesty and that difficult willingness to be vulnerable to work through it. But they had and they continued to do so, and for that Emma was very grateful.

'After you put Thea down...' Nico suggested hopefully, wiggling his eyebrows with playful suggestiveness '... maybe you want to have a nap yourself...?'

Emma glanced around at the pots and pans, pursing her lips. Yes, in this instance, it certainly could all wait.

'I might,' she agreed thoughtfully. 'I *am* rather tired...'

Nico's face fell just a little and she laughed, a sound of complete joy, before she ran up the stairs with her daughter giggling all the way, Nico fast behind her.

* * * * *

COMING
SOON!

We really hope you enjoyed reading this
book. If you're looking for more romance
be sure to head to the shops when
new books are available on

Thursday 20th
July

To see which titles are coming soon, please visit
millsandboon.co.uk/nextmonth

MILLS & BOON

MILLS & BOON®

Coming next month

THE MAID MARRIED TO THE BILLIONAIRE
Lynne Graham

"You took me by surprise… You shocked me," she muttered unevenly, struggling to catch her breath. She was thoroughly unnerved by the sensations that had shimmied up through her taut body and then down again to a place that had ignited with a burst of warmth, mortifying her to the very bone.

Enzo released his breath on a measured hiss. "Relax. For a moment, I was tempted. But nothing is going to happen unless you want it to. I'm attracted to you. I know I shouldn't be but I'm not perfect. In fact, it seems I'm all too human. But you are completely safe with me, *piccolo mio.*"

"Maybe I don't need to be safe…with you," Skye said uncertainly. "You make me feel things I didn't expect to feel. You make me curious. I know, like you said, I shouldn't be in these circumstances. But the truth is, I am and I'm attracted too."

"So…" Enzo breathed a touch raggedly. "What do you want to do about this?"

"We—we could try a kiss…just *one*," she stressed.

Continue reading
THE MAID MARRIED TO THE BILLIONAIRE
Lynne Graham

Available next month
www.millsandboon.co.uk

MILLS & BOON

THE HEART OF ROMANCE

A ROMANCE FOR EVERY READER

MODERN
Prepare to be swept off your feet by sophisticated, sexy and seductive heroes, in some of the world's most glamourous and romantic locations, where power and passion collide.

HISTORICAL
Escape with historical heroes from time gone by. Whether your passion is for wicked Regency Rakes, muscled Vikings or rugged Highlanders, awaken the romance of the past.

MEDICAL
Set your pulse racing with dedicated, delectable doctors in the high-pressure world of medicine, where emotions run high and passion, comfort and love are the best medicine.

True Love
Celebrate true love with tender stories of heartfelt romance, from the rush of falling in love to the joy a new baby can bring, and a focus on the emotional heart of a relationship.

Desire
Indulge in secrets and scandal, intense drama and sizzling hot action with heroes who have it all: wealth, status, good looks…everything but the right woman.

HEROES
The excitement of a gripping thriller, with intense romance at its heart. Resourceful, true-to-life women and strong, fearless men face danger and desire - a killer combination!

To see which titles are coming soon, please visit

millsandboon.co.uk/nextmonth

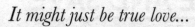